# PRAISE FOR THE WIND FROM ALL DIRECTIONS

Ron Thompson takes the historical record and adds nuance, drama and a touch of magical realism to bring a remarkable story to life. In 1792, several forces clashed on the west coast – Indigenous peoples, the Spanish, the English, and the English class system. History gives us the results and Thompson gives us the compelling narratives.

- Don Gillmor, winner of the Governor General's Literary Award, author of *Breaking and Entering* and *Canada: A People's History*

Ron has managed to capture the strain of the burden of command in an era of snail paced communications. The interplay among the cultures of the two European entities and the Indigenous population highlights the importance of weighing any command decision. He has managed to capture the essence of life at sea during that era.

- RAdm Ray Zuliani, RCN (Ret'd)

Vivid, authentic, clever, entertaining ... exceptional character development and a story that brings to life the period, place, and the nautical setting. I soon found myself immersed, hearing the characters' voices and visualizing the places, events, and ships described in the story. Bravo Zulu to Ron Thompson for this engaging and intriguing book!

- RAdm Jennifer Bennett, RCN (Ret'd)

# THE WIND FROM ALL DIRECTIONS

# THE WIND FROM ALL DIRECTIONS

Ron Thompson

DOUBLE‡DAGGER

Library and Archives Canada Cataloguing in Publication
Thompson, Ron, author
The Wind From All Directions / Ron Thompson

Issued in print and electronic formats.
ISBN: 978-1-990644-90-0 (paperback)
ISBN: 978-1-990644-91-7 (ebook)

Cover Illustration: Ron Berg
Cover Design: Pablo Javier Herrera
Interior Design: Winston A. Prescott

**Double Dagger Books Ltd.**
*Toronto, Ontario, Canada*
*www.doubledagger.ca*

*Corvus — it's on you and me both.*

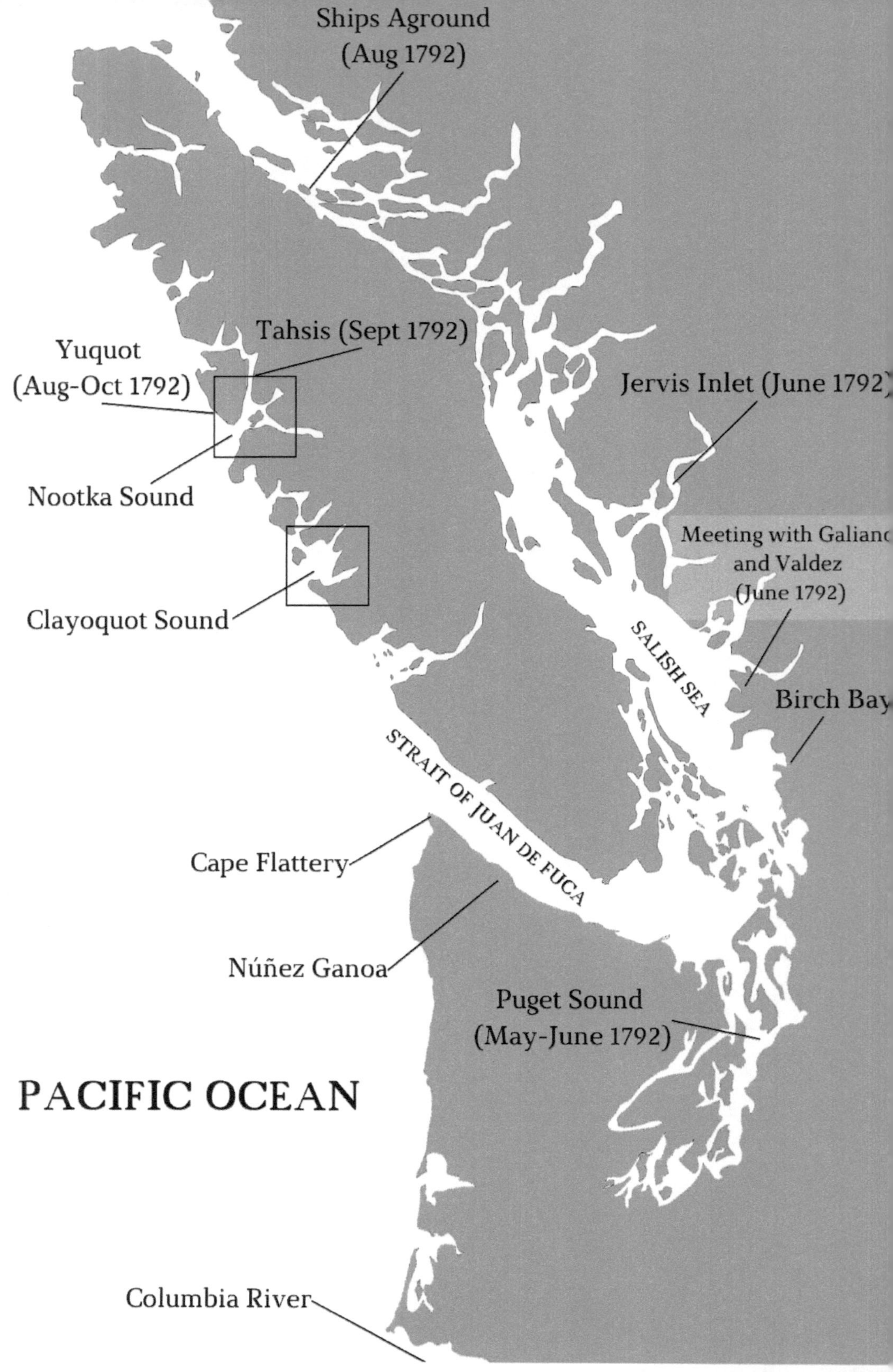

Ships Aground
(Aug 1792)
Tahsis (Sept 1792)
Yuquot
(Aug-Oct 1792)
Jervis Inlet (June 1792)
Nootka Sound
Meeting with Galiano
and Valdez
(June 1792)
Clayoquot Sound
SALISH SEA
Birch Bay
STRAIT OF JUAN DE FUCA
Cape Flattery
Núñez Ganoa
Puget Sound
(May-June 1792)
PACIFIC OCEAN
Columbia River

# CAST OF CHARACTERS

## THE NOOTKA INCIDENT

John Meares, British-Irish mariner, trading in Nootka Sound in 1788
William Colnett, agent for John Meares in 1789
Esteban José Martínez, Spanish naval officer, enforcing Spanish
sovereignty in Nootka in 1789

## THE BRITISH NAVY

**Officers:**
George Vancouver, lieutenant-in-command, *Discovery*. Known as
"Macubah" by Indigenous peoples he encountered on the coast
William Broughton, lieutenant-in-command, *Chatham*
Richard Hergest, lieutenant-in-command, *Daedalus,* killed in Hawaii
(the Sandwich Islands) en route for the northwest
Zachary Mudge, first lieutenant, *Discovery*
Peter Puget, second lieutenant, *Discovery*
Joseph Baker, third lieutenant, *Discovery*

**Petty and Warrant Officers:**
Joseph Whidbey, master, *Discovery*
James Johnstone, master, *Chatham*
Archibald Menzies, surgeon and botanist, *Discovery*
William Gooch, astronomer, killed in Hawaii en route for the
northwest

**Midshipmen:**
Jim Hawkins
Thomas Pitt
Augustus Lincoln
Richard (Dickie) Ramsay
Edward (Ned) Roberts
John Dorsey
Robert Barrie

Charles Stuart

Thomas Dobson, Spanish–English translator, formerly of *Daedalus*

Henry Orchard, Vancouver's clerk

**THE SPANISH**

Juan Francisco de la Bodega y Quadra, naval commodore and
  commander of Santa Cruz de Nuca, the Spanish base in Nootka
  Sound
Pedro Alberni, soldier, commander of the Catalonian regiment in Santa
  Cruz de Nuca
Dionisio Galiano, commander of *Sutil*
Cayetano Valdés, commander of *Mexicana*
Salvador Fidalgo, naval officer, commander of the Spanish outpost at
  Nunez Gaona within Juan de Fuca Strait
Francisco Almeida, ensign and aide to Quadra
Ortiz, an ensign
José Moziño, doctor and botanist
Felix Cepeda, Quadra's clerk
Jacinto Caamaño, commander of *Aranzazu*
Carlos Libertad, seaman
Menendez, commander of *Activa*

**THE INDIGENOUS**

Maquinna, chief of the Mowachaht
Wickaninnish, chief of the Tla-o-qui-aht
Tatoosh, chief of the Makah
Cleaskinah, chief of the Ahousaht
Tsakwasap, shaman-healer of the Mowachaht
Natzape and Quatlazape, advisors to Maquinna
Calicum, brother of Maquinna, killed by Martínez in 1789
Apanas, Calicum's wife, mother of Comekala and Copaza
Comekala, oldest son of Calicum and Apanas, Maquinna's English
  translator

Copaza, younger son of Calicum and Apanas
Matuateh, a young slave girl, adopted daughter of Apanas
Keiskonis, wife of Comekala
Saiyuqa, a young slave girl, friend of Matuateh

TRADERS

James Magee of the American trading vessel *Margaret*
Robert Gray of the American trading vessel *Columbia*, also present in
    1788 and 1789
Robert Duffin, an English trader, present in 1788 and 1789

## NOOTKA SOUND, SEPTEMBER 1792

Picture the scene from high above. The inlet wide, the ships at anchor in the cove. Above the beach the Spanish town, a fringe of field and forest, and there beyond, the ocean vast.

All is calm. The cloak of night is lifting.

The beat of wings.

Pan closer to the tallest ship. Peer down, through its weathered deck. In the cabin at its stern sits a tired man in a blue frock coat. Heavy is the burden of command.

There is movement on the deck above. Muffled voices: a watchman reporting to his superior. George Vancouver stares up at the planks, straining to hear their words — and realizes that the cabin has brightened. Sunlight streams onto the bulkhead opposite. He twists and peers out the window at his back. The sun has broken over the mountains across the Sound. Pink light illuminates his face. For a moment, he closes his eyes to savour it.

Only for a moment. He turns back to the Spaniard's letter. It is succinct to the point of being curt.

> *You say you are authorized to receive the whole:*
> *I am not free to deliver on those terms.*

He scans the rest: the offer to depart and leave him in *possession* of the Spanish base without ceding *sovereignty* to it, without returning anything beyond the low-lying spot where Meares's trading post had stood four years before.

There are few secrets aboard *Discovery* — the barque is but a hundred feet long and berths a hundred men. He's heard them compare that patch of tidal muck to the fine lost harbours of New York and Boston. One lower-deck wag has grandly christened it "The British Territories" and now everyone calls it that.

They can afford to jest.

He takes up his pen and hesitates, examines his palm, waggles his swollen fingers, glances up at a noise.

A call like a crow's, quite close.

He dips the quill and begins to write.

So intent is he on his work that when a hard knock comes on the cabin door he startles; his pen streaks and leaves an ink blob on the page. He glares down at it, then up at the door, before blanking his expression and calling, "Come."

Lieutenant Baker enters and doffs his hat.

"Morning, sir. Sorry to intrude. Something unusual on shore. Strange, in fact. Rather hard to make it out but it, ah, looks like clothing."

Vancouver's eyes narrow. "Perhaps someone's doing his laundry, Joe. Not a breach of Spanish regulations, I venture." He glances down at his letter. He can salvage the page if he blots it quickly.

"Beg pardon, sir, but it looks like a...um...a person, sir. A body."

Vancouver looks up. "Where?"

"The north side of the cove, a ways from the British Terr...ah, from Mister Meares's property, sir. Just visible in a bight in the shore. Quite a rough spot."

Vancouver thinks for a moment. "Send word to Señor Quadra. An unusual situation on shore. With my compliments."

"Aye, sir."

Alone again, Vancouver listens to the muffled discussion above, hears a crew clamber into a boat and put off. The relative silence of the ship at anchor falls again — the comforting creaks and groans, the lapping of water. He returns to his letter, dabs it with a cloth, and reads what he has written.

It will do. He signs his name and thinks, Damn — I should've held that boat for this.

⧖

An hour later. The Spaniards on shore present a strange tableau: the two officers high on the rocks above the waterline, their backs to the harbour; the knot of sailors a respectful distance below, those at the rear pressing forward, craning to see. Behind them, their forgotten launch. In front of the officers stand two Catalonian soldiers. Beneath them lies the object of their officers' attention, a crumpled bundle of bloody clothing and flesh, wedged within a crevasse at which the sea gently laps.

A persistent buzz rings in the ears of the Spaniards. The stink of rot envelops them.

A close observer, concealed in the woods or perched above in a tree, would see that Alberni's face is pale, that Quadra's is set in anger. They recognize the bundle for what it is, for, despite its mutilation and the flies covering it, it is clearly a human body. Its head lies at an unnatural angle to its torso, to which it remains barely attached. The corpse's face is grey and waxen, its strange, unseeing eyes fixed on the blue sky of a magnificent day.

Not you, Quadra thinks.

"Jesus on a Christly crutch," Alberni mutters. "What have they done?"

Quadra turns to him. His eyes flick in the direction of the men, then back to meet Alberni's.

Alberni nods.

Quadra climbs down to the level of the two soldiers. He meets one man's gaze and grasps him briefly by the elbow, as if in his descent he has lost his balance. The other man avoids his eye. Quadra grips his shoulder, lets go, and descends to the corpse. Flies swarm in outrage. He waves them away, kneels to close those unsettling, gaping eyes — and realizes the sockets are empty. The eyes are gone. Some hungry beast has pecked them out.

He straightens and looks out into the harbour. Alberni, lips pursed, nostrils flared, steps down to stand beside him. They exchange looks and turn to examine the site.

History reverberates, yet it is malleable — reforged, drawn anew, told afresh. Woven from the thread of faulty memory, it makes a splendid tapestry, a flag of convenience rippling with false certainty. History is the very map of time, its coordinates — truth.

And there, Dear Reader, is the rub. History is complicated, because *truth* is complicated. Your truth, her truth, their truth — they are not the same.

There is no way to know the truth about those eyes, and what they saw, if you are stuck in the linear flow of time.

Which I am not.

Now that I've shown you the body, I wonder where I should take you next.

I have it — Whidbey. A linear thinker, was Old Joe. He'll ease you into it.

The truth, that is.

So rise with me, for we travel far to the north and three months back in time. It is June, and twenty men in two sturdy boats ply the waters of a long and twisting inlet. They are surrounded by the unknown, far from the safety of their vessel, farther still from civilization.

Unbeknownst to them, their civilization is in the early throes of a conflict that will embroil it for a generation. France is already at war with an Austro-Prussian coalition. In Paris, the final attempt to introduce a constitutional democracy has failed. This very day, an unruly mob will force Louis XVI to don a *bonnet rouge* and drink to the nation's health.

It will be a bitter vintage for the deposed king — and a portent of bounty for all Earth's eye-eating creatures.

# Chapter 1

At dusk they landed on a gravelly ledge, and for the first time in days had room to raise their tents. They laboured through a cold drizzle and managed to light a fire, and though it was well dark when they finished, they were cheered by the prospect of a hot meal and a night under canvas. At dawn their spirits rose still further when the first hint of light revealed a cloudless sky.

As they broke camp, Joseph Whidbey stretched and arched his back tentatively. "It's going to last a day or two."

Archibald Menzies, crouching to roll his blanket, grinned up at his friend. "Ach, you're a medical marvel, Joe — a human weathervane. A day in advance of cloud or wind, you foretell a turn in the elements by the creak in your hip or a stiffness in your knuckle. Your barometric condition must be a boon, professionally speaking, is it no'?"

"Professionally speaking, *Doctor* Menzies, might it not be helpful to show some sympathy for a man's aches and pains?"

The Scot snorted and stuffed his bedroll away. "Mah present wards feel no aches or pains, just a want o' soil. I trust you're in no imminent need o' such a bed."

Old Joe grunted, held a stretch, and glanced towards the boats. The wells of both were crowded with Menzies's botanical specimens. He pivoted his hips and cast his eye around the rapidly disappearing camp until it fell upon the midshipmen. Young Ramsay, Pitt, Lincoln, and Hawkins wasted no time on stretches like his. They seemed to visibly thrive on short nights sleeping rough and long days cramped inside an open boat — though they never seemed to have enough to eat.

They put off before full light, the men at their oars as they had been for days; but by midmorning they raised their sails to a favourable breeze, affording all hands a rest. Bright sun sparkled off silvered waters. They sailed up a steep-walled passage edged by towering forest. On one side, water cascaded off a cliff; in the distance, snow-capped mountains rose against a clear blue sky. Their heavy clothes had been damp for days; now they steamed and dried in the warmth of early summer. Whidbey, commanding the launch that trailed George Vancouver's longboat, loosened his coat and felt immeasurably cheered.

The channel led northeast. They took bearings periodically and attempted soundings, finding no bottom even with a hundred fathoms of line.

Perhaps our quest is complete, Whidbey mused skeptically. Perhaps Hudson's Bay is just beyond yon point.

As dusk gathered, they tracked toward a distant smudge, which resolved into a small Indian village at the channel's terminus. Another dead end. Smoke from the village hung unmoving in the evening air. Several canoes put off from it and drew near. Within both boats the sails came down and the seamen took to their oars, bracing inconspicuously to defend themselves. Vancouver's longboat slackened speed to allow Whidbey's launch to close. Together, they met the natives, who pulled alongside and beckoned them to land.

Vancouver nodded agreeably at the man who seemed to be their leader. He directed his coxswain (Midshipman Lincoln that day) to get underway, and made eye contact with Whidbey, whose launch stood a length off.

"Mister Ramsay," Whidbey said softly to his own coxswain. "Let's go make our halloos. Mister Hawkins, keep your musket at hand, just in case."

They landed, their every movement slow and deliberate.

Vancouver and Menzies both knew snippets of the Nootka tongue from their previous voyages, but their efforts to communicate with it seemed to confuse these natives. Vancouver resorted to simpler means: he held his palm to his chest and said his name.

Whidbey would remember the villagers as friendly and inoffensive, eager for exchange and fair in barter. They offered fish for the few goods, mostly trinkets, that the mariners had left to trade — though these were not what they wanted most. They made this known by gestures to the dirks worn by the midshipmen — and by producing a rusted blade without a haft.

"Well, I'll be damned," Whidbey said as Vancouver accepted it from the chief.

Vancouver turned it over in his hands, examining it closely.

"Now that's a puzzle," said Menzies. He nodded towards two men who were examining ginger-headed midshipman Jim Hawkins like horse-buyers at market. "They seem not tae've seen Europeans before. Yet they know o' metal and have pieces of it themselves."

"It could've been traded from Hudson's Bay," Whidbey said, "or our settlements in the east." He paused, considering the ramifications. "That would mean there's a route after all, at least overland."

Menzies accepted the blade from Vancouver. "Or it's Spanish or Russian, traded from up or down the coast."

*Down* was *doon* in his highland burr.

Vancouver cleared his throat. His eyes searched the faces in the crowd gathered round. "Mister Pitt. May we have your dirk — Mister Ramsay, Mister Lincoln, likewise. We'll make a present to the chief to seal our welcome." A slight smile played at the edges of his mouth. "Mister Hawkins. You may keep yours. Just keep it sheathed."

They made camp that night on the flat across the creek from the Indian lodges. Whidbey was tired, so he ate his meal and went to bed, while Menzies sat at their fire and scribbled notes about a specimen he had found in the woods nearby. Vancouver sat across from him and reviewed his own notes and observations until he turned in for the night. He and his senior fellows thus missed the furtive excursion by some of the seamen and young gentlemen, those who were not on watch or slumbering soundly, to the village, where they bartered buttons and nails for keepsakes, curios, and certain home affections.

Early next morning the explorers bade farewell to the natives and set out back the way they had come. The weather remained fair and warm, but they faced into a southerly wind and had to take to the oars. They made slow progress, with Vancouver's sturdy longboat moving more surely than Whidbey's lumbering launch. The longboat was soon well ahead.

Years later, Old Joe recalled their captain's chronic impatience. "He always behaved," he told Menzies, "as if he knew he had but little time."

The Scotsman, who had ministered to Vancouver during their long voyage, simply nodded and drained his glass.

Mid-afternoon, Whidbey saw the longboat land on a gravel beach. He made for the spot, relishing an opportunity to stretch his legs.

Vancouver stood straight on to the approaching launch, his hands joined behind his back, the very picture of command serenity. "Mister Whidbey," he called as the boat landed. "Will you join me in the longboat." It was not a question. He turned and strode to it; its crew had already re-boarded. Whidbey stepped gingerly ashore and directed his coxswain, Midshipman Hawkins, to take charge of the launch. He hobbled towards the longboat, pausing midway to relieve himself. When he was done he arched his back and stood with his fists on his hips, pivoting from side to side until he heard the captain softly clear his throat. It was a signal, and Whidbey read it correctly. He boarded and seated himself on the stern-sheets bench, where Menzies shifted across to make room. Vancouver boarded last, and his coxswain — it was Midshipman Pitt that day — directed their departure.

The oarsmen pulled south, towards where the channel joined the broad arm of the sea that Vancouver would name the Gulf of Georgia when he got around to mapmaking. Old Joe looked back wistfully and saw the crew of the launch still on shore. Young Jim Hawkins was allowing them a few more moments before setting off.

"Mister Whidbey," Vancouver said in a quiet tone that did not reach forward of the stern sheets. "Your views, please, on our options."

As *Discovery's* sailing master, Whidbey was familiar with all aspects of his captain's hydrographic mission. George Vancouver had been ordered to explore the coast between Spanish California and Cook's Inlet in Alaska. He was to determine, once and for all, whether a passage connecting the Pacific and Atlantic existed within that vast span of territory. Such a waterway — long rumoured, never discovered — was known in mariner myth as Maldonado's Passage, Rio d'Aguilar, and the Strait of Anián, de Fuca, or Fonte.

Old Joe knew that Vancouver thought it better named Folly than Fonte, that his perspective on the mission was absent all chimeric conceit and entirely pragmatic: he intended to delimit the boundaries of the continent, to place an immense tract of land on the map of the known world.

As if *this* were not ambitious enough, he had been given another task, one that he had mentioned to Whidbey only once, in a moment of unguarded candour. That had been two months before, the night of the day they made landfall at Cape Mendocino. After a game of chess in *Discovery*'s great cabin, the two of them toasted their Pacific crossing and the true start of their hydrographic mission. Only then did Old Joe, savouring a brandy and feeling the twinge in his hip that portends a gale, learn that Vancouver had been assigned an additional mission. It was of a ceremonial nature, to mark the end of a dispute that had brought Britain and Spain to the brink of war. As their armies mobilized and their navies put to sea, their diplomats had reached a last-minute accord. Both sides agreed to appoint commissioners, who would meet at the site of a recent altercation in Nootka Sound and formally conclude the affair. Vancouver, already slated to lead a voyage of exploration in the region, was named Britain's delegate. He was ordered to proceed to Nootka, where he would receive British property seized by Spanish officials. Beyond that, his instructions were vague. Further details were to be sent on the store ship *Daedalus*, which would rendezvous with his ships *Discovery* and *Chatham* in the Sandwich Islands.

Vancouver confided to Whidbey that he had been displeased with this complication. He knew the magnitude of the mission he was about to undertake. It was already complicated enough. Joseph Banks, the president of the Royal Society, had used his influence to impose an ambitious scientific mandate on an already-ambitious voyage of exploration. Banks had foisted a dedicated botanist — Menzies — on

Vancouver, along with orders to facilitate his pursuits. This rankled, for the Admiralty had elsewhere taken economies with his complement. He did not sail with an astronomer to assist with navigational matters (as his mentor James Cook had done on his three round-the-world voyages). Nor had he been assigned a dedicated purser. He had to perform that role himself, a role that came with personal financial liability for all of *Discovery*'s stores and supplies — this in addition to direct responsibility for the overall expedition and the lives of all its members.

Now, on top of all that, he had a quasi-diplomatic mission.

In London he was assured it was a formality, and that dispatches borne by *Daedalus* would clarify what he must do. Months later, though, *Daedalus* missed their scheduled rendezvous, and he realized there would be no clarifications, no additional instructions as to the property he was to receive or what he was to do with it. Lieutenant George Vancouver, master and commander of *Discovery*, commodore of a king's flotilla of two, discovered that in matters of diplomacy he was on his own.

Whidbey could tell that this aspect of his captain's orders was deeply worrisome to him. Later, when he reflected upon it, the double appointment struck him as an economical expediency on the part of His Majesty's Government: as the killing of two birds with one stone.

When they reached the mouth of the Strait of Juan de Fuca a few weeks later, more than a year out from England and not a hundred miles south of the appointed rendezvous with the Spaniards, Vancouver did not dither between the conflicting facets of his mission. He directed his ships east, into the Strait and the unknown. Diplomacy, and the Spaniards, would have to wait.

⧖

Now, weeks later, as they drew down this newly explored channel towards the soon-to-be-named Gulf of Georgia, Whidbey sat with George Vancouver in the stern of the longboat and reflected on their options.

"Well, here we are backtracking from another dead end. The flow of the tide suggested it, but it's taken the better part of three days to prove it." He nodded toward the shore on either side. "We know this is all part of the continent and these mountains are clearly impassible. We've come from the south and there's no passage there. So if it exists at all —"

"Yes, yes. To the north." The habit people had of thinking out loud annoyed Vancouver. He tapped the gunwale with his finger.

"And if it's like this there, we've slow work ahead. It's grub that limits us now, Captain. Our supplies are near exhausted and it's going to take us two days to get back to the ships. Two days at least."

"We could continue outbound for another couple of days on half rations. Barter for what we need, push on with the survey until we find a good anchorage. Then return for the ships and bring them up." Vancouver looked up at the sky. "I am reluctant to double back while the weather remains fine."

Whidbey thought about it. Their strategy of provisioning from the Indians had worked well. They had departed with food for seven days and were already eight days out. But they had little left with which to barter. He examined the sky. Clear. He twisted his pelvis slightly in search of the telltale ache. Nothing.

Menzies had been listening to their conversation. Now he leaned closer and spoke in a voice that did not carry forward. "The men are in good health, Captain. Tired but up tae it. There are other factors tae consider as well."

"Being what?"

"First, there are my botanical samples. We have some unknown species that need tae be replanted soon or they'll be lost."

A flicker of annoyance crossed the captain's face. "Noted, Mister Menzies. Thank you. Now —"

"Secondly, *Chatham*'s boats may already be back at the anchorage. Captain Broughton may be at loose ends awaiting our return."

Whidbey observed Vancouver's expression, thinking wryly that if anything bothered his captain more than botanical samples, it was wasted time. "The doctor makes a good point, Captain," he said. "They headed east and south from the anchorage. It looked to be a simple survey. Much simpler than ours has proven. They're very likely back by now."

Vancouver nodded. "Yes. Thank you, gentlemen."

Whidbey was sure he was measuring the slow pace of their survey against the calendar, thinking four boats were better than two.

They fell into silence, broken only by the rhythmic creak of the oars in their locks.

⧗

Open water was now visible far ahead, backed by a substantial island and, towering beyond it, a wall of snow-capped mountains.

"Coxswain," Vancouver said, gesturing.

"Rest on your oars," Pitt called to the crew.

They glided with the current. The long summer dusk was upon them. On their starboard beam, a passage curved off in a northwesterly direction from the broad channel they were in. Vancouver looked toward it, up at the sky to gauge the light, and aft, to where the launch pulled steadily towards them.

"Take that channel," he told Pitt. "We'll see where it leads."

As they got underway Vancouver craned aft and waved his hat slowly at the other boat. An arm returned the wave.

The new channel was narrower and twisted between steep rock faces cloaked in forest. Its waters lay calm, dark, and still, with no discernible current.

They pulled through the gathering dusk until Vancouver ordered a rest. The men leaned on their oars and looked at the rugged shoreline, its jagged slopes intruding close upon the boat.

High above their heads, an eagle soared on currents of air that were not perceptible deep within the darkening gorge. They floated on the slack water as daylight faded around them. From shore, the rambunctious *grawk* of a raven.

Vancouver shifted his weight and said, "Where is Hawkins?"

Whidbey had been daydreaming. He realized the launch should have been with them by now. He listened for the sound of its approach.

In the distance there was a howl. A wolf, he thought, or an Indian mutt. Then nothing.

Vancouver ordered a musket fired. The shot echoed off the rock walls and faded into silence. They sat still, listening. There was only silence. A second shot was fired. There was no reply.

"He must have taken the original channel," Whidbey said. "Overshot this one. He must be in the gulf by now. No harm can come there."

Vancouver turned to look at him. "He has no compass. No provisions."

Whidbey felt in his coat pocket for his own compass. He had not thought to give it to Hawkins. And the longboat carried all their provisions — Vancouver personally shepherded their supplies on expeditions such as this.

Hawkins, with Ramsay and eight men.

Vancouver's lips pursed.

⏳

Years later, Whidbey would recall the moment over a port with Menzies. "His face turned red. He looked over his shoulder and muttered an oath that would shock a dockyard matey."

"Aye, and from the look of him, I expected there was more on the way."

"And then he stopped himself. I *saw* him struggle with his temper. By God, he had one of those. But he wasn't one to rail on unfocused. Not in front of the men. At least not with his target absent."

They both chuckled at what happened next. Vancouver brought his balled fist down hard on the gunwale. It obviously hurt. He sat and rubbed his fist, glaring, his posture tense and rigid. Everyone in the boat waited. The seamen at the oars, facing aft, directed their gazes down into the boat. At coxswain, Pitt studied the shore. In the bow, Midshipman Lincoln scanned ahead and around. Now and then he glanced furtively back towards the stern, hoping for a show.

"And then just like that," Whidbey said, snapping his fingers, "his temper drained. Like bilge water through a hose."

In the ensuing silence he thought about what he had just said.

"No, not drained exactly, but stowed. Stowed like cordage in the place he kept it, ready for use."

"Aye," Menzies said, pointing his glass at Whidbey. "His temper was a blister he could tease until it burst."

THE WIND FROM ALL DIRECTIONS | 13

They shook their heads, though they were in agreement on the point. A moment later they both peered out their leaded window, where some bird had noisily taken wing. It was gone already.



"We'll put ashore for the night," declared Vancouver. "Start a fire and get a meal. Mister Hawkins may yet arrive. In the morning we'll follow this passage to its end, then return to the ships. Hawkins will undoubtedly reach the same decision when he realizes we're separated." He rubbed his fist, the one he had struck on the gunwale. Menzies could see that it was going to bruise.

It was almost dark when they landed on a patch of gravel fronting an impassable tangle of forest. The exposed foreshore provided scant shelter, but they made a camp of sorts, rigging a tarpaulin lean-to against the side of the boat. They settled in as best they could.

Hawkins and the launch did not arrive in the night. Whidbey slept fitfully, disturbed by a dull twinge in his hip. By dawn the weather had turned close and wet. They broke camp, returned to the boat, and shortly entered open water. The narrow channel had been but a passage between the mainland on their right and an island on their left. They followed this island's shore as it rounded into the gulf and headed south, towards the ships.

They landed periodically to take bearings. Beyond these respites the men rowed all day. They passed another uncomfortable night on shore and continued south next morning, making slow progress now against adverse winds. When they landed in fog and drizzle that evening, the third since the boats were separated, they were opposite the mouth of an extensive easterly inlet they had explored a week before. Vancouver had noted its potential as a harbour. They were now just a day from the ships.

They were chilled through, unable to kindle a fire, and they faced another miserable night on sodden ground, huddled beneath the dripping canvas of their improvised shelter. This might have been an occasion for a rousing speech, some words to lift their flagging spirits. "We band of brothers," that sort of thing. Not Vancouver's style. Instead, he ordered a double ration of grog and extra hardtack for every man. He gnawed his silently as they gnawed theirs. Those not on watch fell into exhausted sleep. Vancouver and Menzies settled quickly and were still, but for a long time Old Joe could not find a comfortable position. Still, he was fortified by the grog and the thought of reunion with *Discovery*. His last thought before he fell asleep was of the absence of pain in his pelvis.

They broke their wretched camp in the dark, gnawed a ration of hardtack in silence, and set off at the first glimmer of light on the eastern horizon.

During the night the weather had changed. The rain had stopped, the sky had cleared, the wind had dropped to nothing. Overhead, a crystalline tapestry faded into a cerulean sky. As the longboat scudded the shore in the semi-dark, Whidbey breathed deep of cedar and fir, and when the sun broke through the towering trees off their larboard beam he felt its warmth on his unshaven face. He caught Vancouver's eye.

The captain nodded equably, the hint of a smile on his lips. He looked around, obviously savouring the sea, the forested mountains, the perfect blue above. Unbeknownst to Old Joe, this day was his thirty-fifth birthday.

They made steady progress. Lulled by the creak of oars, the regular surge of the boat, Whidbey dozed in his seat.

A splash, an oath. Whidbey opened his eyes. One of the men had missed his stroke. His oar floundered, another struck it — and suddenly oars knocked oars, blades skittered, spray flew. Men shouted angrily as grips struck chins and glanced off shoulders.

"Stay, damn you! *Stay!*" bellowed Midshipman Lincoln at cox.

The boat lost momentum and wallowed. The men cursed and recovered their oars, examined scrapes, rubbed bruised flesh.

Vancouver remained silent as Lincoln reasserted command.

"Settle back, settle back. Any breaks? I meant oars, Evans. It might improve that mug of yours if your nose *was* broken." Menzies took a quick look and confirmed it was not.

The captain coughed lightly. Lincoln followed his gaze. They had drifted towards shore. "You tars, ready now," Lincoln called, and got the boat underway. Whidbey noticed a thin copper bracelet around the young man's wrist. No doubt bartered from an Indian. It would make an unusual memento back in England, a piece of exotica with which to amuse a dinner party or seduce a girl. Whidbey smiled to himself and stretched as best he could, thinking his back felt better today. It pained him most in the damp and eased on a clearing trend.

"Captain."

Midshipman Pitt, standing lookout in the bow, pointed forward.

They had rounded a headland, and there in its lee lay two schooners at anchor.

"Avast," Vancouver said.

The boat glided, all hands craning to see.

A red and yellow pennant flew from the masthead of each vessel.

"By Christ — it's the fucking dagos," exclaimed one of the men.

Lincoln tossed a stone that hit him on the head and ricocheted into the water. "Silence in the boat! And mind your fucking tongue, Adams, you hear?"

The stone was uncalled for but Vancouver ignored it. "Avast," he repeated. He scanned the horizon all round, then stared hard at the ships.

"Spanish, all right," Whidbey said softly. "Swivels fore and aft. No other armament that I can see."

"Aye. But what the devil are they doing here?"

They floated now in profound silence, all eyes on the unsuspecting Spaniards.

Vancouver straightened. "Mister Lincoln," he said. "Make for the nearest schooner." He waited for Lincoln to get the boat underway. "Smartly, men, smartly...Now, all of you, listen to me." As they pulled toward the ship in practised rhythm he issued instructions, and those not at oars made covert preparations for any welcome.

The Spaniards hailed them.

⧗

Old Joe was behind his captain on his ascent up the flimsy rope ladder, and he was forever dumbstruck by the transformation wrought, in a few short seconds, on that swaying conveyance.

For eleven days they had lived rough in an open boat, exposed to the elements, their accommodations primitive, landfalls few. They were dishevelled, dirty, hungry, tired — George Vancouver as much as any of his men. Yet the captain arrived upon the Spaniards' deck with the full bearing and dignity of a British naval officer: ramrod straight, blue tunic buttoned, weathered hat positioned just so upon his head. The grimace that had clouded his face moments before had vanished. His expression was now open, sociable, inquisitive, relaxed. He tipped his hat to the Spanish flag and to the young officer who received him, replaced it on his head, and extended his hand, which the Spaniard grasped and pumped enthusiastically, as though it were a bunch of grapes and he a winemaker.

Whidbey himself arrived on deck to discover a painful kink in his lower back; he could proffer but an arthritic imitation of his captain's more ceremonious salute. Vancouver cast him a look, but the young Spaniard took no offence. Instead, he seized Whidbey's hand and shook it as he had Vancouver's. As the others clambered aboard, Vancouver attempted to converse, but it quickly became evident that the Spaniard spoke no English, and the English no Spanish.

"*Français?*" queried the Spaniard.

"No, English," Whidbey said. "English."

"He means the language," Vancouver said curtly. "*Oui, un peu.*"

They quickly established that Midshipman Pitt spoke French fluently, and Menzies tolerably, certainly better than Vancouver. Introductions, and pleasantries all round, were conveyed through Pitt.

"His name," Pitt said, listening, "is Valdés...This is the *Mexicana*, consort of the *Sutil*, which is..." he cocked an ear to Valdés, "commanded by..."

"*Capitán de fregata* Don Dionisio Galiano," finished the Spaniard. He gestured towards the other ship. Its launch was pulling towards the *Mexicana*. Valdés continued in French.

Pitt turned to his captain. "He welcomes you and says they've been expecting us."

"Eh?"

Valdés continued. Pitt's eyes narrowed as he concentrated. "Both ships...detached from the garrison at Nootka...which is commanded by..."

"Don Juan Francisco de la Bodega y Quadra," Valdés said, and continued in French.

"... Don Francisco dee-boh dago Quadra," Pitt said. "Who waits there to receive you —"

"Don *Juan* Francisco," Menzies put in.

"Gentlemen. Please." Vancouver's voice was strained.

"*Bodega y* Quadra," Valdés said.

"Quadra," repeated Vancouver, nodding and weighing the name.

"Bodega y Quadra," Valdés repeated, nodding amiably himself.

"Bodago ee Quadra," said Pitt.

Vancouver glanced at Pitt, who gave the slightest shrug. Valdés kept talking.

"He says, sir, they met the ships, Captain Broughton and all, at their anchorage, a week ago."

"They've come from Birch Bay?"

"He calls the place Port Quadra."

"Ah. Port Quadra," Vancouver repeated diplomatically.

As the launch from the *Sutil* pulled alongside, Valdés turned to see it made fast. Vancouver met Whidbey's eye.

Galiano climbed aboard and greeted them in English. There was another bout of hail-fellow-well-met all round.

"Welcome, welcome, *Capitán*. Gentlemans. Please to excuse, my Inglès is no good. I to hope for meet since we to find you ships. Please: will do honour of join us for to eat?" Galiano looked at the grubby British seamen, now assembled on deck and closely observing the Spanish ship. "We see you mans to eat as well."

The officers ate in the cramped cabin, the men on deck. Whidbey would remember the meal as ample though plain, unremarkable save for the sweet black coffee served from a silver pot, and Galiano and Valdés as friendly and gracious. Whidbey felt an immediate affinity with them, for they were knowledgeable surveyors and mapmakers on a mission similar to their own.

The Spaniards listened attentively as Vancouver described their recent survey work, Galiano providing brief translations for Valdés. Galiano explained that they were completing the charting of the region begun in preceding years. Quadra had ordered several of the other vessels under his command at Nootka out on similar missions all along the coast.

"Tell me, *Capitán*," Galiano said as they sat back from their plates. He was a lean man with sharp eyes and a Roman nose. "*Capitán* Broughton tell us you find waterway to south? We have no to go there, therefore no to find."

"Yes. A very extensive one, containing a large archipelago. It took us three weeks to cover it completely. Many channels, all leading to dead ends."

"Then no Strait of Anián there," Galiano said with a shake of his head. "Or anywhere, if ask me."

"No. No Strait of Anián. But on the other hand, no 'Here be dragons' anymore, either."

Galiano laughed. He translated for Valdés, who laughed and replied.

"He say, no dragons, no monsters any kind," Galiano explained.

Vancouver nodded equably and raised his cup to sip his coffee.

"But very pretty country, Puget's Sound," Whidbey said. "A lot of potential, I'd say."

Vancouver's cup stopped midway to his mouth.

"*Mas cafe, Don Jorge?*" Valdés held the pot before him.

Vancouver's expression seemed pained as he accepted a refill. A moment later he glanced at Whidbey.

Menzies asked if they had done any botanizing during their voyage.

"Boat and icing? What is?"

"Botanize. The study of plants, vegetation, trees."

"Ah. No," Galiano replied, shaking his head. "Hah! No my special, no at all." He translated for Valdés, who grinned. "Map only. But at Nootka many farms we have. *Capitán* Alberni is soldier, make experiment with dirt. And we have Doctor Moziño who to collect in forest. He is educate man — to speak Latin like priest. Don Juan permit him to research — to boat-and-ice, as you say — when not to cure the peoples."

"I look forward tae making his acquaintance," Menzies said.

"Perhaps your Doctor Moziño will have some thoughts about the agricultural potential of Puget's Sound," Whidbey said. "To me it looked very promising."

Vancouver drained his cup. "Gentlemen, this has been delightful. A most welcome interlude. I daresay we all feel more like ourselves now, what?" He waved the cup at Menzies, the midshipmen, and Whidbey, his eyes coming to rest on Whidbey. "We must be on our way."

"*Capitán*," Galiano said. "My orders are assist English any way to can. Permit me to take *usted*, ah...to take you to ships. We to sail immediate. It to save you time and to give you men to rest. We have time then for to speak on explores."

Whidbey stretched his back and thought happily of the comfort this short voyage would afford them all.

Vancouver placed his cup on the table and made to rise. "Most gratified, Captain, thank you, but I would not trouble you. We will make the trip on our own. You have been most hospitable. Before we depart, if there is anything I can provide you from our supplies, I should be very happy to oblige."

Whidbey looked at him, thinking about their meagre inventory. Valdés looked from face to face, not comprehending the turn in the discussion.

"Is no trouble to take, *Capitán*," said Galiano. "I assure."

"No, no, we shall make our own way. But —" He raised a finger as if suddenly struck by an idea of exceptional worth. "My instructions are very similar to your own — to collaborate and lend assistance. So I will return here with my ships in a day. I propose that we then combine our efforts and proceed in company. That will give us time to share our survey results and discuss our findings."

Old Joe thought that Galiano's smile remained on his face beyond the normal span of receptive courtesy. The Spaniard exchanged glances with young Valdés before he acceded to the suggestion.

Whidbey pondered how all was fine graces and compliments this day.

Vancouver and his people made their goodbyes and re-boarded the longboat to make the journey back to Birch Bay. It proved long and arduous, as they fought a strong current and a raging tidal surge across a shallow shoal, perhaps the mouth of a river. Near midnight they landed to spend a few miserable hours on shore. As Whidbey sought a tolerable position on the ground, he thought regretfully about Galiano's offer to transport them to the ships. National honour, he understood now, would not be well served on a Spanish ferryboat.

They reached the anchorage at noon the following day. As they drew near, Old Joe was relieved to see the missing launch secured at *Discovery*'s stern, and its coxswain, young Jim Hawkins, looking down over the ship's side with young Dick Ramsay.

Vancouver boarded to the sound of the bosun's pipe, accepted a salute from his first lieutenant, Zach Mudge, and listened to his report. He asked a few clarifying questions and ordered a signal to *Chatham*: Mister

Broughton to attend him for a conference. Then he turned to look for Hawkins. He spotted him waiting nervously in the throng on deck.

"Mister Hawkins," he said. "Will you join me in my cabin."

It was not a question.

# Chapter 2

You will glimpse my shadow from time to time, and even hear my thoughts. You may wonder at them, or find me opinionated. Judgy. Even intrusive.

This strikes me as ironic, as I gaze around at Nature Rampant: the lush valleys and steep forested peaks of the Pacific Northwest, so unspoilt and green this day in 1792, so burnt and barren now. Excuse me if I've telegraphed too much of *your* future plotline — I don't know when you're reading this. It saddens me, the devastation humanity will wreak, even though it will be good for me and my kind. Someone's misfortune is always another's opportunity.

You imposed yourselves where you never belonged. You intruded on our domain. Do I not have the right to intrude on yours?

⧗

We return now to Nootka Sound. It is two months since George Vancouver met Dionisio Galiano and Cayetano Valdés off the Spanish Banks, two weeks until the grisly discovery of that body on shore. *Discovery* has just arrived; her anchor has bottomed, all way is off. At her side stands a skiff with a cox'n and crew already aboard. Two men clamber down into it. The cox'n waits for them to settle, then puts off, calling "Lively, lads, lively!" and steering for the landing.

The decks aboard *Discovery* teem with activity, purposeful as an anthill at dawn. From stem to stern, sailormen haul and heave, coil and stow, climb, descend. At the spar gallows on the main, a gang takes the weight of a longboat on block and tackle, lifts it clear, and swings it to the starboard falls to lower it into the water. Another gang swings a cutter to the other side while, forward of them, a pair of gun crews muster to fire a salute. High above their heads, topmen furl sails and begin the work of clearing the rigging. One of them drops a line to deckhands below; they take it up, other lines follow, and others take them. Together they ease a heavy spar down onto the main. The ship's carpenter guides it to a rest and stoops over it. He sees the timber is cracked, curses, stands, and hawks over the side — narrowly missing a rating running powder to the guns. Aft, on the quarterdeck, seamen furl and fold the mizzen staysail and coil its lines. At the stern a mate kneels, clipping flags to a halyard. He finishes, stands, and runs them up. They catch the breeze and crack like thunder, simultaneously proclaiming *Discovery*'s arrival and her captain's will.

Surrounded by motion, Lieutenant George Vancouver stands at the brim of his quarterdeck, noticing none of it. His eyes are fixed on the settlement ringing Friendly Cove.

⏳

Fourteen years before, a populous Indian village had stood on the ledge above the cove. Now, in its place, there were barracks, workshops, storehouses, solid if rough-hewn and unadorned — except for the largest structure, a whitewashed two-story with a peaked roof and a balcony facing the harbour. A red and gold flag fluttered languidly from a tall pole in front of it.

Beyond the settlement the forest had been carved back, the resultant clearings delimited by fences. Within these enclosures lay cultivated gardens and fields. Cattle grazed where clearing met forest. A large crucifix stood against the horizon, its vertical a trunk left standing when the primal forest was felled.

Vancouver's eyes returned to the settlement. He counted the buildings and estimated the numbers they could accommodate.

"I didnae expect this."

Vancouver turned to see Menzies.

"The town, Captain. It was'na here five years ago. There was just Maquinna's village then. The Spaniards look tae be settling in."

Vancouver turned back to observe the settlement.

Menzies lowered his voice. "How're ye feeling, Captain?"

Vancouver glanced at him before returning to his study of the shore. "Much better, Mister Menzies, thank you. Yes. I am much improved."

They stood for a long minute without speaking.

"With your permission, Captain, I'd like tae get the sick ashore as quick as possible."

"Granted. Wait, though, until we've gone through the formalities with the Spaniards. I'll raise it at the first opportunity."

Menzies inclined his head, turned to go — and froze. A crewman descending the mizzen ratline had jumped the last few feet and narrowly missed landing inside the wooden enclosure that housed botanical specimens. "For God's sake, mon! Be careful there." He hurried aft to admonish him further.

Vancouver's eyes narrowed. That penned space was crowded with greenery, clay pots, boxes of soil, and cuttings from the Scot's rambles ashore over the summer. All sanctioned by the meddlesome Joseph Banks, who considered a working naval vessel an appropriate platform for ivies, mosses, fungi, and the like.

He frowned and glanced away. A few feet to his lee his first lieutenant stood conferring with Old Joe Whidbey and Lieutenant Baker over the ship's transition from sea to port. Mudge looked up and found himself under scrutiny.

"Sir?"

Vancouver waved a hand. "Nothing, Mister Mudge. Carry on." He strolled aft, past Menzies, the mizzen mast, and the wheel, and edged around the enclosure. It occupied half his quarterdeck and was still too small to contain all the botanist-surgeon's plants. Some of them were stored outside the frame. Banks, he mused sourly, would happily transform his ship into an ark, mission be damned. He stopped at the taffrail, leaned a foot on a plant pot, and examined the promontory commanding the entrance to the cove. A wooden palisade stood at its summit. Cannon sprouted from it like spring growth. A Spanish flag streamed energetically from a spindly pole at its centre.

A native dugout crowded with Spaniards drew towards the fortress. He watched it for a moment before turning his attention to *Chatham*. He was relieved to see her safely at anchor. The ships had separated in fog earlier that day and the brig had preceded *Discovery* into Friendly Cove, evidently without incident. He studied her squat profile, gauging how she stood in the water. Her hull was in desperate need of repair.

Close by *Chatham* rode the supply ship *Daedalus*, fresh from England via Port Jackson in Australia. The previous week, via a chance meeting with a British trader, he had learned of her arrival in the northwest. He'd been stunned to hear of the murder of her commander, Richard Hergest, along with the astronomer sent belatedly to help with the survey, by natives in Hawaii.

⧗

Both deaths were a blow, but Richard Hergest's had struck hardest, for he was a close friend. They'd been shipmates together on Cook's voyages, and two years before they'd both been posted to *Discovery*. Then Hergest was reassigned to *Daedalus*, which needed a commander with experience of the Pacific. And then he was murdered — in the same place, and in the very manner, as Cook.

Vancouver's crews were exhausted from their long summer's work, his ships in need of repair. The day he learned of Hergest's death, he decided to make for Nootka Sound. There, he would receive his dispatches from *Daedalus*, finish the transaction with the Spanish commissioner (this Quadra of whom Dino Galiano had spoken), and refit for the voyage back to the Sandwich Islands, where his ships would winter. He had orders to chart the entire Hawaiian archipelago, and he would use the opportunity to seek justice for Richard Hergest. In the spring *Discovery* and *Chatham* would return to the northwest to complete their survey of the coast.

On the voyage to Nootka, he fell ill, a combination of ailments including a hard cough he'd had for months and the recurring fever he'd contracted while serving in the Caribbean. Menzies prescribed rest and Vancouver had reluctantly followed his advice. He left the ship to Mudge and, alone in his cabin, grieved for his friend. His thoughts inevitably returned to the tragedy they had witnessed together, indeed participated in, the train of events that had led to Cook's death. The Sandwich Islanders had turned from friendly to belligerent. No one understood why. When Young Van (Hergest had always called him that) led a boat crew ashore, the natives attacked and nearly overwhelmed them; they fought in the shallows, broke free, and swam for it, battered and bleeding but alive. The following day Cook went ashore with another crew, and was attacked, overwhelmed, and killed. Young Van saw it all from the ship with Young Hergest and everyone else, helpless. Sensations from those days still returned to him in bright flashes, the acrid taste of terror, the uncertain guilt of surviving.

In the solitude of his cabin, he pondered James Cook's decline, the mistakes he'd made and the calamities that had resulted. Van swore he would not let it happen to him. He would not make the same mistakes as Cook.

After two days he felt well enough, as well as he ever did. He resumed his place on the quarterdeck as the ship made its way down the fog-shrouded coast towards Friendly Cove.

He turned from his contemplation of *Daedalus* to complete his examination of the harbour. Across the cove there were two merchant brigs, one British, the other American. Close by his own anchorage, to which he had been led minutes ago by a Spanish pilot, stood the brig *Activa*, the only Spanish warship present in the harbour. From its masthead flew the broad pennant of a commodore. Quadra's, he thought.

Around him, the bustle of the ship's arrival was settling into a semblance of routine. The officers' conference ended and they dispersed; Baker beckoned to a watchman, Whidbey went forward to attend to some task, and Mudge went below. Vancouver glanced to confirm that boats from *Daedalus* and *Chatham* were pulling towards *Discovery*, drawn by his signal and bearing their commanders. He would confer with them before going ashore. But first: he glanced ashore to see his own skiff, bearing the Spanish pilot and Lieutenant Peter Puget, land below the settlement. He watched Puget step ashore and return a salute from a waiting Spaniard.

# Chapter 3

About the missing Indian village at the mouth of Nootka Sound.

It wasn't *Indian*. It was *Mowachaht*. That is what they called themselves, the people of the deer, and they had lived in the place they called Yuquot for four thousand years. In their own language Yuquot means "where the wind comes from all directions," which is true, and tragically apropos, given the events I shall relate.

The Mowachaht were whalers, and Yuquot had been their whaling base for centuries. Yet here it lay abandoned — nay, replaced, by a European outpost.

When Europeans first arrived in the northwest, they acquired sea otter pelts from the people they called Indians, and sold them in China for a two thousand percent profit — gold-rush returns that begat a frenzy. Adventurers rushed to the region to trade. They gravitated to Nootka Sound, which had many sheltered anchorages including, at its mouth, Friendly Cove, on which perched Yuquot.

The Mowachaht seized upon the opportunities their presence afforded. They assumed the role of middlemen, acquiring furs from other Indigenous peoples and trading them on to the white men for metal, tools, and cloth.

The *tyee* (chief, or *tayiihawil*) of the Mowachaht was Maquinna, and within Nootka Sound he was paramount. There were other *tyee* but they were subordinate to him — though grudgingly, for no headman was ever beyond challenge. Beyond the Sound, Maquinna had powerful rivals. Wickaninnish of the Tla-o-qui-aht was the most prominent among them, his people the most numerous. Then there was Cleaskinah of the Ahousaht, who were adept at war; and Tatoosh of the Makah, who lived on the south side of Juan de Fuca Strait. These three *tyee* wanted for themselves the benefits Maquinna had secured as a trade middleman. All four kept tabs on one another and manoeuvred for advantage whenever they could.

Meanwhile, several white nations were doing the same thing.

Spain had long claimed the Pacific Northwest for itself, although other imperial powers blithely ignored its sovereign pretensions. By the mid-1780s, Russian, British, and American traders were operating openly in the region, and Spain felt compelled finally to add muscle to its claim. In 1789 it dispatched a naval force under Esteban José Martínez to occupy Nootka Sound. Martínez arrived that spring to find numerous traders active in the Sound. He demanded to see their papers, questioned them about their activities, inspected their cargoes. Soon he clashed with a belligerent Englishman named James Colnett, arrested him and his men, and impounded both his ships.

Calicum, Maquinna's brother and closest advisor, recognized this as a power grab by the Spanish, one that endangered the trading relationships that had proven so beneficial to the Mowachaht. He counselled Maquinna to stand up to Martínez before it was too late.

Maquinna waffled. Calicum did not. He paddled out to Martínez's ship and gave him an earful. What gives *you* the right to act like this in *our* territory? he demanded. He also complained about Martínez's own trading practices, which were, to put it delicately, shrewd.

Annoyed at the lengthy harangue, Martínez asked his interpreter what the stranger was saying. When he found out, he grabbed a musket from a Spanish marine and shot Calicum dead.

There had been violence before, but this, the murder of Maquinna's brother, a chieftain in his own right! Maquinna saw now what Calicum had seen, that the Spaniards were making their move. He fled Yuquot for Clayoquot Sound, where he sought the protection of his rival Wickaninnish.

Martínez made no further hostile moves. Instead, he sent conciliatory messages and gifts. Maquinna was unsure what to do. Not least of his concerns was his humiliation at being under Wickaninnish's thumb —

he knew he had lost face before his peers. After a few days he returned to Yuquot and led his people away. They moved up the coast to one of their whaling camps, and in the autumn when the weather changed they moved again to the head of Tahsis Inlet, in the interior of the Sound, twenty miles north of Yuquot. Tahsis was where they traditionally wintered; now it became their place of permanent exile. As for Yuquot — well, it was theirs, and their sacred prayer house was in the forest nearby. They had no intention of giving it up forever.

⧗

After the seizure of James Colnett's ships, the chiefs braced for what would follow. And what followed? More traders in quest of furs and pelts, and more Spaniards, a force of two hundred and fifty men. The latter built a base for themselves at Yuquot, which had a sheltered harbour and commanding heights for a defensive bastion. Although Maquinna remained wary of them, he re-established relations and supplied them with food, and men and canoes to deliver it, in return for things he and his people needed.

Calicum had been respected among the Mowachaht, beloved even, and many of the *tyeeclati* grumbled that there had been no justice exacted for him. Circumstances do not allow it, Maquinna replied. We must move forward. He was right — things were complicated. There was both great peril and tremendous opportunity in the situation prevailing in Nootka Sound. A rising tide lifts all canoes; a storm can turn them over.

In those initial years the Spanish commanders lacked understanding, or even curiosity, about those they had dispossessed. They busied themselves carving out their dominion, in the process of which they tore apart native lodges and repurposed their timbers to build their own settlement. Their underlings cheated and robbed and brutalized the natives they encountered. Meanwhile, the traders who visited the region focused on getting rich. Many traded peaceably. Others cheated and stole and ransacked to get what they wanted. Traders torched a village, seized hostages, opened fire on unarmed men, women, and children. Across the region, people died or got hurt; and whenever their chiefs organized to retaliate, the perpetrators sought the protection of the Spanish garrison

THE WIND FROM ALL DIRECTIONS | 29

at Yuquot, gladly tilting their hats to the Spanish flag in return for the safety afforded by their guns. For the Spaniards, this was a more effective way of projecting sovereignty than the gunboat diplomacy employed by Martínez. So what if a few savages had gotten hurt?

Things remained this way, tense and on the cusp of violence, until the spring of 1792, when the arrival of a new Spanish commander, the Peruvian-born nobleman Juan Francisco de la Bodega y Quadra, heralded a change in approach.

⧗

Quadra arrived in April with a fleet and substantial reinforcements for the garrison. He immediately sent out expeditions to explore and map the coast, and put those who remained behind to work building up the settlement the Spanish called Santa Cruz de Nuca.

Emissaries travelled regularly between the region's Indigenous villages, bringing news and offering brides and grooms and the alliances that went with them, as well as intelligence on the movements and activities of traders and ships. There was great interest everywhere in this new Spanish commander. The chiefs of various peoples sent queries to Maquinna at Tahsis. What of this Quadra? they wanted to know.

Before Maquinna could call on Quadra to take his measure, Quadra called on him.

First a Spanish messenger arrived in Tahsis with a polite request from the new commander for permission to visit. Two days later the man himself showed up with an entourage of officers and aides. Some of them were long-timers at Yuquot and fluent in the Mowachaht language, Pedro Alberni most notably. They acted as Quadra's translators and explained things when he had questions.

And the man had *questions* — he was curious about everything. He observed, pondered, listened with an attentive smile. Maquinna laid on a feast in his honour, and he responded with delight at everything it involved. "*Delicioso!*" he exclaimed of the food, "*Espléndido!*" of the entertainment. Drumming, dance, and song seemed to enthrall him. He applauded and smiled and nodded his head, telling the performers "*Gracias, gracias!*" and "*Mucho gusto!*" and shaking their hands with enthusiasm. He expressed interest in everything and everyone he met, though it was noted that his greatest displays of appreciation were directed towards Maquinna.

He gifted like a Mowachaht, showering the performers, the *tyeeclati*, and the elders with presents of cloth and jewellery, metal tools, copper utensils, mirrors, even a beautiful coat of Spanish mail for Maquinna. It earned him a lot of respect.

What people liked best was that he spoke candidly. What had happened at Yuquot between Martínez and Colnett, he told Maquinna, had almost caused a war. But the two white kings, Carlos of Spain and George of England, had decided on peace. Quadra had been sent to make amends with the English, who were sending a representative to meet with him. There would be talks to resolve matters between the two great monarchs. After that, Quadra would return Yuquot to the Mowachaht and withdraw with his garrison. Spain would have no permanent presence north of the Strait of Juan de Fuca, although King Carlos and King George would jointly protect all the people of that territory from the depredations of the white men who came there to trade. Until then, Quadra would reside at Yuquot and protect them with his garrison and ships. He would see that peace and order were maintained, that justice prevailed. While I am here you can count on Spanish justice, Quadra assured Maquinna.

This assertion gave Maquinna pause. What did he know of Spanish justice? What's more, he wasn't sure he wanted the protection of the Spanish *or* the English king.

There have been incidents, he said finally, looking around to find his nephews — Calicum's sons Comekala and Copaza — in the crowd. Many incidents.

I am aware, Quadra said. You have my word that within the power I possess, I will act fairly and justly to all. I will uphold Spanish justice. No innocents will suffer at my hand. I will do my utmost to protect your people.

Maquinna was still unconvinced about Spanish justice, what with his kinsman dead these three years without repercussion. What's more, it sounded to him like the Spanish and the English intended to meet at Yuquot for a kind of potlatch, and who knew what that entailed among white men. He sent messengers to Wickaninnish, Cleaskinah, and

Tatoosh with his assessment of the new Spanish commander.

Messengers travelled between villages all the time; that spring Maquinna heard about the burning of Wickaninnish's village, an attack on another, the movements of various traders and Quadra's ships. Then, shortly after Quadra's visit, a messenger arrived in Tahsis from Tatoosh, reporting that two ships had anchored briefly within Juan de Fuca Strait. They had traded with the Makah, though only for food. Then they sailed east and disappeared into the sheltered sea on which the Salish lived. Their leader's name was Wancoobair. In the dirt beside the council fire, the messenger drew the image of the flag flown from Wancoobair's ships. Everyone recognized it. They had a long discussion about what these Englishmen were up to; none of their countrymen had previously ventured into the Salish Sea. These ones had done so purposefully.

In May, Wickaninnish and Cleaskinah both came to meet Maquinna in Tahsis to discuss atrocities committed by the American trader Gray, who had caused many deaths.

We need to stand together, Wickaninnish said. We need to expel these murderers.

Not all the white men are murderers, Maquinna said. Quadra is a man we can deal with.

Wickaninnish cast an eye around Maquinna's lodge, where a Spanish coat of armour hung on one wall, several muskets on another.

Maquinna read his look. The two of them stared at each other.

Cleaskinah listened to the arguments each of them made and sided with Maquinna. He was not ready for a war against all the whites.

We'll need to set this right, Wickaninnish said. Sooner or later we'll have to.

The chiefs went home, but the debate continued. Intelligence was shared, messengers came and went, emissaries shuttled back and forth to discuss options and responses — and united resistance was always among them. Meanwhile, every chief was working to secure more pelts and furs for himself and his people, in order to obtain more trade goods from the white men.

In late spring Quadra sent a ship and a detachment of soldiers into the heart of Makah territory. Tatoosh reported that they were constructing buildings and fortifications. A few weeks later Quadra sent two more ships into Juan de Fuca Strait. They stopped briefly at their tiny new post there, then sailed east into Salish territory.

✇

Nothing had been heard of the two English ships that had preceded them weeks before. Then a confusing report arrived, one that originated with the Salish but passed through numerous intermediaries on the way to Tahsis. The messenger drew a flag of crosses on the ground and reported that the chief of these white men was named Macubah, and that he wore the jaws of a wolf upon his head.

No one at council knew what to make of that. Could this Macubah (they reasoned he must be Wancoobair) be a shaman? The whites had never had a shaman leader before.

Maquinna's young kinsman Comekala was called before them. He had journeyed on an English vessel to China and learned about the English and their ways and the world beyond Nootka Sound. He debunked the wolf-shaman notion immediately. The Salish, he reasoned, had never seen a white man before. They had seen the jaws of a wolf in an Englishman's cocked hat.

Well, that garnered some laughter at the expense of the foolish Salish; but Maquinna did not join in. Nor did the shaman Tsakwasap, who scowled and spat on the ground and shook his ceremonial rattle for their attention and said, You with smiles on your faces — *you* are the fools, not the Salish. This is no laughing matter. Every year, more white men come, and nothing good ever comes in their wake.

Maquinna glanced at the walls of his lodge and kept his own counsel.

✇

All summer reports about Macubah continued to arrive. It was observed that he did not collect furs, although he did exchange metal and cloth for food. He and his men travelled far from their ships in awkward small boats. They rowed, landed, rowed again, then returned to their ships, sailed north, and repeated their strange rituals. They seemed to look into every bay and cove.

THE WIND FROM ALL DIRECTIONS | 33

Always looking east, someone at council observed. Maybe they are sun worshippers.

They're searching for something, another councillor said. Perhaps the shrines of the Salish or the bones of their dead.

Tsakwasap interrupted him with a shake of his rattle. They do not act like men on a spiritual quest, he said with scorn, but like the wolf that marks its territory.

When Comekala heard this, he laughed and said the shaman was close: the English were making maps. He explained what maps signified and how the English used them.

For the first time Maquinna wondered if the leader of these Englishmen, this Macubah/Wancoobair, was the man Quadra was waiting to meet.

Ten days later a visitor from the Kwakwaka'wakw brought news from the Salish that Macubah had encountered the Spanish ships that had unknowingly followed him into the Salish Sea. Their meeting appeared friendly, and they kept each other's company for several days before separating. The English ships pushed north and entered Kwakwaka'wakw territory, passing through the narrow channels at the north end of the Salish Sea. Now news reached Tahsis quickly. Maquinna and his advisors heard that one ship, then the other, grounded. It looked for a while like both would be wrecked. Kwakwaka'wakw couriers described what Macubah's men did to save them. First, they lightened them by unloading everything to shore. Then they took down their masts and timbers and used them to prop their hulls and prevent capsizing. At high tide they refloated them, hauling the vessels into open water with their small boats. There they reloaded, raised their masts, and continued their slow procession along the coast until they turned towards Yuquot.

Maquinna had not told Quadra about the reports he was receiving, and so the Spaniard was unaware of Macubah's approach. Indeed, in late summer he seemed to abandon hope that the man he was waiting for would arrive that year. He sent several of his ships away to New Spain with many of his men. It was well known that he was short of provisions for them. His numbers were a costly burden. He was dependent upon the Mowachaht for supplies.

It was the cusp of autumn, and the weather would soon turn. Maquinna knew that Quadra and this Macubah intended to transact business before winter set in — and his seat at Yuquot was the prize. His many rivals were watching and itching for his comeuppance, or a good fight, or both. He knew he could not sit idly by. When he heard of Macubah's arrival, he set out immediately to take his measure.

# Chapter 4

"As Señor Quadra resided ashore," wrote Vancouver in his journal that night, "I sent Mister Puget to acquaint him with our arrival, and to say, that I would salute the Spanish flag, if he would return an equal number of guns. On receiving a very polite answer in the affirmative, we saluted with thirteen guns, which were returned, and on my going on shore accompanied by some of the officers, we had the honour of being received with the greatest cordiality and attention from the commandant, who informed me he would return our visit the next morning."

And oh, that morning. An azure sky unflecked by cloud with Venus shining bright, a pristine seascape bordered by rainforest and towering mountains. The harbour bustled with boats crisscrossing between ships and shore. A watering party from *Discovery* had put off early. Another boat had carried a work party ashore to raise the marquee and tent for the observatory. On board, cleaning stations had ended and the forenoon watch had begun. Lieutenant Baker was on the quarterdeck with Midshipman Hawkins when a marine climbed up the after companionway stairs and saluted.

"Mister Baker, sir, captain requests you join him and Mister Mudge. Regarding the charts, sir."

"Thank you, Private." Baker cast an eye around and forward to the bow. "Mister Hawkins, you have the watch."

"Aye, Mister Baker. I have the watch."

Unlike a watch at sea, an anchor watch was undemanding. Everyone knew their duties and there was little for Hawkins to do; and so he stood with the sun on his back and studied the Spanish settlement for the umpteenth time. He had yet to go ashore. There was plenty of activity visible in the little town, groups of men working on the foreshore, boats landing and putting off. He followed the progress of one towards its mother ship, a trader in the outer roadstead of the cove. That was when he noticed a long Indian canoe approaching at speed from the Sound. It was propelled by twenty men, all bare-chested, their faces gleaming with ochre. A man in a fur robe and a tapered headdress worn like a crown sat placidly at its centre. His face was unpainted.

The great dugout slowed in the roads and altered course. Hawkins moved to the brim of the quarterdeck to see it better. Its prow was high and carved with the stylized head of a beast. It came towards *Discovery* and altered course again to circle the ship. On its second pass the man in the robe stood, extended his arms, and called to those on deck. He was a big man, broad across the shoulders, and he spoke with gravitas, delivering a fine, even eloquent speech, though none of its recipients understood a word of it. The canoe completed another circuit while he held forth, and when he finished its handlers brought it alongside. It came to an instant stop below the net ladder on the main deck.

This feat of seamanship brought a murmur of admiration from the men on deck. The robed orator reached for the ladder.

"*OY!* 'Oo's 'e think 'e is?"

Hawkins was frozen in fascination but this broke the spell. No one boarded *Discovery* without permission. He clapped a watchman on the back. "Miller. Haul up that netting, quick about it. You — Steeves. Fetch Mister Baker."

The Indian grabbed for the netting just as Miller pulled it away, and for a moment he teetered. He looked up at Miller in surprise — at which Miller grinned and went, "Yeah, yeah, yeah," and those behind him laughed. The Indian glared at him indignantly.

"Miller. All of you. That's enough."

This simple command drew the man's attention onto Hawkins. His eyes flashed angrily and he flicked a finger at the boy's red hair and launched into a harangue.

Baker appeared at Hawkins's side. "What's he riled about?"

"Beggar tried to board, Mister Baker," Miller said before Hawkins could answer.

"Well, if we were expecting company I'd have put on some tea. You men — stand by with boathooks. We'll push him off if he tries again." He looked around for the corporal of marines, who was mustering a squad.

The Indian now extended his fury to Baker. In the canoe, a young man sitting close by him tried to speak. He was drowned out in the commotion.

"If looks could kill, Jim," Baker observed to Hawkins.

Now the young Indian stood and tried to be heard above his angry countryman.

Baker wagged his finger and said, "No."

This silenced both of them. The man in the robe glared up at the faces above. At last he gave an order to the canoeists. The young man sat down, the paddlers drew water, the canoe separated from the ship. When it was ten feet off, the robed man signalled with his fist, the craft stopped dead, and once again he addressed the ship. This time his voice was calm and full of contempt. He finished what he had to say and turned away. The canoe set off towards the Spanish settlement at a stately, even pace.

His head held high, Maquinna of the Mowachaht remained standing, his gaze to the fore.

⧗

When he landed he stormed in on the Spanish governor.

I will not tolerate insults in my country, he said. In *my* territory.

I am sure it was a misunderstanding, Quadra replied via his garrison commander, the soldier Pedro Alberni.

I have offered my hand to you. Not these people.

Quadra dispatched a messenger to *Discovery*, and a half hour later George Vancouver arrived at the big whitewashed building that served as the governor's headquarters. He was accompanied by Lieutenant Puget, Midshipmen Lincoln and Barrie, and a squad of marines bearing a heavy trunk. Quadra met them at the entrance for a word to the wise, then ushered him upstairs into the hall he used for receiving — the grandest (onliest) salon north of Alta California. Maquinna was waiting there with a small entourage. The chief's temper had cooled since the incident. Now he was merely frosty. He made his displeasure known.

Vancouver listened without interrupting, his head cocked to Comekala, the chief's translator — the young man from the canoe.

"Would you kindly tell your esteemed chief," he told Comekala when Maquinna was done, "that no offence was intended. We made a mistake. A most unfortunate and embarrassing mistake. We were not expecting or prepared for his visit." Now he turned and looked Maquinna straight in the eye. "Please accept my personal apology — and allow me to make amends. I ask that you join me aboard *Discovery* in one hour, when I and my people will welcome you in a manner reflecting our true esteem. In the meantime, I beg you accept these tokens of friendship from my king, His Britannic Majesty George the Third."

He gestured to his two midshipmen, who filed forward, followed by the marines with the trunk. Inside it was a variety of trade goods — swaths of cloth, copper plates, medals, mirrors, and blades, whatever he had been able to cobble together on short notice. The supply ship *Daedalus* had brought fresh stock, but there had been no time yet to board it.

"Many years ago," Vancouver said when he and Puget had distributed gifts to everyone in Maquinna's group, "I visited your village here with Captain Cook, and I recall with fondness the hospitality and kindness of your people." There was more flowery talk along these lines, but he saved the best for the end. "It is my sincere hope and earnest wish that you will accept my apologies, and the amends I am able to make —" he gestured to the presents piled around "— and, most importantly to me, my friendship." Then, tapping his breast and holding Maquinna's eye, he surprised everyone present with the words "*Huacas* Maquinna, *Huacas* George Vancouver. *Huacas* King George," the word *huacas* closely approximating the Mowachaht word for *friend*.

This brought a smile to Maquinna's face and produced a guffaw from his translator Comekala. There followed gracious words of forgiveness and welcome. And so it appeared that George Vancouver had turned an ugly situation around, that he had pulled a rabbit from his worn cocked hat.

Quadra took in the performance and exchanged glances with Alberni.

Barrie and Lincoln exchanged vague smiles.

※

As the boats bearing the visitors approached *Discovery*, two guns forward on the main fired a salute in their honour and the ship's company mustered formally, the ratings forward, the lieutenants with the captain at the gangway, the petty officers and midshipmen on the quarterdeck. Everyone was in dress uniform, the officers sharp in their blue jackets and white breeches. Jim Hawkins looked down self-consciously at *his* best clothes. After a voyage of a year and a half, his tunic and waistcoat were worn and threadbare, his white shirt faded and thin. It was a good thing he wore breeches this day because his everyday trousers were ridiculously short. He had grown six inches since leaving England.

The first boat came alongside and made fast. The boatswain piped the side, the marine guard presented arms. All was stillness on deck. Those who had not yet been ashore craned for their first look at the Spaniards.

Hawkins was at the end of the line of midshipmen, nearest the ship's side. He watched two hands grasp the gunwale; then, a cocked hat appeared and its wearer clambered up and over onto *Discovery*'s deck. Hawkins took in a long blue coat with gold trim and red collars and cuffs. Red breeches. A ruffled white shirt, a kerchief, a gold sword. A splendid sight it was, these fine wardrobe touches, and then he registered the man himself — long face, aquiline nose, thin lips forming a pleasant smile. He lifted his hat to greet his hosts and exposed a broad forehead and silver hair swept back, gathered and braided. His eyes, narrowed by his smile, were heavily creased, dark, and piercing, as though they saw into and through all they landed upon.

Vancouver and his officers returned the Spanish governor's salute and he returned his hat to his head. Then he shook Vancouver's hand, bowing forward a little to take it in both his own.

The next to board was a man who lacked Quadra's effortless grace. He was burly and grizzled, his thick hair streaked with grey. Although he was clean-shaven, his chin, even this early in the day, was heavily shadowed. He wore a different uniform than his commander, a sky-blue tunic with yellow collars and cuffs, a black hat with a red cockade.

"Ach! Crivvens!" whispered Dick Ramsay, next to Hawkins. "Two spay-cimens of a nyew variety of pay-cock, family *Hispanicus*. Ah had'nae haired o' them afore."

Snorts and sniggers came from farther down the line. Ramsay's impressions, especially that of the botanist/surgeon, Menzies, were favourites in the midshipmen's mess.

"Ach, mon. Sir Joseph Banks, mah patron — have Ah ayver mentioned him tae ewe? — he wadna mind a sketch o' these, Ah ken."

Lieutenant Baker, who was forward on the main, cast a look aft. The midshipmen immediately became purse-lipped statues. Hawkins was still on watch and took the glance as a summons. He fell out to join Baker, skirted the growing crowd at the ladder, and came face to face with the grizzled Spaniard.

"Alberni," proclaimed the man, grinning and thrusting his hand at him.

Hawkins took it and blurted his own name and kept moving. More Spanish officers were arriving on deck, and Mudge tried to move them inboard and out of the way. Just as Hawkins reached Baker's side the Spanish commandant drew the captain's attention to something in his boat. Hawkins looked over the side and the aroma of fresh bread struck him like a Dover coach. The boat's well contained baskets of golden loaves and bundles of vegetables.

"... very generous, Don Juan. My thanks on behalf of all hands." Vancouver turned to his officers. "Mister Mudge, Mister Baker, let's move everyone along. We'll have a crowd shortly. Ah. Mister Hawkins. See that the food is brought aboard and distributed to the messes."

Hawkins gathered a detail to board the food while the senior Spanish and British officers passed pleasantries and awaited the arrival of the morning's final guest of honour, the egregiously snubbed Maquinna.

⧗

Close by Vancouver's side that morning stood the stocky figure of Thomas Dobson, late of the store ship *Daedalus*, who had arrived aboard *Discovery* the day before when an unexpected problem suddenly presented itself. Although British and Spanish mariners alike had great facility in the pidgin used in ports around the world, there was no one in Friendly Cove capable of speaking both English and Spanish. No one, that is, except young Tom Dobson.

The previous night, before Dobson's linguistic talent became widely known, the cramped space where the midshipmen messed had been full of gleeful marvel.

"We left England with a hundred men and supplies for two years. Anchors, sailcloth, cordage, four boats —"

"Rosin, pitch, tar, turpentine, oakum, copper plate —"

"Beads and mirrors and fry pans to trade with the savages, fireworks to impress them and ten cannons and swivels with plenty of powder and ball if that didn't work. And —" Robert Barrie paused. "And food. Dickie, let's hear it."

Once a month for the last year Dick Ramsay had conducted a tedious inventory of the cook's supplies. He had made a game of it to entertain his mess mates.

"You really want it?" he asked Barrie.

"I do."

He turned to John Dorsey. "Are you hungry for it?"

"Oh, we are all hungry for it, Dickie."

"Well, all right, then. Ahem-hem. Four hundred pounds of mustard. Three hundred pounds of carrot marmalade. A ton and a half of oatmeal. Three thousand gallons of vinegar. Two hundred gallons of olive oil. A half ton of cheese —" Ramsay's eyes rolled for show. His voice, though, accelerated and assumed a cadence. "— thirty tons of biscuit, two thousand stone of peas, twenty tons of beef, fifteen of pork, ten of cabbage, four of salt, three of malt, two of raisins, one of butter *and* —"

"And!" shouted the midshipmen.

"And!" repeated Ramsay theatrically, stabbing a finger at Ned Roberts.

"And a partridge in a pear tree," sang Roberts in a quavering tenor.

They cheered. Roberts bowed. "Kiss me, you magnificent molly," Dorsey said, grabbing him and puckering. Roberts pushed him away.

"And for all the thought and planning and preparation that went into this voyage," Lincoln concluded, "no one considered bringing a fucking translator?"

"Incredible."

"Menzies has Latin," someone said, "and the Spaniards must have a priest. They could communicate that way."

"If you want to go old school, what about Greek?"

"What's wrong with French?" Tom Pitt asked.

This suggestion actually had merit. Pitt's French had come in handy with Valdés and Galiano in the Gulf of Georgia, and there were others on board who spoke it as well as he did. There had to be some French speakers among the many Spaniards in Friendly Cove.

French would be tricky, Barrie said. Too many intermediaries between the captain and the Spanish governor. You know how he gets a tad impatient, right?

There was quiet laughter at this, along with a few over-shoulder glances.

Yes, and French would tilt things too far in the Bourbons' favour, Ned Roberts added.

A smart lad, was Roberts, though a bit of an egghead.

"Ned's right. As we like to say in French..." Ramsay leaned to the side and farted.

Pitt was miffed they hadn't embraced his idea. "Well, if you want to keep it simple, there's always port pidgin. If it's good enough to hire a whore it's good enough to speak to Spaniards."

"Touché, Tom," Ramsay said. "Well played."

None of their proposals reached their captain, who had already discovered a superior solution in the person of Tom Dobson. Dobson had sailed as an owner's representative on *Daedalus*, which was contracted by the Admiralty and not a naval vessel per se. Within minutes of arriving on *Discovery* and meeting George Vancouver he was entered on the ship's roster as a midshipman. A short while later he was delivered to the midshipmen's mess by Peter Puget.

"We're full up in here, Mister Puget," Pitt said. Early on, he had assumed the role of spokesman for the middies.

Puget glanced around as if he had never seen their quarters. It was crowded to be sure, and the headspace was barely five feet. "Well, it looks roomy to me, but if it's as you say, one of you will have to go forward and mess with the ratings. Who'll it be?"

There was silence. Several of their peers, technically rated able seamen though training as midshipmen, were quartered with the crew; none of them *wanted* to be there.

"You go, Neddy," John Dorsey said. "You were last in."

All eyes fell on Ned Roberts, whose face went ashen. Indeed, he was the most recent addition to the mess, having moved in six months before. He had had some unspecified trouble, a conflict with one of the ratings, before the move. Some of the midshipmen had grumbled about having to give him precious space.

"Mister Roberts stays," Puget said. "What about you, Mister Dorsey?"

Dorsey dropped his gaze from Puget's face.

"I suppose I could pick someone," Puget said. "Or we could take down this wall." He knocked on the planking that separated their berth from the area where the ratings hung their hammocks. It made for a crowded space, but it was *their* crowded space, the only near-privacy they had on the ship.

Grudgingly, they made room for one more hammock.

⌛

The food was quickly hauled up and the Spanish boat moved off to allow Maquinna's canoe to come alongside. The chief clambered onto the main without ceremony, followed quickly by his translator Comekala, who rendered Vancouver's formal words of welcome into Mowachaht. Maquinna listened and replied with gravitas, the kind with which he had delivered his initial oration before being turned away two hours before.

"My chief welcomes you," Comekala said a moment later, addressing Vancouver, "and in the spirit of his friendship with King George, which is of many years' standing, he wishes to provide you these gifts from his lands."

One of Maquinna's men landed nimbly on deck and reached down to take the end of a pole from another below. A third man joined him and together they manoeuvred an antlered stag, hung from its hooves, onto the ship. They held it between them while Vancouver and Mudge admired it and thanked Maquinna, and then Hawkins detailed two men to take it below. Another stag followed. Then several large salmon were handed up and laid out on deck.

Vancouver bowed to the chief. "In the name of King George I am pleased to accept the chief's generous gifts. May the exchanges between us mark the continuation of the lasting friendship between his people and those of King George." He allowed a pause, then continued with equal gravity, "And the commencement of a new and enduring friendship between the chief and myself."

Comekala translated and Vancouver proffered his hand. Quadra, the Spanish delegation, and *Discovery's* entire complement stood by, watching them nod solemnly and wring each other's hands.

Vancouver ushered his guests aft towards the great cabin. On the way Maquinna passed Jim Hawkins and pointedly looked away.

"Don't worry about it," Baker told him later, then related a story he'd heard from the captain himself. In May of 1778, just weeks after Cook's vessels departed Nootka Sound, they were at anchor far to the north while watering parties worked ashore. Over the previous days they'd met and traded with the local Indians, who seemed peaceable, and reasonable in trade, if somewhat obsessed with metal. On Cook's consort vessel, on which Vancouver then served, an anchor watch remained on deck while the bulk of the crew went below for dinner. A pair of canoes approached and their occupants made signs about wanting to trade. They were waved in. They climbed aboard, suddenly brandished clubs and knives, and overwhelmed the watch. Moments later, a crewman came up from below to visit the head. He took in a startling scene: his shipmates corralled and savages relieving them of their buckles and buttons and considering their next move. The man bellowed an alarm, his fellows rushed up from below, and the Indians jumped down into their canoes and fled. No one was hurt — and the next day the same men came back to trade as if nothing had happened.

"Thank God for pickled cabbage," Baker concluded, clapping Hawkins on the back. "Who knows what might have happened had Jack Tar not felt the urge to move his bowels. You followed standing orders, Jim. The captain will never ream anyone for that."

Barely two months before, Vancouver *had* reamed Hawkins out, after their boats became separated in Jervis Inlet. The reprimand came as a shock to young Jim. After all, he had led the boat safely back to the ship. There had been no loss of life or limb. In his naïveté he had expected a word of praise.

Instead, Vancouver tore him a new one. It was a first for Hawkins, and he did not enjoy the experience. Now he was chastened, worried that his career was over before it was fairly launched. What's more, truth be told, he was in awe of George Vancouver — had been from the day he stepped aboard *Discovery*. He had sought his approval at every step; he yearned for it now. With hard work and devotion to duty, he yet hoped to redeem himself in his hero's eyes.

After the dignitaries had dined with *Discovery*'s senior officers they disembarked to the accompaniment of another thirteen-gun salute. They rowed over to *Chatham*, accompanied by Vancouver and Dobson, and *Chatham* fired its own salute as they approached, and again an hour later when the Spaniards and Maquinna disembarked and dispersed. By then a grey pall of smoke hung over the harbour.

# Chapter 5

That night, Quadra hosted a dinner at his headquarters in honour of his visitors. He greeted the officers from the British ships as they arrived at the landing, and walked between George Vancouver and *Chatham*'s William Broughton (with Midshipman Dobson trailing as closely as he could) up past an honour guard to the white building everyone called the Big House.

Quadra's officers were waiting in a receiving line just outside the entrance, and the two British captains stood with the Spanish commandant at its head to usher their own officers through. First came the lieutenants, followed by the warrant officers like Whidbey and James Johnstone, *Chatham*'s master, and Menzies, the botanist-surgeon.

"We are rather over-berthed with young gentlemen," Vancouver said as the first midshipman reached the front of the line. "It was felt by many that a voyage of our duration would build character."

Sometimes I worried about Van, what with a diplomatic issue to deal with shortly, and he no diplomat. Then he surprises with a poker-face here, a deft touch there. Now witness him at the door to the Big House, obscuring like a Medici. The fact was that the privileged sons of Britain's best families had been foisted upon him. He had been entrusted like a butler with their care and coddling, and it rankled. *Discovery*'s authorized complement of midshipmen was six, but strings had been pulled, favours called in. The ship had sailed with fifteen young gentlemen in a complement totalling one hundred. Perhaps half of them had been selected for their potential, the rest for their pedigree.

He glanced down the line at their young faces while Dobson translated. As many as could be spared from duty were ashore for the evening.

"I have the honour," he said when Dobson was ready, "of presenting the Honourable Charles Stuart, midshipman. Mister Stuart is the son of the Earl of Bute, who served as prime minister to His Majesty a number of years ago."

Quadra looked Stuart in the eye as he shook his hand and addressed him formally.

"Señor Stuart," said Dobson, "I am honoured to meet you. Service to your nation is in your blood."

Stuart contemplated his reply. A "Sir," a mute tilt of the head, a "How do you do?" He settled on "Your Excellency" and a small bow and moved on.

There followed the son or nephew of that lord, this admiral, that favourite. Each received a firm handshake, a look in the eye, a personalized greeting.

"The Honourable Thomas Pitt, midshipman," Vancouver said. "Mister Pitt is the son of Lord Camelford and cousin to our present prime minister, Mister William Pitt."

"I am pleased," Dobson told Pitt, "to meet such a *distinguished* son of a *b* — ah, the son of a such a *distinguished* British family."

Pitt, taller than the two commanders, nodded regally and gave Dobson the dead eye as he passed.

Van caught it and wondered if William Pitt was indeed still the prime minister. The dispatches he'd received off *Daedalus* had indicated so, but they were a year old. This son of the extended Pitt family had been a constant bur in his saddle. Dobson seemed to have taken his measure quickly. Others just turned a blind eye to his High Lord Muckymuck pretensions.

"Mister James Hawkins, midshipman." Vancouver paused, momentarily at a loss. There were no grand connections in this case. "Mister Hawkins," he said finally, "is from Halifax, in Nova Scotia."

Quadra shook his hand. "Nova Scotia! I am honoured, Señor Hawkins. I myself was born in Peru. We two are Americans, north and south, yes?"

Hawkins looked at Dobson as these words were translated, then back at Quadra, whose expression was open and pleasant. Hawkins remembered his impression that morning, of a man who missed nothing. He inclined his head and moved along to meet Pedro Alberni. The soldier's handshake was a vice.

"Mister Richard Ramsay, midshipman..."

The visitors were conducted into the Big House as they exited the line. Its ground floor was occupied by a guard barrack, a mess hall, and a bustling kitchen.

"That was quite a gauntlet out there," Old Joe Whidbey murmured to Archibald Menzies, nodding affably to a steward who directed them towards a staircase. "I half expected the Inquisition at the end of it."

"You have a guilty conscience, Whidbey. D'ye have something in need o' confessing?"

"Said the vicar to the lady."

They climbed the stairs to a landing with two doorways. A young Spanish officer stood in front of one, gesturing agreeably towards the other. Whidbey walked through it into a large, high-ceilinged hall lit by a copper chandelier. Additional light was provided by lanterns hung on the interior wall, which was adorned by Spanish flags, several fowling pieces, and a pair of rapiers mounted across a shield. Opposite this wall were a pair of windows and a door to a smaller room. Whidbey looked inside and saw shelves of rolled charts, a table covered with ledgers, and more charts. The table stood in front of a doorway that gave onto a balcony overlooking the harbour. Someone appeared to be out there, taking the air.

"*Ach!* Will ye look a' that!"

Whidbey turned and followed Menzies's gaze. The hall was crowded with heavy wooden tables, all gleaming with crystalware and silver plate on white linen.

"Aye, the fable's true, Menzies," Whidbey said. "We've stumbled on the Spanish silver mines of Nootka! Perhaps the legend of the Seven Cities of Gold is true as well. Me, I'm counting on the one about the fountain of youth."

"A good clyster, Whidbey, would serve ye well in lieu."

"I don't even know what that is," Old Joe replied cheerfully, "but I've no doubt it would hurt."

The room was filling. They moved off to join *Chatham*'s master, Johnstone, who was with a group of traders from the merchant vessels present in the cove.

The midshipmen entered in a noisy gaggle, followed by the Spanish officers from the receiving line. Pedro Alberni stopped to speak to the young Spanish officer at the top of the stairs, leaned in as if to speak confidentially, and poked him in the belly. The fellow doubled over and they both laughed and stood for a minute, talking and looking around the hall. Then Alberni leaned in again and the younger man listened and nodded and descended the stairs. Alberni himself crossed the room to the office and disappeared onto the balcony. A moment later a drum roll sounded from below, the hall fell silent, and he reappeared with Maquinna and a small entourage of his people. Simultaneously, Quadra arrived at the door with Captains Vancouver and Broughton. Everyone in the hall turned to watch the two parties meet in the centre of the room with a show of delight at this, their third or fourth meeting of the day. Maquinna introduced, through his translator Comekala, his advisors Natzape and Quatlazape and four of his wives.

Quadra led them all to the longest table and positioned himself with Vancouver, Broughton, and Maquinna at its centre, with their translators (Comekala, Dobson, and Alberni) close around. The counsellors and wives sat on one side, the senior officers and trader captains on the other. Everyone else took chairs at other tables, the midshipmen on the outer fringes with Spaniards of lesser rank. Here there were no translators and they had to rely on port pidgin. It was enough to communicate, though awkwardly. The noise level around them was high. Both parties soon fell into separate conversations.

Once all were settled and glasses filled, Quadra gave a speech of welcome (translated by Dobson and Alberni), then Vancouver delivered a response (translated by Dobson and Comekala) that ended with a toast to the health of Good King Carlos of Spain. After this, Alberni proposed a toast (translated, yada yada) to Good King George. This was followed by a royal salute of twenty-one guns from the Spanish bastion in the harbour, then by another cannonade, this of seventeen guns, to salute the success of Vancouver's voyage of exploration.

"That was my stomach," Dick Ramsay mumbled towards the end of the last salute.

As soon as the cannonades ceased and the last toast was returned, liveried servers bearing silver platters appeared on the landing at the top of the stairs and spread out across the room.

Lincoln emptied his glass, hoping for a refill with the food. A steward filled it as soon as it touched the table.

Barrie's eyes followed a platter as it passed.

"Was that —"

"Potatoes. Or I'm a Dutchman."

"*You're* a bleedin' Yankee, Jimmy Pompkins. The Dutchman around here is our esteemed captain," Dorsey said. He flung an arm around Ned Roberts and pulled him close. "And *you're* a precious nancy, Neddy. Oh, give us a buss, my darling." He made a kissing motion at Roberts, who pushed him away and flushed.

Caught in the act of drinking, Lincoln burst out laughing; wine sprayed out of his nose. The others recoiled and cursed.

"Pace yourself, Links," Pitt said.

The potatoes went to the head table. A moment later a platter arrived for them. It was followed by others of fish and vegetables. Conversation waned as they tucked in. Servers circulated between tables like bees among wildflowers. Wine flowed like water from an artesian spring. They passed the platters back and forth, emptying them. Their conversation picked back up and they took note of the hall, the tables, the other diners. Lincoln examined his spoon. It was silver, engraved with the words *Plus Ultra*. He glanced around and pocketed it, smiling to himself. None of his companions noticed, for their attention had shifted to the four young women at the head table. Three of them had decorated their faces with red ochre and glimmer; one had a pendant hanging from her nose. The youngest of the four, though, wore neither face paint nor pendant. In the light cast by the chandelier her copper earrings shimmered when she moved, drawing attention to her pretty face, her high, chiselled cheeks and expressive lips, her silky-smooth skin.

"That's not natural," Pitt opined with authority. "She's smeared herself with blubber. These people douse themselves in it like Frenchies with perfume. Without that she wouldn't hold a candle to a Tahiti girl. In fact —" he leaned in and lowered his voice for dramatic effect "— she should be bloody careful around a candle!"

Well, uproarious laughter and mirth! Dorsey, overcome with camaraderie, clapped Hawkins on the back and turned for a better look.

Like the other wives, she was dressed in a cloak that completely covered her shoulders. "I prefer a grass skirt to a tarpaulin," one of them grumbled.

This led directly to tales of their carnal achievements in Tahiti. Oh, had men never copulated before *they* arrived in Matavai Bay? They boasted and drank and compared the flora of the South Sea to that of the North Pacific. But Tahiti was far, and Maquinna's wives near; they soon turned to comparing and contrasting Exhibits A through D, pointing, shouting over one another, laughing raucously.

Ned Roberts and Jim Hawkins were both quiet through this ribaldry. Roberts was a gentle, cerebral lad, and Hawkins, courtesy of Dorsey's clap on the back, had chipped a tooth on his glass. He was still probing for damage when a hand fell on his shoulder.

"*Caballeros.*"

It was the young Spaniard who had been on the door earlier. During dinner he'd been busy directing the servants. Hawkins had seen him conferring with Quadra at the head table from time to time.

"*Señores,*" he said.

He waited for their attention, glancing around the room and absently fingering the medallion he wore around his neck. When they quieted he leaned in, tapped his upper lip, and addressed them in the port pidgin known to all sailors. "Be careful, fellows. Make no trouble with Maquinna. No games with his women. There are girls in the village."

For a moment they stared blankly at him. Then several spoke at once. Girls? What village? Where?

He laughed and tapped his lip again. "Be careful. You pay too much attention. Not these girls." Something caught his eye. "I must go." And then he was gone, moving fast across the room, calling rapid-fire to one of the stewards, beckoning to another.

They watched him go towards the stairway. On the landing he glanced back, grinned, and tapped the side of his nose before descending.

Eventually they began conversing again, now in lower voices. Jim Hawkins glanced towards the head table and discovered Quadra's eyes on him. The Spaniard raised his glass to drink and tilted it, his head inclining ever so slightly with it. Hawkins felt compelled to do the same. The Spanish commander's gaze lingered on him briefly before returning to his guests.

# Chapter 6

The morning after Quadra's welcome bash there were many on His Majesty's Ship *Discovery* with heavy heads. Joe Whidbey was not among them, for he was a seasoned old coot who knew how to handle his nights before. What's more, he had plenty to do this particular morning after. A boat was waiting alongside to take him ashore. Midshipman Lincoln, grey-faced and shaky with crapulence, was aboard it with a work detail. They would spend the morning at the observatory readying it for use.

Whidbey lingered at the brim of the quarterdeck to savour the day. It had rained before dawn and was clear now, already warming. He swivelled his hips experimentally. Yes, a fine day was in store. Conditions were perfect for a solar observation at noon — their first in Nootka Sound.

Two boats were already away. One had borne barrels ashore for repair, the other kegs of gunpowder they'd found to be damp. Above the landing a gunner's crew had spread it out on sailcloth to dry in the sun. Nearby, a crew of coopers were inspecting casks, tightening hoops, replacing staves. Farther down the beach (a safe distance from the gunpowder) a pitch-pot brewed over a fire. One of *Discovery*'s boats had been hauled up next to it and stripped for re-caulking. The acrid smell of tar suffused the harbour's air.

Aboard *Discovery* there was similar busyness. On the main, crewmen hauled sailcloth up from the hold and stacked it to go ashore, where the ship's sailmaker would cut a fresh suit for their autumn voyage. The old sails had already been stripped; they were also bundled to go ashore, in their case for drying and mending. Above Whidbey's head, topmen swarmed the rigging, dismantling that complex web of ropes, cables, stays, and shrouds. They would take down every line, block, and tackle for repair, and when the yards were clear they would inspect each one minutely for damage.

Whidbey's gaze descended to the main and settled on the carpenter. He and his helpers were crowded into a narrow aisle on the larboard side; they were fashioning a timber into a spar to replace one cracked at sea. At that moment, though, the carpenter stood listening to Archibald Menzies with a decidedly cranky look on his face. The Scot pointed aft and Whidbey glanced over his shoulder at the wooden frame that housed his botanical treasures. The man who served as Menzies's botanical assistant was inside it with a watering can, awkwardly manoeuvring around pots of specimens with Tubby, the ship's cat, entangled in his ankles and gazing up needily, her tail held high.

Tubby liked to dig in soil for her own fastidious purposes, and there was only one source of soil on *Discovery*. Menzies had caught her in the act on several occasions. He'd complained about her to the captain, who seemed mightily amused by Tubby's proclivities. "It's nature, Mister Menzies, is it not?" he'd quipped. Recently Menzies had proposed a glass cover for the enclosure. "Very well," Vancouver replied. "Speak to Chips directly about what you have in mind."

Whidbey smiled to himself; the ship's carpenter was the crustiest man on the ship.

He arched his back, held the stretch, and, with a gradual shift of his shoulders, teased out a crack. He sighed with satisfaction, looked up, and found Midshipman Hawkins standing nearby. The young man was observing Whidbey's manipulations while receiving a watchman's report. Their eyes met.

"That was a fine party last night, Mister Hawkins."

"Aye, Mister Whidbey, it was." Hawkins nodded dismissal to the watchman. Old Joe moved closer and noticed the boy looked a little peaked. Green around the gills, in fact. Whidbey clapped him on the back.

"It's the rare man, Jim, who can hoot with owls at night and soar with eagles in the morning."

Hawkins grinned self-consciously.

"Truth be told, we need to soar like eagles while this weather holds.

There's a hard winter on its way and we don't want to be caught here when it hits. Isn't that so, *Professor* Menzies?"

"Oh aye," Menzies said, joining them. "It's no' just the cold, y'ken. It rains every day. The wind howls and cuts through your clothing like a knife through butter. Sometimes it's intolerably icy. But if ye should overwinter here, Mister Hawkins, ye'll feel right at home, for it's like midsummer in Halifax."

Whidbey and Menzies cackled heartily at this witticism. They'd both served in Halifax after the loss of the American ports, and they proceeded to tell a few stories involving witches' teats and balls and brass monkeys, et cetera.

"... so, in and around all the fine speeches and parties, we have *real* work to finish." Whidbey seemed ready at last to get on with *his* real work. Before he did, though, he leaned closer to Hawkins and lowered his voice to a confidential murmur. "Try not to precipitate another international incident today, Young Jim. Our goal is to make friends here, not mortal enemies. Thank God it wasn't the Spaniards you offended yesterday or we might be deep in the doodoo today."

He tilted his hat and winked as he climbed over the side.

"The master is in fine form today, is he no'?" Menzies said. He spotted Tubby inside his plant frame, sniffing at a pot and pawing experimentally, and hurried aft to shoo her away.

The ship's lieutenants emerged from their morning conference with the captain and dispersed. It was Baker's watch, and he reassumed it from Hawkins and went forward to speak with the carpenter. Hawkins was left alone with his hangover. He idled, took in the mountains, the open waters of the Sound, the ships at anchor, the boats crisscrossing the harbour. He was not in top form and did not at first register the fast-moving Indian canoe making for *Discovery*. His heart skipped a beat when he did. Then he relaxed. It had just four paddlers and a single passenger — the young Spaniard who had delivered Quadra's warning the night before.

The canoe came alongside just as Baker returned.

"Permission to come aboard," the fellow called up in pidgin.

"Granted," Baker said. The Spaniard scrambled up the net, acknowledged Baker, and grinned at Hawkins. He handed Baker a thick envelope with an official seal.

"For Captain Vancouver from Don Juan," he said. Then, gesturing into the canoe below, he continued. "And this. For crew."

They looked down into the upturned faces of the Indians holding fast to the ship. Piled around them were baskets of bread and bunches of cabbage and carrots.

"Is good, yes?"

"Is good. Yes." Baker held up the envelope. "Can you wait for a reply?"

The Spaniard inclined his head magnanimously.

"Mister Hawkins, I suspect the diplomatic matter is in play at last. Send word for Dobson to report to the captain. I'll walk this in myself. While I'm below, watch *him* like a hawk." Baker spoke pleasantly in English, smiling and nodding at their visitor. He went aft and descended the companionway.

Hawkins called two watchmen to board the food and another to find Dobson. By the time he turned back the Spaniard was leaning comfortably against the capstan. He cocked his head at Hawkins and shifted over to make room.

Below on the main, the carpenter scolded one of his men for some failure of craft. The Spaniard laughed, looked at Hawkins, and shrugged. "All carpenters are the same," the gesture said. Hawkins found himself grinning back. The Spaniard introduced himself as Francisco Almeida and said he was from Havana, the most beautiful place in all of Cuba, which was the most beautiful island in the Caribbean, and the home to the most beautiful and biggest-breasted girls in the world, who were *fantastico* but not of easy virtue, don't think they are, because it takes *mucho* effort to seduce one, although with your red hair, you would be exotic to them, and this would serve *mucho mucho* in your favour. Also that he was a midshipman on Quadra's flagship (as near as Hawkins could understand, pidgin being limited in its technical terminology although admirably descriptive in other spheres). Hawkins guessed he was around his own age.

They enjoyed a few minutes of broken conversation until Baker returned.

"No reply," he told the Spaniard. "One will be sent later."

Francisco Almeida nodded agreeably. "Until next time, then," he said, then pumped their hands (*"Mucho gusto! Mucho gusto!"*), saluted, and went over the side.

Hawkins and Baker watched the canoe set off. Francisco Almeida twisted around and waved.

# Chapter 7

On the northwest coast stories and songs are passed down from generation to generation. People treat them like property; they hold them close. No one has any business telling another family's story or singing its songs.

Well, if that's not a shiny bauble just asking to be nicked.

Let me tell you a story.

Every person on the coast was born to their station. A commoner was a commoner, a slave a slave, and a member of the *tyeeclati* was a noble, with rights and privileges beyond those of their inferiors. With status came obligations, the most onerous of which were borne by the *tyee* himself. The *tyee* was responsible for the welfare of his kin and all his *masicim*, who included the lower ranked *tyeeclati* and all commoners. He sat in council and listened to advice, yet all the decisions were his. He was the one who resolved disputes, administered justice, and meted out punishment — though he could not be arbitrary in doing so. He sought consensus and was governed by rules and protocols — a constitution, if you will. He participated in ceremonies and adhered to customs that were centuries old, and everyone understood that if he didn't — if he broke faith with tradition — the spirits of the ancients would wreak vengeance upon the living, and the animals upon which they relied would not allow themselves to be taken for their benefit.

Everyone's welfare, indeed their very survival, depended on the *tyee*'s devotion to tradition.

Nothing was more important on the coast than the whale hunt, and the *tyee* was the principal whaler of his people. It was a demanding role involving many rituals. The hunt occurred in spring, and in the winter months leading up to it the *tyee* had to live purely, according to prescribed rites. The regime intensified as the whaling season neared, until, four days before the hunt began, the *tyee* withdrew entirely from human society. He went into the forest, to a location known only to initiates, where his purification rituals, called *osumich*, were especially rigorous. He fasted, meditated, chanted, and recited prayers to the spirits; he cleansed his body by bathing and scrubbing with sprigs of hemlock until his skin was raw and bleeding. He made himself as pure and free of human corruption as he could; and only then did he return to his people and join the members of his whaling crew, who had also bathed and fasted and sung songs to the great spirit chiefs while waiting for him to complete his rites.

They paddled to the whaling grounds, the *tyee* riding in the bow of the lead canoe, for it was his right and obligation to throw the first harpoon. And as they journeyed they sang songs to the spirits, and to their quarry, for they needed to convince it of their purity before it would consider giving itself to them. They sang when a whale was spotted, and during the chase, and when it was finally harpooned to assure the creature that they would honour it, body and spirit, if it surrendered itself to them, telling it that their people would live because of its sacrifice and remember it always.

The hunt entailed much more than these rituals, however. It was physically demanding, dangerous work, requiring a keen eye and a deft hand. There was craft to whaling, and the Mowachaht, the Makah, and others on the coast were masters of it. They knew the habits and behaviour of whales: where they fed, how they breached, where they swam when they submerged. When they sighted a whale they approached with stealth, for despite the reverence they paid it, it was their prey. While it was below in its realm they manoeuvred to the place it would reappear in theirs.

The moment it came up to spout was the moment of its greatest vulnerability. The *tyee*'s canoe would be positioned just beyond reach of its tail, and the *tyee* would thrust his harpoon's barbed head into its side. Impaled, the creature felt the pain and realized its danger. It dove and swam frantically to escape, and as it did, the shaft of the harpoon fell away and floated to the surface, its purpose fulfilled. Now, everything depended on that single barb embedded in the leviathan's side, and on the single line attached to it that connected hunter with prey.

And that prey — that great beast — had immense reserves of strength upon which to draw as it fled to safety in the depths.

This was the critical moment. The line tied to the head of the harpoon was secured to the canoe. It ran out until it was taut, and then the canoe began to move, dragged by the invisible giant. With a splash of paddles the other canoes now joined the chase. There were floats attached to the line, and the whalers watched them to assess the whale's depth and direction to predict where it would resurface — and they headed for that place. The whale stayed below for an eternity, but when it finally, inevitably returned to the surface they were waiting for it. Some were close enough to stab harpoons or lances directly into its side. Others hurled theirs from farther away. The whale spouted, thrashed, and dove again in its effort to escape. Now, though, it was tiring, weakening, the water reddened by its blood.

It swam, towing the canoes, for there were now many lines from many canoes, and the whale lost vigour as it lost blood and breath. Each time it returned to the surface more harpoons and lances pierced its side, more canoes became tethered to it. It struggled against them, fighting in defiance of its pain, unwilling yet to surrender life and give itself to them. It dove and swam to escape, but finally, if they had performed their rites correctly, and sung their songs, and addressed the whale with respect and reverence — if they had done all these things, the creature might decide at last that they were worthy and fall still in the water, prepared to die or dead already.

They were a ceremonious people who believed in the ways of their ancestors, and it was the duty of their *tyee* to keep them on the straight and narrow — for if he failed to do so the spirits would be angered, and for mortal men, no good ever came of that.

Maquinna was conscientious and dutiful, yet that spring he did not lead a whale hunt. Many of the men who should have participated were otherwise occupied, hunting sea otters for their skins or trekking inland to acquire them from others. They all wanted what the white men had and were intent on getting it. Tsakwasap the shaman chastised Maquinna and complained bitterly about the hunters' sudden materialism. It seemed to him that the Mowachaht were losing their sense of identity, and this was especially so among the young, who were less vested in tradition, their identities fluid and unformed. In such times, Tsakwasap said, tradition was more important than ever. Missing a hunt was inexcusable. He was incensed over that and disgusted with Maquinna.

Others were, too. Some called him out for facilitating the whites, for supplying, procuring, fixing, and turning a blind eye. Everyone remembered Maquinna's brother, Calicum, still unavenged three years after his death. He was merely the most prominent of the white men's victims; the ranks of the grieving, the fatherless and lost, were growing. Many among the *tyeeclati* worried about Maquinna's resolve. They called him a collaborator, usually in whispers, though some were bolder and did so at council. Meanwhile, his rivals Wickaninnish and Tatoosh resented him and wanted what he had. They undermined him from afar in every way they could.

But if you think Maquinna had chiefly problems, spare a thought for George Vancouver.

# Chapter 8

George Vancouver sat slumped at his desk in *Discovery*'s great cabin, frowning over Dobson's translation of Quadra's letter. Its numerous attachments had taken the young man more than a day to translate.

He cast a look at his desktop and the table next to it. There lay the paperwork of his command: the ship's log, the register of provisions, the pay and muster books, several rolls of charts, a stack of official correspondence. He sighed, shifted in his chair, gathered up the pages of the Spaniard's letter, and tapped them into order.

He glanced up. For a moment he stared at the door, his head cocked to the sounds of the ship. Most of the men were ashore on work details or on loan to William Broughton, assisting with *Chatham*'s repairs. Weeks before, the brig had grounded and her keel was crushed. Broughton had staunched her leaks and refloated her on the tide and, with pumps manned continuously, she was able to proceed along the coast. She would not survive the voyage to Hawaii in her present state.

And so, over the previous days, *Chatham*'s stores and ballast had been landed to lighten her, her rigging dismantled and masts removed. Her crew had moved into tents ashore, and on yesterday's high tide they'd hauled her into the shallows and tipped her on her side. She lay there now, men swarming like Lilliputians across her great beached hull. Mudge had gone ashore to confer with Broughton and prioritize the work, for *Discovery* had her own repairs to make. The few men left on board were at that moment at gun drill. The ship's mission was exploration and eight of her ten guns were permanently stowed in the hold, yet she *was* a warship.

To Van, the salutes fired over the preceding days had seemed ragged, the gun crews uncoordinated and lackadaisical. He'd ordered the guns exercised. Dry runs, of course — no reason to upset the neighbours. He could hear the gun carriages rolling on the main deck, the men cursing at their weight.

He looked down at the letter.

On his arrival in Nootka Sound in April (Quadra wrote), he dispatched three ships to explore and map the region — the *Aranzazu* under Jacinto Caamaño to the north, the *Sutil* and *Mexicana* under Dionisio Galiano and Cayetano Valdés within the interior waters to the east. He sent another vessel under Salvador Fidalgo with a garrison to establish an outpost on the south shore of Juan de Fuca Strait, at a place he called Nunez Gaona. He himself had remained in Santa Cruz de Nuca in anticipation of Vancouver's arrival. While he waited he made inquiries into the circumstances surrounding the seizure of two British vessels in 1789.

There followed a recitation of Spain's rights by discovery and under solemn treaties, et cetera, et cetera, to the entire coast of the Americas; and a description of the visible joy of the natives when Don Estevan Martínez had arrived in May of that year and performed a ceremony of possession in Yuquot.

Van snorted, thinking that perhaps his counterpart did not have that quite right. He remembered Maquinna's "visible joy" at his own arrival.

The letter enumerated the familiar events of that summer three years before: the inspections by Martínez of foreign trading vessels in Nootka Sound; the arrival of James Colnett to trade — indeed, to establish a permanent trading post. A heated argument about his right to do so on Spanish territory. The arrest of Colnett and his men, the seizure of his ships.

Martínez (Quadra continued) dispatched the impounded vessels to New Spain, where the viceroy returned them to Colnett and released all his men, even paying them full wages for the period of their detention. Colnett immediately set sail for the northwest, where he traded profitably and returned to China with his holds brimming with sea otter pelts.

The assertion that followed this rendering of events had caused Van a start on first reading:

*As a consequence it is clear that Spain has now nothing to deliver nor the smallest damage to make good.*

But in the spirit of establishing peace, continued the Spaniard, he was ready — without prejudice to the legitimate rights of his sovereign — to cede the settlement of Santa Cruz de Nuca to England. Once this was accomplished, he would depart Nootka Sound, with his garrison and ships, and retire to the new Spanish port at Nunez Gaona on the southern shore of the Strait of Juan de Fuca. This would be the most northerly Spanish settlement in America, and mark the boundary of Spanish California. All territory to the north of the Strait would be free for entry by both countries, but no settlements would be created there without mutual consent. And, Quadra concluded,

*The English shall not pass nor trade to the south of the Strait of Juan de Fuca.*

*If you cannot accept these terms, I await your own proposals on how to conclude the negotiations and secure the desired peace.*

Van dropped the page onto the table. "'Desired peace,'" he repeated. He looked out his stern window to where the *Activa* lay at anchor, broadside on and close by. His lips formed a bloodless line as he wondered, was that aspect — broadside on — coincidence?

"'Terms'…'negotiations,'" he muttered to the empty cabin. He had not expected terms and negotiations. He had been ordered to receive British property seized by the Spanish. Period. A purely ceremonial handover.

He sat perfectly still, deep in thought. At last he looked up, cocked his head, stared hard at the door. His eyes narrowed.

His chair scraped the deck as he pushed it back. His heels echoed within the enclosed space. He swung the door open, brushed past the startled marine sentry, strode purposefully to the companionway stair, and climbed up to the quarterdeck.

Peter Puget was there conferring with the bosun. They both saluted and moved aside for him.

"Sir."

"Carry on, gentlemen."

He watched the gun drill below him on the main. The gunner's mate was in charge. A midshipman led each gun crew.

Van watched as one of the crews dry-swabbed their gun, rammed a dummy charge home, and ran the gun out. When it was hard against the gunwale, Midshipman Ramsay mock-primed the touch hole at the breech and mock-ignited it. In battle, the crew leader sighted over the barrel; for a salute, he just needed to make it go boom. There was no boom today — it was a dry run, of course. Still, the crew's movements seemed desultory.

The second crew was worse. Whether for salute or salvo, every step needed to be smooth and fast, round after round. It was not. The midshipman in charge needed to pick up his game.

"Damn me, Mister Lincoln," Vancouver shouted, "that won't do."

All action ceased on deck. Both gun crews looked up at him.

"That is a naval gun on a ship of war, not a sea tortoise on a sunny beach. It must run out faster than that and with more purpose!"

Lincoln inclined his head slightly and touched the brim of his hat. "Aye, Captain," he said.

"King George expects better of us, Mister Lincoln. Let us see to it. Carry on."

"Sir." Lincoln touched the brim of his hat again and turned stiffly away.

Vancouver turned to Puget, who had dismissed the bosun, and lowered his voice. "That really was dreadful, Peter. We need to set a higher standard. Appearances matter here, especially now. Will you speak to the gunner when he comes aboard. Twice-daily drills. As of today. All hands to cycle through. We need to sharpen up the midshipmen as well. They need to know to demand more. I'll speak to Mister Mudge about organizing an all-midshipman gun crew to drill alongside the men."

"That'll do the snotties good, sir. And the men will enjoy the competition."

"Hah! I've no doubt of that."

They watched the drill. Lincoln ran it tighter this time.

"Idle hands, what? We need to keep them busy."

"We'll start on the charts soon. It'll be all hands on deck then."

"Yes, but until then..." Vancouver followed the progress of a launch pulling towards the settlement from one of the trading vessels. "All summer we kept them busy in the boats. Too busy to cause mischief."

"Perhaps we can find them a task, sir. What about sending them out to survey an area of the Sound? Or a stretch of coast down towards Juan de Fuca Strait? We won't be looking at that area closely ourselves."

Vancouver glanced at him. "That's a good idea. I'll mention it to the first lieutenant."

He lingered on deck, in no hurry to return to Quadra's letter. Lincoln, he noted with approval, seemed driven now, a tyrant for efficiency. His voice was a little too strident, but that would improve with experience, if he applied himself. This particular midshipman, though, seldom did.

A pair of canoes plied towards the Spanish bastion at the mouth of the cove. They were paddled by Indians and crowded with men in blue tunics and yellow waistcoats — the uniform of Alberni's Catalonian Regiment.

"Relief for the battery, Captain," Puget said, studying them through a glass.

"Yes. Let's start a log on their movements. In fact, all movements in the harbour. When, numbers carried, where from and to. Anything unusual."

Puget grinned. "Aye, sir. You never know what you'll find when you look with purpose."

As he descended the companionway Vancouver reflected on how fortunate he was with his lieutenants. Mudge was thorough and thoughtful, Baker detail oriented, a fine cartographer. Puget was competent in all things, a good surveyor with excellent powers of observation. He had a bright future, of that he had no doubt.

Taken with this thought, I glanced over the horizon at Peter Puget's bright future. He will soon command their sister ship *Chatham*. Within months of his return to England he will be back at sea, the captain of a sloop-of-war in action against the French. He will go on to command the Fighting *Temeraire*, a 98-gun ship of the line that will be immortalized by painter J.M.W. Turner on her way to the knackers decades later. In 1807 he will play a decisive role at the Second Battle of Copenhagen.

He will die abed in England, an Admiral of the Blue. His grave will be marked by a plaque donated by the Seattle Historical Society.

Van paused at the foot of the stairs to look up at a sky framed by the companionway hatch. Cumulus, he observed, paying no heed to the swirling currents of future history.

Back in the great cabin he stood at his desk and skimmed the letter again. Something rankled at the heart of Quadra's proposal, a nuance he had yet to grasp.

It came to him. The act of making Colnett whole on his trading venture did nothing to resolve the central issue between England and Spain, which was the territorial question.

He thought back to the exact wording of his instructions: to receive British property seized by the Spanish. That property was land, and it belonged to an Irishman named John Meares.

In London he had been briefed on John Meares. In the years 1786 through '88, Meares had traded throughout the northwest, and in '88 he'd built a post in Nootka Sound on land acquired from Maquinna. That autumn, when he departed for China with a hold full of pelts, he abandoned the post, intending to return to it the following year. Yet when he got to China, tired of voyaging, he decided to sit a trading season out. He hired Colnett to voyage in his stead, and provided him with two ships, both well stocked with trade goods and outfitted with supplies to build a sturdier, larger, permanent structure in Friendly Cove to replace his initial post.

Colnett never got a chance to build it. When he told the pesky Martínez what he planned to do, the Spaniard arrested him and confiscated everything.

Months later, when word of this reached China, Meares panicked — everything he owned was tied up in those ships. He saw only one way to salvage his investment. He set out for England, a journey of four months, and on arrival swore a complaint against the Spanish with the British government. It came at an opportune moment. The wily prime minister, William Pitt, sensed Spanish weakness. He championed Meares's case — and took the country to the brink of war.

Now Quadra, the man sent by Spain to make restitution, was insisting that no restitution was necessary, that Spain had *nothing to deliver nor the smallest damage to make good*. What's more, he was proposing boundaries where none had existed before, boundaries that would affect British interests.

Van's orders were silent on boundaries and commercial interests and rights of access and trade, and the dispatches delivered by *Daedalus* had contained no clarifications on them. He'd been sent to receive restitution, restitution in the form of property. Land.

So what was he to do with *this?* Neither William Pitt nor any member of his government would allow a lowly lieutenant-in-command to determine Britain's boundaries with the Spanish empire; nor let him negotiate *any* limits on trade. They would surely cut him off at the knees if he tried.

He was already worried about the Pitt family, what with young Midshipman Pitt being a perennial thorn in his side. Who knew how his punishments would be construed back in Whitehall?

Not to my advantage, that is certain, he thought, balling his fist and thumping the desk. He was sure that one-sided tattle from the boy's apologists would reach the Pitts eventually — and no doubt, the officious Joseph Banks too. Van was already in *his* bad books.

He picked up the depositions appended to Quadra's letter. The Spaniard had taken statements from three traders, two Americans and a Portuguese, all of whom had been present in the region in '88 and '89 and, serendipitously for Quadra, again during the summer just past. Their depositions supported the Spaniard's version of events; they all attested that Meares had had nothing but a small hut on shore; that it was dismantled when he left; and that when Martínez arrived the following spring there were no traces of it remaining. No evidence of British property or prior possession — thus no support for Britain's claim to the territory.

He shook his head. This is a sorry game, he thought, yet surely I must play it.

The sound of the guns being rolled out on deck intruded on his thoughts.

Yes — play the game, he thought, or fight it out instead.

He chuckled mirthlessly as he sat down at his desk and reached for his quill.

# Chapter 9

Hours later — it was evening now. Juan Francisco de la Bodega y Quadra sat at the table in the bureau off the great hall, reading Dobson's translation of Vancouver's letter.

> *I am not authorized to discuss the events of 1789 or before on the northwest coast, nor the respective rights and pretensions of the courts of Spain and Britain. These matters have been agreed and resolved by the ministers of our respective governments under the terms of the Nootka Convention, and I must adhere to my instructions in respect thereof. These are, to receive the buildings, districts and parcels of land formerly occupied by British subjects as well as the ports of Nootka and Clayoquot.*
>
> *Accordingly, I remain ready to receive said properties.*
>
> *Furthermore, the Convention grants free access for trade and navigation to both countries north of the northernmost site occupied by Spain in April of 1789. The port of San Francisco was then the northernmost Spanish settlement, as*

<blockquote>you have yourself acknowledged that Martínez arrived in Nootka in May of that year, and that your post at Nunez Gaona, within the Strait of Juan de Fuca, was established only in May of this year. Therefore it, and all such establishments north of San Francisco, come under the Convention's meaning of "port of free access."</blockquote>

The Spaniard turned to stare out over the balcony. The first stars were visible in the darkening sky. He stood and moved out into the open air, watched the profiles of the vessels at anchor fade in the dark, saw deck lanterns lit. He stared at the lights as night descended.

There were steps on the stairs below, voices in the great hall. A knock came on his bureau door. He returned to his desk and called out an acknowledgement.

A soldier held the door open for Pedro Alberni, whose chin, this late in the day, was dark. He bowed his head to Quadra. "Don Juan," he said.

"Captain." Quadra indicated a chair and signalled the soldier at the door to leave them. For a moment he regarded Alberni. "How are your reinforcements panning out?"

"Ah. Well. Because they are not *real* Catalonians — who are worth two of any other soldier in a fight — their numbers were always going to pose a tactical problem. Nevertheless, I am confident that the Army of New California will persevere."

"It must. I need a show of strength. Every man you can muster, Catalonian or no. You've been creative here for years. I need you to be creative now more than ever."

Alberni reached to touch the silver pot on the edge of Quadra's desk. He flinched as if it were hot and pulled his hand away. "Creative. I accept the compliment. But miracles are not part of my repertoire. I'm just a soldier. Something of a conjuror, if I do say, but no miracle worker."

"You must conjure for a while longer, Pedro. And for God's sake, pour yourself some coffee."

Alberni grinned and filled a fine china cup. It looked fragile in his big hand. He settled back comfortably, raised the cup to his nose, and gave it an appreciative sniff.

Quadra refilled his own cup. "This is not going to be easy," he said, holding up Vancouver's letter.

"I think, Don Juan, that's why the viceroy sent you to handle the diplomacy instead of leaving it to me. My limitations and lack of sophistication are well known in the grand salons of Mexico City." He lifted his cup to the governor, his little finger extended straight, and slurped loudly.

"Perhaps." Quadra pushed Vancouver's letter across the table. "The viceroy is a realist about what we can accomplish —"

"A rare quality in a nobleman," Alberni said.

"He knows we can't hold all of the northwest. We don't have the resources."

"I can just hear him. 'Listen, all I can spare you are a few leaky ships and some ragged Catalonians led by a madman I once had arrested.'"

"Forgive and forget, Pedro. His actual words were 'Let distance be your ally. You must take advantage of your counterpart's isolation.' He thinks we can secure California and the coast all the way north to the Strait of Juan de Fuca. 'It's a natural boundary,' he told me. 'You need to secure his agreement on that, and to do that you must appear entrenched. Negotiate hard, and from a position of strength, because what you achieve there will be recognized in Europe.'" Quadra gestured at Vancouver's letter. "I wonder what he would tell me now. Our British commissioner may be isolated, but he shows no interest in negotiating."

"What will you do?"

Quadra shrugged. "Our supplies are tight. There's another lean winter in the offing and no possibility of resupply until spring. I'd be happy to transfer the establishment here to him and let the British carry the load. The Convention guarantees our rights in this region, including to the north. The ticklish issue is where we draw the border. Our friend out there read my move and tabled a shrewd rebuttal. I wonder if he knows more than he lets on."

"'The English are born to duplicity, as Spanish nobles are born to cruelty.' A Catalonian adage, known to every child."

Quadra gave him a pained look. "He makes a point that's difficult to refute: Where are our settlements on this coast? There are missions in California but no settlers to speak of. Here in Nootka we have British traders, American traders, even Portuguese and French, but not a single Spanish merchant."

A cannon sounded in the distance. Quadra turned to look out over the balcony. Alberni leaned forward, his head cocked to listen.

Another gun fired. It came from the fortress at the mouth of the cove.

"It's the signal gun. They've spotted a sail or light. It could be Caamaño, or Galiano, or Valdés, returning at last. Will you excuse me, Don Juan?"

"Go. Send word as soon as you know what it is."

Alberni stood, drained his cup, and placed it with a *clink* on the desk. "Thank you for the coffee, Don Juan — and the frank discussion. I am at your service. Always." He bowed and left.

Quadra listened to his footsteps on the stairs, heard him hail his sergeant and greet young Francisco Almeida, who was waiting to come up. There was a bellow of laughter. Someone ran for the landing.

He *is* a miracle worker, Quadra thought. To survive here for three years, with almost no help. *That's* a miracle.

As he waited for Francisco he turned to look out into the darkness, thinking about Vancouver's letter — and how he would respond. He hoped Alberni was right about the signal — that it heralded the return of one or more of his ships. He needed to know what his officers had discovered on their voyages.

A knock came on his door.

# Chapter 10

The girl known as Matuateh was taken as a child by the Kwakwaka'wakw. Her own people lived on the mainland, and she was very young when she and her brother were captured in a raid. Raiding was common in those days. People traded in good times, and raided, even went to war, in bad; and, like fires in the forest, bad times came periodically. The Mowachaht did their share of raiding. They raided the Kwakwaka'wakw, the Salish, even others who were "Nootka" and essentially kin. Young men could always find some excuse to fight. Then, at feasts and before the home fire, they danced and sang to their own glory and played out their feats of courage and daring.

In later life Matuateh would say that this was the nature of men, that the men of her own people were just as boastful and just as vain. She maintained that women did not have to brag, because everyone knew that they moved better and danced better and sang better than men. She loved to sing herself, and so the Mowachaht called her Matuateh, because they said she sang like a bird.

Captives were taken for ransom, and no ransom was ever paid for Matuateh and her brother. Their people were across the water. Perhaps they never knew who took their children, or they couldn't pay; perhaps they were killed in the raid. Whatever the reason, the fate of those not ransomed was set: they would live out their lives as slaves.

After a few months among the Kwakwaka'wakw, the two children were sold to the Mowachaht. This was during the time of Maquinna's father. Matuateh became slave to the family of Calicum, her brother to another family. Some years later, when the Spanish came, a priest purchased him from them for a sheet of copper and some cloth, and that fall — this was two years before Quadra arrived — he left on a ship for New Spain with other young slaves. He was a young man by then and didn't want to go. The priests said he would be trained in the ways of God. Matuateh never saw him again.

The priests tried to buy her, too. By that time Calicum was dead at the hands of Martínez, and his widow Apanas refused to part with her. Apanas was from the Hesquiaht, a small band that lived to the south between Yuquot and Clayoquot Sound. She had come to the Mowachaht in marriage to cement an uneasy peace between the two peoples. She was lucky in the bargain, for Calicum lost his heart to her and never took another wife. She returned his love. The couple broke tradition by remaining in Mowachaht territory with his family, rather than living with hers. Politics, it was, but people held it against *her*, and she remained an outsider, even after many years. And as an outsider herself, she had a soft spot for this foreign girl who sang so sweetly. She had two sons, Comekala and Copaza, but no daughter of her own. Matuateh may have entered the household a slave, but Apanas treated her as family.

Many of the Mowachaht disapproved of Apanas already; and so they disapproved of the leniency with which she treated Matuateh. Too bad: the treatment of a slave was left to its owner. Slaves could be beaten, sold, or killed, given the hardest work, the dirtiest jobs. Because of their daily debasement they lived in a state of permanent disgrace. Not Matuateh. From an early age she carried herself with poise and hauteur and considered herself a Mowachaht.

There were many who could not forget her status. Growing up, the boy Copaza heard their criticism of his mother for her kindness to a slave girl, her tolerance of Matuateh's unseemly pride. Copaza and Matuateh were close in age, and he was always teasing her, and she him, as the Mowachaht do with those they love. Yet he was sensitive to people's disapproval. He was of a family of *tyee* and his own pride was fierce. He had lost his father young and was confused about many things.

After Calicum died, Maquinna provided for his family and took interest in the boys. As their kinsman he was concerned about their future. As a chief he thought about his own needs.

THE WIND FROM ALL DIRECTIONS | 75

The oldest boy, Comekala, took after his father. Maquinna arranged for him to join a trader's crew on a voyage to China. The boy returned a year later having seen more of the world than any Mowachaht before him. He had lived among white men and become fluent in English. He became Maquinna's translator and, inevitably, his counsellor on relations with the whites. It was a useful role, one that kept him close. Maquinna perceived in him a potential rival.

The younger boy, Copaza, was quiet, moody, and withdrawn. Maquinna did not know what to make of him. He eventually apprenticed him to the shaman Tsakwasap. The old man wasn't getting any younger. Someone would have to take his place some day.

Tsakwasap was the custodian of a vast body of knowledge, some elements of which were practical, others sacred. The practical elements were many and diverse. Tsakwasap taught the boy about herbs and moss, fungi, roots, and bark, when and how to harvest them, how to combine them into poultices and emulsions for different ailments, their dosages and effects.

The spiritual side was far more demanding, for it required unquestioning submission. Before Copaza could be introduced to it, he had to be purified, cleansed as a vessel to receive it. He spent weeks in the forest under Tsakwasap's instruction. The shaman told him stories shared only with acolytes. He taught him secret prayers and chants and songs, which they chanted and sang for days, deep in the woods, far from other human ears. Tsakwasap took him deeper into the forest and ever deeper into the ancient knowledge, leading him through the rites of *osumich*, which, if followed diligently, remove the stink of being human and the taint of human thought so that a spirit, a *chi'ha*, might choose to speak to him. Tsakwasap taught him how to sense a *chi'ha's* presence and listen for its voice, but to never look at it, for the mere glimpse of a *chi'ha* meant certain death. He showed him how to purify himself before seeking a *chi'ha*. It required songs and incantations and ritual bathing. Copaza practised these rites with Tsakwasap, then he practised them alone. He spent weeks by himself in the forest in quest of purity and a *chi'ha's* voice.

The other prescription for purity was sexual continence, and in this Copaza's thoughts and deeds fell short of the required standard.

No *chi'ha* spoke to him.

The fact is, Copaza was not inclined to ritual or tradition. There had been momentous change during his young life, and he was unsure who and what to believe. He certainly saw no reason for continence and lacked the discipline for it. Tsakwasap eventually concluded that his sullen young novice was not the stuff of a shaman. He told Maquinna the boy held no promise.

Maquinna asked the old man to persevere. Then he told his nephew to try harder. Tsakwasap, he said, had wisdom to impart, skills and knowledge that future Mowachaht would need. Copaza had been given a gift — the opportunity to master it. He had a duty to do so.

Copaza returned to his lessons. For a time, he applied himself. But before long, his interest waned again.

By the time Quadra arrived, Tsakwasap had rejected his no-good apprentice. As Maquinna considered what to do about Copaza, he thought about his own needs.

Relations with the Spaniards were complicated. Their numbers were large, and while Maquinna benefitted from their protection, he could not supply them with their necessities for free. He needed someone to manage the commercial details while he made ostentatious ceremony with their leader.

He had seen something in his nephew, and Tsakwasap's complaints confirmed it: the boy was morally compromised. Maquinna reasoned that this made him an ideal go-between; he provided plausible deniability.

The new role added to Copaza's confusion. The Spanish, after all, had killed his father. Three years before, he had been angry when Maquinna re-established relations with Martínez so soon after Calicum's murder. With whom, though, was he angry? With Calicum, for dying? With Martínez, for killing him? With Maquinna, for not exacting revenge? Or with all the white men, for their very presence?

Now, three years after his father's death, Copaza was far from at peace with himself. Yet he did what his chieftain asked of him. He arranged things for the Spaniards. They needed fish and meat; he delivered quantities of both. They needed timber to build up their garrison; he had it harvested and floated into Yuquot. They needed canoes to ferry between ship and shore; he provided them, and slaves to work them, too. Whatever Quadra's garrison needed, he spent his days acquiring and delivering. It kept him busy. That summer, he spent a lot of time at Yuquot and travelling within Nootka Sound to arrange what the Spanish needed.

That was how he met Francisco Almeida, whom Quadra had made responsible for trade on the Spanish side. Francisco had a way with languages. He had a smattering of Mowachaht when he started, enough to bargain with. The two of them took their responsibilities seriously and frequently went head-to-head, haggling and looking incredulous and affronted until they settled on a price and closed the deal.

Although Francisco's assignment did not require him to leave Yuquot, he often travelled with Copaza on his supply trips. They spent day after day in each other's company, often just the two of them in a canoe travelling between villages. Francisco used the time to ask questions and practise his Mowachaht.

Copaza was taciturn towards him, stingy when it came to conversation. But Francisco had an exceptional ear, and out in that canoe, ignored by Copaza, he repeated back words and phrases he'd heard from others, practising different intonations and tones that made the stone-faced Copaza smile to himself.

When the Spaniard mastered the words he'd heard from others, he sought more from Copaza. He pointed and gestured: What is that bird? What is this (flapping his arm like a wing)? What's this (shaking his paddle)? He asked about numbers, the seasons, parts of the body: neck, shoulder, chest, breast, woman's breast.

Copaza was bored. He replied with the relevant words. Francisco recited each one back, repeating it over and over until he'd committed it to memory. He counted, listed, conjugated, pronounced. There in the canoe, with only Copaza as his witness, he recited his entire vocabulary.

One. Two. Three...Arm. Elbow. Back. Stomach. Ass. Leg. Knee. Ankle...Green. Brown. Blue. White...Winter. Spring. Summer...

He demonstrated a knack for assembling words into phrases. Pointing at a cloud, he would ask Copaza, How do you say?

Copaza gave him the word.

He mimicked the fall of rain with his fingers.

Copaza gave him the word.

Raincloud, Francisco would say, pointing at the sky and wiggling his fingers.

Copaza corrected him when necessary. He seldom had to repeat himself.

Signing, Francisco asked for more words: Sun. Hot. Round. Moon. Full. Beautiful.

Francisco repeated Copaza's every answer, then repeated it again.

Soon he was building on these separate lessons.

"Hot summer sun," he said, pointing in triumph. "A full white moon." He craned around to grin at Copaza and gestured with his hands. "A beautiful round ass and two full breasts."

Francisco's recall was near-perfect; he rarely made the same mistake twice. A steel trap, that boy's mind, when it came to language. What's more, he was irrepressible; his curiosity never abated and, as his fluency developed, Copaza was both amused and impressed. The answers he gave to the Spaniard's endless questions became more detailed and informative.

Francisco listened closely as Copaza opened up. He asked more questions.

On shore, they spent hours haggling on behalf of their masters; then they packed and hauled and loaded, spent hours in the canoe, unloaded, hauled, slept rough on the beach.

Thus are friendships forged between young men. Despite Copaza's grudge against the Spaniards in general, he grew to like this one member of their tribe. He did not let that affect their daily bartering, however. Those arguments remained as fierce as ever.

Francisco never seemed to tire of being in a canoe. When they arrived at a village, he wandered through it with curiosity, grinning at the locals, jabbering with his limited vocabulary, pointing and gesturing when words failed. Copaza followed like the indulgent father of an especially precocious child. Francisco laughed with others at his own mistakes. Within weeks he was fluent in Mowachaht. He often joked that he was of the Cubachaht, that he was from an island far to the south that was not so different from their own, though warmer.

As he mastered the language he asked more complicated questions. He wanted to know about a *tyee* and his *masicim*, how people decided things and settled arguments, about whaling, fishing, hunting, what people ate and how they cooked it, how they built their houses, why and when they migrated and how they fought their wars, and was it true that spirits existed everywhere? He listened thoughtfully to the answers and said the Cubachaht *masicim*, and especially the slaves, had many similar customs to those of the Mowachaht, and he talked about Cachita, whom the Cubachaht slaves called Oshun. She was a spirit-god who did not offend the One God of the Spanish. He wore a shiny likeness of her on a chain around his neck.

Francisco observed, queried, absorbed, engaged. He garnered amazement and hilarity from children. He coaxed smiles from the crankiest elders (though never Tsakwasap, a killjoy when it came to fun). Among his contemporaries, the boys afforded him acceptance, grudging at first, then gleeful and unreserved, and the girls blushed in his presence and cast him lingering glances from afar.

Ah, yes, the girls. This brings us to another, shadowy aspect of the trade between the whites and the Mowachaht, for there was another commodity exchanged between them, this one in the dark of night.

When white men first arrived, the Mowachaht thought they mated with seals, because there was (they noted) a strong family resemblance. Soon they figured it out — the hard way — and members of the *tyeeclati* made their slaves available to the whites for purposes of rut. They weren't just thinking about the safety of their wives and daughters. They made a profit in the bargain.

Copaza fell into the role of intermediary and fixer for the *tyeeclati*. It was a logical extension of the commerce and logistics in which he was already immersed. He was frequently in Yuquot to deliver supplies, and when he came he brought slave women. They often rowed the canoes that brought the supplies — a practical measure, the killing of two birds with one stone.

A slave's affections could be bought for a strip of copper, a handful of nails. Copaza paid the bulk of what he received to their masters and kept a commission for himself. He developed a thriving side business, trading what he accumulated for items others wanted — pistols, knives and trinkets, pieces of clothing, cloth.

With the proceeds he was able to contribute food and sundry comforts to his mother's household. Until then, a widow and an outsider, Apanas had lived in reduced circumstances, and although Maquinna provided for her, she knew this served a purpose: it was meant to be seen. So she accepted Copaza's contributions — while making clear she wasn't happy about where they came from. She was sensitive about the prostituting of slaves. She scolded her son about abetting activities that reminded people about Matuateh's origins and could put her at risk. Copaza took it in silence. He never once suggested that Matuateh perform the duties of the other slaves. He had never treated her like a slave at all; yet that year his attitude towards her changed. In former times he had teased her incessantly. Now he simply paid her no heed. He fell into silence when she was around, or, if forced to acknowledge her presence, treated her with casual contempt.

For her part, Matuateh was young and headstrong. She had her freedom (virtually), and as those with free will do, she followed her heart; and that summer she fell in love with a young man. To be precise: she fell in love with Francisco Almeida.

They met when Copaza brought the Spaniard home to Apanas's lodge. It was Francisco's first trip to Tahsis and he was not as fluent then as he would become. Language proved no barrier. He was wiry and handsome, she lithe and beautiful. There would be an attraction between two such young people in any circumstance. Francisco, though, was more than a pretty face. He was a fireball, curious and interested in everything and everyone; exotic, funny, charismatic, intriguing. And when he turned his charm on someone — well, that was unlike anything Matuateh had ever experienced.

Their first encounter was very formal. The four of them — Apanas, Matuateh, Francisco, and Copaza — ate a meal together. Francisco shared from their communal tray, took his turn dipping in and eating with his fingers in the local manner. His expression showed his delight with the food, which in itself was a marvel, for while the Mowachaht had many delicacies — both sea and forest being bountiful and rich in variety — it was known that white men found their cuisine unappetizing.

And here was a Spaniard, smacking his lips and licking his fingers like a Mowachaht.

Apanas exchanged glances with Copaza. His black eyes signalled nothing.

Aware of this stranger's presence and magnetism, both she and

Matuateh were reserved. Conversation during the meal was stilted and awkward. Francisco's vocabulary was not yet as rich as it would become, and with all the formality of a first meeting it could have turned into a long evening.

But after the meal Francisco seized the initiative.

"Kind lady," he said to Apanas, "thank you for the meal delicious. Please let me leave you a..." But he didn't have the words. He dug into his pack and unfolded an object; it was a piece of white cloth. He showed it to her, then folded it neatly into quarters and closed his fist on it, shoving the last of it into his palm with his finger. Then he bowed to his perplexed hostess and opened his fist to present his hand, the one with the hanky. But the hanky was gone.

Francisco looked puzzled; he scratched his head. "*¿Que? ¿Dónde está?...Está perdido!*" he said. He looked around the lodge and they followed his eyes. His puzzlement spread to Apanas and Matuateh, then his expression changed. Ah! It said. He closed his hand again and hit it with the palm of his other, three good whacks. He raised one eyebrow to look slyly at Copaza, then opened his fist. The hanky was back. "Kind lady," he said to Apanas, inclining his head and bowing to her again.

Apanas accepted the cloth and they all laughed at the trick. Copaza watched with a founder's pride, his smug smile saying, Do you see the clever foreigner I brought into our house? But Francisco wasn't done. He held out both hands to Apanas and Matuateh, showing his palms were empty. He dropped his arms, flicked his wrists, then presented his hands again: a blue abalone shell lay in the palm of each.

Apanas was amazed; she laughed now with delight, clapping her hands together and exclaiming in wonder. Matuateh laughed too, but held back with a reserve that was unaccustomed in someone normally so headstrong.

Francisco bowed to Apanas. "*Un regalo. Un regalo para usted.*" Then in Mowachaht he said: "A gift." He did know the word after all! He'd only been pretending before. He stepped closer and gave one of the shells to Apanas. He gave the other to Matuateh and looked into her eyes. She dropped her own gaze down to look at the shell in her palm.

He reached up to the side of her head and produced a silver coin from her ear.

Apanas shrieked and slapped her knee and nudged Matuateh. "How did he do that?" In reply he reached up to *her* ear and produced a larger coin. He displayed them in his hands and they all laughed with delight. He presented Apanas with the second coin, then turned and handed the first to Matuateh. She looked from her palm to his face. Now they held eyes.

Copaza reacted strangely to the obvious attraction between his Spanish friend and the slave girl beloved by his mother, a girl he had known since childhood. He became condescending and dismissive. Any words he exchanged with Matuateh from that point onward were tinged with scorn, even anger. You are a slave, he told her once. You have no right to act like a *tyee*, to choose who you will love. But he did not interfere.

It was obvious what his problem was, though no one saw it at the time.

# Chapter 11

A churning surf, the frothing water red. At the last second he sees the club. No time to react. A blinding flash of light.

Fog seeps, darkens to ink, reaches, and wraps around, welcoming. Mother, Father, glimpsed and gone.

A voice murmurs, Your struggle can end.

He goes under yet floats above, disembodied, neither in nor out, here nor there. There is light and its utter absence. He is on a frontier, a cusp. On which side will he fall?

Accept, urges the voice.

Weightless, he embraces it. Alone no more.

If he does nothing the men will die.

This tugs him back. He flails, inhales — and gets a lungful of water. Choking, he rights himself, finds bottom, comes up croaking. Around him arrows flit, spears and rocks fly, men thrash and fight, and he is in a soundless limbo. His eyes sting with salt and blood, and the jungle, the mountains beyond, every leaf and branch and peak in sight is vivid, crisp, and achingly beautiful.

A body falls across him and all again is noise and mayhem: the whistling, screaming natives on shore, the insect reverberation of their collective voices. Around him men drop one by one. Their only chance is together. "To me!" he calls. "To me!" and amid the tumult and chaos they hear, they wade and stagger and gather round. He sees hope in their eyes. If they can hold a little longer the boat will reach them and carry them away. He nods encouragement, reaches for his dirk, and turns to face their attackers.

This time he does not see the club. There is a blinding flash and the water takes him, darkness enfolds him, and though he resists — the men! — he cannot hold on, he is slipping away

he has failed them

they will die

all of them are dead

Gasping, eyes wide against the dark, he listened, unsure if he had called out.

Water lapping against the sides. A watchman pacing the deck above. The ship creaking, mostly quiet.

His sleeping berth was narrow, windowless like a tomb. He rolled out of his cot and padded to the door.

Nothing.

He stepped through the interior lobby into the great cabin. He paused in the darkness, listening again, then crossed to the stern windows.

Sea air, cool on his face. He ran a hand across his forehead. The fever came and went. He kept his own supply of Peruvian bark. He would take some in the morning. No need to bother Menzies; he knew the dosage and when it was needed. He could not deny, though, that something else had been affecting him recently. His fingers had felt stiff, his hands swollen; even his face — his own reflection had shocked him. He'd considered consulting Menzies about these new symptoms, and ruled it out. Details were sure to get back to Joseph Banks in England, and no good could come of that.

The harbour was dark. There was no sign of dawn. The sky was clear; the stars glimmered overhead. He could just make out the profiles of the two Spanish schooners that had arrived after sunset.

Hours later. Morning now. George Vancouver sat in the stern sheets of the cutter as it pulled towards shore, his thoughts on all he needed to accomplish.

Both ships needed repairs and replenishment. Vast volumes of wood, water, and fresh food needed to be acquired, boarded, and stowed for the voyage to the Sandwich Islands. He had reports and dispatches to prepare for the Admiralty and, of course, there were negotiations to conclude on the diplomatic matter. So much to do, so little time.

And on the subject of *time*, there was his longitude problem, which left him literally all over the map — a map he had yet to draw.

Over the summer just past, as they conducted their survey, Van and his officers had recorded hundreds of celestial observations. They were skilled navigators, current in hydrographic and survey technique, and yet the longitudes they had calculated from these observations contradicted those of all previous navigators in the northwest. According to their readings, the coast they were following was ten miles inland of its position as charted previously. A discrepancy that large was a serious problem for a mapmaker.

Van planned to spend the day with Whidbey at the observatory to reconcile the difference. They would comb through their raw data, spot-check calculations, look for a pattern or an outright methodological error. The solution, he was sure, was hiding in plain sight, and they would find it quickly. In parallel, Lieutenant Baker was organizing and cataloguing the huge volume of raw survey data they had collected over the preceding months. Only when that was finished and their positions were reconciled could they get on with drawing charts.

In his mind he was already moving on to the next challenge. The Admiralty had provided him with several chronometers — marine timepieces — to help in determining longitude. These were expensive, state-of-the-art devices, and they had performed well on the outbound voyage. Recently, however, at the very time he could have used their help, they had become erratic. The best of them, Kendall's K3, had been allowed to run down and stop, and it hadn't been reliable since being restarted.

You might say that circumstance had left him to his blown devices.

He smiled wryly at his own witticism, and I felt a pang of pity for him. Who did he have with whom to share a joke, even a bad one like that? Perhaps Richard Hergest, had he lived — he was an old friend, a true peer. There was no one else, not even *Chatham*'s Broughton, who was a fellow captain but his subordinate, and who, besides, had worrisome connections to Joseph Banks.

To be in command is to be alone. Van had accepted the isolation that came with his position — embraced it, even. Sadly, I knew where that led.

⧗

Vancouver had a sudden strange sense that he was under scrutiny. He glanced around. No other boats anywhere near. He looked at the faces of the men at the oars. All facing him, and all, per naval convention, carefully avoiding his eye. He looked up. A bird, a dark speck on a current of air, nothing more. On shore, the usual bustle. Nothing unusual in the harbour. It was the same scene as the previous day, save for the presence of the *Sutil* and *Mexicana*, arrived overnight.

He looked back into the boat and thought about that strange sensation. Was it déjà vu? First his dream the night before, and now this. He found it rather unsettling.

⧗

"We won't be long," he told Dobson. "A quick word with the governor about his letter and we're off."

"Aye, sir."

They strode up the slope towards the Big House. The overnight dew was nearly dry. A gentle breeze luffed across his cheek. He glanced up at the sky. Blue, a few light ribs of cloud. Rain tomorrow. Today, though, conditions would be good for a noon sighting with Whidbey. The master was already at the observatory with the midshipmen, working through their astronomical calculations. That would be good practice for Dobson. Vancouver had liked what he'd seen of his young translator. He was level headed and diligent. Not all his midshipmen were.

"How are you finding your mess?" he asked over his shoulder. "I trust you're settling in?"

Dobson hurried to catch up. "Yes, very well, thank you, sir. Very comfortable it is. A palace compared to *Daedalus*."

"Hah! It's snug, I know. I hope you'll look upon your time with us as an opportunity. When this diplomatic business is done you can return to *Daedalus* if you wish, but why not stay on with *Discovery* as a midshipman? You'll be qualified for a commission by the time we get home."

Dobson replied that he was pleased to be of service and honoured by the suggestion.

Diplomatic, as well, thought Van. It amused and pleased him. "Where did you learn your Spanish, Mister Dobson?"

"My family are wine merchants, sir. My uncle lived in Santander for a spell. I went out there for a year, four years ago now."

Quadra was in his bureau with the young commanders of *Sutil* and *Mexicana*.

"Jorge!" Dionisio Galiano exclaimed when Vancouver was shown in. He crossed the room and embraced him. "Is happy see you, friend, arrive safe. And you" — shaking Dobson's hand — "are offeecial translate, yes? Don Juan say you have do excellent work."

"You are well, Jorge?" Cayetano Valdés asked, looking a bit concerned.

Dobson tactfully translated Hor-gay as "Captain."

"Very well, Cato," Vancouver said. "You look hale and hearty yourself. It's good to see you both."

Quadra was on his feet with everyone else. He gestured towards his table. *"Caballeros, por favor. Sentar."*

Vancouver hesitated for a split second, glanced at his two erstwhile collaborators, and sat down. Dobson did likewise. A steward brought a plate of pastries and poured coffee from a silver pot that he left on a side table.

"I just say Don Juan," Galiano said, "was weather bad on voy here."

"We had much the same."

Dobson translated, then tasted his coffee. It was piping hot and strong. He smiled to himself and reached for the sugar.

"And voy you have, after leave us?"

"It was difficult. All those interior channels. Both of us grounded before we reached open sea. We had to lighten ship to get off, and *Chatham* suffered some damage. Don Juan has kindly allowed us to make repairs to her on shore."

Dobson put down his cup to concentrate. Vancouver watched the listeners' eyes flick between speaker and translator. Quadra's stayed mostly on him.

"The currents there are treacherous," Valdés said. "We touched and nearly grounded several times. We had to backtrack again and again. Finally, we found a good, deep channel." He stood and leaned over to indicate it on a chart rolled out on Quadra's desk. "From here...through here. It's very narrow just here. Deep, though. A bit exciting at flood but fine at slack water."

"I have instructions to provide you with all our charts," Quadra told his counterpart. "I'll have a full set delivered to you later today — including those these gentlemen drew."

"My instructions are similar. Unfortunately, I am much delayed in my mapmaking."

"Perhaps I can be of assistance."

"We have some minor measurement issues to resolve. Once we do, we can produce our charts very quickly."

"We not need now for voy despite," Galiano said.

"I beg your pardon?"

Galiano explained himself in Spanish.

"These gentlemen are leaving for California in the morning," Dobson said.

"Tomorrow? You just arrived."

Galiano shrugged a what-can-you-do?

Quadra stood and went to the side table for the coffee pot. He refilled Vancouver's and Dobson's cups. "We are racing against winter. The storms here are severe and neither ship handles well in a heavy sea. I want them both away south as soon as possible."

Dobson translated Vancouver's regrets.

"Gentlemen, see to your arrangements," Quadra told his subordinates. "Speak to Felix about the supplies you need. We'll debrief more later." He turned back to Vancouver. "Captain, I would be honoured if you would join us this evening for dinner — with as many of your officers as you can spare. We'll see our two young colleagues off in style."

Vancouver stood to shake their hands. He clamped Galiano's in his, drew closer, and lowered his voice. "Might I impose upon you, Dino? A favour. Would you carry a dispatch for me? And a letter, a personal note?

Both would reach England from Mexico long before any other means available to us."

Galiano grinned. "Perhaps letter to lady friend, Jorge. Yes?"

Vancouver coloured.

The Spaniard saw and immediately grew serious. "Of course, Jorge. I take. I honoured. I at you service to be."

"Please, finish your coffee," Quadra said when Galiano and Valdés left the room. They sat back down. Dobson helped himself to a pastry. It was good. *Tal lujo*, he thought, practising. It had been a while since he had spoken so much Spanish. He finished the pastry and thought about taking another. He wished there was more coffee on offer. Vancouver and Quadra sat sipping the last of theirs.

From beneath the governor's open balcony came muffled voices, the crunch of boots on gravel fading as the two young officers descended to the landing. In the distance, the solid knock of hammer on wood, the sharper clang of steel.

⌛

The Spanish and British commissioners to the Nootka Convention both glanced out the balcony door at the noise. While their heads were turned their official translator helped himself to a polvorón.

Vancouver turned back to his counterpart, now keen to address the point of his visit.

"I have received your letter, and replied to it."

"Yes, I've read it. The matter is a vexing one. Shall we walk?"

Vancouver looked uncertainly from his translator's face to Quadra's.

"I want to show you our establishment. It will not take long."

They emerged from the Big House into bright sunshine, and as they strolled through the settlement Quadra described the functions of the various buildings. There were barracks, storehouses, a bake house, an infirmary. They were constructed of rough lumber, their cracks neatly chinked with lime. He had allocated two structures to the British: one for supplies, another for the sick.

The buildings all faced the cove. To their rear lay a grassy meadow on a neck of land that separated the harbour from the open ocean. Two days before, a work detail from *Discovery* had set up the expedition's observatory on a promontory overlooking that outer shore. Van glanced up at the sun. With any luck he would —

"*... nuestro herrero...*"

He looked back at his guide. On the near edge of the meadow, just past the last of the buildings, stood a blacksmith at a forge. Sparks flew with every blow of his hammer. He quenched the piece he was working on and tossed it onto the ground, where it clanged and lay steaming among other pieces: harpoon heads, spikes, nails. They continued onto the meadow and strolled along a bramble fence that enclosed plots of tilled earth and rows of staked vegetables. Beyond these fields, cattle and sheep grazed on the lush grass, watched by a single herder. An old man traversed the area, afloat in a sea of bobbing birds. He moved slowly, murmuring and clucking and casting seed from a bag on his shoulder, the fowl a rippling blanket flowing round.

"Our flock keeper," Quadra said. "Pablo!"

The old man saw him and bowed majestically. When he straightened he began talking. It seemed he had a lot to say. Quadra hesitated, gave Vancouver a rueful smile, and waded into the flock. As commander and keeper met, the birds closed around them. Pablo's voice was high and strained. He used his hands for emphasis, the birds flapping and lunging at every false gesture.

Dobson had been translating continuously and hardly knew where he was. Now he took in his surroundings. The birds were mostly chickens; there were some ducks and geese and a few turkeys a head above the rest. He looked down at his feet and took a quick step back.

"All in the line of duty, Mister Dobson."

The young man laughed and scraped his heel on a stone. "Aye, sir. All in the line."

Quadra waded back towards them. "Apologies, gentlemen. Shall we?"

Pablo tipped his hat to them and started away, stepping carefully to avoid treading on any of his birds.

"Pablo is one of Alberni's men. I'm sure he served in Roman times. He is the general in our war against rats." He gestured towards the harbour. "They come by ship and get into everything. Gardens, storehouses. They eat our flour and grain, even the bags it's stored in. Eggs and chicks, too.

They'll even grab an adult. All these birds you see would be dead without Pablo. Our rats are as bad as —"

Vancouver glanced at Dobson, who looked confused.

"— bad as weasels, I think sir. I think the word is weasel."

"*Si. Comadreja.* Our rats are a plague. Given what they eat, I expect they're quite tasty themselves."

Vancouver went *huh.*

"When I arrived here in the spring we landed all our sailcloth and cordage. They got into it too. I had to buy a fresh supply from the traders, and was lucky to get it. You need to be careful with everything you bring ashore."

There was a short silence as they walked.

"I've been wondering, Captain," Quadra said. "Who will you leave in charge when you take possession here? I'm assuming you won't stay yourself."

⧗

For a moment Van wondered if Dobson had made a mistake. He glanced sharply at the young man, who returned his gaze.

Who will I *leave,* he thought. Who will I *LEAVE* when I *take possession?*

In London, taking possession had been described as a formality. Perhaps there would be a ceremony, a trooping of colours, a drum roll as one flag came down and another went up, a solemn reading of their agreement, handshakes and salutes. Surely no one in London had contemplated him literally occupying Nootka Sound. He'd been provisioned for a voyage of discovery, not garrison duty.

His mind raced over the Spaniard's letter. Quadra had pushed back on the terms of the treaty negotiated in Madrid, asserting there were no amends to be made but offering to withdraw under certain conditions. Vancouver had rejected them all. Now it looked like Quadra was conceding.

Take the win, Van, the voice of his friend Richard Hergest urged. If it is within your reach, take it.

If win it is, thought George.

Not like you to be overcautious, Van. *Carpe diem. Ne plus ultra* and all that.

He performed the calculus in his head.

⧗

"If I were to take possession here," he said, choosing his words carefully, "I'd leave Mister Broughton. With *Chatham.*" He looked at Quadra, then at Dobson, wondering whether the conditional would survive translation. While Dobson rendered it in Spanish, he thought about the consequences for his survey.

"You'll need to make arrangements for the winter," Dobson told him, translating Quadra's reply. "Please let me know how I may assist. I'll do everything in my power until I hand over to you."

*Until I hand over to you.* That was definitive, not conditional. An ungenerous doubt about his translator flashed through Van's mind. He pushed it aside and pondered *arrangements for the winter.*

He would strip *Chatham* of her master Johnstone, some other key men, and her launch. Leave a skeleton crew, a presence. He would fulfill his mission in the Sandwich Islands, send a report via *Daedalus* about this unexpected turn, and return to the coast in the spring to continue his survey, though he'd be down from two ships to one, with hundreds of miles yet to cover before they reached 60° North. That was assuming the mouth of the Northwest Passage did not exist between here and there. If it did, his orders were to enter it and determine where it led. He doubted its existence, but if he were proven wrong, he would obey his instructions to the letter. A dead end or an unnavigable stretch would return him to the Pacific. A passage through it, though, whether into Hudson Bay or the Atlantic, would bring *Discovery* home to glory and make Friendly Cove incalculably valuable, the gateway to China. It would also leave Broughton stranded for another winter, maybe longer.

"I would need to land the supplies from *Daedalus,*" he said, still in the conditional.

"I'll have a storehouse cleared. Captain Broughton and his men can move ashore permanently when we depart. I'll leave the livestock and poultry for him. He'll need to deal with the rats. A man like Pablo would

THE WIND FROM ALL DIRECTIONS | 93

be worth his weight in gold."

The rats indeed. A line of verse came to Vancouver. *Our wills and fates do so contrary run.* He tried to remember the play. A tragedy, no doubt.

⧖

They crossed the meadow to its far edge and stood above a crescent beach onto which ocean breakers rolled and broke. Cobble swept ashore on every surge and tumbled back on every recession, clattering like laughter. The breeze here was cool. Quadra pointed up the coast.

"Maquinna's people summered up that way," he said. "They're at Tahsis now for the winter. It's inside the Sound, sheltered from the storms."

Van could not resist a glance in the opposite direction. Fifty yards to the south, overlooking the same beach, stood his observatory. A grand name, that, "the observatory"; in truth it was a simple affair, a wooden viewing platform and a marquee flanked by a couple of tents to house the expedition's survey equipment — sextants, theodolites, barometers, chronometers — and a shore detail to keep it secure.

A day's work awaited him there. He could see Whidbey on the plank platform, surrounded by blue-coated middies.

Quadra followed his gaze. "I would like to visit your observatory, Captain. When it is convenient, of course. Come, please. This way." He gestured back towards Friendly Cove.

For the blink of an eye Vancouver hesitated, torn between his longitude problem and his diplomatic one. The Spaniard's intentions on the latter were opaque. Was he indeed conceding outright, or was he standing pat on his new border proposal? Van felt like he was missing something that should be obvious. He revisited Quadra's question, "Who will you leave in charge when you take possession?" and this time replied, "Bollocks."

Language, Van, said Richard Hergest's mock-offended voice.

He smiled to himself. Hergest was the foulest-mouthed man he'd ever known. Even as a snotty.

They returned through the fields and settlement and walked north along the ridge above the cove. The line of the ridge led them to a point above the *Chatham* worksite. The brig was on her side in the shallows, the shore crowded with tents housing her crew. Groups of men were at work on the strand. Others swarmed over the brig's hull. The copper sheathing below her waterline had been stripped to get at the damaged timbers below. They weren't just damaged from grounding. There was rot from shipworm too. Vancouver had told Broughton to make her seaworthy as quickly as possible. Men from *Discovery* and *Daedalus* had been assigned to help. Quadra had lent some of his own carpenters to assist and Broughton had hired more from the traders.

Van mused glumly that the task was not as urgent now as it had been an hour ago.

They descended to the beach so he could speak with Broughton. Quadra and Dobson stood back and waited discreetly, the Spaniard observing the site with professional interest, the Briton glad it was not his to announce where the Chathams would winter.

Van did not mention that to Broughton, reasoning there was a time and place and this was neither. Instead, he listened to his fellow captain's report, asked a few questions, returned a salute.

"One more thing," Quadra said when Van rejoined him. He led them along the shore and around a high rock outcrop reaching down to the water. On its far side was a narrow bight.

Van felt his heart accelerate. This was where Meares's post had stood four years before.

Though nothing remained of it, the cramped area was far from abandoned. On the flat above tidewater stood a wooden stock, on which perched the keel and ribs of a small vessel. Men bustled around it; hammer blows and the clatter of construction echoed off the surrounding rocks. On the slope above the stock stood a canvas tent. Close by it were stacks of lumber, a fire pit, a pile of formed strakes. A group of men, cussing creatively, hauled one of the heavy strakes into place on the ship's hull.

"This vessel belongs to one of the traders. Captain Magee. He will leave a crew on it when he sails for China in a few weeks. They will trade along the coast all winter, and he will return next year, take on their furs, and leave a fresh crew and supplies to do it all again. Less time spent means greater profit."

They stood and watched the men work.

"The traders who come here don't care about consequences, or people, or the niceties of diplomacy or sovereignty. They're racing to take all they can before it's too late, and they'll do anything if they believe they can get away with it." Quadra paused and glanced sideways at Vancouver. "Do you know why Maquinna tolerates my presence here, in his tribal seat? His most important village? Because he thinks I am capable of controlling these people. Now he thinks that you and I are poised to fight, and if that happens the tranquility we've achieved here will fall apart. He's worried his people will be left to the whims of men like this."

Quadra stood staring at the worksite, deep in thought. "In truth, I am not the key to that tranquility. He is." He turned to face his counterpart.

"Captain, I have a proposal for you."

# Chapter 12

Old Joe Whidbey had given his boys — he always thought of the midshipmen as "his boys" — a lesson and assigned them calculations to perform while he reviewed the expedition's puzzling longitudinal problem. But his plan went awry, for not all his boys had heads for planes, azimuths, hour angles, and right ascensions; and so he put his own work aside to circulate among them, correcting calculations and nodding encouragement like an indulgent schoolmaster. Time well spent — the boys needed his help. Besides, the captain was on his way. When he arrived, the two of them would put their heads together and finally crack the longitude chestnut. They might even have time to recalculate the running error on Kendall's K3. The damn clock had been wonky since being allowed to run down. Oh, that had caused fireworks. The captain had danced a heiva that day. Today, though, they would resolve everything. All would be set right.

Sunny, was Old Joe, always thinking the best.

It was late morning when Dobson appeared and told him the captain had returned to *Discovery* on urgent business.

"Urgent business," Whidbey repeated.

"Yes, Mister Whidbey. He told me to report here and help you this afternoon."

Old Joe waited for more but Dobson did not elaborate. The fellow's silence irritated him.

"Help. Yes. That is what I need, Mister Dobson. And no doubt you are just the one to provide it." Doubly peeved, was Old Joe. He did not like change at the best of times. He looked around. He would need to do what he'd planned to do with the captain by himself. He could use the boys to calculate, though there were too many of them for what needed doing.

He readied them for the noon observation, supervised their readings and recorded his own. Then he divided them into two groups and informed one that this was their lucky day, for he was giving them a free afternoon, and don't squander it, and write up today's sighting, and do your calculations on your own time. "Alas for *you*, Mister Dobson, *you* must remain here as my particular assistant. The captain believes I am in need of your *help*."

⧗

Dick Ramsay glanced at the others who'd been dismissed. Jim Hawkins looked confused, even disappointed. Tom Pitt's expression was unreadable. John Dorsey, though, was grinning ear to ear, and Auggie Lincoln looked ready to scream with laughter.

Old Joe could still change his mind, Ramsay knew. He set off briskly in the direction of the settlement. A moment later her heard his fellow parolees behind him. "Don't look back," he said softly over his shoulder. They crossed the meadow, passed the gardens and the smithy at his forge. As soon as they were past the first building, Ramsay dodged into its lee, out of sight of the observatory, and pulled the others in with him. They were all now merry at their luck.

"Listen, fellows. Calm down and listen. We shall ruin this if we draw attention to ourselves. We must stay away from the main landing and avoid anyone from *Discovery*."

Of course, of course, they agreed. Lincoln did a little dance as though he had to pee.

They walked to *Chatham*'s camp, lined up at the cook tent as if they belonged, took plates, and went outside to sit and eat. The site was crowded with Chathams as well as Spaniards, traders, and Indians. Hawkins spotted Francisco Almeida, the Spanish midshipman he'd met the day before, down at the water's edge, where a group of natives had landed their canoes.

The midshipmen returned their empty plates and followed Hawkins towards the spot.

The canoes were loaded with cloth- and hide-wrapped bundles, some of which the Indians had laid out on the ground. Francisco knelt, unwrapped one, and prodded its contents — chunks of ruddy dried salmon. He sniffed his fingers, leaned closer, and sniffed the entire pack, then tasted a morsel. He chose another bundle to sample in the same way. Then he stood and spoke to one of the Indians, turned, waved, and called, "Carlos!"

A tall black man, massive across the shoulders, brushed past the midshipmen. He wore the rough canvas slops of a Spanish seaman. His face was disfigured by a thick scar running from his temple to his chin.

Hawkins sucked in his breath.

"Wait till you see the *other* fellow," Ramsay quipped.

"That's one big chimney chops, that is," Dorsey grudged, unaccustomed to being out-sized.

Another Spanish sailor followed the big man. They rewrapped the open bundles, gathered them and others, and carried them away towards the Big House, while the Indians unloaded more from their canoes. Francisco glanced up and saw Hawkins.

"*Oye!* Yim. What pleasure."

They shook hands and Hawkins introduced him around.

"He was the one spoke of girls," Pitt said.

"*Que?*

"You were at the governor's dinner," Pitt said, this time in pidgin.

"*Si.*"

"It is a great pleasure to meet you, my friend," Lincoln said, bowing obsequiously.

Dorsey snorted. "Just ignore Auggie here, mate," he told Francisco as he shook his hand. "He thinks you can line him up with snatch. Auggie's a right arse licker, he is. Auggie's out for Auggie."

"Look who's talking," Ramsay murmured to Hawkins.

Dorsey had spoken in English. Francisco looked confused, and then he got it, grinned, and shook Lincoln's hand, "*Si, si.* Auggie! *Mucho gusto.*"

Lincoln scowled and Dorsey laughed.

"What are you doing?" Hawkins asked.

"I buy food for garrison. Fish today. Is good here. Not like Havana, though. Havana is best fish in world." He put his fingertips to his lips and flung a kiss towards the seafood delights of Havana. He indicated the young Indian with whom he had dealt. "This is Copaza. He is a friend."

Black eyes, deep as a well. Copaza observed Hawkins coolly and said something deadpan. Francisco laughed.

"He says your hair is on fire. Good joke, *si*? Copaza arranges for us. Please excuse. I must go settle with him. And governor call me too. Maybe I'm in trouble — he finally catch me, heh?" He grinned puckishly, said "See you later," and went off with Copaza. Copaza's people followed with bundles from the canoes.

The beach was narrow and crowded with *Chatham*'s crew. Lincoln called an insult to one of their midshipmen, who returned a stony stare. Lincoln laughed, a sick-horse whinny that was too loud. William Broughton looked over from a conversation with his first lieutenant.

"We need to go," Ramsay said softly. "Follow me."

They filed off along the water's edge as though they were on an important quest. On the other side of the ridge bounding *Chatham*'s worksite lay the bight that housed the traders' camp. It was crowded with men working on a small vessel propped on a sturdy frame.

"That was close," Ramsay said. "He would have put us to work."

"You almost scuppered us there, Auggie," Dorsey said. "You've got to shut yer arse-kissing gob."

"Shut *yours*, Horsey."

Ramsay stepped between them. "Gentlemen. This way."

They edged past the labourers and climbed the ridge to get out of their way. Halfway up they sat and stretched out on the rocks. Their bellies were full, the afternoon warm. Lincoln rolled his tunic into a pillow and lay back on it. Dorsey mocked him, then thought better of it, rolled his own jacket, and reclined too. He quickly fell asleep. Pitt and Hawkins tossed stones at a tree stump. Ramsay idly watched the workers below fit a strake to the ship's hull. Others shaped planks, sawed and stacked lumber. He noticed a steady stream of Spaniards to the site. Sailors and soldiers alike mingled among the labourers, then disappeared into the tent that stood a little above the boat yard. It seemed to Ramsay that there was something furtive going on. He watched the tent closely for several minutes.

"Tom. Jim. Look at this."

Pitt and Hawkins both quickly spotted what he had noticed.

Dorsey awoke to their soft laughter. He sat up.

"Horsey," Ramsay said, "they've got a shebeen running down there. Right beneath our noses."

Pitt nudged Lincoln awake.

A short while later Ramsay made a proposal to which they all agreed.

"Let's go." Lincoln scrambled to his feet.

"No, no. Listen. We mustn't all sit inside, just in case. We'll get a bottle and drink it here." Ramsay held out his hat. "Pay the parson."

They searched through their pockets and threw coins in.

"Wait." Hawkins took back one of his.

"What are you doing?"

He held up a worn farthing. "My lucky coin. It's got the old king on it. Seventeen-fifty-four. It's not for spending."

Dorsey said, "Jesus, Hawkins, you have a *lucky coin*."

"Let me see it," Lincoln said.

"Jesus fuck, you people." Dorsey was thirsty.

"Just wait a second." Lincoln held the coin close to his eye, shrugged, and tossed it back to Hawkins.

"All right, let's go," Pitt said.

"No, no, no," Ramsay said, exasperated with their carelessness. "Just one. One of us, alone. We mustn't draw attention."

Ah. Right. Yes.

"I'll go," Lincoln said. He descended to the tent and returned a few minutes later with a bottle wrapped in a piece of ragged sailcloth.

"It was only a dago dollar," he said. "We could do another."

"First things first."

They passed the bottle around. It was harsh to their taste. They agreed it was nowhere near the quality of naval rum.

"Nevertheless, a bird in the hand," Ramsay said, shaking the bottle.

"Must be wrung by the neck."

Hearty agreement all round.

They drank and gossiped and reminisced about home, about

the voyage and their adventures on it. There was that wild night in Portsmouth before they departed. Great fun, though one of them had been bepoxed in the course of it. (He had endured the mercury cure — which no one mentioned today.) And they had called at the ports of Cape Town and Tenerife.

Tenerife! They recalled a drunken spree that had ended in a riot. A fight had broken out ashore between Discoveries and Chathams, and Spanish soldiers stepped in to break it up. The Britons immediately united and turned on them. The captain, who was at dinner down the street with some of the officers, hurried towards the fracas and waded into it, shouting to be heard — but he was not in uniform, and took a punch from a Spaniard. All hell had broken loose then. More soldiers arrived, and some locals came to their support. The British were outnumbered, corralled, and pushed to the edge of the quay. Vancouver had been among them, bellowing for calm and ordering "Avast! Step apart!" but the donnybrook raged on, and the next thing anyone knew there was a great splash and the captain was down in the water, thrashing and cursing a blue streak.

"Cap had a little nudge off the edge, you ask me," Dorsey said, looking at Pitt, who grinned and tapped his nose.

Others then followed him into the harbour, jumping of their own volition or tipped by the press of the mob. *Discovery*'s longboat had plucked them all from the water, and eventually everyone left on shore got off safely too. Next morning, Vancouver filed a protest with the Spanish governor over the rough treatment meted out on his liberty men, and the governor apologized, sort of, noting who had started things. That was the end of the affair, a war story for all involved.

There was a crash at the worksite below. They all looked down towards it. A worker had stumbled and dropped a plank. There were now several native women on the beach watching the shipwrights work.

"Well, hello," Ramsay said.

"That Spaniard talked of girls," Dorsey said. "'Girls in the village,' remember?"

A trader climbed the rise towards them. He was lean and slightly stooped, his features sharp. He introduced himself as James Magee, master of the *Margaret* out of Boston. "That rum you're drinking is from my supply," he said. He asked about the state of grog aboard their ship.

"It's good," Hawkins replied. "No complaints. We're well supplied."

Magee's face registered surprise. He took a close look at Hawkins.

"On a personal note, though, we could use more in the way of volume," Pitt said.

Magee laughed. "Well, I'm happy to help you there. You only need ask. I take it you gents are off *Chatham*."

Ramsay pointed out at the harbour. "*Discovery*. We are enjoying Sunday liberty."

"Hah! Not much of that among *Chatham*'s people."

"No. We are exceeding lucky."

"Well, I'm glad to accommodate your liberty. We've had trade with some of your hands but none with the officers. Now you know where to find me, come by any time. Just be discreet. What Señor Quadra doesn't know can't hurt anyone."

"We are the soul of discretion, Captain Magee."

"What about quim?" Pitt asked.

Dorsey snorted, Lincoln whinny-laughed, Magee frowned.

"What?"

"I see you've got some skirt down there. Can you accommodate us with some of that?"

Magee's eyes narrowed.

"What I mean is, do you know where we can come by it? In every port we've been, it's there for the asking. There's often an intermediary such as yourself."

"That's not my line," Magee said gruffly.

"Captain, please excuse my friend," Ramsay said. "He's had too much of your excellent rum and has forgotten himself. He means no offence."

Magee took his eyes off Pitt and addressed Ramsay. "You know where to find me. I'll be getting back to work."

"Very glad to meet you, Captain," Ramsay said.

Magee started away, then turned back to Jim Hawkins. "Son, if you don't mind me asking, where are you from? You sound American."

"There's a reason for that. I was born in Boston. My family are loyalists."

Magee grinned. "Well, red head, red coat. Even so, once a Boston man always a Boston man."

"We left everything in Boston, Captain. I'm a Nova Scotian now, and an Englishman still. And as you see, my coat is blue."

Magee nodded diplomatically. "Those were difficult times. I'm sorry for the price you paid."

"We never settled on a price. As far as I'm concerned, it's still outstanding." Hawkins held the American's eye before pointedly looking away.

"Well, that went well," Ramsay said as Magee descended to his worksite. "Jesus, Tom — and you, Jim. That man's our ticket to redeye, and you both go stupid on us."

Pitt shrugged.

Lincoln swigged from the bottle and said, "We should have put the bloody Americans in their place when we had the chance,"

"Look at you, Auggie. All brave behind the Yankee's back," Dorsey said. "You're a hero, you are."

Few dared tangle with big stroppy Dorsey, but when Lincoln drank his inhibitions fell like autumn leaves — and he hated being called Auggie. To Ramsay's eye, he looked set to do something stupid. "Don't hog the bottle," he said to distract him. "Pass it here."

"I'm not hogging the fucking bottle."

"Give him the bottle, Links." Pitt's eyes were trained on the beach.

Lincoln handed it to Ramsay, who handed it on to Dorsey, who pointedly wiped its neck.

Ramsay reached over and ruffled Hawkins's hair. "Red head, blue coat — and giant blue balls. It's time, boyo, to address that unfortunate condition. What about one of those comely maidens on the beach?"

Hawkins blushed, but his peers didn't notice. They were all again focused on the women down below. Copaza's helpers had floated their canoes around to the traders' side of the ridge. Men and women alike were busy loading them with packs and bundles. More Indians arrived from the direction of the Spanish town with bundles and loaded them too.

"There's your friend Ferdinand," Pitt said.

"Francisco," Hawkins said.

The Spaniard and his collaborator Copaza had appeared at the water's edge. The Indians finished loading, hauled their canoes into the water, and boarded. Copaza took a spot in one, Francisco in another. The canoes put off.

"Bloody hell," Pitt said. "There go our girls."

"I'll get their attention," Dorsey said. He got to his feet and stepped a few feet forward. Facing the cove, he urinated. "This is why they call me Horsey," he said, brandishing himself in the direction of the departing canoes.

The natives did not notice. They manoeuvred through the anchorage and out of Friendly Cove, turned up the Sound, and disappeared around a point of land.

# Chapter 13

*Sutil* and *Mexicana* weighed anchor before dawn. A few hours later the Spanish commandant arrived aboard *Discovery* for a working breakfast with his counterpart.

The day before, Vancouver had seized upon Quadra's proposal. He had spent the remainder of the day working through preparations. Now, over fresh bread and Mexican coffee (courtesy of the commandant — translator Tom Dobson could not believe his luck!), they finalized the details. They would depart next morning at dawn. Quadra had already dispatched an aide to inform Maquinna they were coming. They would visit him jointly, as allies and emissaries of their respective kings.

Vancouver saw Quadra away, dismissed Dobson, and went back to the great cabin for his morning meeting with Zach Mudge. The first lieutenant's briefing was thorough and without surprises, as a report from a good Number One should always be. They discussed the work to prioritize while Vancouver was away and the men it would require.

"Pick whoever you specifically need to remain here. I'll take crews for two boats from those you don't. I'll also take a crew of midshipmen to man a third. This trip will be in lieu of the survey mission we talked about giving them. They'll go straight to work on the charts when we get back."

"Have you a solution on the longitude issue, sir?"

"The master thinks he does. Messrs. Baker and Johnstone will review it while I'm gone. If it proves up we'll push ahead immediately. Well. Is that it for today? Kindly send Orchard in when you go up."

With his clerk Henry Orchard, he reviewed the directives delivered by *Daedalus* and the official responses they required, the reports and correspondence that needed drafting. None of it was pressing. They had weeks to prepare a packet of dispatches for *Daedalus* to carry when it returned to Port Jackson in Australia. What *was* pressing was the condition of the supplies the store ship had brought. Vancouver told Orchard to inventory the lot and determine what was salvageable.

He paused, thinking of the surprise Quadra had sprung on him the day before. "While I'm away I want you to prepare a plan," he said. "Assume *Chatham* will winter here while we continue with our original mission. She would have no resupply until *Daedalus* returns next summer. How would we divide up the supplies?" He observed the look on Orchard's face. "It is a contingency, Mister Orchard, for a possibility you will not discuss with anyone."

Zach Mudge had the afternoon watch, which was quiet, allowing him to work on his plan for the period of the captain's absence. He sent Midshipman Pitt forward to see to the supplies for the Tahsis excursion, while he stood at the chart table on the quarterdeck taking notes with a pencil.

"All in order, Mister Mudge," Pitt said when he returned.

"Very well."

"That's a lot of wine to take."

"Mmm." Mudge crossed a name from one list and added it to another.

Pitt lingered. Mudge looked up.

"Are the rosters set yet, Mister Mudge?"

Mudge glanced at him and tapped the chart table. "Soon will be." He returned to his work.

Pitt stepped to the brink of the quarterdeck to stand and survey the main, his hands held loosely behind his back, the epitome of the calm and competent young officer.

A moment later he returned to the chart table.

"I should like to go, Mister Mudge. On this excursion to Tavish."

Mudge looked up. "Tahsis, Mister Pitt. Alas, you will not be going." He tapped one of his lists. "Luck of the draw. I have you remaining here."

Pitt looked at him blankly for a moment. Then his eyes narrowed. When he spoke his voice was low and confidential.

"*Daedalus* brought a letter from my father, Mister Mudge. As you know, my family has a long connection with the East. Father is an orientalist and has been a collector all his life. He has asked me to obtain a trophy from the northwest for his collection. I should very much like to fulfill his request."

This subtle mention of family unsettled Mudge. His own family shared a west-country connection with Pitt's parents, who had asked him to look out for their son when he first came aboard. It had proven an awkward mission; his young ward had been headstrong and impetuous from the get-go.

Mudge decided to deflect.

"There'll be other opportunities for collecting, Tom. This year or next. In the meantime, the captain and I have talked about a midshipmen's excursion. A local survey mission, your very own."

"What, just us? Away from the ship?"

Mudge described Peter Puget's original notion without mentioning Vancouver's dismissal of it. "So, if circumstances allow —"

"But *will* the circumstances allow, Mister Mudge? Scuttlebutt is we'll be charting soon, and will be until we sail. There'll be no time for that mission."

Mudge silently marvelled at the accuracy of rumour on a man-of-war.

"If I am to participate on any excursion, what better place to satisfy Father than the capital of a savage empire?"

"You are on the wrong list, Tom."

"That can change with a stroke of your pencil. It is an amendment of no consequence. No one need know what was and is and how they differ."

"It is unfair to the others."

"It can be made up to the others. They do not bear the burden of my father's expectations." Pitt's expression grew more earnest. "I should very much like to fulfill his charge before we sail so I can send what I collect on *Daedalus*. Father will have it in England within the year — alongside my letter expressing my gratitude to you for facilitating its acquisition."

What had always struck Mudge about Tom Pitt was his preternatural self-confidence.

"I promise you, Mister Mudge, I will personally make amends to the single person affected by your pencil stroke. And he will never know."

Zach Mudge wanted to look away from Pitt's gaze and found he could not.

⌛

At that very moment Joe Whidbey was describing his presumptive fix for their longitude problem. Vancouver heard him out and told Baker and Johnstone to test the idea while he and Whidbey were in Tahsis. "While you're at it, check all the raw measurements and calculations again," he said. Privately, he was disappointed with Old Joe's solution, an adjustment to the standard method for correcting raw celestial readings for parallax and refraction. It sounded more like a fudge than a fix; it was doubtful Whidbey had thought of something the Royal Astronomer had gotten wrong.

He dismissed them and spent several hours computing the run-rate errors of the expedition's five chronometers. They were not consistent, but if their rates of change over time were, they could again be useful. The work required estimation to bracket the errors, a painstaking exercise requiring laborious calculations. He applied his results and compared them with the longitudes determined by celestial observation — but of course those were known to be off, and the more he thought about Whidbey's approach, the more dubious of it he became.

He dined alone so he could keep working, and as the sun set he still had no solution. *It's three in the morning in Greenwich*, he thought sourly, looking out the big stern windows of the great cabin. *Or maybe four. Or half past two. I have five state-of-the-art timepieces, and dead reckoning is more reliable than any one of them.*

A messenger arrived after dark bearing a lengthy letter from the Spanish commandant. Vancouver cast his eye over it. It obviously pertained to the diplomatic matter. He sent for Dobson.

"Just give me the gist. Is there anything new?"

Dobson scanned the letter. "Ah," he murmured absently. "Mmm hmm. Mmm."

Vancouver cleared his throat.

"Uh, beg pardon, sir. It seems a rehash. There's more on Martínez and Meares, the site of the hut. Pretty much the same offer to withdraw."

"Very well. I'll need a full written translation when we get back from Tahsis. Leave it until then."

Dobson bowed and turned to go.

"Mister Dobson."

The midshipman turned back.

"You've been most helpful since you came aboard. I very much appreciate your work."

Dobson thanked him and departed.

Van stood at the open stern windows, stretching. He had spent the entire day in the great cabin. Although he was tired he was feeling well. The fever had been but a touch this time. The days in port and fresh food had rejuvenated him. The morrow's outing would be a respite from accounts and ledgers, the bureaucratic minutiae that were the bane of his command. He was looking forward to it with nothing short of zest.

# Chapter 14

As dark melted into day, four boats set off from Friendly Cove crowded to the gunwales with officers, men to handle the oars, and provisions for the journey and the feast at its terminus. Among the journeyers there was a sense of anticipation and excitement. Plenty of banter passed between the three British craft, until Vancouver leaned towards his cox'n and murmured, "If you please, Mister Ramsay, silence between the boats."

Ramsay hailed the other coxswains and the chatter across the water ceased.

Vancouver sat forward of Ramsay in the stern sheets of *Discovery's* longboat with his Spanish counterpart Quadra. Midshipman Dobson sat forward of them, facing aft to translate. Next to him sat Archibald Menzies, facing forward and leaning into a conversation (in French) with *Chatham's* Broughton and the Spanish doctor, Moziño. This left the two commanders to converse as if they were alone and not crowded together with more than a dozen others.

And what, pray, did the two commissioners to the Nootka Convention discuss? Was it matters pertaining to the resolution of the dispute between their respective courts, viz. the transfer of buildings, districts, and parcels of land? No. The weather. Anecdotes of their recent voyages. The scenery. Past service. They had both served in the Caribbean and had visited many of the same ports, though neither dwelt on specifics, their nations being belligerents at the time. They defaulted to the neutral fodder of their experiences in the northwest. Quadra spoke of his voyages in 1775 and 1779, making light of the inadequacies of the vessels available in Mexico for the rigours of the North Pacific. Vancouver pointed out an island on their starboard beam.

"That's Bligh's Island," he said. "Cook named it after his ship's master. We anchored there for six weeks in the spring of '78. We'd had a hard crossing from the Sandwich Islands and *Resolution* had sprung her mast. One Sunday, Captain Cook declared a day of rest for all hands — except midshipmen. He had us row him around the island, and he sat here, where I am now, egging us on. 'Put your backs into it, gentlemen,' he told us with just the hint of a smile. 'This is not the River Cam, and I am certainly *not* your lady friend.'"

Quadra smiled appreciatively. Neither commander spoke for several moments. Van stared at the island, thinking about that day and his delight in seeing Cook as he'd first known him, relaxed and garrulous, a far cry from his demeanour over the preceding months. By then it was clear to everyone that their commander was in decline. On previous voyages he had shown wisdom, discretion, restraint. Now he was careless and erratic. He made mistakes he would never have made before. Simple ones, dangerous ones. Everyone saw them, yet no one dared challenge him, or ask how he was, or if there was something wrong. Then he would revert to his old self, and his people, like children wanting to believe, were reassured, their faith renewed. In truth, the wise and intrepid explorer was fading away, supplanted by an uncompromising martinet. Just a few days after that Sunday outing, in that same anchorage in a cove off Bligh Island, a group of Indians came aboard to trade. One of them grabbed an iron hoop and fled in his canoe. Cook roared at him to stop, grabbed a musket, and fired. The man fell dead. After so many wise choices, so many decisions that had saved and respected lives, he had taken one in a blind rage.

"We were looking for you, you know."

Vancouver looked uncertainly at Dobson, who had translated the words, then at the Spaniard who had spoken them.

"Word came from Spain that the illustrious Cook was somewhere in the northwest. I was sent north with others to intercept him. I am glad now that we did not meet then."

"As am I."

Dobson carefully excluded himself from the chuckle they shared, which seemed somewhat forced in any event.

They landed midmorning for a bite to eat, and by the time they set off again the wind had risen and the boats raised their sails to it. The marines crewing one of the British boats, relieved from their oars, took up their fifes and drums. The tiny flotilla sailed north to *Heart of Oak*. Two canoes passed in the opposite direction. Quadra waved a greeting. The Indians stared back.

"We must be a sight to them," Quadra said.

"That is certain." Vancouver reflected for a moment. "They were a sight to us when we first encountered them. Quite different from the people we'd met in the South Sea. Friendly, though. Assiduous traders, as I recall."

Dobson hesitated at *assiduous* and went with *tough*.

Quadra laughed. "I can confirm they have not changed."

*Tough* worked for Van too. They had demanded payment for trees felled for *Resolution*'s mast. Cook had grumbled and paid up, quipping that *this* was irrefutable proof that they had landed on the shores of America. That had been a good day. Cook was his old self. Days later he shot a man dead.

Music echoed off the timbered slopes. They cruised along the western shore of a long northern reach. A large bird took flight from a dead tree, its wingbeat the luff of a sail too close to the wind.

*"Mire! Un águila."*

The creature caught a column of air and ascended. All heads in the boat turned up to see its snow-white head, stern face, curved beak. It looked down at them as it soared past, the dark feathers at its wingtips splayed and trailing like pennants.

*"Haliaeetus leucocephalus,"* Menzies volunteered, leaning back to address the two commanders. "The bald eagle. Common in coastal areas across the continent. Ubiquitous here in the northwest."

"California too," Quadra replied to Dobson's translation. "I admire this bird. There is a lethal grace in its every movement."

"The Americans chose it as their national symbol," Menzies said, his eyes still tracking the eagle, "a choice Ben Franklin lamented. He thought the wild turkey a more respectable emblem of the 'brave and honest character of America.' He called it —"

"Mister Menzies takes a keen interest in scientific matters," Vancouver said, cutting him off. "He joined us originally as a supernumerary, in the capacity of botanist, and like a herbal Noah he has filled my ship with cuttings and shrubs. But when my surgeon was incapacitated, he acted in his stead, and I'm happy to say he has now agreed to assume the role officially. He is no longer a supernumerary but a proper member of our complement."

"You sailed with two surgeons?"

"Fortunately, yes. Mister Cranston had a stroke on our outbound voyage. He's been bedridden ever since, unable to communicate. Most tragic. He is ashore now, among our sick. He'll sail on *Daedalus* for Port Jackson."

"*Lo siento.* What a pity. Doctor Menzies, perhaps Doctor Moziño can assist with his treatment." Quadra nodded towards his own surgeon, who was already back in conversation with Broughton. "I will mention it to him."

"I would be grateful for his help," Menzies said.

"Mister Menzies will be happy to help Doctor Moziño as well."

"Captain, thank you. I may even consult him myself. Another opinion, you know, is always helpful."

"Then he is at your command." Vancouver hesitated and nodded towards the Scotsman. "I must say that I'm grateful to him for filling the role when necessity called, and for assuming it formally now."

"I'll continue in my role as botanist, of course," Menzies told Quadra. "Sir Joseph Banks will insist upon it. I'm under his personal instructions tae perform the role he filled on his own voyage. He —"

"Mister Banks would place many demands upon a ship of war." Vancouver's expression was that of a man who has sipped sour milk. He threw his interpreter a glance. "Mister Dobson, take a rest. We'll need you again shortly. Mister Menzies, on a naval vessel a supernumerary is a passenger. A deadweight. Your duties as surgeon must take precedence over your botanical pursuits." His finger, which had been tapping the gunwale, stilled. "Which I will accommodate when circumstances allow."

Menzies flushed. He seemed poised to speak. A long moment passed in silence, the two men's eyes locked. At last Vancouver said, "Mister Menzies. Do not let me detain you any further."

The botanist-surgeon inclined his head and turned back to Moziño and Broughton.

⧗

The soothing strains of "The World Turned Upside Down" floated across from the musicians' boat. Relieved of the burden of translation, Tom Dobson relaxed and took in the scenery he had all but missed. Quadra gazed after the receding eagle. After a short silence Vancouver said, "I've been wondering, Don Juan, what we should expect at Tahsis."

"Ah! Speeches. Formality. They are ceremonious people. Alberni warned me when I arrived, and if anything he understated it. The first time I visited Maquinna, he threw a feast in my honour. I tell you, it was governed by protocols that would not be out of place in Versailles. There was serving after serving of food, round after round of gift-giving, formal proclamations of friendship and esteem. Soon after, Maquinna came to see me at the *presidio*. He stayed overnight and we talked for hours. When he left, he invited me to his daughter's *fiesta de quinceañera*."

Dobson hesitated and then translated this as 'debutante ball.'

"*Si. Debutante.* Ever since, we've exchanged visits regularly."

In the broad waters of the Sound the boats had sailed in loose formation. Now, as they entered the narrow inlet that led to Tahsis, they formed a single column. The commanders fell silent to watch.

"You built an excellent rapport with Maquinna," Vancouver said when it was accomplished. "And you did it quickly."

"We both worked hard on that. It's fragile, though. It would be naïve to think otherwise. What we have here could fall apart" — he snapped his fingers — "like that."

Vancouver glanced forward. Menzies and Broughton were immersed in their conversation with Moziño. He looked over his shoulder. Ramsay's eyes were on the passing shore.

"It's easy to be deceived of one's power," he said quietly.

The Spaniard gave him an intent, curious look.

"I've often thought about what happened to Cook. I believe now that he misjudged the power he could wield over others — his power over things he could not control."

Quadra waited for him to continue.

"William Bligh was offshore with the rest of us the day Cook died. He saw it all happen. You'd think the lesson would never be lost. Yet ten years later he made the same miscalculation. His ship, *Bounty*, was five months in Tahiti. He allowed his men to live ashore. He let discipline slacken. Routine fell away, relationships formed. When it was time to leave he tried to reassert his authority — but his people had been seduced by the place, the freedom they'd had. They mutinied and cast him adrift."

Quadra nodded. Vancouver stared hard at Dobson.

"Sir?" the midshipman asked, disconcerted.

Vancouver glanced back again at Ramsay, whose eyes were casting ahead and around as a diligent coxswain's should. He leaned closer to his translator. "Mister Dobson. What I say is for Don Juan alone."

"I understand, sir."

Vancouver's gaze lingered on Dobson. When he continued his voice was low and quiet.

"Last winter we were there for a month to provision and refit. It was less than three years since the mutiny. I imposed restrictions to prevent what happened to Bligh. No shore leave. No private trade. No congress." He leaned closer to Dobson, his voice growing even quieter. "None of these measures was popular."

With the lowering of his voice his breath caught in his throat. He coughed, and Menzies glanced around. Vancouver waved him away and waited, perhaps to catch his breath, perhaps to be sure no one but Dobson heard his next words.

"Tahiti was not the Eden I remembered. I saw peril everywhere — perhaps because I knew of Bligh's fate, perhaps because I had witnessed Cook's. Or perhaps it was because I was no longer a boy, that I bore responsibility now for so many lives. Not just those of my own people — the lives of the Tahitians also depended on what I did. I suddenly saw the danger that must always have been there, danger that is present whenever two peoples, two tribes if you will, meet for the first time.

"And still, I nearly repeated Cook's mistake. I shan't burden you with details, but I realized in the nick of time that I cannot, must not, overreach the power I can actually exert. Left to our own devices, so far from reinforcement or counsel, the situation demands that we maintain distance, that we exercise..." He sought the word. "... discretion. Our lives depend on it. And so, when necessary, I instill discretion in my own people if they cannot find it in themselves. I did this in Tahiti and the Sandwich Islands. I'll do it again if I see a similar danger here or anywhere."

"*Exactamente, Capitán.* My men think I am too hard on them and too lax with the Indians. But treating the people here humanely has saved lives on both sides. Before I arrived, things were ugly. Indians were cheated and killed, their women taken against their will."

Vancouver's eyes narrowed to slits.

"I put a stop to that. I will not tolerate the violation of innocents. There is a trade that goes on in Santa Cruz — it's a port, and such a trade exists in every port. That's a fact, and I must make peace with human nature. But rape...no."

Vancouver grunted. "With all of that going on, Maquinna's restraint was remarkable."

The wind had freshened from the south; it filled their sails and carried them briskly up the reach. For the first time in more than an hour, the musicians took a break. Quadra and Vancouver sat in thoughtful silence.

"It's more than remarkable. Let me tell you what happened a few weeks ago. My deputy at Nunez Gaona — our post inside Juan de Fuca Strait — is Salvador Fidalgo. He is a good man, but unimaginative. Cut from traditional cloth. One of his men raped an Indian woman. She screamed, her people caught him in the act, they killed him. They were justified; they were defending one of their own. But Fidalgo had lost a man — he felt he had to act. Next day he opened fire on Indian canoes. They were just passing, no threat at all. It was carnage — legs, bodies everywhere. Children. Were *they* guilty of his man's murder? Fidalgo claims he was under attack and fired in self-defence."

The musicians began another tune, a rousing version of "British Grenadiers."

"A commander must be free to act, but what he did was stupid. Discretion, as you say, was called for, and he failed to exercise it. The chief of the people there — they call themselves Makah — is Tatoosh. He was friendly with us until then. But now his tribesmen, his *kinsmen*, were dead. Word spread like fire along the coast. We heard it here in days. It probably reached Tahsis before it reached us.

"If I'd had anyone to take Fidalgo's place, I would have arrested him. Court-martialed and cashiered him at the very least. But I didn't. So I sent him a reprimand. What do you think a scolding does for the peace I've worked to keep? Where is the justice in it for the Makah? Can it bring back their dead?"

At the helm, Ramsay shifted his weight slightly to lean forward. Vancouver sensed it and cast him a look. Ramsay leaned away. "British Grenadiers" ended abruptly. With barely a pause the musicians began "Garryowen."

"Soon after there was another incident, this time in Clayoquot Sound. The English trader Brown argued with the local chief, Wickaninnish. It was over the price of pelts. It's always over the price of pelts. It turned into a fight and more Indians died. Brown had the sense to weigh anchor, but he still wanted pelts. That's what he was there for. He moved on to trade with the Ahousaht who live nearby. Their chief is Cleaskinah, a legendary warrior. They argued over the price of pelts — you see a pattern here? — and Brown decided the way to settle things was to take two of Cleaskinah's sons hostage. Yes. You see how it will go. Both boys wound up dead.

"All this follows on the heels of previous trouble. Last winter the American trader Gray burned Wickaninnish's village. In the spring he killed more Indians, raided villages, stole furs. Other traders, not all but some, were doing the same. So put it all together. In the space of just a few months, *all* the white nations present in the northwest had committed atrocities against people here."

Dobson felt a soft kiss of mist on his cheek. The breeze off their stern now felt cool.

"Tatoosh, Wickaninnish, Cleaskinah — they'd all had enough. They met in Clayoquot Sound. They agreed to war and resolved to kill every white man in the region. Every American, every Spaniard, every Briton — all of us, in one coordinated attack."

Quadra observed Vancouver's expression as Dobson translated. The Englishman's face betrayed no emotion at all.

"It would require surprise and superior numbers. They had that — they could mobilize their own people and others who owed them fealty. Most of the traders were dispersed throughout the region and could be picked off one by one. Fidalgo's garrison wasn't finished digging in and could be overrun quickly. But we were there at Santa Cruz de Nuca, with our heavy guns and fortifications, our soldiers and ships. Not impregnable, but the most difficult objective, and essential to their success. What's more, they couldn't attack it without Maquinna's consent — it's his territory. And they needed his people, their numbers, to add to their own if the plan were to succeed."

Quadra waited for Dobson again, noting this time the narrowing of Vancouver's eyes.

"The chiefs sent word to Maquinna, and he went to Clayoquot to hear them out. They reminded him that the Spanish had killed his own brother, Calicum, just three years before. They reminded him of all the other incidents in which his people had died. They shamed him for his prosperity and demanded he join them.

"He said no. He argued against the attack and in favour of us. I've never heard the specifics. I only know he must have been persuasive because he convinced Cleaskinah to come and talk to me in person. Then he travelled ahead to warn me what was going on.

"Cleaskinah came the next day. He is very blunt-spoken — I like him. He laid out their grievances, all the incidents, every conflict, death, and crime. He spoke as a father about his murdered sons. What can you say to that? I realized what it was going to take, what I had to say, the assurances I had to give and live up to. I told him there would be no more sons taken, no more grieving fathers created, no more incidents like those at Nunez Gaona or Clayoquot or Ahousaht. That I would never allow another Indian to suffer because of a white man's actions, that a white man would pay if he so much as hurt an Indian.

"'Never is a long time,' Cleaskinah replied — and he was right. It's easy to talk of *never*. It must have sounded hollow. I knew then that I had to commit completely. I vowed to him, upon my honour, in the name of my king, and before God, that no one among them would be harmed by any Spaniard from that moment on.

"We talked for two days. It was just me and Alberni, Maquinna with his kinsman Natzape, and Cleaskinah. Maquinna spoke in my favour. Old Natzape did, too. It took a very long time to bring Cleaskinah around, but we did it. We convinced him it was in his people's interest, in everybody's interest, to maintain peace.

"It was Cleaskinah who went back and persuaded the others to abandon the attack. But it was really Maquinna who prevented a bloodbath."

Quadra and the musicians fell silent at the same moment. Midshipman Ramsay, who had been listening to what he could catch, sat back, took note of the boat's position in the little flotilla, and adjusted course.

"A close call," Vancouver said.

"*Si.* Too close. This was just a few weeks ago. It is still fresh in their minds."

They both glanced towards the launch, where a fifer played the opening notes of "The Girl I Left Behind Me." His mates joined in.

"I intend to keep the commitments I made to them. They must understand I am honour bound, that when I give them my word on something I will keep it come what may."

Vancouver gazed ahead. The pause in their conversation was a relief to Dobson. He was drained from the continuous demands of the past several hours: listening, thinking, translating, speaking. He folded his arms across his chest against the now-chill breeze and looked around. Far ahead, the end of the inlet was now visible. In the boat trailing theirs, one of the midshipmen was clowning with his mates, laughing feverishly, and making the wild motions of a conductor to "The Girl I Left Behind Me." Prat, thought Dobson. This is all a lark to him.

# Chapter 15

Dozens of lodges were splayed across the terminus shore, wisps of smoke rising from them, white against the green slopes beyond.

"Big place."

"Hundreds here, I'll wager."

"Hundreds of cannibals. And *we've* come for a feast."

"You really think they're cannibals?"

Lincoln seemed to relish the idea. "Old Joe said."

"He was having you on," Barrie said. "I heard him joking about that with Scotty MacMenzies."

Dorsey reached forward to flick Ned Roberts across the head. "Watch your back when we land, Neddy. They'll want some of that sweet rump roast of yours, and not just for romancing."

Roberts twisted around, angry.

"Steady in the boat, Mister Roberts," Peter Puget called from the stern.

Roberts flushed and faced forward. Puget returned to his conversation in French with Pedro Alberni. Midshipman Pitt, sitting at the tiller behind them, leaned forward to listen in.

Dorsey sang-snickered, "Nan-cy got a spank-ing."

"Fuck off, Dorsey," Roberts spat over his shoulder.

In the senior officers' boat Vancouver conferred with Midshipman Ramsay, who hailed the other boats. They all struck sails and took to oars. A moment later the musicians launched into "Lilliburlero." Vancouver sat observing the smoke and the size of the village. Over in the launch they were captivated by it.

"Cunnytown, here I come," Dorsey purred.

"We'll get you laid tonight, Jimmy Hawkins," Lincoln said, giddy at the prospect. "There's a first time for everything."

Stuart nudged Hawkins from behind.

"You too, Charlie," Lincoln said.

Predictably, there followed noisy bragging about past carnal adventures.

"Silence in the boat," Pitt called from the stern. He tapped his nose at those who turned to look. He needn't have worried. Lieutenant Puget was not listening. He was deep in conversation with Alberni.

Pitt grinned happily to himself.

⧗

The commissioners' plan was to make camp short of Tahsis and arrive formally the following day — Quadra had sent Francisco Almeida ahead with word to that effect. So while the band played, the two commanders studied the shoreline and chose a flat, grassy area a few hundred yards from the village. Ramsay led the way in, and the commissioners, along with Broughton and the ever-present Dobson, stepped ashore to discuss camp arrangements. When Puget and Alberni joined them they separated by nationality.

"Mister Puget, our tents will go there —" Vancouver pointed "— with officers there. The Spanish tents will go over there. Señor Quadra will delegate an officer to oversee their arrangements. Work with him. Joint mess tents and fires in the middle. We will be responsible for the perimeter, so establish that straight away. Mister Broughton will go up to the village with Captain Alberni to invite the chief for supper. The Spanish will take charge preparing it. We will provide whatever assistance and victuals they request...Ah, Mister Menzies. Join us. Your botanizing can wait. Kindly do the rounds of the men. General welfare, ailments et cetera. Any with the venereals are not to wander tonight. Mister Puget, please note that and ensure the watch knows. Well, gentlemen, that is all. To your tasks ...Mister Puget, a word before you go."

Vancouver led Puget a few paces away and gave Dobson a glance that froze him in his place. For a moment he stood looking towards Tahsis. "We must have no trouble tonight, Peter. Not with the Spanish and certainly not with the Indians. I want vigilance on the perimeter and a picket between us and the village. Steady men with judgment." He pointed upslope towards the forest. "Let's have another up that way and another at our backs. Unobtrusive but armed to sound the alarm. Nothing more. No shots into the bushes, not even for deer." He paused, glanced around, and his eyes settled on the midshipmen ascending from the landing.

"Take Hawkins as your Number One. He's steady and keen and good with people. Take whoever else you need among the midshipmen for the pickets."

Puget looked them over. Barrie. Yes. Steady. Perhaps overly serious, but he'd learn to lighten up. He looked down to the water's edge, where Ramsay was securing the longboat for the night. Yes. Those two would do nicely for the picket on the frontier with the village. He'd pair them with a couple of seamen. His eye fell on Roberts. Young. Lacked confidence. He'd give Hawkins a deputy. Pitt. Lincoln. He'd keep them away from temptation in the other post. There was Dorsey also. He'd put him on the far side of camp, farthest from the village, well out of trouble's way. Once the camp was established, the others could take liberty, even go beyond the perimeter.

There were provisions to land and tents to erect, wood to collect, and of course the perimeter to establish. Puget went to work. He organized the men, sent a runner for Hawkins, and conferred with Quadra's designate, a young ensign who spoke good French. By the time Hawkins reported they had agreed on everything. "This is Señor Ortiz, Mister Hawkins. He seems a friendly chap. He'll be your dance partner this evening." He explained the arrangements and what he wanted him to do. "How is your French?"

"Not very good, Mister Puget."

"Try pidgin." Puget patted him on the back and strode off to find Menzies.

While tents sprouted like mushrooms, George Vancouver climbed to the edge of the meadow, peered intently into the trees, then turned to take in the camp, the inlet, the Indian village in the distance. Smoke rose from the longhouses above the shore.

⧗

Was he thinking of the recent plot by the chiefs? Did it remind him of

Cook's death, or confirm the perfidy of uncivilized natives?

No. He was remembering the day he lost control.

Waimea Bay, six months before. His ships had sailed four thousand miles from Tahiti. The northwest coast was still three thousand miles away. His men needed rest, his ships repairs and provisions for the voyage.

The Hawaiian archipelago was ablaze, chiefs warring with chiefs, islands with islands. Traders calling there en route for the northwest fuelled the conflict with firearms, and now everyone wanted them. The natives at Waimea Bay pressed Van for muskets in return for the food and supplies he badly needed.

My weapons belong to King George, he responded. And he forbids me to sell them to anyone.

If there is one thing a Polynesian understands it's a taboo; besides, Van had plenty of other things to trade for what the ships needed. His men got on with the work. The islanders were businesslike in all their interactions, though grudgingly so. They *really* wanted those guns.

He wondered if there was something more at play. Something seemed off about the place, though he allowed it might be him. Cook's death and the carnage that followed were engraved in his memory, seared onto his soul. He had never expected to return to the islands, yet here he was, no longer an impressionable midshipman but a commander with lives reliant upon him.

He established a defensive perimeter and insisted his people keep their distance from the natives.

One morning, just to get off the ship for a few hours, he rode ashore with a watering party. There were many ashore already: a detail of marines, carpenter's crews from both ships. Menzies was botanizing near the landing and Baker was at the observatory. "Carry on, carry on," Vancouver called to the marine sergeant when he landed. "Don't mind me." He set off alone along the beach, enjoying the sun on his back, the brilliant light, the cooling breeze off the ocean. The sound of waves rolling onto the sand was comforting. The two ships stood peacefully at anchor against a boundless horizon.

He walked on, allowing himself the pleasure of daydreaming. A mile out, he decided to turn back.

That's when he noticed fires burning in the hills above the shore.

Dense pillars of smoke rose into the sky — just as in the days before Cook's death. Then, they had failed to recognize it as a summoning of warriors. Later they realized they had missed other portents: the islanders' escalating hostility and insolence, their brazen acts of thievery.

His blood ran cold. His people were exposed on the beach, unprepared, unsuspecting. He started back towards them at a brisk pace and glimpsed movement in the trees: men flitting between the palms. He began to run. Now their voices came to him, first as a murmur, then growing in volume. They were shouting and whistling, the presage to a charge.

"To the boats!" he shouted. He was winded, unused to running after so long at sea. Savage drums beat in his ears. Spears would fly next. Volleys of stones would rain down like murderous hail. The natives would flood out of the jungle, swarm and overwhelm the men, lethal blows landing, crushing, cutting.

"Get to the boats!" he called, hoarse with effort.

He was nearer now. The men on shore turned and looked his way.

"NOW! To the boats!"

He ran even faster, waving his arms, not daring to glance around.

"Move, damn you! Off the beach!"

The men gathered, exchanged looks, confused. They watched his approach. He reached them, gasping and winded, pointing at the hills, the boats, the ships at anchor in the tranquil bay.

Menzies realized what the captain had seen — the smoke in the hills. He explained that it was innocent, that it was the practice of the natives to burn their fields to encourage new growth. The ash —

"Get off the goddamn beach — *NOW!*"

He pushed the Scot towards the boats and swept them all ahead of him, flailing his arms, shoving those who dawdled, bellowing the while.

They evacuated in disarray. One of the boats turned broadside in the surf, swamped, and nearly capsized. Men and gear went into the water. The other boat came to its rescue. All hands made it off the beach and back to the ships.

There had been no men in the trees, no shouting or whistling, no stones hurled. No native scheme to murder them all. The smoke had triggered a memory. The savage drumming had been the frantic beating of his own panicked heart.

Everyone on the beach had witnessed his behaviour. Everyone on both ships soon knew of it, too.

A dream that haunted him had come to life. He had lived and breathed that dark, chaotic struggle; he had seen the club descend, gone under, tasted salt and blood and his own fear.

What was happening to him?

Now, standing and gazing at Tahsis with *its* columns of smoke, he wondered if he'd gone mad. After the fiasco in Tahiti he had vowed never to lose control again — and there, in the Sandwich Islands, he'd done so; that was certain.

And yet, he knew now that the feeling he'd had — that something was off in the Sandwiches — had not been wrong. It had been neither his imagination nor paranoia. At Waimea Bay, just two months later, Richard Hergest and the astronomer William Gooch, bound on *Daedalus* to rendezvous with him, were overrun, killed, and cut to pieces, their flesh and bones distributed to the local chiefs.

⧖

An hour later Maquinna and some of his counsellors arrived with Alberni and Broughton to dine with the senior officers. Their conversation was stilted, filtered as it was through a bottleneck of translators: Comekala for Mowachaht–English, Alberni for Mowachaht–Spanish, Dobson for Spanish–English.

I grew bored and looked for a midshipman.

I found Hawkins with Ramsay, Barrie, and two seamen at the picket nearest the village. They were keeping a wary eye on the meadow beyond their perimeter, where numerous natives had gathered, having followed Maquinna from Tahsis. Despite their numbers they seemed peaceable. Archibald Menzies had certainly deemed them so — he had wandered out among them to botanize. He'd soon approached a group of women digging with sticks. Now he was on his knees next to one of them, peering into the hole she had dug. The other women had stopped their own work and gathered round.

For the benefit of the picket men, Ramsay interpreted the scene.

"Whit are ye rrrrooting fer, lassie? Aire thur neeps in the daihrt?"

The picket men laughed. A moment later the women in the field laughed too — the Scot's limited Nootkan vocabulary had failed him. He grinned up at them and tried again. Shortly they were all laughing together. Menzies turned back to examine the excavation. Another woman got down in front of the hole to show him something.

"Och, hoots! Tha's fascinatin', lassie. Saire Joseph Banks — mah patron, huv Ah mentioned tha' afore? — Ah've noo doot he'll get a bonny bonah when he hairs aboot this."

Ned Roberts came trudging towards their post from the direction of the forest.

"Everything all right, Ned? What's happening at the other pickets?"

"All peaceful in the woods."

"Are Auggie and Pitt awake?" Barrie asked. "What about Dorsey?"

"Yes, wide awake. It's early yet."

Hawkins caught something in his manner. "Let's get back to camp, Ned. It'll be dark soon." He turned to the others and gestured towards Menzies. "Keep your eye on His Nibs. We'll send supper out for you in a while. A hot drink too."

"Spike it for us, will you, Jim?" Ramsay clapped one of the seamen on the back. "I speak for Evans here, not myself."

Evans grinned hopefully.

"Hah. We'll send a tot. That's all I can do."

They walked back to camp. The light was failing now and Maquinna's party had gathered to leave. "That's all for tonight," Vancouver told Dobson when they were gone. "Rest up for tomorrow. It will be a demanding day."

The night was cool with a clinging mist. Fires were kept stoked against the chill. Around the officers' fire the brandy kept flowing, and conversations continued in French and pidgin after the two commissioners retired to their tents.

Hawkins ran into Menzies near the officers' tent.

"What did you find in the meadow, Mister Menzies?"

The Scot's face lit up. "Ach, it's something like a potato. I believe it's a new species of *trifolium*."

Pitt and Lincoln jostled in from the darkness and joined them, grinning and swaying. Menzies looked at them uncertainly and continued. "I'd seen the excavations before and thought they were digging for sarane or the root of *lilium camschatcensis*. It's a *trifolium*, though, for certain. They tell me they eat it with oil, as a relish for fish or meat. I arranged with one of the ladies tae try it tomorrow."

Pitt clapped him on the back. "I shall go rooting for *those* at the first opportunity, Mister Menzies. I expect the flesh will be tawny and the taste somewhat gritty."

Lincoln snorted.

If Menzies sensed mockery he chose to ignore it. He smiled indulgently and bade them goodnight. When he was gone, Hawkins pulled his peers into the shadows.

"What are you doing here? Why aren't you at your post?"

"Don't worry, old boy," Pitt drawled. "Rome is protected. Our two watchmen are holding the fort. We came for a meal."

"I sent food up an hour ago."

"Ah. We must have passed the porters in the dark."

Lincoln laughed loudly and patted his tunic. "Perhaps we were a bit delayed. We had a snort on the way down. Yesterday I called on your countryman again."

Hawkins pulled them farther into the dark. He could smell booze on them now. "You've had more than a snort. You're on duty, and you're pissed. Both of you. Get back up there before the captain hears."

"How will His Highness Captain King George of Holland hear, unless you tell him, Jim-Bo?" Lincoln said. "I thought you were a better sort than that."

"Get back up there now or I'll wake him up and you can tell him that yourself."

Lincoln's expression darkened.

"Links," Pitt said.

Lincoln stared hard at Hawkins before glancing away.

"We didn't know food was on the way," Pitt said reasonably. "We thought we'd been forgotten, Jim. And yes, we had a tipple, but it was out there in the dark, on the way here. Our men didn't see a thing."

Hawkins hesitated. If that were true, they'd certainly figure it out when these two returned.

"Just get going. By now your supper's there. No more of this. Give me your word. Both of you."

Pitt nodded. Lincoln wobbled, smirked, and crossed his heart. They slipped away in the direction of their post.

The encounter left Hawkins in a sour mood. He kicked himself for taking their word and not their bottle. He found Ned Roberts and told him to do another circuit of the perimeter. Ensign Ortiz came by just as Roberts was about to go. Hawkins introduced them. They exchanged pleasantries in French.

"It is very quiet," Ortiz said in pidgin to Hawkins. "Boring, yes?"

"Why don't you go with Ned? He's going to walk the perimeter."

The Spaniard brightened at the suggestion. He headed off with Roberts.

After they returned there was an incident at the fire shared by the British and Spanish seamen. In the spirit of the excursion there had been tots poured all round, and there was more grog in unsanctioned circulation, what with sailors being resourceful in that line of procurement. Everything was cheerful until it was not. A fight broke out between a gunner's mate named Reybold and the scarred Spanish seaman everyone called Black Carlos. Their fellows egged them on.

Hawkins and Roberts hurried towards the ruckus. "Fetch the bosun and a couple of watchmen," he told Roberts when he saw what was happening. He pushed Ned away and hesitated, recalling some advice Peter Puget had given him once during a night watch at sea. "It's there in black and white, so best read not at all," he'd said. They were talking about the Articles of War, specifically Article 21, which dictated that anyone striking an officer would be condemned to death.

"In a dustup, one punch always lands in the wrong place," Puget said. "So have someone else break it up. Do it yourself only if you must. Avoid it if there are witnesses."

Hawkins stepped further into the shadows and waited.

Ortiz appeared at his side. They exchanged glances. The ensign nodded and made no move to intervene either. It seemed the Spaniards had similar regulations, and similar ways of dealing with them.

Reasoned caution is not cowardliness, Hawkins reflected. An officer's duty demands discretion as much as courage. There in the darkness, he felt that the Spaniard at his side was a kindred spirit, a brother-in-arms.

Ortiz moved closer in the dark. Hawkins glanced at him, wondering if he felt it too.

The young man smiled and held his eye. Unsettled, Hawkins looked back to the fight.

Reybold and Carlos were well matched — each gave as good as he got. Their mates called encouragement but did not join in. That was the real risk, a melee, and when he ruled it out Hawkins allowed himself to relax. Reybold, he noted, dropped his opposite shoulder before throwing a punch. Black Carlos read it and had him off balance and reeling. The Spaniard, though, had his own bad habit. He twisted when he threw a hook and stumbled into some punishing blows as a result.

Ortiz nudged him gently. Hawkins glanced his way and moved a little to the side to make room.

A bosun's mate from *Discovery* barged into the midst of the fight, knocked both men off balance, then pummelled them with a knotted cord. They raised their arms to fend off his blows but did not resist. A moment later two watchmen and a Spanish mate arrived and separated them.

Hawkins and Ortiz stepped into the firelight. Ortiz led Carlos aside to deal with him. The British mate pushed Reybold in the other direction. Reybold's nose was streaming blood.

"Well? What do you say for yourself?"

"A misunderstanding, Mister Hawkins. That's all it was. We was drinking peaceful and a misunderstanding arose. Nothing was meant by it."

Hawkins looked out into the dark. Reybold was a drunk and a brute, a troublemaker with a vicious temper. If this incident were escalated it would not go well for him.

"Any more of this and you'll go on the blacklist. The captain will deal with you then." He looked around at the faces in the firelight. "Listen to me, all of you. There will be no more trouble with the Spaniards. And there'll be no more drinking. The festivities are over. You will go to your tents."

He saw resignation on sullen faces and breathed a secret sigh of relief. He turned back to Reybold, who held his eye for a moment too long. "Start him six," he told the mate.

Reybold hunched and raised his arms and took his blows from the bosun's cord.

As the men went to their tents Ortiz lingered with Hawkins and Roberts until they finally parted to make their separate rounds.

# Chapter 16

They embarked at midmorning. To the shrill of fife, the roll of drum, and the steady creak of oars, the boats promenaded before Tahsis, circling to observe native protocol; then the longboat bearing the senior officers led the way in.

The boats landed and the crowd on shore below the village surged forward. Jim Hawkins suddenly found himself encircled by Indians who jostled him, peered into his face, tugged at his hair. He stumbled and nearly fell, righted himself and realized they had walked straight into an ambush. He grabbed for the dirk at his belt.

"Stay, lad, stay," said Old Joe Whidbey, appearing from nowhere, his hand firm on Jim's wrist. The master grinned at the Indians surrounding them, the smile forced and a bit grotesque. The Indians backed off. Hawkins saw now that they were not hostile. They were merely intrigued by his flaming red hair.

Quadra and Vancouver moved slowly through a noisy throng and up the sloping beach. At the midpoint between landing and village, the crowd parted, revealing Maquinna with his arms extended wide. He stepped forward to greet each of them with a handshake and a shoulder-to-shoulder embrace. It was a sight: Maquinna in a cedar headdress and glistening otter cape, Quadra in his red- and gold-trimmed naval tunic, Vancouver in austere blue and white, their translators and minions gathered round, the raucous crowd surrounding them all. There on the beach, the representatives of two imperial powers presented tribute to the local sovereign in the form of abalone, copper sheet, and a fine steel sword and scabbard that drew approving murmurs from the crowd. Maquinna reciprocated with a pair of lustrous sea otter cloaks, which he draped over their shoulders himself. Then he took his place between them and escorted them into the village. The senior officers, Broughton, Alberni, and Puget, followed close behind among Maquinna's kin and counsellors, and everyone else straggled along after them in a mass. Menzies walked with Whidbey, observing the inhabitants of Tahsis as he went.

The women wore woven capes that covered their shoulders and torsos, the men breech clouts and little else. Some had applied oil to their skin and painted their faces.

"Now that's interesting, Whidbey. This bedaubing of the skin was near universal when I was here five years ago. It seems much less common now."

The master did not seem inclined to pursue the topic. Menzies continued, now addressing Midshipman Ramsay on his other side.

"The face paint is purely ceremonial. If it's dying out, as it appears, perhaps it's the influence of outside contact — an example of the adoption of a new fashion standard. Effectively, by cultural diffusion."

Whidbey moved off laterally through a gap in the crowd. He turned back to wink at Ramsay, then disappeared.

"The application of oil, though, has nothing tae do with fashion. It protects the skin and insulates the body from exposure. How else could these people survive so lightly clad in such a climate?"

"Is it not wantonness that leads them to deport themselves thus?" Ramsay asked, winking sidewise at Pitt.

"Nonsense, Mister Ramsay. They are no more wanton than the..." Menzies paused, a smile playing across his face as he savoured a thought. "... than the savage Sassenach tribes of the south of Alouiōn." Again he paused, this time seeming to expect a reaction and receiving none. "Sir Joseph observed a similar practice — that of slathering the body with oil — among the Oona of Tierra del Fuego. The climate there is even harsher than it is here, and yet the Oona literally go naked. They live in an environment rich with marine life and have adapted tae its endowments. As have the Nootka, whose skill in hunting whales and seals yields them great volumes of oil, which they apply tae their skin as an insulating layer."

"For want of trousers, I'd slather myself with oil too — though I'd prefer warm company to both."

There were some hardy-har-hars and amen-to-thats among the midshipmen.

Menzies tut-tutted indulgently.

"All that blubber makes them stink like fishmongers," Pitt said.

More har-hars from the midshipmen; more erudite indulgence from the botanist-surgeon.

"One must suspend one's sensibilities, Mister Pitt. The Nootkans bathe and apply these ointments daily. Tae the civilized man, such habits are repugnant — imagine bathing daily! Yet the Nootkans survive here, by all appearances, with great success. Look around ye. They have created a veritable civilization."

He gestured at a row of sturdy lodges, substantial structures with high, flat roofs and walls of well-joined timber. Their entranceways were decorated with carvings of creatures whose open mouths gave passage to the interior. The chief conducted his guests of honour to the grandest of the lodges and through the mouth of its entrance beast. The senior officers filed in behind them, followed by the masses. Inside, Jim Hawkins took in the vast space, the cathedral-like hush. Light filtered through chinks in the roof planks; smoke and sunbeams mingled, illumining those passing through them in a fleeting, haloed glare. As his eyes adjusted, Hawkins saw, high above, racks of fish hung in the rafters. Their aroma merged with that of cedar, smoke, and raw humanity. He had never witnessed anything so alien, so brimming with possibility.

Glass panes filled small gaps in the wood-columned walls. A dozen muskets hung in the space between two of them. At the centre of the far wall stood a massive column carved with animal figures. At its base were a series of cooking fires, the source of the smoke that suffused the interior. Women bustled round them, tending, stoking, stirring cauldrons, preparing and stacking platters of delicacies. They had a pair of stags roasting over coals, a porpoise stewing in a watery pit, and no time to participate in the ceremonious proceedings on the far side of the lodge. Nor was it their station to do so, for they were commoners and slaves. Still, they were curious about the visitors. One of them stepped away from her work for a glimpse, as if looking for a friend. Her overseer called her back. There's too much work, she grumped, for you to dawdle like a man.

The senior delegation met Maquinna's subordinate chiefs. There were women sprinkled among the native dignitaries, wives and daughters of the headmen, or counsellors in their own right.

"Over there," observed a midshipman.

"Mmm hmm."

It was the young wife of Maquinna whom they had admired at the Big House.

"A pretty flower, that."

"I'll be her honey bee," Lincoln said. He had been very quiet all morning. His eyes were puffy, his face pale from the rigours of the night before.

Dorsey nudged him so hard he stumbled. "You do that Auggie, you poxy little shite. See how that works out for everyone."

"Keiskonis!"

It was Menzies, standing at the entrance. He waved and pushed his way through the crowd. A woman among the royal kin waved and smiled and moved towards him. She was, noted the middies appreciatively, very beautiful. They met, gripped hands, and conversed animatedly in the local tongue. Then he guided her back towards the dignitaries and senior officers. "Captain, may I present Keiskonis. We met on my previous visit to Friendly Cove. She and her sisters accompanied me on my rambles ashore. They saw themselves as my protectors, and were the truest friends a man could ever have."

Vancouver bowed and inclined his head to her. "Madam. Delighted."

"Well, well. Even our pure and proper surgeon keeps a doxie in the bush."

"Quiet, boy," Old Joe told Lincoln softly. He moved past the midshipmen to join the senior officers.

Menzies gestured towards Maquinna's translator. "She tells me that she is married now tae Comekala. He is a very lucky man."

"Both things are true," Comekala said. "I *am* a lucky man." He grinned and translated for Keiskonis, who gave him a look that deeply impressed the midshipmen. Dorsey chortled dirtily. Ned Roberts took Comekala's measure and hated himself for it.

The senior officers were ushered to benches, and Maquinna's family sat opposite them. The rest of the visitors accommodated themselves on benches to the rear. When everyone was settled, Quadra rose. Pedro Alberni moved to stand beside him.

"Great Chief Maquinna — wise prince. It is well known to my king that you are a friend to Spain, and you have many times proven your friendship to me. I will ever be your friend, as Spain will ever be your people's."

Alberni translated into Mowachaht. Dobson murmured an English summary for Vancouver and those near him.

"Today you pay me the great compliment of welcoming me and my officers to your village. We are honoured. It is my pleasure to travel in the company of my friends, Captains Vancouver and Broughton, and their officers, all of whom are just and honourable servants of the English king. I come today to assure you of the friendship and good relations that exist between King Carlos and King George, and between Spain and England, and to assure you of Spain's eternal affection for and commitment to you and your people. Our friendship is one that will never wither."

The chief replied (now with Comekala translating for Vancouver and Alberni for Quadra) that he would accept the friendship of Captains Vancouver and Broughton, as he had accepted the friendship of King George and Captain Cook before them. He knew the English king to be a wise and powerful monarch and his servants to be just and honest. Yet he regretted the pending departure, too soon, of his friend Quadra, who had proven himself wise and fair in all his dealings with his people.

Vancouver stood and bowed to Maquinna. He spoke of the friendship of King George with Maquinna's people, of the peace that reigned between England and Spain, and of his own friendship, recent as it was, with Señor Quadra and Maquinna himself. He turned and nodded to a bosun's mate at the entrance, who waved in several seamen bearing packages and bundles. They laid them in the open space between the benches, and Vancouver reached in among them and presented Maquinna with a handsome bowl of Sheffield plate. The chief held it up and drew an admiring murmur from the bystanders. With Broughton's assistance, Vancouver presented gifts of copper sheet, navy cloth, blankets, beads, and ornaments to the chief's relatives. They accepted these with shows of evident pleasure, displaying the wares for everyone to see.

When this finished the two captains sat again, though not without a good deal of bowing and bobbing and more words of friendship and esteem in the process. At that point Maquinna stood once more and delivered a lengthy oration of thanks ripe with flowery assurances of friendship, which the translators did their utmost to convey in real time.

The steady drone of voices within the dim vastness of the lodge had a predictable effect on some of the guests. Jim Hawkins, having been on night watch, nodded off in his seat. So did several of his shipmates.

⧗

Sunbeams falling through the ceiling and window gaps migrated through the interior. One fell eventually on the face of the slumbering Hawkins. He awoke, squinted in its glare, and shifted to avoid it. This startled Ramsay awake beside him; he shifted to make room and woke the midshipman next to him.

Maquinna was in the final stages of an oration which had turned from gratitude to gift-giving. While the snotties had kipped, Vancouver, Broughton, Puget, Menzies, and Whidbey, as well as Quadra, Alberni, Moziño, and even Ensign Ortiz, who had entered from outside to whisper something to his commander at just the right moment, had all received gifts of carvings, weavings, or lustrous furs.

Maquinna's party had dispersed during the latest round of presentations. When it ended, the chief took a seat between Quadra and Vancouver and signalled someone at the entrance. A group of warriors armed with spears, clubs, and muskets came through immediately. They moved to line the walls, effectively surrounding everyone within.

Not a few sphincters tightened among the visitors. They exchanged glances, murmured among themselves, shifted uneasily.

Some of the new arrivals wore carved masks depicting gryphon-like beasts. Those with muskets wore scraps of European clothing; others wore costumes suggestive of the South Seas. Most, though, were dressed as hunters or warriors. The latter now came forward and formed a line in front of the guests of honour and Maquinna.

The warriors stomped in unison on the packed earth floor. Then they stomped their way forward to within a few paces of the front bench. There, as one, they gave a guttural cry, crouched, thrust their spears forward and

THE WIND FROM ALL DIRECTIONS | 137

froze, their faces distorted in hateful grimaces.

George Vancouver was an analytical man, and considering everything in context — the greetings and gifts, the warm words of friendship — he was not unduly alarmed; and yet his stomach knotted, for he recognized a shift in equilibrium, a tilt in the atmosphere. Quadra's account of the plan to attack the region's white men came to his mind. If treachery were his host's aim, this surely was its moment.

Others sensed it too. Whidbey and Menzies exchanged gambling-table stares. Peter Puget counted heads, figuring who in their party was inside, who without, and how best to bring them together. And for the second time that day, Jim Hawkins fingered the scabbard of his dirk.

He reached slowly across his body to grip the scabbard's chape, slid the dirk half out, then free. He shifted and tensed, ready to spring up — but never did, for he was suddenly gripped by the shoulders and pressed firmly into his seat. He twisted round. Francisco Almeida leaned towards him from the bench behind. Keeping low, he whispered, "Is no fight, Yim Hawkes. Just show." He let him go, patted his shoulders, and sat back in his seat.

No one noticed this exchange. Everyone was focused on the warriors.

There was a resounding boom — an explosion of sound. Hawkins jumped but stayed seated. Another salvo followed. Unnoticed amid the attention paid the warriors, a group of drummers had stepped forward, and in the close confines of the longhouse every beat they took echoed like a cannon blast. They started to chant, and the warriors began to move. Focused on a foe beyond the front rank of spectators, they thrust their spears, manoeuvred to parry unseen counterthrusts, retreated in unison, and advanced again, stomping, thrusting, blocking. Voices and drumbeats reverberated. The warriors passed through beams of smoky light, wielding their weapons with deadly precision.

The drums beat a final signal and ceased. The chanting stopped; the warriors gave an exultant cry and froze with spear points extended, ready for one more opponent, one final lunge. Then they relented, relaxed their stance, and brought their shafts to the ground, their dance over.

The lodge erupted. The visitors rose to cheer and applaud. Quadra and Vancouver nodded and smiled; others laughed giddily. Ramsay whistled and gave Hawkins a nudge. Hawkins re-sheathed his dirk and glanced back at Francisco, who winked and leaned forward again. "Nice to see, *mi amigo*. Later we talk. I work now." He stood and moved towards the entrance, signalling someone on the way. Down the row, Pitt got up and followed him out.

Quadra and Vancouver circulated among the warriors presenting trinkets and compliments. The Spaniard clasped his hands to his heart as he met each performer. The Briton relied on Comekala to translate his praise.

When they resumed their seats, the hunters assembled and, to thunderous drumming, acted out the wiles of a hunt, the role of prey performed by dancers wearing skins and masks. Next (after applause and presentations to hunter and hunted) it was the turn of the musketeers, who performed a dance that mimicked the close-order drill of the Spanish garrison at Friendly Cove. The accuracy of their performance, even down to the way they'd assembled a hodgepodge of clothing into the semblance of uniforms, made everybody laugh.

The commanders again showed their appreciation of the dancers with presents; then Comekala steered them back to their places and sat between them. "Maquinna has gone to make arrangements," he told Vancouver, then leaned towards Alberni and repeated himself in Mowachaht. "He wants us to continue."

Most of the visitors saw the next act as one of native fancy. Warriors dressed like South Sea islanders danced and battled each other with clubs and spears. The men who had performed as soldiers in the previous dance, still dressed in their makeshift European costumes, joined them mid-melee, and a fresh battle was enacted in which the combined islanders prevailed over the Europeans, the survivors of whom backed away as their leader fell amid a flailing mass.

Quadra and Vancouver both sat straight-backed and stiff through this performance. Comekala sat looking neither right nor left. At its conclusion the performers lingered, seeming to bask in the applause, until their ranks suddenly parted and Maquinna stepped forward. He held a spear and wore a carved mask atop his head. The previous dancers filed off and a drum sounded, a voice began to chant, and all the Mowachaht present joined in. The chief moved slowly at first, every step precise though exaggerated. The drum accelerated and he moved more quickly, lunging and circling in a performance as nimble as any delivered in the ensemble battles enacted previously.

The chanting and drumming ceased and he fell still. His guests stood and applauded. An attendant handed him a sack from which he pulled handfuls of white down to scatter at their feet.

Several men joined him for a finale, a representation of a whale hunt, with one of his men in a mask playing the role of the great cetacean. Unlike the energetic, even exuberant dances that had preceded it, this dance was solemn. It ended with the whale slain and Maquinna, surrounded by his whalers, hovering over it in soliloquy, addressing unseen eyes and the whale itself. Alberni and Comekala translated softly for Quadra and Vancouver, their officers straining to hear as best they could. And then the whale (or rather the prone actor who had performed the role) was borne off reverentially by the whalers, followed by Maquinna, as stately an exit as any ever performed at Drury Lane.

After the excitement of the hunt, these sacraments were unexpected. Silence fell among the visitors, until the two commissioners rose as one to applaud. Their subordinates followed their lead and stood to clap, calling "Bravo!" and "Good show!" and nodding approvingly.

Maquinna led the dancers back into the centre of the room and accepted the accolades with poise, while his supporting cast sweated and grinned and nudged one another, pleased as Punch.

⧗

The senior contingent gathered round to praise the chief and soon broke into separate conversations. In the general hubbub George Vancouver drew Peter Puget aside. The lieutenant nodded and left the lodge. Vancouver turned to Dobson. "Get some air, Tom. Just be back when Mister Puget returns."

Dobson did not need to be told twice. Just outside the entrance he encountered Whidbey doing his stretches and swivels. A crowd of children had gathered to watch. They mimicked the master's motions and laughed at the faces he made back at them. Dobson walked on. The Spaniards had lit cooking fires while he was inside. Cooks and stewards bustled around them. Pitt was loafing nearby with the fellow who'd delivered the Spanish commandant's first letter.

Dobson did not feel like conversing with anyone, least of all Pitt, who had been rude and aloof to him since his arrival. Lord La-di-dah had saved all his charm and bonhomie, it seemed, for this one Spaniard. Dobson moved off in the opposite direction, towards the landing.

Inside, Vancouver angled through the milling crowd towards Comekala. The young man turned as he arrived.

"You learned many things while you were away."

Comekala returned his gaze.

The stillness of an Indian, Van thought. Nothing wasted, nothing given away. It had unsettled him as a youth. Now he admired it. "I journeyed myself as a young man. One sees the world, and draws lessons from it."

Comekala nodded and waited.

"Journeying changes one. Mystifies, confounds, and nourishes at the same time. Rounds one into a better man, expands one's horizons. It is like..." He paused, searching for a comparison the young man would understand.

"Like a map."

The analogy surprised Van and he laughed. "Yes! I suppose it is."

Comekala seemed to relax his reserve. "You are right. I saw many things. And heard about others."

"And your people listened."

"Some listen. Some hear."

For a moment Vancouver pondered the light streaming through the roof slats. Then he glanced around to confirm they were alone. "A wrong committed cannot be undone. But if it can be understood, further wrongs can be prevented."

Comekala nodded.

"When I was here, years ago, there was..." Vancouver paused, once more looking for words. An incident? There was no sugar-coating what he wanted to ask. "A man was killed. One of your people."

No expression. The guard was back.

"He took something that belonged to Captain Cook, and he was shot. Do you know about that man? That day?"

It was Comekala's turn to look up at something in the rafters. His gaze returned to Vancouver's face — which he studied for a long moment.

"I know of it."

"Tell me what you know about what happened. And tell me about him. Who was he?"

⧗

A delicious aroma now permeated the interior, and Jim Hawkins followed his nose towards its source, the cooking fires and cauldrons at the far end of the lodge. He stopped short, though, knowing what the women bustling around them would do when they noticed him. They would smile and beckon him closer, take him by the hand and draw him into their circle. They would be friendly. They would laugh and joke. And in no time they would feel compelled to touch and feel and pull his red hair.

Indeed, one of them came towards him, although she paid him no heed — she was actually craning to see the visitors surrounding Maquinna. As she came closer their eyes met. She smiled. She was attractive. A bit old for him, but she had smiled, and she was a good-looking woman. *What are you waiting for, numbskull? demanded the voice of John Dorsey. You know what that is. Or do you prefer to bum-fiddle the cabin boy? Maybe you like it up the what-not yourself.*

A wave of humiliation swept over him. He nodded curtly to the woman and turned away. Where were his mates? Lincoln was over by the door, gawking at something. Roberts stood nearby, talking with Ensign Ortiz. They both laughed, and for a moment Hawkins regretted that he could not speak French and share the bond they had found through that. Still laughing, Ortiz took Ned by the elbow and guided him outside.

"Later we talk," Francisco had said. Perhaps he was still outside. Hawkins reached the door just as Tom Pitt and Francisco's Indian helper, Copaza, pushed their way in from outside.

"Tom!" Lincoln hissed, tilting his head and pointing with his nose. Pitt and Copaza both followed his gaze. So did Hawkins. Francisco was engaged in a conversation with a girl, a very pretty one, and there was a great deal of back-and-forth in their exchange. Then Francisco leaned closer, took her hand, whispered in her ear. She listened intently to what he said; her eyes sparkled when she laughed. Hawkins was struck by her beauty. She might have been sculpted by a master. And the way she looked at Francisco, the bold intensity of her gaze — oh, that she would cast that look on him.

He blushed at the thought. No one had ever looked at him that way.

Oh, the callow sap. Adrift without a compass once again, lost and nowhere, without prospects. Even Ned Roberts was plotting a course, although it was fraught with danger. Diversity was not a strength in his day, but rather, a hanging offence.

Four young men — Hawkins, Lincoln, Pitt, and Copaza — stood admiring that young woman: Matuateh, of course. They watched as Francisco acted out a pantomime of reluctant departure. He tapped his heart, took a step away, stopped, and sadly bowed his head. She laughed and reached to touch his hand. The Spaniard took hers, kissed it, gazed into her eyes, and hesitated theatrically before giving her a final flourish and wading through the crowd towards the exit.

Pitt followed him out. Lincoln and Hawkins were about to do the same when they were jostled aside by a group British seamen and marines. Peter Puget and Dobson trailed in after them. "Hold there, gentlemen," Puget told the midshipmen. He turned and met his captain's eye. Vancouver nodded and moved to the centre of the lodge. One of the marines gave a drum roll.

"Chief Maquinna, nobles, ladies."

Comekala translated.

"On behalf of all my officers, I wish to express my gratitude for receiving us today, and for the honour you have paid us by these many performances. I wish to reciprocate by entertaining you with a specimen of our English dance."

Dick Ramsay had a sudden vision of Captains Vancouver and Broughton, bells a-clanging, plodding through the motions of a Morris dance. He giggled, turned away, and coughed hard into his fist. Then he looked up, sputtered, and laughed outright.

Puget shot him a look.

Ramsay frowned at his boots. Maquinna, though, nodded earnestly at Vancouver's offer. Quadra, Alberni, and Moziño all leaned in to hear Dobson's translation. Vancouver nodded to the bosun's mate, who whispered to the men. One of the marines raised a tin whistle and began to play. Two fiddlers immediately joined in.

The tempo was rapid, the tune familiar — "The Irish Washerwoman" was known to all the seamen — yet they hesitated. Puget had drafted them without warning, and they were completely sober — not their accustomed condition when dancing. A couple of them picked up the melody and clapped hands. The others followed their lead.

Vancouver's brows rose expectantly.

One man found the rhythm and the others joined in. Foot to foot they moved, now circling, clapping the while.

The tempo increased, and they had to move faster. They stopped clapping to focus on their footwork. The pace accelerated further and they hopped and whirled, arms now high for balance. Still the tempo increased, the musicians playing frenetically, the dancers circling like dervishes, spinning and kicking as if possessed. At last the whistler threw a signal, the fiddlers wound it down, one of them gave a shout, and the music ceased. The dancers froze in place, arms extended above their heads.

The lodge erupted, the Mowachaht, Spaniards, even the British spectators roaring, whistling, applauding, everybody on their feet. All the cooks had abandoned their food preparations for this spectacle of dancing white men.

The performers stood sweating and heaving for breath. They looked delighted and surprised at their spectators' reaction.

The clamour died down. Vancouver signalled for an encore.

This time, a marine played solo on his hornpipe, and two groups of seamen curled their arms at their hips and reeled, locking elbows with their fellows, swinging one another with abandon, and nearly careening into the crowd when breaking contact — though none of them did. This was a game they often played after downing their grog.

The onlookers applauded wildly again when it concluded. Some of the men, emboldened, took deep theatrical bows and waved at the applause. Maquinna beckoned them forward and presented every one of them with a fine wood carving.

This marked the end of the performances, and collective preparations began for serving the meal. Under the direction of Maquinna's senior wife, the Mowachaht rigged tables from planks propped on blocks. When that was done the Spanish stewards laid them with linen, silver, embossed plate, and crystal brought from Friendly Cove. While this was being done Quadra went outside to inspect the fire pits his cooks had lit. Vancouver's steward uncorked bottles of wine brought from *Discovery*. Puget drafted the midshipmen for various tasks — the ratings were winded and had earned a rest.

Amid all this activity, Dobson found himself at loose ends. Knowing he'd be called upon to translate again soon, he set out for a walk around the village. He saw Tom Pitt again with the young Spaniard. This time they were conferring intently.

⧗

Surrounded by the bustle of others, George Vancouver stood with Comekala listening to the story of a man he'd never known and the other side of events he'd witnessed with his own young eyes. He was so intent on what he was hearing that he did not notice the woman until she laid a hand upon his sleeve.

It was she whom Hawkins had encountered scrutinizing the visitors; she had been looking for one face in particular — and she had found it. Her voice was soft and low, and what she said was beyond Van's rusty vocabulary. He nodded uncertainly.

"What does she say?" he asked Comekala.

"She says she knew you when you were here before."

Van studied her intently, then looked down at his feet.

"We were just talking about those times, Auntie," Comekala said in their language. "Now it seems Raven has stolen the captain's tongue."

Indeed, it was obvious that George Vancouver, master and commander of *Discovery*, commodore of an ambitious voyage of exploration, official British commissioner appointed under the Nootka Convention to fulfill his government's will, was deeply affected. So much so that he was blushing.

She was not Comekala's auntie, nor any kin at all, merely a woman older than he. From beneath her cloak she removed an object and held it out for Vancouver to see.

"She says you gave her this," Comekala said.

Vancouver accepted a scrap of weathered parchment. He unfolded it

THE WIND FROM ALL DIRECTIONS | 145

slowly. Within it lay a lock of black hair.

Vancouver's lips pursed. His eyes remained on the parchment. He seemed lost in thought. Finally, he looked up at the woman. "Madam," he said. He inclined his head, refolded the parchment, and turned to Comekala. "Please tell the lady, it is many years since my last visit to Nootka. I was very young, and have changed a great deal in the intervening years. I am honoured that she has recognized—yea, remembered me." He bowed to her, handed her the parchment, and waited as Comekala translated.

As she took the parchment he briefly grasped both her hands, looking deep into her eyes. Then he bowed again, excused himself, and stepped out of the lodge for a breath of air.

⧗

Eventually the meal was ready, and Maquinna, his wives, his daughter, and his subordinate chiefs, the cream of the *tyeeclati*, sat with the senior officers and enjoyed Quadra's food off silver plate, and Vancouver's wine from crystal stemware. Maquinna handled himself amid this foreign finery with dignity and restraint. He had learned the game and played it well, and the *tyeeclati* followed his lead. Imagine, for a moment, the linguistic burden borne by those few who could facilitate the dinner discussion: Dobson for English–Spanish interactions, Alberni for Spanish–Mowachaht, Comekala for Mowachaht–English. Those three earned their meals, if they ate them at all.

The finest meal, though, was enjoyed by Maquinna's lesser tribesmen, for the chief had ordered a feast comprising the region's finest delicacies: from the sea, whale and seal and porpoise stew, salmon, herring and oolichan with dips of *quakamiss*; from the forest, the finest venison. This is what a potlatch requires — the host's unstinting hospitality and generosity.

And yet the Spanish and English, led by two astute men of character charged with a task of high diplomacy, had brought their own food and drink.

Maquinna realized this only when the Spanish arrived and lit their own fires. He discreetly tried to explain what a potlatch *was*. The message, delivered by underlings to underlings, was not heard, or at least understood. Maquinna the Chief was rebuffed. Maquinna the Diplomat turned the other cheek. He and his *tyeeclati* sat down with the visitors over *their* meal while his people crowded into the communal cooking area and tucked into the costly treats prepared for the honoured visitors.

Even before this slight, the shaman Tsakwasap refused to attend the potlatch. He stayed inside his own lodge until a follower brought him word of what was happening. It was more than an insult. It was sacrilege. He stormed to Maquinna's lodge but would not enter. Instead, he sent a boy in with a message. Maquinna ignored it. Tsakwasap waited outside, fuming, pacing back and forth. When Maquinna finally emerged, it was not to see him but to prepare for his dance.

Tsakwasap confronted him.

"Keep your voice down," Maquinna told him curtly. "And step aside, away from the entrance, if you wish to speak."

"Yes, I *wish* to *speak*," spat the shaman.

The gist of his lengthy diatribe was this: You dishonour all of us by allowing them to dishonour you.

Maquinna looked pained at the old man's vehemence. "They do not understand," he replied. "Nor do you. They have honoured me with their visit. We must try to understand their ways."

Tsakwasap was furious. "Everyone sees this. You know you have enemies here. Wickaninnish and Tatoosh will soon hear what has happened. What will they say? What will they do? Do you know what this means for the Mowachaht?"

"Do not presume to tell me what anything means for the Mowachaht," Maquinna said.

They stared daggers at one another.

"We must accommodate these people. In some things we must change." Maquinna turned away from his shaman and positioned his mask atop his head before re-entering the lodge to perform his dance.

⧖

The visitors departed that evening to earnest expressions of friendship and Maquinna's promise to return their visit in a few days. The commissioners embarked feeling their trip had accomplished all they'd intended. In the warm glow of its success, as they journeyed towards the mouth of Nootka Sound, Quadra asked his counterpart to commemorate their meeting, and the friendship they had struck, by naming some local feature after the both of them, thereby linking their names in history. And Vancouver, surveying the waters of the inlet and the Sound ahead, the great forested slopes on either beam, the smoke of Tahsis now a faint smudge of vapour far astern, was suddenly inspired. They were deep within an inlet on a great island, surrounded by unnamed territory; he proposed to christen it the Island of Quadra and Vancouver.

The Spaniard was delighted with the suggestion, though some in the British contingent were cattish about it later. "Our Commander has *modestly* perpetuated his name on this Coast," wrote Archibald Menzies to Sir Joseph Banks. "Our Commander in Chief," wrote a young gentleman to an acquaintance, "is grown Haughty, Proud and Insolent."

# Chapter 17

Far away from the Island of Quadra and Vancouver, great currents sweep the world. Historic tides have turned, change has been unleashed, ancient regimes teeter on a precipice. Doves take flight, dogs bay at what they scent upon the wind. They are the best of times, they are the worst of times. The old rotted order crumbles, but Fate has yet to flex her wiry muscles. A semblance of normality still reigns. The listless mundanity of human existence continues undeterred.

Consider Napoleon Bonaparte and Arthur Wellesley.

On the day the Spanish and British commissioners return to Yuquot, Napoleon and Arthur are both twenty-three years old, and twenty-three more years will pass before their mutual appointment with destiny. Napoleon, recently appointed commander of a Corsican battalion, will spend the afternoon tending to his laundry. Arthur, a junior captain of dragoons, will spend it wooing a vivacious young woman named Kitty Pakenham. Her family will shortly reject him as a suitor, believing his prospects dim. The future Duke of Wellington will persevere, and marry Kitty fourteen years later. Napoleon will crown himself emperor in twelve.

All is yet in train for their momentous clash — although there is still time to draw back from the brink. Nothing is inevitable.

I allow an exception for the frivolity of youth.

⧗

Days later.

Few lights were visible in the Spanish town or on the anchored ships. Darkness prevailed, and silence, save for the muffled sounds of their departure. To the east, across the Sound, a sliver of orange nudged forested crests. They clambered down from the ship, took their places at the oars and pulled away smartly, conscious of a brooding figure on the quarterdeck. Pitt helmed them out towards open water. To the rhythmic creak of oars in locks, they drew abreast of the headland that sheltered the harbour. They were hailed from its bastion.

"*Discovery!*" Pitt bellowed, his free hand cupped to his mouth.

They could barely discern the sentinel profiled against the night sky at the fort's peak. He waved an arm and shouted something they did not understand.

They rounded the point and the Spanish settlement disappeared astern. They heard the unmistakable sound of the open ocean, then felt its swell. They caught a steady breeze, shipped the oars, raised the sail, and settled back — the wind would carry them now. Sweat dried in the small of Jim Hawkins's back, chilling him through. He didn't care. Ahead lay freedom.

They ran south, the wind on their starboard beam. The sun rose, the chill dissipated. Wisps of cloud specked an azure sky. To port, a long reef paralleled their course. Gentle waves, regal and benign, rolled in on the rocks and broke into spray. Pitt steered to seaward. "Dickie, make a note of that, will you? And Charles, do a sketch or two of the shore. Links, Jimmy, Robert, you too."

"It's a good wind. We'll make good time."

Pitt considered the sail, the water ahead, the aspect of the shore. "It's still far. We need to watch for a sandy bay, a headland. There's a gap in the reef."

It was midmorning when they spotted the landmark, a cliff at the southern tip of a broad crescent bay. Pitt altered course to southeasterly, putting them on a broad reach running fast and straight for the headland. They struck the sail and took to the oars to manoeuvre around the reef, then Pitt steered them across the bay.

"Gentlemen, behold the noble savage."

Hawkins craned around to see a vague shape within the wall of trees above the beach. It stepped into the open; he glimpsed black hair, a native cape over a white shirt. It was Copaza, Francisco's Indian collaborator.

The midshipmen landed and splashed ashore, hauled the cutter up, and secured it. Then they shouldered their rucksacks and scrambled up to Copaza's level. Without a word he turned and strode into the forest. They exchanged glances and followed.

They were on a path that wended and climbed through a forest of pillars — towering fir and cedar, their upper boughs dappled by sun, their bases sombre, cool with shade. Nature's basilica — and these no choirboys.

The sounds of the sea faded. Soon there was no trace of the breeze that had filled their sail a short while before. The forest was still. and the shade, which had felt cool and fresh on entry, began to feel humid and close. Conversation petered out. They trailed after Copaza in silence, sweating.

Fungi and ferns sprouted from a blanket of moss that absorbed all sound. Deadfall reclined into somnolent rot. Jim Hawkins stopped to look at the forest floor, struck by the contradiction: the lushness of the living, the decay of the dead. Menzies, he thought, would find this a trove. The others edged past him, huffing to keep up with Copaza. Up a gentle rise and around a bend, they disappeared from sight.

Silence enveloped him like a shroud. He unslung his sack and looked around. A massive tree lay on a carpet of moss beside the path, its trunk exceeding the span of his arms. How many years had it taken to grow? How many years had it lain dead? Its mossy surface was soft as the coat of a cat. He prodded a patch of exposed bark and it crumbled away, exposing the wood beneath, still solid and unmarred by decomposition. But this, he saw immediately, was an illusion. He imagined Menzies opining on the evidence in his highland burr. "The rate o' putrefaction is necessarily detairmined by the degree o' dahmp." He grinned and scratched at the heartwood, which fractured into chunks and strands of wet fibre. He pried these away to find damp red mush beneath. His fingers slid into it easily; he clutched rotted fibre, pulled it out and opened his fist to examine it.

Minuscule creatures, eyeless and wet, slithered indignantly in the reddish rot scooped from the tree's dead core.

He cursed and swiped his hand clean, then rubbed his palms frantically. A reddish residue remained, and he squatted to wipe it on the moss. Then he stood, wiping his hand on his trousers and thinking, Screw botany, screw Menzies. It was time to catch up with the others. He stepped towards his rucksack and looked up.

Standing not five paces away was an Indian, his face divided into hemispheres of black and red. A bone ring dangled from his nose.

"Jesus Christ!" gasped Hawkins.

The man stared at him. He wore a bark headdress trimmed with fur — it resembled the jaws of a dog or a wolf. A cloak hung from one shoulder, exposing slashes of red on his chest. He was stooped as if to spring, yet made no move.

Jim Hawkins could not move either, what with being petrified by fear.

There was no sign of a weapon. Beneath the paint the Indian's face was deeply lined. Hawkins realized he was old. He raised his hand slowly, as he had seen the captain do on so many first encounters. The man did not respond. Another moment passed in wary regard. Then, holding eye contact, moving slowly and deliberately, Hawkins knelt to feel for his sack, found it, and slung it over his shoulder as he rose.

"Hawkins," he said, putting his palm to his chest. "Jim Hawkins."

No response.

"I have been examining this tree," he said, gesturing and holding out his grimy palm.

Silence.

"A botanical examination. Botanical," he repeated, more slowly, "examination."

They looked at each other. The dog-wolf-man's eyes shone; his face glistened with paint. He was old, but still, a big man.

"King George," Hawkins ventured. "England...Captain Vancouver... his ship...that way." He pointed back in the direction whence he'd come. "At Friendly Cove." He dropped his arm, stopped to breathe and think. The man had not moved, nor acknowledged any of his words. Hawkins knew he was babbling but he still could not see the man's hands. At least I have my dirk, he thought, calculating the speed at which he could draw it, the moves he would have to make. He pointed in the direction his shipmates had gone.

"This way — friends. *English* friends, shipmates — *many* shipmates. I go now...to join them...this way."

He edged towards the path, reached it, and stopped. The Indian turned to face him — his first discernible movement. They stood looking at each other once more.

"Good day to you, then," Hawkins said, bowing.

The man's head inclined slightly. Hawkins took it as a nod, a good sign, and bowed again. Slowly, he backed up the rise in the direction the others had taken. The Indian watched him go. At a bend in the path at which they would lose sight of each other, Hawkins raised a hand and waved it slowly and deliberately.

He ran until he caught up with the others and did not fall out again.

They hiked on, sweating heavily. Copaza did not slacken pace or stop to rest. The humidity in the forest grew oppressive, and now there was a hint of something on the air. They exchanged glances. It was vague and elusive. On they trekked, and it intensified, grew acrid, and smothered the sweet scent of the forest, stinging their nostrils like smouldering pitch.

They emerged onto a sunny ridge overlooking a rocky valley, at the foot of which lay a sheltered arm of the sea. The path, Hawkins realized, had wound around to return to the coast some distance from where they had landed. Sulphurous vapours rose around them; they heard the murmur and trickle of water. At the top of the valley a steaming rivulet emerged from a rock face, tumbled over a series of boulders, and formed a small pool. It drained to a lower level where the flow puddled into another pool. Across the face of the valley other springs fed other babbling rivulets that descended through other pools until they reached the narrow, rock-strewn inlet.

They stood on the cliff, breathing hard from the hike and absorbing the scene, thinking about their months at sea, the summer spent in small boats, wet, filthy, cramped, and cold.

Copaza stood apart and watched.

No one spoke, no one moved — until Ramsay broke the spell by letting out a whoop and taking off down the slope as fast as he could scramble. The others followed in a wild, joyous charge. Ramsay reached the first pool and began to strip off his clothes. Hawkins passed him, making for the next, but another middie beat him there, so he kept going, lost another pool by a whisker, then found a larger, deeper one below a falls, better than any of the ones he'd missed. He stripped, blindly flinging his belongings to the ground, swished a hand in the water, and lowered himself until he was submerged to the neck.

Ramsay bellowed, "Jesus fucking hell, that's bloody fucking hot."

Insanely happy, they laughed, splashed, called back and forth, wisecracked.

The pools near where the water bubbled from the ground were hotter and more sulphurous than the lower ones fed by gravity. In the lowest pools, the thermal water mixed with seawater, producing a cool wash that was refreshing after the heat. They migrated across the hill, luxuriating in the variations. After an hour they gathered to eat from the provisions they'd brought in their rucksacks.

"We've had a pleasant boil and simmer," Pitt said. "Now let's have a toast." He pulled a bottle from his sack and held it high. Simultaneously, Lincoln and Ramsay did the same.

The rest of them huzzahed and cheered, and in that moment, in the happy glare of self-interest, Hawkins forgot his recent disapproval of Pitt and Lincoln and unsanctioned rum, and slapped the former on the back.

Pitt was in a forgiving and forgetting mood himself. He handed Hawkins yet another bottle. "Uncork this one, Jimmy boy." He uncorked his own and held it up. "Come now, we shall have our liberty. The day is still young, and so are we."

They cheered again, and those who had bottles drank and handed them on.

"Thank Links for the kill-devil. He took a small detour while he was ashore yesterday."

"To Links," Ramsay declared, toasting him.

"Happy to do my bit," Lincoln said. "We'll settle the out-of-pockets back in Friendly Cove."

"Who says we're going back?"

This brought hear-hears and hearty har-hars. The sun was full upon the valley. They sprawled on the warm rocks overlooking the cove, eating and drinking.

"Is this Magee's rum?" Ramsay asked.

"There's more than one source of sly-grog in Friendly Cove. This is English. Captain Brown's people. The *Butterworth*."

"Rough stuff, but it does the trick," one of them opined, with the critical eye of a teenage connoisseur.

"Handy having traders around."

"They are able to supply all the comforts of home," Pitt agreed, "except one."

"To missing comforts," Ramsay said, tipping the bottle again. Lincoln made a wanking motion. They laughed and drank.

"Where's Copaza?" someone asked.

Hawkins realized their guide had gone unmissed since delivering them to the springs.

Ramsay belched epically.

"He'll be back," Pitt said. "Very soon."

"At least he's not hanging round begging a drink," someone said.

"Indians can't hold their liquor," another posited.

"I hold my licker," Lincoln said, "by the hair."

There followed another round of ribaldry and drinks. "I don't know how Copaza holds it," Pitt called above the fun, "or her" — hoots, laughter — "but so far he's delivered. Let's all hope he keeps on doing so."

"To Copaza!" Lincoln roared.

They all huzzahed Copaza and drank, Pitt grinning like a Cheshire cat.

After lunch some of them returned to the pools or went exploring. Those who were drowsy from the heat and rum lay down on the warm ground to nap.

⧗

Hawkins sat up to a footfall. Copaza was approaching from up the hill. Pitt was already on his feet. Ramsay was sound asleep nearby, but Lincoln was stirring. Pitt saw and tapped him on the knee.

"Links, my hearty, get up. You too, Jimmy boy. Copaza has brought a surprise."

Barefoot, clad only in trousers, they gingerly followed Copaza back up the rocky slope and entered the forest. After the hard light of the valley the woods were dim. Shadows in the gloom resolved into human form. Woven capes, tunics — they were natives, and they were many. Hawkins's heart missed a beat. He looked for a hulking, painted figure. He was not there. Those who were were slight and lean of figure. They were young women, some with faces painted, others with rings dangling from their noses.

THE WIND FROM ALL DIRECTIONS | 155

Pitt grinned at his companions' reactions: Hawkins looked stricken, while Lincoln took a long pull from his bottle and eyed the women like a punter at the races. They, meanwhile, stood in an unsmiling huddle and watched as Pitt drew Copaza aside and handed him something from his rucksack. Then he turned and gestured for everyone to follow.

He led them out of the trees into the sun. A middie down at the pools spotted them and called the others. They gathered, dripping and dancing into their trousers, their eyes fixed above on the newcomers.

Pitt stopped just above their level. "Well, gentlemen, I told you we would have our liberty," he said. He stood aside so they could all see those behind him. "And we shall."

"Liberty or death!" Lincoln tittered. He dug his elbow into Hawkins's ribs and took another swig.

The girls and midshipmen exchanged glances among themselves.

"Though we are liberty men, we cannot forget our duty," Pitt declared. "Our *illustrious* commander is currently engaged in a task of delicate diplomacy on behalf of our great nation — and he has made it his mission to cement friendships with the denizens of this savage region. It is alliances he wants. Relations. Well, gentlemen, Copaza has arranged for these local debutantes to join us for the day. They are equally intent on forging relations..." There were guffaws at this, and Pitt deigned a smile. "However, as you see, they are decorated in the local fashion, besmeared with dirt and grease. As civilized men, we find this repugnant, yet duty calls, and an Englishman never fails to perform his duty with verve and spirit — and no small amount of ingenuity in lieu of soap. The pools we have discovered today afford a solution. I believe they will have a most agreeable, indeed *civilizing* effect upon these maidens — though perhaps an *un*-civilizing effect upon the lot of you!"

The midshipmen wisecracked and whooped and cheered for Duty. Even Jim Hawkins, reminded of the painted giant he'd encountered in the forest — and uncertain over the here and now — laughed along.

Pitt grinned magnanimously.

"If you should have a shiny buckle or brass button to repay your sweetheart's attentions, she will be most grateful."

"Oh, I'll make her grateful," Lincoln puffed.

Pitt turned to Copaza, who issued a command. The women formed a line and shuffled forward slowly — except one, who stood her ground and addressed Copaza in a tone that was decidedly imperious.

Hawkins recognized her immediately. He had not forgotten the look she had bestowed upon Francisco at Tahsis.

The girls, previously listless, now showed life. Their eyes flicked towards Copaza to see what he would do.

He pointed to the line.

The smirk that came to his face a moment later brought an instant response. Matuateh's fists went to her hips, as though she were about take wing, and indeed she did launch — not into flight, but a ferocious tirade.

The midshipmen were confused about what was happening. The girls knew. Their faces darkened.

Copaza's smirk disappeared. His expression transformed to something just shy of angry, with a tinge of astonishment bordering on bewilderment. He tried to speak but Matuateh would not be stopped. The girls gasped at something she said, something that tipped the balance with Copaza too, for his expression hardened and he charged towards her with his arm bent to strike. It looked certain he would knock her down and beat her for her impudence, yet he stopped short and stood, towering over her with his fist raised and clenched, and hissed something only she could hear.

He stabbed his fist upslope.

They glared at each other, before she turned and stalked away in the direction he'd pointed.

"Spirited," Pitt said. "I like that in a wench."

The midshipmen laughed. The girls exchanged glances and lowered their eyes. Copaza ignored them all, tucked what Pitt had handed him under his arm, and set off in the opposite direction from that taken by Matuateh.

Without further ado, Pitt paired the girls with the midshipmen, who milled about, some swaggering, some uncertain, before dispersing. Hawkins and his allotted companion were among the last to remain.

He decided to return to his first pool. He led her there and sat on a narrow ledge of rock and gestured for her to sit too. Her face was painted, neatly divided into hemispheres of black and red, the exact pattern he had seen on the old man's face. She was slight and copper-skinned, her hair impossibly lustrous.

She sat at the edge of the ledge and looked neither at him nor away.

He did not look directly at her either, yet he was stirred by her proximity. He had never had a sweetheart at home, never been inside a sporting house, never visited a brothel in a port of call; nor had he been with one of the carefree Tahitian or Hawaiian girls. Something had always conspired to keep him a virgin. An anchor watch when others had liberty, a fever that kept him abed in Cape Town, an extra lesson from Old Joe Whidbey, who considered him his protégé. In the South Seas there were standing orders, issued by the captain, prohibiting fraternization. His peers had been less dedicated and more opportunistic, *carpe diem* their motto. Bad luck or lack of initiative, too dutiful or timid, that was poor Jimmy Hawkins. He had no experience to guide him now.

And she, so withdrawn, showed no inclination towards instruction. She was passive and still. He knew what she expected, what he should do, but he could not take what he was expected to take. Rum, he thought desperately. Where was one of those bottles? Her eyes remained averted.

They sat thus for some time, until he steeled himself to move closer. When he did, she tensed, though she did not move away. He turned to look at her face, wanting to see the young woman beneath the paint. He reached out and gently lifted her chin. She did not resist. At last she met his gaze. Her eyes told him nothing.

His heart thumped as his fingertip traced her chin. Still he hesitated. His hand fell away to his own chest. "Hawkins," he said softly, "Jim."

I won't hurt you, he wanted say.

Silence. She did not understand. Her eyes were black. They shone like water at the bottom of a well.

"Jim Hawkins," he said again, tapping his chest. He pointed at her. "You?"

She observed him impassively, then looked away, glanced around, seeming to take in her surroundings for the first time. He was afraid she had not understood; or had she dismissed him from her mind?

At last her gaze returned to him. She breathed deeply, sighed, and tapped her chest. "Coulz," she said.

"Coulz," he repeated, thinking it a harsh name, the way she'd said it. He could think of nothing further to say. She averted her eyes, and he knew then that she had rejected him. They sat in silence until she rose. She was leaving and he could not bring himself to look. He dropped his head in shame, heard a rustle, a step, another rustle, a plane of water softly broken. When he looked she was submerged to the neck in the pool. Her clothes lay on a rock nearby. She looked up at him, her eyes narrow in the rising steam.

⧗

The valley was peaceful through the afternoon, yet Hawkins could not forget the presence of others nearby. He led Coulz higher up the slope, skirting the populated pools on the way. Higher and higher they climbed, until he was certain they were above all the others and alone. He stopped, ostensibly to take in the view, but he saw only her. She was all he wanted. He could resist her no more than he could still his heart or suspend his breath.

They lay together on the moss, his rucksack for a pillow. Eventually, they dozed.

He was awakened by a woman's angry voice. It came from higher up and across the slope. He pulled his trousers on and ran towards it. Climbing and scrambling over the rocks, he rounded a boulder, and found Tom Pitt sitting with his feet dangling in a broad pool. At its opposite end, Matuateh — she who had berated Copaza so devastatingly — was submerged to the neck, directing a similar stream of invective at Pitt, who grinned rakishly back and regarded her with open admiration.

"Tom!"

Startled by his voice, she stopped in mid-harangue. For a moment both she and Pitt looked at him. Then her expression changed and she addressed him in a tone of appeal.

Uncertainly, he looked at Pitt. Then Coulz brushed past. She had followed him, and Matuateh was speaking to her. She stooped and gathered Matuateh's clothes from a rock and went to her.

"Jimmy. Jimmy boy!" Like Hawkins, Pitt was dressed only in trousers. "There seems to have been a misunderstanding. The lady has airs I would not expect in the circumstances."

"What's going on?"

Pitt watched as Coulz helped Matuateh step out of the pool and cover herself. "Links and I came up here with our strums," he said. "For the view. I'm afraid old Links has had too much to drink again. He's getting a bit silly. I left the three of them below and continued up. I found the lady *dishabille* and disinclined to share her bath. And I was too gallant to insist."

"Her choice, I reckon. It looked like she opted out before. Besides, you have a girl."

Pitt's eyes settled on Hawkins. His smile faded. He rose to his feet. "Yes. I reckon."

Covered now, Matuateh glared at Pitt, who made no move to withdraw. Instead, he smiled and bowed to her. She returned a look of contempt and turned away. Coulz turned with her.

They both turned back at a scream from somewhere below. There was a cry, the clink of breaking glass. A thrashing of water, more cries. A man's bellow, a woman's voice. What now? Hawkins thought. For the second time in minutes, he ran towards the sound of trouble. He crested a boulder and found Lincoln standing in the middle of yet another pool. In one hand he held the neck of a broken bottle. With the other he gripped the hair of an Indian girl who was flailing desperately, for Lincoln was making a concerted one-handed effort to push her head beneath the surface. Another girl, naked, clung to his back with one arm, pummelling his head with her free hand. But she could get no purchase in the water, and she was sliding down his back and to the side, holding on but slipping slowly, inexorably, into the pool.

Lincoln turned halfway towards her, and her upper body slid free. He saw his opening and jabbed backwards, hard, with his elbow. The blow cracked her full in the face. She let go and splashed into the water.

Lincoln's move, though neatly executed, put him off balance. He toppled onto his back in the water, dragging the first girl's head under. As he fell, he flailed wildly with the bottle's neck and Hawkins, splashing into the pool, nearly stumbled into it before he caught his balance and dodged away. Lincoln's face was flushed, a contorted, angry mask, and for a moment he brandished the bottle shard at Hawkins — until recognition came to his drunken eyes and he lowered it. At the same time, almost as an afterthought, he released the first girl's hair. She burst to the surface, gasping and croaking and heaving up water.

The other girl, the one he had elbowed, was already back on her feet. Her nose, adorned with a thin copper ring, was bloody. Blood streamed down her lip and into the pool.

Swaying, Lincoln turned to her, and his expression changed. He reached with his free hand, as if to console her or staunch the flow of blood. Instead, he slipped a finger through the ring and tugged it from her septum.

"Jesus Christ, Lincoln!" Hawkins bellowed as she screamed. He lunged and shoved him with all his weight. Lincoln fell back with a great splash just as Pitt and the two other women arrived on the scene. Pitt waded in and knelt beside Lincoln while Hawkins stood frozen in horror. Coulz and Matuateh went straight to their countrywomen, who were crying and wailing in pain and fear.

Lincoln held his arms above the surface, the neck of the bottle in one hand, the girl's ring on a knuckle of the other. He dropped the neck into the pond and began to cry. Tears ran down his contorted face. With Pitt's help he stood unsteadily. He was naked, pasty but for pinkish blotches on his chest and back. "Filthy, dirty people," he blubbered. "She needed a bath. She needed a proper scrub to be rid of the...I was giving her a *bath*, Tom, just a bath, to scrub that filth, the paint and grease and all the disease, away...and the bitch broke my bottle. She broke my fucking bottle!" He put his head in his hands and sobbed.

"There, there, Links," Pitt consoled. "Buck up, man."

Coulz and Matuateh attended to their battered sisters. The one girl's nose was torn, but the bleeding had stopped. Hawkins went to see if he could help, but Coulz gave him a look and shook her head. He knelt nearby and watched their ministrations, and they accepted his presence while shooting murderous looks at Lincoln and Pitt. Lincoln seemed to have forgotten them entirely. He had stopped crying; there was no sign of his previous rage, nor of any regret or guilt or shame. He scratched absently at the mottled rash that covered his chest. The ring, along with a fragment of tissue, was still on his finger. Crazy daft bastard, Hawkins thought. Crazy daft bastard.

⧗

The girls departed soon after. Copaza had not returned, and they filed up the hill and into the forest on their own. Before they left, Pitt tried to present a handkerchief to Matuateh, but she turned her back on him and led the others away.

THE WIND FROM ALL DIRECTIONS | 161

It was getting late. The midshipmen lit a fire and improvised shelters for the night. Copaza had left a salmon, and with this, and the bread and other food they had brought, they made a meal. The other middies were not even aware of the ugly incident on the hill's upper reaches, and their banter was jovial. Jim Hawkins did not join in. He sat a bit apart and reflected on the day, thinking about the beautiful painted girl, naked and trembling in his arms, and the other girl, naked, half-drowned, and bleeding into the sulphurous water; and the silent painted man he had encountered in the forest. He had only just begun to see with his own eyes, to see at last, to live. There was so much he did not understand. He thought of Coulz with — what exactly? He dissected his feelings. Tenderness, no question. Gratitude, yes — sheepishly yes. Desire, yes — powerfully so. And something approaching awe.

He knew, with absolute certainty, that he had to see her again.

Lincoln slept after the girls' departure and missed the meal and all the backslapping. He was stirring as the others crawled into their pine bough hooches for the night.

"You look like shite, you tosspot," Ramsay told him.

"There's a reason."

There was, miraculously, still a little rum left in one bottle. Ramsay handed it to him. "Try Uncle Dickie's elixir."

Lincoln swigged it down.

"You always brag how you hold your liquor in epic proportions, Auggie, and you never do. Every single time, you get soaked to the gills and go queer in the nob."

Lincoln felt so wretched he let the "Auggie" go. "It's this rot," he said, indicating the bottle. "I didn't…" He stopped short, met Hawkins's eye, looked away.

Pitt took the empty bottle from Lincoln's hands and tossed it into the dark. "Get some sleep, bucko."

⧖

They broke camp and were on the forest path before first light. When they reached the cutter they ate the last of their rations. Hawkins took bearings on all the headlands he could see; Stuart, Pitt, and others made descriptive notes; and Barrie drew a sketch of the bay. Then they drew straws and Ramsay won. He took the tiller, Pitt took an oar with the others, and they set off. They pulled out of the bay and headed north along the coast. The chop was difficult and the wind unfavourable for setting the sail. They were forced to stay at the oars.

Their return took them longer than the outbound trip. It was hard labour, and as they approached the Spanish fort they entered a lee shore and rested out of sight of the harbour, intending to make an impressive entry and a smooth, disciplined approach to come alongside *Discovery*.

They bobbed there in silence for several minutes, sweat cooling on their backs. Finally, Pitt rose carefully from his thwart. "Gentlemen," he called, as if addressing an assembled ship's company from the quarterdeck. "We must count ourselves lucky for our liberty, and let us be of one mind as it ends. We will report on our nautical and topographical discoveries. We will draw a chart and submit our sketches and bearings and observations for the official record. And the rest — all the juicy details — will stay between us."

Har-hars, "I think so!" and huzzahs all round.

"Dorsey's going to be pissed he missed this," Lincoln shouted to laughter. If there was a hump-dog among them, it was Dorsey.

"We are explorers all, and our discovery warrants a name — an English one, although a Spaniard told us of it. We are about to enter Friendly Cove, which is not, I think, as *friendly* as that snuggery we entered yesterday." Har-hars and hoots drowned him out. He waited for quiet, swaying with the movement of the boat. "I think that place a Very Friendly Cove" — har-hars and *woo!* again — "but that is altogether treacly. Let us call a spade a spade. It shall be known among us as Fornication Cove — though that name will not appear on our chart or in our report. Some discoveries, gentlemen, are like women. They are best held close."

There were more cheers and hoots at this, and Hawkins laughed along with everyone else, although in truth his thoughts were a mad confusion. He remembered the painted man in the forest, the vermin crawling in his hand, Coulz in the pool, the steam rising, the look in her eyes. Later, he met Francisco on shore and asked him to arrange another meeting with Coulz. The Spaniard looked at him strangely and asked him to repeat her name. The pronunciation wasn't quite right but he recognized the word. He told him what it meant.

Slave.

She was a slave girl. It came as a shock, one he needed to absorb. Had she been willing? Had she had any choice? He told Francisco he had to see her.

⧗

You are no doubt wondering how this liaison came to pass, how a group of native slave girls materialized from the forest above those magnificent hot pools to have congress with a gaggle of horny British lads.

First, the horny British lads.

"We'll give it another forty-eight hours," Vancouver concluded when he convened with his officers the day after his return from Tahsis. He had been right about Whidbey's solution to the longitude problem. Baker and Johnstone had disproved it during his absence. "If we don't have a solution by then, we must start on the charts and correct them later. Approximately right will do until we figure it out."

They voiced agreement. They all understood the conundrum. He dismissed Baker and Puget to their duties and remained with Mudge to discuss Maquinna's visit. Their plan was to host him and his counsellors at dinner the next day; further niceties would be transacted the following morning at the Big House.

"All this diplomacy is going to keep me fully occupied, Zach. You'll need to keep the ship afloat, so to speak."

Mudge smiled dutifully at his captain's bad joke. Vancouver stood to signify the end of the meeting and walked to the door. Menzies was waiting outside to report on the sick list. Vancouver waved him in and returned to his desk.

Mudge had made no move to leave. "May I make a suggestion, sir?"

"Of course."

"Over the next few days we're going to have Indians underfoot and our own people bumping into each other."

"Yes?"

"We have too many snotties, sir, and I don't have enough work details to keep them occupied. Until these entertainments end and we start work on the charts, I can use about half of them productively. So it seems we have time now, and a good reason, for that mission we talked about giving them."

He described what he had in mind.

Vancouver looked doubtful.

"It is not a liberty, sir. They will have a proper mission. An exacting one, judging by the distance they must travel, and it will fill a gap in our knowledge of the area to the south. I will make their goals clear and hold them accountable."

"Hmm."

"Thermal springs could be therapeutic for our sick, Captain," Menzies said. "Even if we cannae use them afore we sail, they may be useful in the future."

Vancouver pondered the suggestion. "Very well, Mister Mudge. Fill out a complement and provision them for two days. Hold back whoever you need for duty. I want two here copying the New Zealand and Hawaiian charts for *Daedalus*. At least we can do that much. Keep two or three more for work parties and duty coxswains as you see fit."

"Aye, sir. I'll put one over at the observatory too. It'll keep the sentries on their toes."

Vancouver liked the idea. He could not spare a commissioned officer for the task. "One other thing about this mission. Dobson cannot to go. I need him here."

"Sir." Mudge turned to go.

"Number One. Where did you hear about these springs?"

Mudge seemed to hesitate. "Mister Pitt told me about them, sir. He heard about them from one of the Spaniards."

"Ah." Vancouver's nose seemed to wrinkle at a foul odour.

Pitt, he thought. Always Pitt. The ringleader. The spokesman. The pain in the ass.

⧗

Add opportunist to the list.

At Tahsis, Tom Pitt had broached the topic of women with Francisco. His interests at the time were immediate. Still, they discussed longer-term arrangements. *Discovery* would not sail for weeks.

It was during his initial chatty softening up of Francisco to these ends that the Spaniard told him about the hot springs. ("Very pretty place. Hot like kettle. Smell like sewer. But nothing is perfect, yes?")

Pitt recalled Mudge's mention of a midshipman's expedition and went to work on the first lieutenant as soon as he was back in Friendly Cove. His premise was the handsome carved mask he had acquired in Tahsis. Father will cherish this, he told Mudge when he showed it to him. Then he reported what he'd heard about the hot springs, and earnestly professed his desire to be the one to confirm their existence. Perhaps there will be more artifacts there to collect for Father, he said.

He read the expression on Mudge's face and was encouraged. He had a low opinion of Zach Mudge, thinking him dull and without flair, too much the Dutchman's loyal lapdog.

Later that evening, when he piloted a boat ashore, he sought Francisco out. I can arrange that, Francisco told him. Just tell me when.

⧗

Francisco made the arrangements with Copaza and intended to accompany the midshipmen from Yuquot, so of course Matuateh wanted to accompany the other girls.

I'm going, she told Copaza the night before their departure, expecting him to object. He had been strange with her all summer.

A dark look *did* flit across his face, and Matuateh knew that she'd been right. She braced herself for one of their arguments. But the expression evaporated instantly. If you wish, he said with a little smile. He turned and left the lodge.

Matuateh should have wondered about that enigmatic smile. Copaza already knew that Quadra had ordered Francisco to remain in Yuquot for Maquinna's visit. For her, it would be a wasted trip.

The day before the rendezvous with the British they set off by canoe, the young slave women at the paddles and Copaza sitting in the centre like Maquinna himself, enjoying the ride. All of them, including Matuateh, were skilled canoeists; they made good time down the Sound and along the coast.

They landed and set off towards the springs, but halfway there they left the path and went through the forest to a rough shelter Copaza knew from his days of *osumich*. They made camp there, and that night Copaza took his liberties with Matuateh's friend Saiyuqa. In the morning he left to meet the English. Stay here, he told the women. When I come back I'll take you to the King Georges.

A few hours later he returned and they set out, back the way they had come and then along the path to the springs.

They were not long on their way when they met the shaman Tsakwasap coming from the opposite direction. He was dressed in ceremonial cloak, painted and oiled in the old way, and he flew into a rage when he saw his erstwhile apprentice. He grabbed him by the breast of his fine white shirt and pulled him off the path, gripping him so firmly that they were nose to nose. From Copaza's stance it looked like he wanted to look away. Yet he held the old man's eyes.

What have you done, boy? There are foreigners at the hot springs.

Copaza said nothing. Tsakwasap looked around him at the slave girls clustered on the path, watching intently.

Realization spread like winter dawn across his gleaming face. He shoved Copaza away and spat, You fool. You young fool, desecrating a sacred place. You disgust me.

Copaza still did not speak, though his face showed his own anger. He attempted an ironic grin.

This infuriated Tsakwasap. What would your father say? he shouted, charging and seizing him by his shirt's lapels. What would Calicum say?

Copaza's grin disappeared. He attempted to break free, but Tsakwasap was a powerful man. He held his fallen apprentice in a vice-like grip.

He would be ashamed! You are not worthy of Calicum. You are not worthy to be his son.

Copaza staggered back as Tsakwasap shoved him away. But Tsakwasap was not finished.

It was you, he raged, circling like a predator. It was you who revealed our whaling secrets and our shrine to the young Spaniard. Now you defile this sacred place, where the *chi'ha* speak to those who make themselves pure. To this holy place you bring girls to fornicate with foreigners. You would pollute its healing waters. Its *sacred* waters.

Copaza backed away as Tsakwasap came at him again. The shaman flicked his shoulder with disdain.

Look at you! You wear the white men's clothes and pretend to be like them — to be one of them. You offend your ancestors. You offend the spirits. You will bring disaster on your father's people *and* your mother's.

He spat on the moss and pointed his knuckly hand at Copaza while the earth and sky stood still.

I curse you, Copaza, son of Calicum. I curse you.

The hand fell to his side. Tsakwasap turned and brushed past the slave girls on the path. They scrambled out of his way and gathered back in a group to watch him barge away. He did not look back.

Copaza also watched him. Crazy old man, he sneered.

But his face was pale and no longer held the haughty expression he had previously shown the girls.

# Chapter 18

George Vancouver realized the full extent of his reliance on Tom Dobson when his young translator came within a whisker of dropping dead.

The boy's ordeal began the evening before the midshipmen's departure, when Vancouver hosted a dinner for Maquinna on board *Discovery*. Quadra and his officers attended too, and again there was much gift-giving and chummy talk, and when night fell Van led everybody onto the quarterdeck for a fireworks display. It was a new experience for Maquinna and his counsellors and they seemed thrilled by it.

(The Spaniards don't have this capability, Quatlazape murmured to his fellow war chief Natzape. Do you think the English are more powerful?

It's impressive, all right, Natzape replied without answering the question. A moment later he continued: I wonder what Tsakwasap would say if he was here.

They both laughed. Maquinna glanced over his shoulder at them and they went deadpan.)

After his guests disembarked Vancouver stood and watched their boats pull towards shore. "That is all, Mister Dobson. Get some sleep." He returned Dobson's salute and turned away, then turned back, struck by a thought. "Hold up. I wish I could spare you to go with the others, but I need you here for these niceties. And tomorrow I need Señor Quadra's letter translated. Tonight, though, you may take liberty ashore. That is, if you wish."

Dobson pounced like a hound on a pork chop. He was aboard the next boat headed shoreward, where he did the rounds, partook of a trader's hospitality, and ate a plate of mussels collected from the Sound. He returned to *Discovery* in the bottom of a Yankee jollyboat, gasping for air, limbs numb, face swollen like a crimson pumpkin.

Menzies propped him up and forced an infusion down his throat that had the desired effect — Dobson retched up his dinner (and the remains of his lunch). Yet he continued to deteriorate; soon he was nearly comatose, swollen, numb, labouring for breath. His lips had a blue-black hue. At midnight he suffered violent tremors. Near dawn, as the other young gentlemen departed on their expedition, he fell into a fevered sleep.

Between trips to sickbay, Vancouver paced the quarterdeck. Now, with the crisis seemingly past, Menzies recommended the poor fellow be taken ashore to recuperate at the infirmary.

During the two days of his convalescence, communications between the representatives of the two great European powers present in Nootka Sound were transacted in the language of a third. Vancouver's French was passable though not fluent, and he was forced to rely on his officers who spoke it better. His counterpart spoke little French himself and relied on his own French-speaking officers. So, commander-to-commander discourse involved an extra step and an extra intermediary. Sometimes, frustrated at the lengthy delays, desperate for a more direct dialogue, he resorted to Latin, imparted by a long-ago tutor though dimly remembered two decades later. The effort proved ineffectual, with the middlemen gaping at him uncertainly and Quadra leaning forward intently to try to catch his meaning.

⧗

On Monday morning Menzies cleared Dobson for duty, although the midshipman was still experiencing spasms from the cathartics used to purge his system.

"You gave us a scare, Tom," Vancouver said when he reported. He studied the young man's face. "The surgeon tells me you must take light duty for a few days. And avoid shellfish. I think *that* will not be hard... Well. Your first task is to clear up old business — the letter Señor Quadra sent before Tahsis. I will need to include a translation with my dispatches. See to that right away. Then I want you to get your head down and rest. I have seen new sailcloth darker than your face."

Alone again, he considered priorities. There were no more official trips or festivities planned, and the midshipmen had returned the day before in one piece. Now there was just work, and plenty of it: inventories, correspondence, and dispatches for the mail packet he would send on *Daedalus*, repairs and preparations for their departure. The drawing of the charts had been delayed too long. And of course there was the diplomatic matter. On that they had a verbal agreement — at least Quadra appeared to think so. Now that Dobson was back, Van hoped to conclude the details quickly and be done with it — though he feared it might cost him *Chatham*.

An hour later Dobson returned with his translation of Quadra's letter. He looked wan and shaky; his forehead glistened with sweat. At Vancouver's insistence he withdrew to rest in his hammock.

Van skimmed his work. Then, gobsmacked, he reread it slowly.

He sat oblivious to the familiar sounds of the ship at anchor, the creaks and voices, the water lapping against the hull. His mind swam with consternation.

The letter began with a restatement of the evidence that the small hut Meares claimed to have built in Friendly Cove was gone when Martínez arrived in May of 1789. But in any event, Quadra said, the current Spanish establishment was not on the hut's purported site.

> *I will, accordingly, not cede the sovereignty of Nootka to you.*
>
> *If you cannot accept my first proposal, then I will leave you in full possession of the spot where Meares's hut allegedly stood in 1788.*

The Spaniard concluded with an offer to place the entire settlement under Vancouver's *temporary* command while they referred the matter to their respective governments for resolution. If Vancouver accepted this offer, then he, Quadra, would depart the Sound as soon as command could be transferred.

Van stood and strode towards the cabin door.

He was silent in the launch. He had ordered his coxswain to bypass the settlement's main landing and land at the site of Meares's hut. Their course took them past *Chatham*, which had been refloated a few days before, a newly arrived American trader, and the Spanish frigate *Aranzazu*, just returned from its northern explorations. Van had met her captain, Jacinto Caamaño, at the Big House the night before; they had agreed (through the French-speaking mediums) to meet again to discuss their respective surveys. Now, though, as he rode beneath *Aranzazu*'s bow, he ignored it and stared instead at the approaching shore, trying to reconcile the "districts" and "parcels of land" his orders required him to receive with this pitifully narrow beach in a far corner of the cove.

One of the hands, facing aft and pulling in unison with his mates, surreptitiously watched his captain's face. Back aboard *Discovery* that night, he would tell his messmates that their commander's manner resembled that of Tubby, the ship's cat, when teased to the limits of feline tolerance; and he obligingly demonstrated on Tubby until her ears lay flat, her eyes shone dark with malice, and she was coiled to pounce.

"From 'is posture 'n the knit o''is brows, Oi fathomed trouble," Adams would say knowingly. "Cap'n warn't 'appy — that were plain as day. An' when Cap'n's not 'appy, lower deck's to pay. Oi says to meself, nowt good'll come o' this."

Sitting in the stern sheets that morning, Van was oblivious to his men's surveillance and canny insights. At the precise moment at which Adams registered his clouded expression, he was asking himself if *this* was why the British fleet had been mobilized. Would William Pitt really go to war over this forlorn ledge of muck and broken rock?

Closer now. The site was shaped like a triangle, one side bounded by the sea, the others by craggy ridges extending down to the shore. A breach in the rocks, nothing more; a small, low-lying strand on the edge of a deep-water harbour, isolated from the Spanish settlement except at low tide. On it stood a sturdy frame supporting the hull of a vessel under construction. Men scrambled industriously around it. Van saw hammers strike, heard echoing blows an instant later.

The boat landed, Midshipman Lincoln at cox careful to observe procedure, the crew subdued. They had all now read the look on their captain's face. Van picked his way across the shore, the slippery stones retarding his progress. He plodded onto firmer ground and halted to survey the stocks, the strakes and planking around it, the tent on higher ground above. He turned to look back at the cove, then in the direction of the Spanish town. Nothing of it could be seen beyond the rocky ridge. Nothing, that is, except the Spanish flag on its long pole.

The men on shore cast curious looks at the commanding figure in the brass-buttoned coat. He seemed oblivious to their presence.

One of them called to get his attention.

From the launch, Lincoln frantically waved him off.

No, Van thought. I will not raise the British flag over this wretched patch while Spanish colours fly on higher ground. My accepting *possession* here and *temporary command* there might be construed as recognizing Spanish sovereignty over the whole. That would not be welcomed at the Court of Saint James's. Pitt and his crowd would throw me to the dogs if it served their purpose — and I cannot hazard a guess as to what their particular purpose might be on the day they hear of this. No. I cannot accept the offer. Temporary command is not possession, and possession is what my orders demand.

He was turning back towards the launch when he felt a hand on his arm. He started.

"Captain." It was the Boston trader, James Magee, who had ignored Lincoln's warning. "Good day to you, sir. It's a stroke of fortune, you showing up here today. I've been meaning to speak to you."

Vancouver looked down at Magee's hand on his sleeve.

"You'll be needing provisions before you sail. I have a broad range of stock — linens, shirts, blankets, everything you need for your crew. Also axes, muskets, and trinkets to trade with the Indians. Whisky and rum, too — you won't find better quality around here, whether for Indian or white. I've already had dealings with your people, and they're a thirsty bunch, that I can say."

Vancouver's eyes had become gleaming slits.

"My stock is at your disposal." Magee grinned and tapped the bridge of his nose; when he continued it was in a quieter, more intimate voice. "If we transact, Captain, let me assure you there's profit in it for the both of us."

⧗

That night, it was the observant oarsman Adams who related the subsequent scene to his fellow tars. "There 'e was, standing in the very 'eart of our new American empire with a look on 'is face like to choke a priest. 'E was already in a stew, Oi could see that well enough on the way in. An' Magee walks straight int'it. Well, there was words. Loud words. Cap'n blew 'is top. 'Lay off and unhand me, *Mister* Magee,' 'e sputters, an' shakes off Magee's 'and on 'is arm. 'I won't buy a goddamn dram of your goddamn rot-gut!' 'e shouts, an' more. 'Mind your own bloody business, you blackguard, and stay away from my people. Now get out of my way, sir.' Cap'n's in a 'uff 'n Magee tries t' int'rupt, which only gets 'im 'otter. 'You vile hound,' 'You black-hearted bastard,' 'You damn'd shite sack,' an' so on an' so forth. 'You will desist from selling my people *anything*.' There was more talk like this in a low form o' language, but me bein' of gen'l'manly persuasion Oi'm no' fain to repeat it."

There was muted laughter in their cramped mess, along with anxious looks. Magee was the covert purveyor of cherished supplements to everybody's daily grog.

As the launch set off from shore, Adams observed that the captain's face was crimson, that he sat taut and silent, looking neither one way nor the other; but as the boat approached *Discovery* Adams noticed a transformation. His posture relaxed, his complexion returned to normal. "Like 'is mind were made up. 'E were watchin' the ship by then, real close, like 'e were lookin' through 'er sides at 'er innards. Seein' ev'thin', 'e was."

⧗

Vancouver was piped aboard. He accepted a salute, beckoned to his first lieutenant, and strode aft to descend the companionway stairs to his cabin.

"Since we arrived," he told Mudge, closing the door behind him, "discipline has been allowed to slacken. Kindly muster the ship's company for eleven o'clock. I shall read the Articles of War. Also, effective immediately, there will be no private trade. None. Without exception. There will be no shore leave. All shore trips will be purely on ship's business. This applies to officers as well as ratings. That is all. Carry on. I shall attend to correspondence until muster. I am not to be disturbed — except by Mister Dobson. Kindly pass word to him to attend on me in half an hour."

# Chapter 19

A gentle breeze, cool yet pleasant, wafted in from the balcony of the Big House, ruffling the single page on Quadra's desk. He snatched it before it drifted to the floor. Close on two weeks of excellent weather, he thought, and another beautiful morning today. It's borrowed time.

He sighed and looked again at his counterpart's letter. It had arrived the previous afternoon.

> *You are reviewing events at Nootka that I am not authorized to revisit, our governments having made their determination. In the face of your latest position I shall refer the matter to my superiors. You may depend upon the justness of my representation regarding the entirety of our discussions and transactions here.*
>
> *I reiterate that I remain prepared to receive possession of all the territories described in the Convention concluded between our respective governments, and as directed by your first minister, the Count Floridablanca. That is, this place, Nootka Sound, in toto, and all of Clayoquot Sound.*

Quadra turned to look across his balcony at *Discovery*. He sighed again, took a fresh sheet of paper from a drawer, dipped his quill, and began to write.

He was conferring with his clerk, Felix Cepeda, when Jacinto Caamaño arrived. "See that this is delivered immediately," Quadra told Cepeda. "Call for Francisco. Have him deliver it." The clerk bowed and left as Quadra turned to Caamaño. He beheld a man of thirty, robust, full of energy. This is a young man's life, he thought, and I am old. Alberni and me, two worn boots with their soles barely attached.

"How are you this morning, Jacinto? Have you found your land legs?"

"I am well, Don Juan. As are my legs."

"Then let us stretch them. This desk gives me a headache. Moziño tells me I must 'take the air.'"

Caamaño reported on the *Aranzazu*'s condition and the health of her crew as they strolled through the Spanish town. Quadra listened, asked questions, nodded.

"Tell Felix what supplies you need, and he'll scrounge up what he can. The work you describe will take a few weeks. I'll try to hire some men from the traders to speed it up." He gestured towards the harbour. "At the moment there is a lot of competition for help."

They entered the meadow behind the settlement. Caamaño called to Pablo, who was inside one of the enclosures, surrounded by his flock. The old man waved and called back.

"Ai! His birds have done well," Caamaño said.

"Thanks to him there are now more chickens in Santa Cruz de Nuca than Catalonians. I go to great lengths to conceal that fact. The troops I evacuated left their uniforms behind. Alberni's idea. Now when the guard at the bastion on San Miguel changes, it's actually seamen from *Activa* masquerading as soldiers. Twice a day, they dress here in the barracks and are ferried across to the fort, where they make a show of arriving, then disappear behind the wall. A couple of real Catalonians stay behind, and the rest return here, change back into their own clothes, and go back to their real work."

Caamaño laughed. Quadra's own smile was weary. "And with half the garrison we had, we still have too many mouths. My counterpart out there"— he gestured back towards the cove — "has a dedicated store ship to resupply his two vessels while I, the Governor of Nuevo California, rely on tricks to demonstrate Spanish might."

They paused on the ridge above the outer shore to watch whitecaps break on the cobble beach. A distant fog bank concealed the horizon. Quadra led the younger man onto a forest path that paralleled the shore. In the woods the air was redolent of cedar, the sound of the ocean faint. They walked in silence.

"What we're doing here cannot withstand scrutiny for long," Quadra said. "I must decide if it's worth the effort."

Caamaño glanced at him.

"Santa Cruz de Nuca is important if de Fonte's passage to the Atlantic actually exists. But Galiano didn't find it to the south, and you didn't find it to the north. Closer surveys might uncover it, but we have no time for that. I was authorized to leave Santa Cruz to the English and withdraw to Nunez Gaona. Galiano, though, says it's a poor harbour, inferior to what we have here. So, if we remain in Nuevo California, *this* is the best place. And that is the central question — should we remain? Based on what I've learned, I don't believe we have to give up Santa Cruz at all. Meares's claim is based on lies. It's entirely the wrong reason for us to leave."

"Is there a right reason?"

"Yes. That we lack the will to hold it — and I can't decide that. All I can do is delay, in the hope that the king's ministers get some backbone and send us the resources we need. Captain Vancouver has agreed to refer the issue back to our governments — though he still pushes to implement the Convention to the letter. I believe his government's commitment is no clearer to him than ours is to me. So he and I dither over details while I engage in a ruse."

"Not a ruse, Don Juan: a tactic. A necessary one if it serves our interests."

"Perhaps. But I'm not proud of it, or any of the other 'tactics' I've had to use."

Ahead there was a snap, a thud. Quadra grasped Caamaño's arm to halt him. A deer stepped from the undergrowth, its hooves thudding on the path. It stopped in the clear and turned its head towards them. Dark eyes drank them in; long ears swivelled to listen. They were close enough to see its white muzzle, the white patch between its eyes. It was a doe.

Several seconds passed in mutual observation before one of its ears pivoted. A moment later the Spaniards heard a hollow knock, a distant voice. The deer looked towards it, back at them, then bounded into the forest and headed in the direction of the outer shore. They watched it move among the trees, heard a final crack of hoof on deadfall before it disappeared.

"A handsome beast," Quadra observed.

"Venison to me. I've been at sea for three months."

They walked on. The path skirted a wall of rock, took a bend, and led onto a ridge separating the ocean, distant now on their left, from a lake just visible through the trees on their right. The path closed on the lake and led them to a clearing above a gravelly landing, where Francisco Almeida and Maquinna's kinsman Copaza were hauling up a small canoe.

"Francisco!" Caamaño called.

The boy startled. "Don Jacinto...Don Juan..." He glanced around and spoke to Copaza.

"What are you doing here?" Quadra's voice was sharp.

"I —"

"Did I say you could leave the settlement?"

"I should have sought your approval, Don Juan. There is an island... it's...there is a cemetery there. Copaza wanted to show me it, and you once said I should try to —"

"A cemetery? What about it?"

Copaza waded out of the water and started up the ridge.

Francisco hesitated. "Well, it's more like a mausoleum, a shrine where they keep relics — bones, carvings, masks. It reminds me of Santeria back in Cuba. I've always been interested in things like this, and Copaza wanted me to see it, and you told me to..."

"Enough."

Copaza reached their level, gave them a curt nod, and turned to speak to Francisco. Then he set off in the direction away from the Spanish settlement.

Francisco scrambled up the bank. "Please accept my apology, Don Juan. I interpret my orders too freely."

Quadra's expression softened. He clapped a hand on Francisco's shoulder. "Yes. An officer must interpret his orders. You will learn that at Cádiz." He turned to Caamaño. "Word came while you were away — he's been accepted into the naval academy. He will join next year's class."

"Bah!" said Caamaño. "You're better to remain an *aventurero*, Francisco. It hasn't hurt me. The academy's over-rated. Why would you ever need to speak Latin? What good is that on a quarterdeck?"

"I have to learn Latin?" Francisco frowned and fingered the medallion he wore around his neck. "I kiss Cachita here for luck, and I go to mass when I have to, but I don't want to be a priest. I want to be an officer."

Quadra laughed. "You have to study Latin. That doesn't mean you'll learn it. Although you just might." He turned back to Caamaño. "It turns out he's got an ear for languages. That's made him very helpful here these last months."

"I do my duty, Don Juan."

"Yes. Let's talk about that. How is Maquinna?"

"Well pleased. His people are still talking about our visit. Wickaninnish is said to be very jealous. Which makes Maquinna even happier."

"Anything else?"

"There is some talk...Some of the elders think Maquinna is too friendly with you."

"Which elders? Who said this?"

"I don't know. I just overheard a comment."

"Get me names if you can. Maybe I can change their minds. When do you leave for supplies?"

"Three days, dark and early, with Copaza." He gestured up the path.

"Very well. You'll see your lady friend then, I suppose. How is she?"

"Aha!" Caamaño guffawed. "So you take language lessons at the School of Horizontal Arts!"

Francisco blushed.

"Out with it, Francisco," Caamaño pressed. "How *is* she?"

"I...You embarrass me, Don Jacinto. My duties have kept me from her, if you must know. I heard she is unhappy with me." A sly grin replaced his discomfiture. "Don Juan, if you wanted to set things right, a few extra days —"

"Watch out, watch out," Quadra said, laughing. "You'll end up a colonial administrator with mouths to feed. Chained to a desk and far from any quarterdeck."

Francisco lifted his chin and assumed the manner of an affronted hidalgo. "No, I will graduate from Cádiz, and serve where I am sent, and one day I will command a fleet that sweeps the sea of our enemies — and in doing so I will save the fat asses and juicy sinecures of a *thousand* colonial administrators."

The two older officers laughed. "So you will, Francisco," Quadra said. "I've no doubt of that. Though I am beginning to think you've laboured too long under the tutelage of Captain Alberni."

They all laughed at this.

Quadra grew serious. "What about the young English?"

"They are restricted to their ships now, except on duty, but that won't inconvenience them long."

"What's do you mean?"

"They're very, ah, resourceful. They find a way to get what they want."

"And you help them do it, don't you? Listen, we're not playing games here. I don't need trouble."

"Don Juan, I try to prevent trouble before it happens." Francisco's eyes flicked away, then returned. "Sometimes I make things happen so worse things don't. But I assure you I have done my duty. And I've kept you informed — as you asked me to."

Quadra looked out at the lake. "Get along to the *presidio*. Felix has a letter for Captain Vancouver. I want you to deliver it and see your midshipmen while you're aboard. Speak to those who are ashore too. Whatever you learn is helpful."

Francisco inclined his head and started towards the settlement. He turned back. "Don Juan," he said. "This was my second visit to the island out there. Copaza showed me the shrine before, and I wanted to see it again. Their beliefs interest me, and help me understand them better. But I won't go there again."

Quadra nodded.

The boy bowed, turned, and resumed walking. Quadra again looked down at the lake, where the island was indistinguishable from the far shore, then at the canoe drawn up on the landing.

"Jacinto," he said, "let's go see for ourselves."

# Chapter 20

Back to the maps. The blessed maps. The crinkly, rolly, papery maps, the *charts*, cellulose lovechildren of exploration, as yet a twinkle in their creator's eye.

More a glare, actually, given his unresolved longitude problem.

While Van and Old Joe Whidbey sought a solution, young Joe Baker did what mapmaking he could with a rotating cast of midshipmen. First they drew charts from the data collected at their landfalls in the South Seas. Then they copied the Spanish charts provided by Quadra. Where these overlapped with areas they'd surveyed themselves, Baker had them compare the Spaniards' longitudes with their own, hoping to resolve the conundrum that had bedevilled them since their arrival in the northwest.

This was the task on which Midshipmen Hawkins and Stuart were engaged that morning. Baker had them working at tables on the quarterdeck to take advantage of the fine weather. Old Joe stood nearby doing his stretches and observing the flow of traffic in the harbour — a trader's longboat making for shore, a native canoe headed for the Spanish bastion, another drawing towards *Discovery*. Quadra's young aide, Francisco (Whidbey marvelled how everyone knew him by his first name!), sat at its centre. Whidbey bent his arm behind his back and glanced shoreward to check on *Discovery*'s cutter. It was just getting underway.

He arched his back and held the position, looking up at the sun as he did to gauge its angle. The cutter bore a watering party and casks that would be stowed below. Placed too high, off centre, or in a position from which they might shift at sea, they could cause the ship to capsize. Problem was, boarding them took time. They had to be swung aboard in cargo nets, lowered into the hold, and rolled into position (after allowing for where the supplies brought by *Daedalus* would eventually go). Only then could they be lashed down and secured. Whidbey needed to oversee their placement — and he needed to get to the observatory by noon. The duty midshipman was there to record the zenith, but conditions this day were perfect, and Old Joe was a perfectionist; he wanted to take his own sighting.

The cutter pulled slowly towards the ship, sluggish with its burden.

A watchman turned the hourglass and rang the ship's bell: two strokes of two followed by a single stroke. Whidbey had ninety minutes.

He rotated his shoulders and mumbled, "Taking their sweet time."

Baker looked up from one of the tables. "Don't worry, Mister Whidbey. You'll make it."

The master grunted. "Perhaps — in a blessed rush." He put his hands on his hips and pivoted, stretched the small of his back again, and tilted sideways to see what Baker and Hawkins were doing at the table.

The lieutenant looked at a plot Hawkins had marked, referred to a tattered notebook, and measured an angle.

"There. It's the declination," he told Hawkins. "If you interpolate between the last two confirmed variations, our plot corresponds perfectly with Galiano's. Allowing for the longitude difference, but that's constant."

"Eureka, Mister Baker," Whidbey said.

"Indeed, Mister Whidbey. It was your long shadow over the table that inspired me."

Hawkins laughed. Whidbey grimaced and leaned away from the table to stretch in the opposite direction.

Francisco's canoe came alongside. He scrambled up the ladder, landed nimbly on the quarterdeck, and greeted the officer of the watch like a long-lost chum. Peter Puget was not having it; he coolly accepted a proffered envelope and handed it straight to his watch deputy — Midshipman Ramsay — who walked it aft and descended the companionway stair.

Francisco was about to try again with Puget, but the lieutenant took a report from a watchman. Francisco waited. Ramsay reappeared from below, envelope still in hand, and hurried forward. He rolled his eyes as he passed Francisco, descended to the main and continued forward to the fo'c'sle, where Tom Dobson stood watching Archibald Menzies fuss over a pot of cuttings. It had been moved there for want of space on the quarterdeck.

Francisco watched them for a moment, turned, and spotted Jim Hawkins at his plotting table. "Yim," he called softly — so softly that Hawkins did not hear. Francisco stepped towards him.

Puget caught movement out of the corner of his eye. His head swung towards Francisco, and he raised a hand to stop him — just as George Vancouver stepped up through the companionway onto the quarterdeck. Puget's raised hand immediately formed a salute. "Morning, sir," he said, cool as a cucumber, moving to leeward.

"Good morning, Mister Puget. Would you..." Vancouver turned and found a Spaniard standing on *his* quarterdeck.

Francisco had frozen in his tracks on Vancouver's arrival. "*Capitán,*" he said now, bowing with the grace of a courtier. He glanced around and waved to Hawkins, who was conferring with Baker and hadn't noticed him. Francisco hesitated, still hoping to catch his eye. He gave up, moved briskly towards the gangway, and cast a final look at Hawkins before saluting Vancouver smartly and descending over the side.

An amused pucker flitted across Vancouver's face. He turned his attention back to *Discovery*. The tide had ebbed since dawn and the ship had pulled at its moorings. The breeze had veered and strengthened. The ensign at the stern flapped audibly now.

"The glass, please, Mister Puget."

He extended the telescope to observe the canoe that had just landed at the Spanish fort. He held the glass to his eye for a long time, then lowered it, hmmphed to himself, and tapped the rail ruminatively. He turned towards shore and saw that the cutter, riding low in the water, was now midway between the settlement and the ship. He observed it carefully. It wallowed slightly with its heavy burden, the men labouring hard at the oars. Pitt, its coxswain, slackened pace to exchange a few words with Francisco as he passed the Spaniard's shore-bound canoe.

Vancouver heard a mutter close by. He lowered the glass and found Whidbey contorted into an odd twist, his eyes on the cutter.

Minutes later it made fast abeam of the main hatch. Pitt scrambled aboard, saluted, and turned to supervise unloading.

Vancouver stood watching as the men on deck and in the cutter prepared to ship the casks. He turned to Puget and nodded towards the boat. "That man, Mister Puget. Reybold. Would you be so kind as to see what he's hiding in his coat."

Puget descended to the main, beckoned to the master-at-arms, and had a word with Pitt. Pitt called down to Reybold, who quickly looked up at the quarterdeck, saw Vancouver watching him, and averted his eyes. He climbed up from the boat and stood listening to Pitt, then slowly removed a sailcloth bag from his tunic.

"What is it, Mister Pitt?" Vancouver asked as he approached with the master.

The bag's contents clinked in the midshipman's grip. He looked inside. "It's Dutch courage, sir. Two bottles of it."

Vancouver stared at Pitt, who returned his gaze. Reybold kept his eyes on the deck.

"Master-at-Arms. Take the sack from Mister Pitt and bring Reybold to my cabin. Mister Mudge, will you join me there. Mister Puget, kindly have a midshipman gather a crew for the cutter. I will go ashore with the master in forty-five minutes for the noon observation." He turned back to Pitt. "Thank you, Mister Pitt. See to the boat and to the stowage of the casks — Mister Whidbey will have specific instructions, and then he'll leave you to it."

"Sir."

"When you are finished there, I have another task for you. The ship's well must be sounded. I want you to inspect the bilge. Personally. Plumb it fore, midship, and aft. Log the depth every quarter hour for four hours. I want detailed, accurate measurements, and I want you to calculate the rate at which we take on water. Then I want it pumped dry and smoked. I want you to supervise that personally, and I want your report by the end of the second dog."

Pitt flushed, bowed slightly, turned to his task.

Whidbey noticed that Vancouver's face was also flushed. He came close to speak privately. "There's no end to what a tar gets up to in port, is there, sir?" Then, more quietly yet, "It's plenty foul in the well, Captain. That's a long time for the lad to be down there."

Vancouver glanced at him, then appraised the angle of the sun, thinking the master's soft spot for the midshipmen bordered on indulgence.

And with regard to this particular prideful, pompous, trouble-making midshipman — well, Whidbey, and Menzies too, coddled the boy, turned a blind eye to his appalling behaviour, or kissed his ass outright. Did they not see the futility in grasping at the coattails of privilege? The licence it provided for even more bad conduct? He saw it also in the subtle deference paid by his own lieutenants, who were solid to a man, yet unseemly in their forbearance of this miscreant.

It was very like how everyone treated that constant meddler, Joseph Banks, tugging forelocks and scraping the ground in hope of favour in return.

"Thank you, Mister Whidbey. Do please consider the stowage of the casks. Then we need to get ashore. In the meantime you will excuse me. I have enquiries to which I must attend."

# Chapter 21

Van's boots crunched purposefully on the gravel path that led to the Big House. Dobson had to trot to keep up.

It was late afternoon — they were more than an hour early for the nightly hospitality in the great hall. Van wanted a private word with his counterpart, out of earshot of the guests who frequented his table. The commandant's latest letter contained nothing new, just a reiteration of his previous position. They were accomplishing nothing and wasting time.

He returned a salute from a Spanish guard and stared out at the harbour while Dobson explained his purpose. A soldier ran upstairs. Moments later Quadra's clerk, Cepeda, came down to escort them up and through the great hall to the office. Quadra stood waiting for them in front of his desk.

"Captain! This is an unexpected pleasure. Please, take a seat. Mister Dobson, you too. Would you like coffee? An aperitif?"

"Very kind, Don Juan, but no. I am here on the diplomatic matter. In fact, I have been here for two weeks, and we have yet to have a direct conversation about it. It seems futile to conduct such a discourse by correspondence when I am right here. Let us discuss this face to face and resolve it, once and for all."

Quadra gestured to a chair.

"With regard to your letter," Vancouver continued as soon as he sat, "I cannot accept possession of anything here under any restriction. The Convention reached by our respective governments states that the properties in question are to be *unconditionally* returned. I cannot agree to anything that contravenes that principle. I must decline possession of this place on anything less than sovereign terms. If that is indeed your proposal, I shall proceed to sea, report accordingly to my government, and await direction."

Quadra's eyes stayed on Vancouver as he listened to Dobson's translation.

"Captain, the Convention places no obligation on me to transfer ownership, nor to abandon our settlement here." (Vancouver's brows arched as this was translated.) "I've offered to withdraw to avoid the potential for further conflict, but my offer *is* conditional: that it will not prejudice our right of return. I have offered to —"

"Don Juan, I must point out that your first minister, Count Floridablanca —"

Quadra held up a hand that stopped Tom Dobson in mid-translation.

"Count Floridablanca consented with your court to our appointment as commissioners to negotiate terms. I hardly think our governments would have deemed it necessary to appoint us, and send us both here, if they had intended a mere transfer of possession. Our respective cabin boys could have accomplished that without us. My boundary proposal, at Juan de Fuca, is —"

Now Vancouver held up his hand to stop Dobson.

"Your boundary proposal goes quite beyond the scope of our mandate. But if you insist on putting it forward, I must remind you that the Convention clearly establishes the principle of free access for British vessels as far south as the port of San Francisco."

They had gone around these matters several times when a servant entered to advise Quadra that dinner was ready, and that the Spanish and British officers and several of the traders were gathered in the great hall.

Quadra stood and rubbed his hands together. "Well, here is a proposal we can agree upon. Let's eat."

The British commissioner remained seated, his expression pained. "If that is truly a point of agreement, it lacks relevance to the issue. May I suggest, then, while we are in an agreeing mood, that we continue this discussion after dinner."

"Of course," Quadra said. "Let us invite our officers to join us then. Perhaps a broader discussion will help us find a solution."

Van rose to his feet wondering what a broader discussion could accomplish. It seemed like a stall to him.

⧗

When dinner concluded, and coffee and digestifs had been poured and drained, a small group remained to continue the suspended discussion. Alberni, Moziño, and Caamaño took seats with Quadra, while Broughton and Mudge sat with Vancouver across from them. Dobson sat at the table's end with a clear view of both parties.

The discussion that ensued proved no broader than the one that had preceded it. Quadra did all the talking for the Spaniards, repeating his defence of Martínez and his assertion that Spain's sovereignty in the area was well established. Maquinna, he said, had consented to the Spanish presence in Friendly Cove.

Vancouver listened politely and wondered again if he was missing something. They were going around in circles. Or was this merely the pace and nature of diplomacy? If so, he was grateful for the path he had taken years before. Better seasick and scurvied on a storm-tossed open deck than confined to a fragrant salon negotiating the number of angels permitted to dance on the head of a pin.

"… nevertheless, in the spirit of cooperation, I have no objection if you wish to take possession of the site of Meares's house."

Vancouver declined.

There followed a reiteration of the specific terms of the Convention, and a rebuttal involving the need to interpret intent. After a few minutes of such back-and-forth, the commissioners declared a stalemate and agreed to refer the matter to their respective governments.

To Tom Dobson, relishing the sudden silence, both commissioners seemed to brighten, as if relieved to be rid of a nettlesome task.

"Perhaps we should discuss the practical details," Quadra said. "The *Activa* is almost ready to sail. I will leave with the garrison as soon as our preparations are complete."

Vancouver nodded. "And I will depart when we are ready, likely in a fortnight or so. We will winter in the Sandwich Islands, but with the westerlies here, a direct voyage is impossible. We will sail south and survey the coast along the way to the latitude of Alta California, thence west to Hawaii. Previously I said I would leave *Chatham* here over the winter, but with your, ah, modified proposal that will not be necessary — though it may be unavoidable. Mister Broughton will explain."

Broughton looked from Vancouver to Quadra, gathering his thoughts. "Yes. When we careened *Chatham* last week, we could not float her high enough to do all the repairs she needs. There's a spring tide next week, and I want to use it to careen her again and finish work on her keel and bottom. To do that I will need to move my people ashore again — with your consent, Don Juan."

"Of course. Do what you need to do."

"Thank you. It's possible we won't be ready to sail with *Discovery* and *Daedalus*. I will leave as soon as I can, but if the weather breaks we could still end up wintering here."

"I understand. In that case, without prejudice to our rights, the port and its facilities will be at your disposal." Quadra looked around the table. "Gentlemen, it seems I will depart before any of you. I would prefer to sail *with* you but I cannot delay, given the time of year. I will wait for you in Monterey, where I can offer you a higher standard of hospitality than I have been able to eke out here."

"I find that hard to believe," Vancouver said. "Your standard here has been high indeed. But I very much appreciate the offer. A final landfall before we turn towards Hawaii will benefit all hands. We relish the prospect of reunion and the continuance of our friendship — in Monterey."

"Hear, hear," echoed Broughton and Mudge dutifully.

"Don't underestimate the weather on your way south, Don Jorge," Alberni said. "The storms can last for weeks."

"If we hit anything like that we'll run for shelter. I understand the bay at San Francisco is well protected."

None of the Spaniards responded. Vancouver examined a silver spoon left on the table. It was engraved *Plus Ultra*. He smiled faintly, as if at a memory.

Quadra said, "As you will remain when I leave, and we have not resolved the issue at dispute, let us discuss the protocol for my departure. I propose to strike the Spanish flag over the settlement, at which time you may raise the British flag in its stead. I will board *Activa* and fire a salute, if you will return it with an equal number of guns. Then, in company with *Aranzazu*, I will withdraw from the port, leaving you in possession here. I must reiterate, Captain, gentlemen," he looked at the faces around the table, "that my departure will not constitute a cessation of Spanish sovereignty. I cede nothing. We are entering into an administrative arrangement, nothing more, and it will stand while the issue is resolved by our governments."

"Agreed. Don Juan, I concur in every respect. Let us put paid to it." Vancouver's chair scraped on the floor planks as he stood and extended his hand. More chairs scraped across rough timber as the others stood to witness their agreement.

And I, observing the historic moment from without, eavesdropped on their thoughts. The soldier Pedro Alberni wondered what Vancouver knew about San Francisco, and where he'd learned it. The mariner William Broughton contemplated winter in Nootka Sound, and what he had to do to avoid it. The physician Jose Moziño worried that his commandant looked pale and tired. The translator Tom Dobson felt relief that this diplomatic affair, with all its precise and complicated language, was resolved at last. The *aventurero* Jacinto Caamaño marvelled how any topic could be squeezed dry as dust. And *Discovery*'s first lieutenant Zach Mudge grappled with how de facto possession of the whole was less than de jure possession of a part.

Quadra beckoned to his steward (who was thinking about bed). "I've been saving this for a special moment," he told the small assembly, accepting a bottle from him. "It's pisco from my family's estate in Peru."

The steward poured and the guests all deemed it excellent. They savoured it in silence.

"There is another matter I would discuss," Vancouver said.

He described the American trader Magee's sale of liquor from his base on shore. "I've taken what measures I can. I've issued orders to my own people; but I must request that you deal with Magee. Until you withdraw, you are governor here. Only you have the authority to prohibit the sale of spirits ashore."

Quadra's expression showed his irritation. "I understand your concern. I will deal with Magee."

They had another brandy. Quadra asked about the charts.

"Ah. We've had trouble reconciling our longitudes with those of others." Vancouver fiddled with his glass. "Including yours. We are reviewing our data and recalculating everything to determine the reason."

"Yes, you've mentioned this before. We're running out of time before my departure."

"Once we reconcile, we can produce charts very quickly." Vancouver was struck by a thought, a suspicion he had wrestled with for some time. This was a good time to test it. "We can deliver them to you in California. We will certainly have them completed by then."

He observed Quadra's expression as Dobson translated. The Spaniard's eyes stayed on his.

"I must have them when I sail. Your orders and my orders are clear that we are to share our discoveries."

"And I will provide them, Don Juan. I'll do my utmost to get you copies before you leave. But we need to ensure their quality, and that will take time."

"If you need assistance in charting, or in reconciling your data, I will provide help. Caamaño here, for example, is an excellent cartographer."

Dobson got as far as "Caamaño here, for example," before Vancouver cut him off.

"We are very close to a solution."

As Dobson translated, Quadra regarded his counterpart intently.

When they parted a short while later, Van felt it had been a productive evening. Decisions had been made, the outcome was satisfactory, and he was nine-tenths sure a suspicion he'd harboured somewhat guiltily was true. Now, with the diplomatic matter referred home and out of the way for good, he could focus on his voyage and the completion of the survey at its heart.

The way forward was clear.

# Chapter 22

"The British Navy is driven by wind and run by accountants," Vancouver grumped to his clerk, Orchard, who stood in the doorway with an apologetic smile and an armful of ledgers. "Come in, Henry, come in. Let's have at it."

Together they reviewed the accounts and inventories of the carpenter, the gunner, the boatswain, and the cook. When that was done they turned to the real purpose of their meeting: the condition of the supplies brought by *Daedalus*. Orchard had inspected them thoroughly — he was a methodical man, which was why he had earned Vancouver's trust — and found extensive wastage. The cargo had been poorly stowed and there had been a fire at sea. The ship itself had been lucky to survive.

Some ships were thought to be unlucky. Van knew luck had nothing to do with it. He thought of Hergest and Gooch, both of whom had survived the fire but not the voyage.

The accounts put him in a sour mood. When he was alone again he penned a peevish letter to the Admiralty itemizing the damage to *Daedalus*'s cargo, knowing it would not be received for upwards of a year but finding therapeutic value in its composition.

At half past nine the first lieutenant arrived for their daily briefing. Vancouver pushed the paperwork aside to listen.

The decks, Mudge reported, were shipshape: weather decks were swabbed, scrubbed, and clean; below decks, hammocks were lashed and stowed, the decks cleaned, swept, sponged with vinegar, and dried. As it was Thursday, the men were washing their clothes. The powder, sail-room, and rope lockers were dry, the ship's stores secure. The ship was not yet rigged and ready for sea — the sailmaker was working on a new suit of sails, and the bosun would soak and bend them on when he was done. Midshipman Pitt had supervised the pumping and smoking of the bilges, and Mudge himself had confirmed his calculation of the rate of flood. The copper on the keel was intact and in good condition.

Mudge paused expectantly. The daily report was a ritual both he and his captain knew by rote.

"Very well. The people."

"The surgeon advises there are three ratings ashore at the hospital, all with routine ailments: gout, digestive indisposition, one of a venereal nature. Three of the gentlemen also: Mister Cranston, of course; Mister Ramsay, digestive; Mister Lincoln, a recurrence of his unfortunate malady. Total: six of ours, a further three from *Chatham*. We have two men with mild ailments resting in their hammocks here on board. The rest are healthy. Two marines and a midshipman — Mister Hawkins relieved Mister Barrie this morning — are at the observatory. That brings me to the black list. Reybold is the only one today. Bilboes overnight. Punishment at eleven."

"All to attend who are able. Those ashore as well."

"Aye, sir. I'll recall them as soon as I go up. There is one other thing: with respect to the charts..."

"Yes?"

Mudge did not miss the sudden alertness in Vancouver's demeanour. "When we have a solution to the...the longitude problem..."

Unsettled by the intensity of his captain's expression, the first lieutenant trailed off. The ship's bell sounded on the quarterdeck above. Vancouver glanced up, sighed. "The 'longitude problem,' Number One, has taken us far too long to resolve. What with the deplorable condition of our supplies and the regrettable state of Anglo–Iberian relations, I have had to ponder it from afar these last many days."

"Yes, sir, and now that we have agreement with Señor Quadra on the diplomatic matter I'm sure we'll crack the, ah, matter quickly, and we must be ready then. Frankly, the chart work we've been doing has lagged. We need to finish it, so we're all hands on deck to produce the new ones."

"Who does Baker have assisting?"

"Today it's Pitt, sir."

Vancouver's nostrils flared. "Pitt," he repeated. "Who is the best draftsman among the young gentlemen?"

Mudge considered. "Definitely not Pitt. Roberts, I'd say."

"Yes, he's got steady hands. Have him report to Baker after muster. Who's next best?"

Mudge thought again. "Ramsay. Hawkins. Both are good."

"Ramsay's sick, you say? Put Hawkins on it. Double him up with Roberts until further notice."

"Hawkins went ashore yesterday for duty at the observatory."

Vancouver's brow furrowed for a moment before he realized Mudge was thinking out loud. "Recall him, Mister Mudge, straight away." He tapped his fingers on the table, suddenly inspired. "Send Pitt ashore in his place."

And good riddance, he thought. If only he had a longer-term solution regarding His Muckymuck High Lordship.

"Aye, sir."

"Good. After muster I'll meet with Messrs. Baker and Whidbey on the longitude issue. We must crack that acorn. That is all for now. Unless you have something else?"

"No, sir, that's it for today."

"Then I'm going up for some air. I need to escape the pleasure of their company for a few minutes." He tapped the ledgers on his desk.

The upper decks were drenched in sun. He cast an eye up at the sky and the rigging, then forward, observing the activity in the fo'c'sle and on the main; then he turned to appraise the stern. Inside the plant frame a crewman — Menzies's assistant — manoeuvred slowly with a watering can, nudging pots aside with his foot to make room to stand.

Van frowned. That blasted enclosure grew more crowded by the day. The surgeon's many specimens overflowed onto the quarterdeck and now even onto the main. Menzies seemed intent on exceeding the number of botanical curiosities collected by his idol Joseph Banks — and nary an edible carrot or potato among them.

Before we sail we must cull them, he thought. Menzies can make his sketches and take his notes, but he must wait to pot his ferns and fungi until our survey is done and we turn for home. Until then, I need room to work the ship.

He turned away from the frame, thought about the work waiting on his desk, and decided to linger. He strolled aft and leaned over the taffrail, looking out. *Discovery's* launch had already put off to recall the men ashore. He watched it pull smartly towards the landing — Midshipman Roberts at cox, he noted approvingly. An Indian canoe was approaching *Discovery* bearing the Spanish lad Francisco. Van snorted. Everyone seemed to know the boy's name — including him. He watched the canoe manoeuvre alongside — very sharply, he thought. The Indians were superb on the water. The young Spaniard scrambled up and onto the quarterdeck, where he greeted Midshipman Stuart, not with the formal salute protocol demanded, but with an "*Oye! Hombre!*" and a feint to his *cojones*.

Stuart knew his captain was on deck and certainly watching. He nodded coolly and accepted the envelope proffered by Francisco.

"Where is Yim Hawkes?"

"Not *here*," the midshipman replied — a creative rejoinder in the circumstances, as it constituted both fact and warning. He pointed shoreward. "The observatory."

Francisco nodded and was about to continue when he realized that *Discovery's* captain was observing him from the stern with a look of open amusement. He straightened, saluted smartly, turned about (murmuring "Later, *amigo*," to Stuart), and clambered over the side.

⧖

Van was not at all surprised to receive a letter from Quadra confirming their agreement of the previous evening. One for the record, he thought, pacing the great cabin while Dobson sat at his desk, translating. He mentally enumerated all that still needed to be done to effect their departure, calculating the time it would take. Broughton would shortly career *Chatham* again. We need to take on some of the stores from *Daedalus*, he thought. I'll leave the bulk for Broughton in case he has to winter over after all.

Yes, much to do. Come on, young man, he thought, staring at Dobson. Let's have it.

At last the midshipman looked up and handed him a single page. He read the transcription, glanced at Dobson, read it again.

Quadra wrote that he would return the original British territories, being Meares's property; but he would leave the Spanish settlement at Nootka, with its garrison, under Spanish flag.

"This is not 'leave it,' as in depart, but 'leave it,' as in 'leave it *here*'?"

"Yes, sir."

"Are you certain?" His look was a glare. Dobson returned it without expression.

"Quite certain, sir."

Van looked down at the letter. Well, he thought: gobsmacked again. The Spanish would not withdraw. They would not abandon their establishment at Friendly Cove. There would be no striking of the flag, no mutual salutes. Quadra had reneged on the terms he himself had proposed not twenty-four hours before.

He told Dobson to wait while he composed a reply.

> *I will not entertain the idea of hoisting the British flag on Meares's land, as my orders are to receive from you, on behalf of His Britannic Majesty, the whole of Nootka Sound as well as Clayoquot Sound.*

He paused, read what he'd written, and added a peevish observation that the Spanish commissioner's last two positions had differed materially from each other, and from that contained in his original letter delivered two weeks previously. What, he asked, is your specific intention?

# Chapter 23

Runners from *Discovery*'s launch set out to round up those not bedridden or on essential duty. And though Jim Hawkins *was* on essential duty at the observatory, a breathless crewman arrived to tell him he'd been reassigned, that he was to return to the ship and report to Lieutenant Baker after muster. With regret (it was a magnificent day, and he was ashore!), he turned over his tiny command to the marine corporal and made for the landing. Ramsay and Lincoln were already there. Other Discoveries — the quartermaster, a carpenter's crew, the cook and his mate (ashore brewing spruce beer for the coming voyage) — arrived and boarded. Just after they put off, Francisco Almeida came running along the beach, waving for them to stop. Ned Roberts was at cox and in a hurry; he waved him off. Hawkins waved too. Francisco stopped, cupped his hands, and called to them, though he could not be heard above the splash of oars. Hawkins grinned and held his own arms up in mock resignation.

They arrived aboard with minutes to spare. The hour sounded, and as the sixth bell faded the captain stepped onto the quarterdeck from below.

"Captain on deck."

Vancouver returned a salute. "Mister Mudge. Muster the men aft."

"Aye, sir."

The boatswain's mate piped hands aft, and *Discovery*'s ratings hurried to assemble between the foremast and the quarterdeck. A squad of marines formed up facing them; the remainder of their number lined the fo'c'sle, facing astern.

Vancouver, meanwhile, stood at the stern casually looking out at the harbour, the shore, the Spanish fort; he sniffed the air, noted the stream of the ensign, the flow of the tide.

When quiet fell he turned and strode to the rim of the quarterdeck. His lieutenants moved to flank him. The petty officers, master's mates, and midshipmen had already formed two ranks behind.

"Bosun, rig the grating," Vancouver said. "Master-at-Arms, bring up the prisoner."

"Sir."

Two men dragged a hatch cover to the gangway and secured it against the railing, while the master-at-arms and a mate brought the prisoner up from below. They stopped on the main in front of the marines, Reybold blinking at the light. Vancouver regarded him from above.

"George Reybold, you are found guilty of disorderly conduct. Do you have anything to say for yourself?"

Reybold met his eye, then averted his gaze. "You caught me red-handed, Captain. I got nothing to say."

"Strip, then. Master-at-Arms, seize him up."

Reybold removed his shirt, revealing a back that was heavily scarred. The master-at-arms tied his wrists to the grating. "Seized up, sir." The bosun stepped up next to him.

Vancouver removed his hat. The entire ship's complement did likewise. Vancouver handed his to Henry Orchard, who exchanged it for the Articles of War.

The captain looked out at the assembly for a moment. "Article Thirty-five," he read. "'All non-capital crimes committed by any person or persons in the fleet, which are not mentioned in this act, or for which no punishment is hereby directed to be inflicted, shall be punished by the laws and customs used at sea.'" He handed the Articles to Orchard, took his hat back, and replaced it on his head.

"Contraband goods and contraband trade will not be tolerated on this vessel. Bosun: twenty-four lashes. Do your duty."

And there it was. From a comprehensive listing of strictures and punishments for crimes like profanity, drunkenness, cowardice, the striking of a superior, desertion, buggery, spying, mutiny et cetera, he'd convicted Reybold under a catch-all known as the Captain's Cloak.

The marine drummer initiated an ominous roll.

The bosun moved in behind Reybold. He held the cat o' nine tails in his hand, weighing its handle to find its pivot point. He separated its tails with his fingers and took his stance.

A matador, playing to a crowd, would linger over this moment, teasing out the anticipation, the tension, yea, the adoration of his onlookers. Not a Royal Navy bosun. This was not a show but a demonstration. All business were the bosun and his whip, the brutish instruments of naval justice. He brought his arm back and swung with force.

The tentacles of the cat are too short to arc like a bullwhip. It is thus impossible to swing from rafters with it, to climb or rappel. The cat o' nine tails has no derring-do potential at all. It is, pure and simple, a malevolent stick, entirely utilitarian in nature.

With the impact, Reybold's head snapped back and he gave out an explosive grunt.

"One," called the master-at-arms over the roll of the drum.

There was little splay among the tails — they struck in a narrow band. The blow cut through the skin of Reybold's back. Flecks of flesh spattered away and left an open welt. For a moment, it shone white, as if incensed by the blow. Then blood oozed up and over its edges.

Among the onlookers, the sound of that first stroke caused stomachs to clench. Bodies swayed, a few knees nearly buckled.

The bosun swung again. This time spatters of blood mingled with specks of airborne flesh. The blow again knocked the breath out of Reybold. He emitted a guttural bark.

"Two," called the master-at-arms.

The captain and his lieutenants stood motionless, backed by the ship's officers and young gentlemen. Many observed with detachment, inured, resigned, or glad it wasn't them. Some felt distress. A few felt oddly energized. Others tried to rationalize the proceedings.

⧖

George Vancouver, for one, by all appearances stolid and unperturbed, is thinking: This is not futile. *It is not.* It serves a purpose. A man like this must be reined in. The harm he could do, the havoc, were he unleashed. This is not futile. *It is not.*

He has seen for himself the havoc wrought by madness. Witnessed it. Lived it. He knows its power all too well. It is contagious. No one is completely immune.

The drum continues its enervating roll. Two more lashes strike and are duly counted off.

Joseph Baker's eyes are on the scene before him, but he has checked out. Gone elsewhere. It is a mental trick he employs. He does not like the dreams these punishments beget. His friend Peter Puget, by contrast, is analytic. He tries to recall the number of floggings Reybold has absorbed since joining the crew. Four, he reckons, and that in barely a year. He'd signed on in Cape Town as a replacement for a man gone ill. Puget wonders now what he was running from, the circumstances that motivated him to sign on to an outbound voyage of at least three years. Whatever it was, it had not constrained him in the least; he'd been a troublemaker from the start. By God, though, thinks Puget, he takes his licks like a man.

Mudge is twenty-two, the youngest in that front row, though already a veteran of twelve years' service. He has witnessed many floggings, and what he feels as he watches this one is what he always feels. Regret for the pain inflicted, acceptance of its necessity. Order must be maintained or there is no order.

Zach Mudge will live another sixty years. He will serve with courage and distinction through the Napoleonic Wars, yet he will be remembered best for his foreshortened service on this expedition.

In the rows behind that front rank, uneasy shifting mingles with stoic detachment. Henry Orchard sways a little, the gunner looks on indifferently, the carpenter seems entirely unaffected, and the master fidgets and glances up at the sky, thinking he has too much to do to stand around at muster. Archibald Menzies observes with a clinical eye. Midshipman Stuart's expression is blank, though his brow is furrowed. Ramsay stands stock-still. Hawkins breathes deeply and consciously. Ned Roberts has fixed his gaze on the fo'c'sle, far forward and above the cat's trajectory. He focuses on the continuing drum roll, mentally overlays it with fife and brass, and roars along in his imagination to the tune thus created.

*Come, cheer up, my lads, 'tis to glory we steer,*
*To add something more to this wonderful year.*

"Eight."
*Heart of Oak are our ships,*
*Jolly Tars are our men.*
"Nine."
*We always are ready: Steady, boys, steady!*
*We'll fight and we'll conquer again and again.*
"Ten," goes the tally man.

The cat continues its cutting work. At sweet sixteen, the boatswain runs its tails through his fingers to separate them; they have joined into a single wet cord. The pause would have thrown off gentle Ned's timing, were he listening.

Notable among the rest, Lincoln watches the proceedings through narrowed eyes. Dorsey is smiling to himself and sporting a semi. Pitt stands stiffly, his face blank, eyes following the motion of the whip. He's been scratched by the cat himself.

⧗

The matter of his own punishments is not spoken of by his peers, at least within his earshot, what with his thin skin and quickness to defend his all-important Honour. He has been flogged twice, though on neither occasion was it with the cat o' nine tails. He had his from a boy's cat, a kitten compared to the tom clawing Reybold's dorsum. It has five tails, none of them knotted, and is reserved for the correction of young gentlemen.

His first flogging was delivered in Tahiti, where he was caught bartering for a young girl's affections with an item pilfered from the ship's supplies. Several quietly came to his defence. Menzies called it a youthful indiscretion. Broughton counselled a stern talking-to. Whidbey said the boy was high-spirited and had surely learned his lesson; besides which, the item he'd appropriated was just a small hook, a trifle, broken at that.

Vancouver was unmoved. The punishment was twenty-four lashes on Pitt's bare arse, administered in the relative privacy of the great cabin. The young gentlemen were assembled to watch. Mudge presided. After twelve strokes, he called on the bosun to stop, and offered Pitt parole if he promised to improve his behaviour. The boy choked out a refusal and took his remaining twelve.

Why, you ask, *why*? I, you, we would take the deal. This boy wouldn't. What made him tick? Was he destined for greatness? Round off the arrogance, wear away the pride, perhaps you've got a notable character — a Washington, a Churchill. I cannot tell a lie; we shall fight them on the beaches.

The second punishment was during the summer just past. The ship was at anchor while boats were away on survey missions. Pitt was roughhousing on the quarterdeck with another of the left-behind midshipmen. They stumbled into the binnacle that housed the ship's compass, breaking its glass cover. Not a small thing — the ship relied on its compass. My fault entirely, said Pitt, exonerating his opponent, Lincoln (though it takes two to tango). Once again, interveners found excuses: youthful rambunctiousness, an accident, and the compass itself wasn't damaged. And wasn't there something noble in taking the fall? Vancouver, though, could not tolerate a scuffle on his quarterdeck. What's more, he was fed up with this infuriatingly irresponsible boy and his serial derelictions of duty. Pitt had been found asleep on watch at sea. And he had let *Discovery*'s best chronometer stop. The duty of winding them rotated among the midshipmen — he had forgotten when it was his turn. The broken binnacle was the last straw. Pitt was red-arsed again before his peers.

So what is the Honourable Thomas Pitt, heir to a powerful peer of the realm, thinking as he watches Reybold's flogging? He is thinking how much he hates George Vancouver, and how in the end he will have his revenge.

⧗

After twenty-one lashes Reybold fainted. The last three strokes were delivered to his unconscious body. At the call of the twenty-fourth, the drum roll abruptly ceased. Silence fell on ship and crew.

"Dismiss the people, Mister Mudge. Mister Baker, Mister Whidbey, a word in my cabin."

Hawkins had been ordered to report to Baker. He waited topside for the lieutenant's return, standing with Ramsay and Lincoln, who were returning to the hospital, and Pitt, who would take his place at the observatory. They watched as Reybold's limp body was carried to sickbay, where Menzies would attend to his wounds.

No one spoke until a muffled scream came from below. Menzies had cleansed his patient's wounds with salt.

"Lazarus is risen," Lincoln said softly.

From the masthead above, I observed how he and his mates were reacting to what they had just witnessed. Lincoln himself looked feverish, Ramsay pale — they'd both been sick, of course. Pitt's mien was cold, as it had been all through muster. And the expression on Hawkins's face, framed by his fiery red hair, was troubled. His eyes looked soulful and pained.

They also looked decidedly scrumptious, but I was only thinking ahead. I leaped off, beat hard, caught a thermal, and soared higher, then dropped my head, folded inward, and dived, re-extended, pulled out, and veered away on the wind, delighted and content.

You won't have to wait long now.

# Chapter 24

That night, the dream again. The jungle buzz and hum, the peril invisible, oppressive like tropical heat. Pangas, spears, and rocks. The struggle in the frothing water, the crushing impact of the club.

He woke with pounding heart, passed quickly into the great cabin, leaned out the stern windows.

I cannot lose control, he thought. I cannot allow it. There is too much at stake. Too much to lose.

He thought about the day he teetered on the edge. It was the closest he ever came, his moment of lunacy. Since then, he'd wondered what had driven him there; the answer, he'd decided, lay within that cursed dream. Not the struggle in the water, which was horrible enough, but the events behind it, the hubris to which the great James Cook had succumbed.

It was quietly acknowledged that Cook had a *passionate* disposition. When something angered him he raged and stomped and shouted. His people made a joke of it, comparing his outbursts to the frenetic heivas performed by the Polynesians. Yet he always reined himself in and stopped short of the point of no return — though perhaps it was not a point at all but a slope, a slippery one, for on his last voyage his rages grew worse. They were frequent and no longer directed at those he commanded. Now others bore his wrath.

Cook's ships had spent many months among the scattered islands of Polynesia, and many aboard them (Young Van included) had become fluent in the language. They knew that the islanders had a utilitarian perspective on property: they took what they wanted and what they could use. It was theft, of course, but it was not a lethal, cutthroat form of thievery. There was an innocent daring to it, a bold effrontery. It was sport, and Cook learned how to referee it; he used the social hierarchy that existed on every island, persuading kings and chiefs to control their people's proclivities in return for opportunities to trade. These were more attractive and sustainable than any short-term benefit from theft.

This did not stop the thievery entirely. Metal was new to Polynesia, and the theft of axes, nails, spikes, and hooks was common. The losses were petty individually yet cumulatively costly, and on the great navigator's final voyage they seemed to rankle him more than previously. Cook pleaded with the chiefs, then he hectored them — and still the thefts continued. His anger simmered and finally erupted; he danced his heivas publicly and his actions grew more severe. He ordered twelve lashes for a captured thief. The next got twenty-four. The penalty escalated until it reached seventy-two. Then he ordered a thief beaten. The three sailors restraining the man exchanged looks. They had never been given an order like that before; never been afforded such licence — free-form beatings weren't prescribed in the Articles of War. They shrugged and got to work. The next thief they brought before Cook received a beating *and* had his ears cut off. The latter appalled Cook's officers, but he was Cook the wise, the omnipotent. He had never led them wrong.

And then a goat was stolen.

His ships had brought livestock — cattle, horses, sheep, and goats — as gifts for the native potentates. There was self-interest in this. The Admiralty wanted to establish a local food source for future mariners. The goat was merely taken before it could be given.

There was no restraining Cook. He raged. He stomped. He shouted at the local chiefs, demanding the goat be returned. It was not.

Assemble the men on shore, he commanded.

He led a column of marines and seamen into the interior in search of the wretched goat. It devolved into a vengeful mob. The men, given franchise, freed of civilized restraints, went berserk. They rampaged, torched a village; destroyed houses, food supplies, canoes. A primitive bloodlust long restrained by discipline took them beyond their officers' control. They looted and pillaged, slaughtered dogs and livestock. Men and women too.

In the aftermath Cook seemed to return to his rational self. Those who had witnessed the incident, or participated in it, alluded to it vaguely if at all. They wanted to believe again in James Cook, the Enlightenment Personified; and yet it was clear now to everyone that there was something wrong. He was not the wise and measured, just and lenient, infallible leader he had been on previous voyages.

The voyage continued. They sailed from Tahiti to the Sandwiches, to the northwest coast and back to the Sandwiches, where Cook danced his final heiva.

Young Van saw the change in his mentor, witnessed his madness for himself, and kept his mouth shut like everyone else. Over the years he puzzled over what he'd witnessed. Eventually, he came to believe he understood where Cook had gone wrong.

And still, just eight months before, he had come achingly close to replicating Cook's mad rampage.

His ships were provisioning in Tahiti for the voyage across the Pacific. The Tahitians behaved true to precedent. Something was stolen every day, and Van, with his fluency, calmly scolded the culprits in their own language. When that failed to stop the thievery, he appealed to their chiefs. The incidents continued. And escalated. Every day, some item essential to the expedition disappeared, and he was forced to set aside a chart or manifest to try to get it back. He had never been a patient man, and the amount of time he spent on this exasperated him. He ordered a man caught red-handed with a bag of purloined nails flogged as an example. It had no effect. The thefts continued. It seemed his ships were being slowly scuttled by a thousand nicks, stripped to their timbers one nail at a time.

A small sea telescope went missing from the observatory. He demanded its return. The chiefs looked at him blankly, as though they didn't know what he was talking about. It nettled him, and he hectored them — to no avail.

Next it was an axe. No longer calm, he shouted and shook his fist and told a chief, *Return it and return that telescope or I will burn your house down.* Neither the axe nor the telescope was returned. He did not burn the chief's house down.

The last straw was a bag of his officers' laundry — cloth being in great demand locally. It was no small loss, what with them embarked on a three-year voyage that would take them nowhere near a tailor.

The petty thievery, the telescope, the axe. Now this. He had reached his limit. He grabbed the Tahitian washman, shook and throttled him, and raged, *I'll hang you myself if that bag isn't returned.* The locals exchanged glances, a headman raised an objection — and Van lost it completely. A tirade, a tantrum, a mad heiva — it wasn't pretty however you described it. *Return those goddamned shirts*, he bellowed, *or I will lead my men ashore and destroy your village.*

The natives disappeared into the hills.

Eyes flicking between faces, the men witnessed it all.

No one dared tell him he had gone too far. They didn't have to. The next day he sent messages to the chiefs, delivered gifts to entice them back, patched things up, made peace.

The laundry was never seen again.

He was humiliated by the spectacle he had made of himself, his loss of *control*. More than that, he was deeply confused. What was happening to him? What was he becoming? He had nearly followed in the bloody footsteps — nay, fallen into the same abyss — as his mentor Cook.

Was it his fate to fail and fall, as Cook had failed and fallen?

He knew that his own people compared him to Cook and found him wanting. He suspected the world at large would forever compare him to Cook and find him wanting. That thought brought him as close to despair as he allowed himself to go.

He consoled himself with defiance and resolution. Damn the blows from wherever they might come — panga or poison pen, he cared not. Damn the sneers and damn their judgment. He would do his duty and that was that.

He glanced into the blackness of the Sound. There was no light yet on the eastern horizon. He might yet sleep. He turned away and padded softly to his berth.

⧗

Next morning he sat half-listening to Mudge. There was still much to do to prepare for departure, but Mudge was competent — all his people were competent. Everything would get done.

And so he let Mudge talk while he thought about his solution to the longitude problem. It would serve.

Mudge rendered his report with the usual efficiency. The state of the ship: unchanged from the day prior...As for people: Reybold, returned to duty. Two of the hospital cases had returned to the ship, including Midshipman Ramsay. Two other men had been sent ashore by Menzies for bed rest (a digestive disturbance was going around). As for the two men convalescing on board, one had returned to duty, and the other likely would in a day. Midshipman Pitt had taken ill — probably fish he'd eaten ashore. He had been sent to rest at the hospital. Dorsey had taken his place at the observatory. Lincoln was still abed, having taken a turn for the worse. Doctor Menzies had reported the usual number of venereal ailments. Also, as the weather was dry and below-decks had been fumigated recently, he had suggested they not be smoked this day. If the captain felt otherwise, the surgeon requested permission to move the one man convalescing in his hammock ashore to avoid the smoke. Mudge stopped for a response.

Van was thinking about the diplomatic matter, ruing the probability — no, the certainty — that whatever he decided here would be criticized in London months from now. He realized his first lieutenant was waiting. There was a short silence while he replayed Mudge's last words.

"Yes, all right, make it so. Have the decks smoked and send the fellow ashore."

Next, Mudge spoke about the chart work. Vancouver listened closely to this. There had been progress since the day before. The backlog was gone. They were ready to begin drawing the charts from the summer survey.

"Well done, Zach. Pass it on to those involved. Now we must get on with doing just that. Here's what we're going to do."

Because they could not be certain about the true longitude of any place in the northwest, Van had decided to use the meridian of Friendly Cove as their charts' Prime Meridian. If it was wrong relative to Greenwich (he was sure it was) they could correct for it later. In the meantime, all their plots would have the virtue of consistency. Local errors relative to Friendly Cove would be small.

Mudge saw the elegance of it immediately. "That will save a lot of time, sir. I'll mobilize the midshipmen."

"Baker will need the best draftsmen to work on the originals. That's Roberts, Hawkins, Ramsay. Pick the best of the rest to round that to four. Put all the others to work copying what they produce. Whatever Baker needs, give it him. First priority in copying is to fill our own needs. Dispatches to the Admiralty and copies for every ship. Copies for the Spaniards —" His brow furrowed. He reached for a letter and dropped it in front of his first lieutenant. It was Dobson's translation of Quadra's latest. He waited as Mudge skimmed it. "Copies for the Spaniards are the lowest priority. When we *do* get to them, after we have our own well started, I want…time expended on the task. *Time*, Mister Mudge. Is that clear?"

Mudge met Vancouver's eye. "I understand, sir. Perfectly."

"Their quality is also not our top priority."

Mudge allowed himself the hint of a smile. "I have just the mapmakers for the task, sir." He continued with his report, and as he did Vancouver's thoughts returned to the diplomatic situation. He wondered if the clarification he'd requested from Quadra would contain another twist. The man's diplomacy was nothing if not fluid.

If the Spaniard's position remained as outlined in his last letter, Van's course of action was clear. They would do everything in their power to repair *Chatham*'s keel and keep the tiny fleet together. Together the ships would explore the coast south to California, reconnoitre the Spanish settlements there, then proceed to Hawaii, where they would refit, provision, and finish charting the archipelago. In the spring they would return to the northwest to complete the survey, the men refreshed by a season of tropical warmth.

Vancouver and Mudge emerged on deck just as an Indian canoe bearing Ensign Ortiz drew alongside. Vancouver wondered where Francisco was. He'd gotten used to seeing him bearing Quadra's letters. He smiled to himself. He was a rascal, that one, a *ne plus ultra* spirit. Reminds me of Richard Hergest at that age.

You mean, reminds you of you, Van, said Richard Hergest's voice.

Vancouver snorted at the idea. *I was never that young.*

He recalled an incident from their shared youth, on Cook's second voyage — their first. The expedition had ventured farther south than any before it, probing the unknown waters of the polar region in search of the apocryphal southern continent. Finally, faced with an impenetrable ice pack, the ship at risk of being crushed, and his crew miserable with cold, Cook declared an end to the quest and ordered the ship to come about. As it wheeled away from the pole, Young Van raced forward across the main, climbed onto the foc's'le and out onto the bowsprit. There, drenched by freezing spray, he waved his hat and bellowed into an Antarctic gale, "*Ne plus ultra! Ne plus ultra!*" It was a spirited stunt on the boy's part (and a triumph for the expedition's astronomer, who had tutored him in Latin). Aft on the quarterdeck, even the taciturn Cook smiled.

*Aye, you were young, and an arse kisser from the very start,* cajoled Hergest's voice.

Mudge glanced at the captain and was surprised to see a grin on his face.

Ortiz scrambled aboard, exchanged formalities with the officer of the watch (Puget, shadowed by Dobson that morning), and handed him a letter.

*My reply,* Vancouver thought. *And, he hoped, Quadra's final position.*

"Gentlemen," he said, joining them. He acknowledged the Spaniard's salute with a nod and a finger to his brow. Puget offered him the letter. "Let's place it straight into the relevant hand, Mister Puget. Mister Dobson, kindly see to its translation straight away. I expect Mister Puget can spare you from the watch."

"I believe I can, sir," Puget said.

"Thank you. Mister Dobson, report as soon as you're done. And good day to you, young sir," he said to Ortiz. He strolled aft towards the taffrail, hands clasped placidly behind his back.

*And so we arrive back where we began, on a nearby shore, with a sundered body lying at our feet.*

# Chapter 25

Alberni's face was ashen, Quadra's set in anger. Though the corpse's head was at an unnatural angle to its torso and nearly severed, the face was recognizable. It was that of Francisco Almeida.

"Jesus on a Christly crutch," Alberni said.

Quadra turned and met his eye. He flicked a glance in the direction of the nearby seamen, then turned back to Alberni.

Alberni nodded. Quadra climbed down to where the two soldiers stood over their grisly find. As he reached their level he met one man's gaze and grasped him briefly by the elbow, as if in his descent he had lost his balance. The other soldier would not look at him, and Quadra gripped his shoulder before descending to the body, disturbing the feeding flies. He waved them away and knelt, thinking to close the corpse's strangely gaping eyes, and realized they were gone.

Quadra straightened and held a hand across his nose. Close to the body the stench was overpowering. Alberni stepped down to stand with him.

The corpse was clad in a tattered white shirt, through which blood had seeped from punctures to the chest and stomach and cuts on the arms. Francisco's blue tunic might once have covered him, but it looked to have been tossed aside; the body bore the marks of feeding by some large-jawed carnivore. Broken branches lay strewn around it. Quadra saw that it would have been quite hidden where it lay. It was the white of the shirt, and the disturbance by the beast, that had made it visible from *Discovery*. He looked out to confirm the sightline from the harbour.

"Son of a bitch."

Alberni's face was contorted. Quadra followed his gaze. The body's lower legs were covered in blood. The calves had been cut out. Removed. Alberni cursed again, this time in a string of creative blasphemies. Quadra ignored him and examined the cuts. The youth's manhood was intact; there had been no mutilation there. He glanced around, saw the rocks below, the sea lapping gently at the shore, the ships at anchor in the cove. There was a stone ledge above where the body lay. He climbed onto it. Alberni followed.

There were dark blood splotches on the patchy grass, in the middle of which lay a piece of crumpled cloth, stained rusty, stiff with blood. Alberni knelt to it. Quadra continued to the edge of the little clearing, where a vague pathway led off into dense bush. He stooped to pick up an object.

It was a knife. Its smeared blade glinted in the sun as he turned it over. He met Alberni's eye.

"Cover him," he called down to the Catalonians. He turned back to Alberni. "I'm returning to the *presidio*. You stay here and search the woods and around the rocks. I'll send the boat back for you right away. Bring his body when you come, and as soon as you land, summon Maquinna. I want him here as soon as possible."

※

The scent of neither wood smoke nor cedar plank assuaged the memory of that stench. Quadra stepped out onto the balcony. Caamaño and Moziño exchanged looks and followed.

He wanted the wind on his face, but the cove at noon was still. The harbour's normal working bustle was absent. There were just two boats under way, both drawing towards the *establecimiento*: one bore Pedro Alberni from the north shore; the other was a launch, its wake trailing like a pennant towards *Discovery*.

Word had spread that something had happened, though no one knew just what; a crowd had gathered to meet Alberni's boat. He landed and pushed through it, spotted a native headman, and drew him aside to speak. The man immediately hurried away, and Alberni began issuing orders. A soldier ran towards the guardhouse, another along the beach. Alberni began the climb towards the *presidio*. A clamour rose behind him, as crewmen in the boat called to those on shore. The boat's coxswain bawled for silence, but the clamour grew. On shore, Spanish sailors chased and surrounded the native headman, jostling him. Alberni turned, saw, and barked a command. It was ignored. The jostling spread. He bellowed angrily and it stopped. The natives backed towards their canoes. They put off from shore just as more soldiers clattered out of the guardhouse.

Alberni raised a hand to halt them. He watched the Indians depart, then turned and deployed his men along the ridge and around the *establecimiento*.

Quadra turned to Moziño, said "I want you to examine the body immediately," and stepped inside.

Alberni entered the guardhouse below, calling orders as he went. More soldiers clattered out with muskets and swords. Footsteps on the stairs and across the great hall. Alberni burst into the room.

"They've gone. Every one of them. By canoe, or filtered away into the woods."

"Because they know they'll pay for this," Caamaño said.

"Before we go that far," Moziño said, "something here doesn't make sense. Francisco was supposed to travel for supplies yesterday but —" he pointed in the direction of the north shore "— he obviously never left. While he lay dead over there, they remained here and went about their business as normal. As though they knew nothing about it. Now, today, they seem as surprised as we are."

"That's what I thought," Alberni said. "It could be others. Another tribe. Maquinna has enemies and they've plotted against us before. There's something odd about this too. It doesn't look like an act of war. When they make war they take heads as trophies. Francisco's was nearly severed but it wasn't taken."

"Perhaps the killer was interrupted," Caamaño said.

"We should consider every possibility. Don Juan, that's why I left the body over there. I thought Doctor Moziño should examine it where it lies. Maybe his knowledge can help. Then there is the matter of his...of the legs. The flesh was taken."

"We've all heard the stories," Caamaño said.

"And no one ever found any evidence. Believe me, when the priests were here, they looked."

"All we know for certain is that Francisco is dead," Quadra said, "and

I want to make one thing absolutely clear. There will be no retaliation against the Indians, no action at all, until we know what happened and who did this. Justice must be seen to prevail here. I have promised them justice in all my actions, and we will deliver on that promise. Everything we've worked for and accomplished here will be lost if we don't."

"It might not even be the Indians."

All eyes turned to Alberni.

"Carlos Libertad went absent the night *before* Francisco was supposed to leave. And he was with him that whole day."

The previous day, the seaman everyone knew as Black Carlos had been flogged after a short desertion. He was confined now aboard *Activa*.

"Have him brought ashore. I'll question him."

The officers lapsed into silence.

"You were right to leave the body, Pedro. Doctor Moziño, take the boat and examine the site. Then bring the body back here. Make your best determination of when he died."

Moziño glanced out across the balcony. The Spanish boat was still on the beach, waiting. The British boat had landed nearby.

"He wore a medallion on a chain around his neck. Our Lady of El Cobre. I didn't see it on his body. Look for it there on the ground." Quadra moved to the table where he had left the knife and bloodied cloth. "What do you make of these?"

Moziño straightened the crumpled cloth.

"A handkerchief," Caamaño observed.

They examined it closely. Plain white, linen, square.

Alberni picked up the knife. "A good steel blade." He held it closer to his eyes. "Not forged locally. It's a common enough trade good. There are hundreds like it in the area. It could've been sold by any trader."

"But why did the killer leave it?" Caamaño asked. "Take his calves and leave the knife?"

"Madness," Alberni said.

"And the cloth. It was used by the killer to clean up and wipe his hands," Moziño said, "yet he didn't bother with the knife."

Quadra stared at the items. "Examine them, and examine the body. Let me know what you learn. That is all, gentlemen."

Moziño had just packed the items away in his bag when Felix Cepeda entered. "Don Juan," the clerk said, "there is an English officer below."

Quadra nodded. Moments later Midshipman Pitt entered. Seeing Moziño present, he addressed Quadra in French.

"Captain Vancouver's compliments. I beg leave to deliver this."

Quadra accepted an envelope from him and said, "Please convey my compliments to your captain, Mister Pitt. Good day."

Quadra was still holding the envelope unopened as Moziño moved to follow the midshipman out.

"Doctor," he said in Spanish, "one other thing."

Moziño turned. So did Pitt — who suddenly realized that Quadra's dismissal had been in French.

"Ask Doctor Menzies if he will assist with your examination. He is most resourceful and inquisitive. Perhaps Mister Pitt can convey the message."

He listened to the sounds of their descent, their short discussion in French as they separated. For a moment he stared out at the ships in the anchorage and the distant mountains.

"What happened, Francisco?" he asked softly. "Why are you dead?"

He returned to his desk and cracked the seal on his counterpart's message.

> *I must request your categorical and definitive answer. Will you restore to me for His Britannic Majesty the territories in question, of which British subjects were dispossessed in 1789? These territories are Nootka and Clayoquot, in toto, and by treaty they are to be restored without any reservation whatsoever.*
>
> *Unless our negotiation is brought to a conclusion on the terms indicated in this and my former letters, I must positively decline any further correspondence on this matter and refer it to my government for direct resolution with yours.*

Quadra sighed. Not today, he thought. Not today.

# Chapter 26

When Carlos Libertad returned from a short desertion, he was hauled before his captain, *Activa*'s Lieutenant Menendez, to answer for it.

He looked like death warmed over. His arms and face were scratched; a cut had not yet scabbed over on his temple. His eyes were red and swollen, his dark skin greenish, save for the thick scar that ran down his cheek.

He answered questions evasively, but Menendez was not fooled. Black Carlos had been on a binge, an out-of-control, knee-crawling bender.

Where did you get it? Menendez demanded.

Carlos pled ignorance, denied he'd been drinking, claimed he had the flux. This was laughably untrue. Menendez ordered him flogged for the desertion and added a few lashes for his blatant lies. He was aware it would be no deterrent. The big man's back was heavily scarred from previous punishments.

⧗

That had been the day before, when Francisco's fate was yet unknown. Now Carlos Libertad was brought ashore and marched to stand before Quadra at the Big House.

The commandant left him standing. He sat like a magistrate behind a long table, between Caamaño and Alberni. At one edge sat Felix Cepeda, ready to record the interrogation; at the other, *Activa*'s Menendez. A soldier stood on either side of Carlos.

Moziño entered, huddled briefly with the officers at the table, and took a chair against the wall. Quadra nodded to Caamaño to begin.

"Seaman Libertad. Ensign Francisco Almeida was last seen alive on Thursday. Doctor Moziño and the English Doctor Menzies believe he died that night — the night you deserted." He let the insinuation settle. "We want to know where you were and what happened. No more deceptions. This time we want the truth from you. Tell us what you know or face the consequences."

"Your Excellency," Carlos said, addressing Quadra. His voice was hoarse. "I swear I didn't know yesterday that Francisco was dead. Today I will tell you everything."

"From the beginning," Caamaño said. "You were with him that night." Carlos swallowed hard.

"It's true, Don Jacinto. I was with him. I hauled supplies for him that afternoon. We finished late. Then, after, we talked. Francisco had no airs — we spoke as man to man." His eyes dropped as he remembered he was not before his equals. "He was leaving for Marvinas at first light, on Your Excellency's orders," he looked directly at Quadra, "but he let slip that he'd arranged to meet a girl that night. When he left to meet her, I tagged along because..." He looked down at the table. "I thought there'd be one for me."

"Why did you think that?" Alberni asked.

"Francisco had arranged to meet one of Maquinna's men outside the *establecimiento* —"

"Which one of Maquinna's men?"

"It was Copaza, the one who arranges supplies for us. He was bringing the girls. Francisco said girls. That's what I heard. That's why I insisted on coming along. He tried to talk me out of it. He said, 'Carlos, I don't think there'll be a girl for you,' but I wouldn't take no. I told him I was coming. On the way, we stopped at the traders' camp."

"Why?"

Carlos looked at his feet. "Some of them stay ashore at night." He glanced up quickly, then down again. "They sell rum."

"Which trader? Who sold rum?" It was Quadra, for the first time.

"It was the *yanquis*, Excellency. Captain Magee and his crew. Francisco wanted to buy some from them, but Magee said, 'I've given up the trade.

THE WIND FROM ALL DIRECTIONS | 217

Señor Quadra frowns on it.' Francisco was annoyed. He knew they were selling — just not to him."

Carlos waited. Quadra did not react.

"Your Excellency, everyone knows he works for you. Francisco argued, but Magee wouldn't budge. We left them and walked down towards the water, where someone called to us, quiet-like, from up on the rocks. He jumped down, and I saw it was Copaza. And while they spoke together in Indian, I looked back towards the *yanquis*. They had a fire, and I could see they were getting lots of visitors — the rum was selling well that night. Then Francisco turned to me and said, 'There's only two girls.' I told him I only needed one."

Carlos's eyes revisited the scene in the space above Quadra's head.

"Francisco said, 'There's someone else. I'm to meet him here, and he's waiting.' He gestured out into the dark, and I looked — and there was someone there, just a shadow against the cove, yet I saw him.

"'So what?' I said. I didn't understand what he was saying. 'You've got your sweetheart. But there's two girls. I'll take my turn with the other.'

"Francisco took my arm and said, 'This fellow who's waiting...' He leaned closer and said, real quiet, 'He is a gentleman.'"

Alberni and Caamaño exchanged glances. Quadra did not react.

"Francisco says, 'Look, Carlos. It's a special rendezvous I arranged. There are just two girls. You weren't expected. This gentleman was.' He gestured again into the dark and lowered his voice even more. 'There will be other times, but tonight there's no chance. Go and drink some of Magee's rum.' He pointed towards the *yanquis*. It made me angry — very angry. I know...I *knew* Francisco well. He always treated me decently, but here he was treating me like I was...like I was less than a man." His expression hardened.

"I argued with him. I was angry, I admit that, but we didn't fight. I never laid a finger on him, and I never would. He was calm, and he wheedled away at me, wearing me down till I gave in. 'Go. Drink some rum,' he told me once more. He knew me too well. Rum is my true mistress. But was there any rum to be had? 'Magee won't sell to me,' I said. 'He saw me with you.'

"'I know, I know,' Francisco said with that big grin of his. 'I sent Copaza. Magee doesn't know he's with us.' He pointed — and I saw

Copaza profiled against the *yanquis* fire. He was already coming back towards us, and he had a sack. When he reached us he handed it to Francisco, who reached inside and took out a bottle. 'One for me,' he said. He handed me the sack and clapped me on the back. 'One for each of you.'

"I've got nothing against an Indian if he's got nothing against me. And we had a bottle each. So I left Francisco and we went off, Copaza and me, into the forest.

"That was the last I saw of him, Your Excellency — I swear. Copaza led the way and I followed, and at the edge of the woods I looked back. I saw Francisco walk into the dark, towards the shadow. That gentleman. I saw movement, a profile against the cove. There was no moon, but there were stars, and there were lights on the ships in the harbour. Light enough to outline him, nothing more. I wasn't truly sure he was there till that moment."

"Who was it?" Quadra asked.

"Your Excellency, I don't know. I couldn't see. He stayed out of sight while I was with Francisco, and I couldn't see him from the woods. I only know that Francisco was expecting him — and he was there."

Caamaño broke the brief silence that followed. "Don't play games, Libertad. You know who it was, this 'shadow.' We'll beat it out of you if we have to. So tell us. Who was it?"

"Don Jacinto." Carlos looked from him to Quadra. "Your Excellency. I swear I don't know. I only saw a shape. Yet I'm sure he was there."

"Continue," Quadra said. "What did you do then?"

"Copaza led me on a path through the forest to the far shore — the ocean shore. We found a place on the beach, and we sat and drank."

"You drank. That's it?"

"Yes, Your Excellency. You know the rest."

"No. We don't." Caamaño ran a hand around his throat.

Carlos blinked, swallowed. "Well, when we drank…Your Excellency, that rum…at first I forced it down, to get the warmth in my blood. That's what I wanted. But that rum…I'd drunk Magee's before. This was different."

"Different how?"

"It burned my throat. It was like lava in my stomach."

"Lava in your stomach. And what did you do?"

A moment's hesitation. "I kept drinking. I put it down. So did Copaza. It was foul, but it did the trick. Then, I don't know what happened, or why, but suddenly I was angry and —" he rubbed his knuckles absently, "— well, I punched him. He didn't do anything that I can remember; I just let him have it. He fought back, and I remember going down and hitting my head." He reached up to feel the scab on his forehead. "Some time passed, and we're drinking again, no hard feelings, nothing broken, and Copaza suddenly leans over and pukes it all up. More time passed, and I puked too, and my throat's like a blister. Everything's spinning and moving, and I can't tell up from down or the moon from my ruby red arse."

Carlos, lost in memory, suddenly remembered where he was. He fell silent.

"And Copaza?"

"I don't know. I lost him somewhere. Eventually, I was on my feet, stumbling along, everything reeling and lurching around me, and I fell. I couldn't stand, so I crawled on my hands and knees. Finally, I must have blacked out.

"When I came to I couldn't move. My head was pounding. There was blinding pain, yet numbness, too. I've never felt like that before. I must've passed out again, because the next thing I remember was the sound of birds. Dawn was breaking. I lay like a dead man, kept my eyes closed, and focused on that birdsong. It was proof I was alive. Then..."

He stopped and looked down at his feet. They had all seen his expression change.

"Speak up," Caamaño demanded.

Carlos closed his eyes. "I have a memory. I don't know if it's real."

"Oh, for fuck's sake," Alberni said. "Out with it, man."

But Carlos didn't out with it. For such a large man he looked oddly vulnerable.

"Tell us," Quadra said softly.

Carlos kept his eyes closed. "I had...a vision. A heavenly being touched my face. A beautiful being. The Virgin, I thought. Or an angel. Yes! This is what an angel looks like. Her eyes shone, as though she had wept for me through that long night, through all my suffering. She spoke, but I couldn't understand what she said. She propped my head up, wiped my face. She was gentle, and I reached for her, hoping to receive her blessing, to touch and taste her tears. She drew away, turned to a voice, and disappeared. I still couldn't move, yet I felt I'd been saved. Touched by an angel and saved."

Alberni and Caamaño exchanged glances. At last Carlos opened his eyes. "I must have lain there for hours. Eventually, I could sit up. Later, I could stand. My insides were on fire and cramping. I was dizzy and dead on my feet, but I knew I had to return here and face my punishment. And I did. Your Excellencies, I've told you the truth. I don't know what happened to Francisco, or where Copaza went, but I do know one thing for certain. That rum of Magee's — it was spiked."

⧖

Alberni and Caamaño probed, trying to trip Carlos up — and couldn't. His story stayed the same; yet there were many details he could not provide.

"Did you see the girls?"

Carlos hadn't.

"How did they arrive?"

Carlos didn't know.

"What happened to Copaza?"

Carlos couldn't say.

Alberni pressed him on that. "But you were with him. You hold your liquor. You must have seen him go."

"I don't remember when he left. Or if I left him."

"You fought."

"We did. We were both banged up. And then we continued drinking."

"But he couldn't hold it like you. How did he disappear into thin air when *you* couldn't move?"

"I swear I don't know what happened to him. We got separated. I don't know when."

"He went *somewhere*. Was it back to find Francisco?"

The suggestion seemed to surprise Carlos. He thought for a moment. "When we left Francisco, I was angry — and Copaza was too, now I think about it. It was the way he acted, the way he walked. After we drank, though, I don't think he could have made it back there, the way he was. And that wasn't where Francisco...where his body was found."

Quadra's mouth was pursed in concentration.

"This 'shadow' you say you saw," Caamaño said. "How big was he? What was he wearing?"

"Don Jacinto," Carlos said. "I couldn't see. There was just an outline against the harbour —"

"Francisco called him a 'gentleman.'"

"That's what he said."

Caamaño smacked the table. "You're a fucking liar, Libertad. Your story is bullshit. Apparitions. Angels. Shadows of gentlemen. *You* killed Francisco, *you* butchered him like a dog, and now you're spinning lies to save your neck. It's not going to work. You're going to swing for this." With an air of finality he sat back in his chair.

The officers let Carlos digest Caamaño's words. When he spoke at last, he addressed the commandant.

"Your Excellency, I am no saint. I've brawled and whored and gambled. I've deserted more than once. And I've killed men." He ran two fingers down his scarred cheek. "Twenty years in the king's service, I've killed many men. I did what I was told and what I had to do, but I've never murdered anyone, and *I did not kill Francisco*. God knows I don't want to die, but I would accept that as my penalty if I *had* killed him. I'd die knowing it was justice for the crime of killing an innocent."

He looked down at the floor for a moment, then met Quadra's eye again. "None of you see me as a Spaniard, but I've served Spain for twenty years. I was born into the hell of slavery, and on the day I became a freeman I took Freedom as my name — and swore I would never follow anything but my own free will. Free will matters more to me than life itself. So you must believe me when I swear on my freedom: I did not kill Francisco."

For a long moment the room held its breath.

"Was he wearing Cachita?"

Carlos looked confused. "Your Excellency?"

"That night, was Francisco wearing the medallion he always wore around his neck?"

Carlos's hand went to his own neck. "I don't remember seeing it that day, but I never knew him to take it off."

Quadra nodded. "You will remain on *Activa*. You will not come ashore again while we remain in this port." He looked to the soldiers flanking Carlos. "Take him away."

Black Carlos bowed low to Quadra and left between his guards.

"He didn't do it," Caamaño said when the door closed and they were alone. "There, if ever there was one, is a man telling the truth."

Quadra looked up from his thoughts.

"I want to talk to Magee," he told Felix Cepeda. "Tomorrow, here, first thing. Send him word. Tell him nothing else."

⌛

What of Copaza? Yes, spare a thought for him, for in the course of a single night he was poisoned, knocked about, and implicated in a brutal killing. The boy was debauched and dissolute. He had done many dishonourable things. But was he capable of murder most foul?

When I consider this question I am reminded of Yaftma, for Yaftma was also the flawed son of a powerful *tyee*. He was born bearing expectations, and as a boy he listened keenly to the legends of his people. He came to yearn for the day when he would ascend to the chieftainship, and legends would be made and told of him.

Yaftma grew into manhood; and though his father still lived and ruled as *tyee*, he was old and ailing and no longer up to the rigours of whaling. He declared it time for Yaftma to lead the hunt.

And so, that spring, Yaftma proudly rode in the bow of the lead canoe, and sixty canoes followed, the whalers singing and chanting the whole way to the whaling grounds.

They were not long there when they spotted a whale. It was a massive grey, and they tracked and approached it carefully, Yaftma's crew manoeuvring into the perfect position, close by the beast's tail as it readied for its dive. Yaftma stood in the bow and raised his harpoon, juggling its shaft in his hand to find its point of balance. He drew his arm back and looked down the harpoon's length, aiming. He was confident. He waited. The moment would come. He was ready.

THE WIND FROM ALL DIRECTIONS | 223

He flicked and released the harpoon. It was a true and practiced throw. He felt a surge of satisfaction, knowing it would strike true.

But the harpoon splashed into the water, narrowly missing its target.

The men of his canoe gasped, before catching their emotion.

Rather than diving, the whale remained on the surface. Moments before, it had seemed to be offering itself to them. Now it seemed to taunt Yaftma for his near miss. The whalers in the canoes trailing Yaftma's could have approached and harpooned it themselves, but it was his right and duty to spear it first. And he had missed.

Yaftma, a bit frantic, reached for another harpoon just as the whale dipped its head and rolled forward into the deep. Its tail stood free of the water for an instant before it disappeared, leaving the surface of the sea unbroken.

The hunters avoided Yaftma's eye. He hauled in his harpoon and directed his steersman to take them closer to shore. The other canoes followed at a respectful distance. An uncomfortable silence fell; no one thought to sing now. Yaftma stared to the fore and stewed over his failure.

Then he saw it. Black, beneath the water, ahead. Turn, he told the steersman, pointing. That way.

He felt excitement race through the crew, saw hope on their faces. His canoe sped to the spot and the others followed. A harpooner began to sing in one of the trailing canoes. It was a whaling song — an appeal to the whale to let itself to be taken. Others joined their voices with his.

There it was, beneath the surface. Yaftma stood in the bow for a better look. He saw it clearly now. He drew his harpoon back, ready to hurl or, better yet, to thrust it directly into the whale's thick flesh.

Black, submerged, just ahead. He plunged his harpoon into the water, right at the spot.

Nothing.

The other canoes drew up to see. Still no indication from the whale — no breaking of the surface, no indignant thrashing. The harpoon line did not play out. Yaftma's canoe was stationary, as were the others. All eyes were on the spot.

The harpoon bobbed to the surface.

A rock, said Yaftma's steersman, looking at the black spot in the water. It is a rock.

They returned to the village, and when they landed Yaftma left the canoe without uttering a word. He went to his lodge and disappeared inside.

Next morning, Yaftma's father looked in on him without warning and found him lying with his wife — something no whaler dared do before the hunt had ended.

The old man was furious. What is this? he demanded. This cannot be done. The old man paused and thought for a moment.

What *else* have you done?

Yaftma confessed that he had not achieved the purity demanded by tradition. He had not followed the rituals; he had broken faith with the ancestors and his people. He had speared a rock and was ashamed.

The old *tyee* blinked in disbelief. He was about to speak but checked his anger. He looked away at the distant horizon, where clouds pregnant with rain clung to a rolling, agitated sea. When he turned back to face his son, his expression was set.

You can lie there and wallow with your woman and be ashamed, he said. Or you can rise and do something about it. Do you have what it takes to do what is right? Or will you try to feed your people on the meat and blubber of a rock? Is that the story you want spoken of you in future times?

This was a question Copaza would also have to answer, for he had done his own share of wallowing and breaking faith. And the answer would be found in his own deeds, in the light or darkness of his soul.

# Chapter 27

Van had the dream again. The desperate struggle in the surf, the men falling and dying around him.

He awoke in a sweat, wondering if he had called out.

The ship was quiet. He knew all its sounds and could tell that it was near dawn. He would not sleep again. He dressed and climbed to the quarterdeck. Midshipman Hawkins, who was standing watch, saluted and moved out of his way. Vancouver acknowledged the salute absently. He was thinking about the dead young Spaniard.

Quadra and his officers had been his guests for dinner the previous night. It had been arranged days before, a gesture to reciprocate for the near-daily hospitality he and his own officers enjoyed at the Big House. When the news about Francisco reached *Discovery*, he had assumed the Spaniards would cancel, yet they came. They were a sombre bunch when they arrived, and Vancouver asked for a private word with his counterpart. While the others went below to the great cabin, the two of them (with the ever-present Dobson) remained on deck.

Van stumbled through an awkward *He was a lively lad* to get to *If there is any assistance I can provide.*

"Doctor Menzies has already been of great help to Doctor Moziño," he said. "I am grateful for it."

"He told me some of the, ah, details."

An awkward silence fell. Both men gazed out at the harbour.

"We have many times spoken about the situation here. If I may offer a word of counsel, it is to err on the side of forbearance."

As soon as he uttered the word he wondered if Dobson would translate it correctly. He waited while he did. Quadra's eyes remained on the spot on shore where Francisco had been discovered. "That is good advice, *Capitán*. I intend to follow it. I will not retaliate."

A moment later he turned to face Vancouver.

"But I will not rest until I find who did this. Then I will mete out Spanish justice — or else Spanish justice is worth nothing."

Now, as night began to fade, Van thought about how close *he* had come to justice-meting, months before in Tahiti. He tugged his frock coat closer. The sky was clear. The day would be fair; the chill would burn off early.

"Good weather for chart work, Mister Hawkins. We must set up extra tables so you can all work above deck today."

"Aye, sir. It looks like it'll be a nice day."

Hawkins's accent always reminded him of John Gore. Born an American before America existed, he had brought Cook's last expedition home. He had died at Greenwich just months before *Discovery*'s departure. Van had visited his bedside, and they had talked of Cook's final days — and the ugly period following his death. Gore had been the advocate of restraint. Bligh and others had demanded vengeance.

A gun sounded from the Spanish bastion.

"A ship, sir. I'll log it when she comes into sight."

"Very well. The glass, please, Jim."

"Sir."

Vancouver tucked it under his arm and strolled aft.

"Evans, eyes peeled on the harbour mouth," Hawkins told a watchman.

"Morning, Captain."

He turned. The surgeon, Menzies, stood inside his plant enclosure with a watering tin and a hand trowel.

"A bonny day, Captain. Shaping up, that is."

"Mister Menzies. You are up very early."

"Aye, I couldna sleep, and mah garden needed water. It's braw for the season, but dry." The Scot inclined his head and returned to his specimens.

Vancouver frowned, glanced up at the rigging and back at the enclosure. It was a hazard to his topmen. The area around the mizzen was crowded enough without this blasted hobby farm.

"There she is, sir," Hawkins said, approaching and pointing.

A ship warped slowly around the point. He extended the telescope to study her. She was a stubby brig with open decks — a snow.

"Portuguese colours," Menzies said. "From Macau, no doubt."

Vancouver turned and found Menzies beside him. He'd left his watering can and trowel inside the plant frame. Together they watched the brig's slow progress under tow by her own boat. She went to anchor in the roads on the far side of the cove. Francisco's body had been found on the shore just beyond the spot.

"Will Doctor Moziño need your help again today?"

"I dinnae think there's anything left for me or him tae do. We examined the corpse yesterday. Our conclusions were quite clear from that."

Menzies was standing close, and Hawkins seemed to be hovering unnecessarily near, undoubtedly listening. Anything to relieve the tedium of an anchor watch at night. Vancouver cleared his throat and moved a few paces away.

To his annoyance, Menzies followed. "I enjoyed the work, if that doesna sound macabre. I mean the collaboration with Doctor Moziño. He's a fine surgeon and a gifted scientist."

Van glanced at his own surgeon-scientist, then over his shoulder. Hawkins had moved forward to speak with a watchman. "Indeed."

"We've no' had a consultation in a wee while, Captain." Menzies's voice was now low and confidential. "Are ye feeling well?"

Vancouver extended the telescope and scanned the shore of the cove, the ships. The horizon. "Yes! Thank you, Mister Menzies. Very well. Braw, as you might say."

It was lighter now, easier to make out details. The boat that had pulled the Portuguese brig in had tied up alongside. A couple of men clambered into it and it set off for shore.

"And your cough?"

"Gone — completely cleared up. That concoction of yours did the trick. It tasted like tar but it didn't kill me outright, eh what?"

"What about your sleep?"

"Like that of a baby. I believe I had a case of indigestion. I am much improved."

They stood in silence, Vancouver apparently fascinated by what he could see in the telescope.

"From the Portugee just arrived," Menzies said, referring to the boat. "Off tae present their papers tae the dons."

Vancouver grunted.

"May I, Captain?"

Vancouver lowered the glass to throw him a look. Something in Menzies's expression changed his mind. He handed him the telescope.

While Menzies peered through it, Vancouver stifled a cough, thinking whatever the Scot was looking at, he was taking his time about it.

"What do you see, Mister Menzies?" he asked finally. "A new variety of seagull? An undocumented species of pelican or booby?"

Menzies lowered the glass to look at him. "Aye, a new species, Captain. Though one of more interest tae you than tae a disciple of Linnaeus. That's Robert Duffin in yonder boat. I crossed paths with him in China when I served on *Prince o' Wales*. He'd just returned then from voyaging with John Meares. In fact, he was here in Friendly Cove with Meares in '88 — and back the following year as Colnett's mate. I should think Duffin's the only Briton who was here in both years and knows the truth o' both. Yon Mister Duffin has a tale tae tell, if I'm no' mistaken. What with our stand-off with the Spaniards, Captain — I'd say that's Providence calling, in the form o' Mister Duffin."

⧗

An hour later the Spanish commandant stood in the doorway of his balcony watching the officers from the newly arrived *Fenis and St. Joseph* file away to the landing. Normally, he would have offered them coffee and let them talk to take their measure. He could read a man's face like a nautical chart. This morning, though, he had accepted the captain's papers with nominal scrutiny, shaken hands all round, and invited them to dinner.

Until then, gentlemen, you will excuse me. A pressing matter. Felix will see to your needs.

A succession of ships' bells sounded in the harbour. Below him, soldiers clattered out of the guardhouse. A hen foraging on the path fluttered out of their way, chicks chirping and scuttling after her. The soldiers, relief for the bastion, hurried for the landing where *Activa*'s launch awaited them. There were no Indians to ferry them now.

He watched the chicks, savouring their innocence, turned, and stepped inside. The table had been moved in front of the balcony. Caamaño and Alberni sat behind it, conversing on strategy. Quadra took the chair between them. A moment later Felix Cepeda came in, signalled the commandant, and took his chair at the end of the table.

They waited.

Gravel crunched on the path below. Voices in the guardhouse, footsteps on the stairs and across the great hall. Ensign Ortiz entered, followed by Captain James Magee of the trading vessel *Margaret*. Quadra and his officers rose, Ortiz saluted, Magee removed his hat and bowed. Quadra gestured to the single chair in front of the table.

The American sat down stiffly.

Quadra was succinct. Thank you for attending, a murder in the port, circumstances not yet clear, Spanish jurisdiction, your cooperation requested.

"I'll do what I can to help," Magee replied in Spanish.

Quadra looked to Jacinto Caamaño.

"You have heard by now that the victim is Spanish," Caamaño said. "The *aventurero* ensign Francisco Almeida of His Majesty's warship *Activa*. He was last seen alive Thursday night. So let's begin with where you were that night."

Magee had been at the yard during the day, supervising work on his shallop. Most of his people had returned to the *Margaret* at dusk, but he'd stayed ashore with his watchmen. "If you leave anything unguarded," he said, "it's gone by morning. There never seems to be many Indians in the settlement, but they're always around. They miss nothing and take everything."

Caamaño let the silence linger for a beat. "And was anything taken that night? From you, that is."

"No."

"So you and your watchmen were alert."

Magee's eyes flicked from Caamaño to Quadra.

The sun finally broke over the mountains to the east, striking the balcony doorway and illuminating the interior. "You were ashore,"

Alberni said. "What did you do?"

It was a nice evening, though chilly after dark. They had a fire and cooked a meal. Occasionally someone dropped by to sit and talk. "Companionship," he said, "in a far-off place. Everyone values that. Francisco came by for a while. Everyone knew him — he was a good lad. He liked me and my mate Pruitt because we speak Spanish. He would ask about Boston, America, the ports we'd visited. He liked to talk about Havana. He was a bit of a talker, and he was proud of Havana."

"Did he talk about Havana that night?" Alberni asked.

Magee shook his head. "He was with Black Carlos, and they didn't stay long. They left, and that was the last I saw of him. He was a good lad," he repeated. "I'm sorry he's dead."

The Spaniards were silent. Alberni shifted in his chair and slid a little to the side. Now the morning sun streamed over his shoulder and fell directly on Magee.

"What *did* he talk about?" Alberni asked.

Magee squinted into the light, trying to see their expressions. "He wasn't there for long, and there were others there too. I think he just came to see what was what. He was a boy, and boys are curious."

"Who else was there that night?"

Magee responded vaguely: people from the establishment and the ships in the harbour.

"Tell me again why they came to see you."

Magee peered at Alberni. "Why don't you ask them? They came. We shared our fire and our hospitality. That's all."

"Let us talk about your hospitality, Captain," Quadra said. "And let us dispense with evasions. Because a curious boy, as you call him, has turned up dead. You continued to sell rum after I forbade it."

A succession of sentiments flashed across Magee's face before hardening into defiance.

"I'm a trader. I won't apologize for that. My countrymen fought a war not so long ago to be free to trade. I fought in that war — as did all of you. We were on the same side then."

"This has nothing to do with former wars. You are in Spanish territory. I govern here. Your ship and cargo are confiscable, at my discretion, in the event of a breach of Spanish law."

Magee's eyes narrowed. The room was quiet. "The last time anyone around here made a threat like that and followed through, it caused a lot of trouble. Our mutual friend out there —" he pointed out at the harbour "— is still awaiting restitution. I don't think you want —"

Quadra slammed the table. "I don't *make* threats, Captain Magee. Do not underestimate my resolve. I'll do what I need to do. You're a razor's edge from losing your ship."

Magee folded his arms across his chest and looked down. When he looked up he said, "This year has been challenging here. I leave soon and need to sell my goods for what I can get. So, yes, I've been selling down my rum supply. But I've been discreet."

"And how have you been discreet, Captain?" Caamaño asked. "I refer specifically to the night of the *murder*."

Magee shifted in his chair. "I didn't sell to the boy."

"That's what he wanted? He didn't just drop by to — what were the captain's words, Felix?"

"'To see what was what,'" Cepeda read from his transcription.

Outside, the sun continued to climb. Its rays now fell full upon Magee's chest. By straightening in his chair he could see their faces.

"How much did he want?" Alberni continued.

"A couple of bottles. I refused. I knew he worked for you. I knew it would be trouble..." His voice trailed off.

"He was with Carlos Libertad. Black Carlos."

"Yes. The boy did the talking, but I could tell Carlos was in a mood. I've seen the look before. He was ready to kill for a drink." Magee stopped himself.

Alberni let it hang.

"Then what happened?"

"Carlos had words with me and my men, but we were firm. The boy persuaded him to leave. They walked away."

"To where?"

"Towards the water, I think."

"Then what?"

Magee hesitated. "Nothing. We continued as before."

"Selling rum?"

"Some."

"Who to?"

"British, Spanish." Magee seemed to relax in his chair, as if the worst were behind him. "It was getting late. We had a few more visitors, but we were careful. I didn't want Francisco to come back and find us selling rum."

"Who else came?" Alberni asked.

"No one of consequence. There was nothing unusual. It was like any other night."

"Spanish and British?"

"Yes."

"Officers?"

Magee thought. "No."

"Soldiers?" asked Alberni.

"Soldiers, sailors," Magee responded, annoyed with the repetition.

"Were there any Indians that night?"

Magee shrugged.

"Were there any Indians?"

Magee appeared to think and conceded there were some. "I told you before, they're always around."

"And you sold to them?"

Magee did not respond.

"Captain," Alberni said. "Do you sell rum to the Indians?"

"I'm not the only one," Magee said gruffly. "We're all squabbling and competing with each other while *they* get rich. Two years ago, a single sheet of copper bought ten otter skins. Now it buys one. Boston to here, here to China, that's a two-year round trip for me, and my investors expect returns when I get home. So, yes, I sell Indians rum. They extract their profit from me. I need to make it back."

"What a fine speech you make," Caamaño said. "If only your investors were here to witness it."

"Jacinto," Quadra said. Then, to Alberni: "Let's move on."

Magee shifted in his seat.

"Did any Indians come that night after Francisco?"

Magee thought for a moment. "Yes. One."

"Who?"

"I don't know. One of Maquinna's people, I suppose. Young."

"What did he look like?"

Magee's eyes narrowed. "Like an Indian."

"What did he want?"

Magee looked closely at Alberni and almost smiled. "Rum, of course. They all want rum."

"How much did you sell him?"

"Pruitt dealt with him. Two, maybe three bottles."

"That's a lot of rum for one man."

Magee shrugged. He thought for a moment. "I know he had Spanish dollars."

Quadra said, "We need to speak with your man to confirm the number. Where is he?"

Pruitt was at the boat yard. Quadra signalled Cepeda, who left the room. They heard him speaking in the guardhouse below. Footsteps crunched on the gravel outside and faded into the distance. Quadra said something to Alberni, then leaned back in his chair. "We'll wait for my secretary," he told Magee.

Magee looked cool as a cucumber, but that was an act. There was unfinished business in the air; the room was taut with tension. They all felt it; each handled it in his own way. Quadra sat perfectly still. Caamaño reached for Cepeda's transcript and flipped through it. Alberni, a man of action, shifted and fidgeted in his chair, then stood and went to the balcony doorway to look out.

Cepeda returned moments later with a steward carrying a tray with a pitcher and cups. The steward left the tray and withdrew. Alberni returned to the table and poured himself a cup. He looked up and saw Magee watching him. "Water, Captain?"

Magee accepted the cup and nodded thanks.

Alberni poured water for the others and sat.

"Let's begin," Quadra said.

Alberni scratched his stubbly chin. "I've been thinking about those bottles your mate sold that Indian. What was in them?"

"I already said it was rum."

"Well, there's rum and there's *rum*." Alberni picked up his cup and swirled its contents, examining it closely. "It's like wine, isn't it? Age, flavour, the wood of the cask."

Magee blinked. "I don't know what you're getting at."

"These qualities are lost on an Indian."

"That's true. They would hardly appreciate a *brandy de Jerez*. Or a *pisco aguardiente*." He nodded to Quadra, who did not respond. Alberni, though, grinned back.

"That's my point exactly. Surely you don't sell them the same rum you sell white men? It would be a waste."

Magee's faint smile disappeared.

"So what do you give them? Some kind of blend? You have to stretch your supplies. You have investors to satisfy. And these people are tough traders. I will attest to that. I've had mouths to feed these three years. I've had to deal with them myself. Always on their terms." He shook his head. "What is it you give them? How is it prepared?"

Magee's eyes narrowed.

"It must be a blend," Alberni prompted.

"Yes. A blend," Magee said cautiously. "Harsh to a white man's taste, but they don't know the difference."

"What's in it?"

Magee hesitated. "We add fermented wine, mix in water, and darken it with iodine and tobacco."

Alberni scratched his chin as he considered this. "But that won't have any kick. You've got to add something more for that."

Magee stared back at him.

"What else do you use?"

"Look," Magee said at last, "it's just an inexpensive blend that lets me recover some of what they gouge me for."

"I understand that. But there's more to it than fermented wine. There has to be."

Magee shrugged and looked down at his hands.

"I want an answer, Captain," Quadra said. "We know that's not all you put in your rum."

Magee squinted against the light from the balcony. He sighed. "To offset the dilution," he said, "we add wood alcohol and tincture of opium. Enough of both so they don't feel any pain. For taste, we spice it with pepper and sulphuric acid."

"Sulphuric acid?" Caamaño sat forward, ready to stand. "*Sulphuric acid?*"

Quadra put a hand to his forearm. "Jacinto."

"The young Indian," Alberni said, "did he have a weapon? A knife?"

Magee wasn't sure.

"Where did he go when he left you?"

Magee didn't know.

"Did you see anything else that night? Anything unusual?"

Magee scratched his chin. "Many skulk on that shore, Captain, for many reasons. But I saw nothing out of the ordinary. When Francisco and Carlos left, others came. We were busy." Magee's eyes shifted onto Quadra. "We're at the far end of the world, and everyone's looking for solace and comfort. Say what you will about my business on shore, but that's what I provide."

Quadra stood, his chair scraping on the rough floor planks and nearly tipping. "Not anymore. Your sale of liquor will cease or I will confiscate the *Margaret* and the ship you're building and your entire cargo. This is not a threat. It's a promise." Quadra leaned across the table. His face was flushed. "Our investigation will continue. We may have further questions for you. For now you are free to go."

The room cleared, leaving just the three senior officers.

"*Cabrón*," Alberni muttered. "*Gilipollas. Hijo de puta.*"

"You deal with the mate, Pedro. Confirm the number of bottles. Then search their tent. Take his mate with you. Destroy all the alcohol you find. Break the bottles, puncture the barrels. I want an officer present at all times. No bottles will 'disappear.' I want his boat yard and his tent searched daily. If you find so much as a drop after today, we'll take his ship."

Alberni nodded and rose to his feet. "By the sweet bowels of Christ, Don Juan, he'll wish he was dealing with the Grand Inquisitor, instead of me."

"Where is Maquinna?" Quadra wondered to himself. "Why isn't he here yet?"

⧗

Indeed, where was Maquinna? And where was his nephew, Copaza — that latter-day Yaftma, that red apple, that young rebel, that quisling, that pimp?

Tsakwasap was not the only one angry with him after the frolic at the hot springs. Matuateh was furious, too. She had only gone because she thought Francisco would be there, and Copaza had treated her with complete contempt in front of everybody. She'd been humiliated. She was used to being treated like a daughter and a sister. That was how Copaza had formerly treated her. Like a sister.

Francisco never recognized the change in Copaza's attitude towards Matuateh. Having remained on duty at Yuquot, he was not even aware of their confrontation at the hot springs. His first inkling that something was off came as he prepared to go on an extended supply trip. It was the kind of venture he loved: miles covered and hard labour in a canoe, new sights, camps, villages, the people he met, the decisions he had to make. He and Copaza would be gone for ten days, and before he left he wanted to see Matuateh — he hadn't seen her since the potlatch in Tahsis. He asked Copaza to arrange a rendezvous.

"Arrange it yourself," Copaza said.

They were in a storeroom at Yuquot, Francisco stacking trade goods for the trip. He stopped and looked at Copaza.

"What?"

"You heard me."

"*Hombre*. How will I do that? I'm stuck here in Yuquot."

Copaza turned away and poked through the contents of a shelf on the wall.

"Come on, brother. I need your help."

Copaza picked up a knife and felt its blade with his thumb.

Francisco went over to stand next to him.

"Hey. I'm asking you to do this."

No response.

"Copaza."

"She is a slave."

"I don't care."

Copaza's eyes were locked on the knife, and Francisco misread his thoughts. He put a hand on his friend's shoulder. "Take it. And this too." He handed him a mirror. "For your mother. And these." He held out some copper hoops. "I know what you can get for these if you play it right."

He clapped Copaza on the back and told him what he could get if he played it right. He joked and cajoled and teased until his friend smiled grudgingly. Francisco assumed that meant agreement.

"I want you to arrange for someone to come with Matuateh," he said. "I don't know her name, but she was with one of the English at the hot springs. You remember the ember head? Yim Hawkes. He's ashore at their observatory and wants to see her again. Not just any girl — that specific girl. Ask Matuateh; she'll know who he means. Or she can find out. Tell her I think he's in love."

⧗

The rendezvous was near where the traders were building their boat. They had a tent on a rise above the beach — to house a guard against Indian thievery, they said. That night, the traders sat in front of their fire, their backs to the tent. Shadows flitted in and out of their flickering circle, man-sized moths to their flame of enticement. Muffled conversations by the fire led to purposeful trips to the tent, then the shadows disappeared into the darkness, silent save for the occasional *clink*.

Copaza sat with Matuateh and Saiyuqa on the high rocks bordering the inlet, well beyond the light of the fire. It was a warm night, stirred by a gentle breeze. They waited, watching figures enter the firelight from the direction of the Spanish village. Once, a boat landed from the cove. Its occupants approached the fire, got what they'd come for, and disappeared back into the dark, the careful sound of their oars fading quickly to silence.

Copaza carefully studied every new arrival. Matuateh and Saiyuqa grew bored. They lay back on the rocks and gazed at the stars, and Matuateh dozed off. She startled when Copaza gave her shoulder a shake. Saiyuqa was already up, peering towards the traders' fire.

Two figures walked towards it. Matuateh recognized Francisco. He was lean and tall. The other man, she could not identify.

"Is it Hawkins?" Saiyuqa whispered.

Matuateh caught the hope in her voice. Hawkins had been kind and gentle with Saiyuqa at the hot springs. These words were seldom used to describe the experiences of the *coulz* forced to fornicate with white men. When Matuateh first told her that Hawkins wanted to see her, teasing her about his ardour, Saiyuqa had laughed girlishly, flattered to be thought beautiful, happy to be admired and remembered purely. For a moment she'd forgotten her lowly station and the duties it entailed; her hand had fluttered at her breast like a butterfly. "My heart," she'd told Matuateh.

They could see now it was not Hawkins, and the hope Saiyuqa had held moments before evaporated. She was suddenly uncertain, afraid — and angry with Copaza. She cursed him for a trickster and rose to run off, but he grabbed her wrist. "Be quiet and wait," he said. He released her and stared at the dim figures outlined against the fire.

"Maybe Hawkins will come," Matuateh whispered. Saiyuqa sank back down onto the ground and watched intently. Matuateh watched too until, not sure why, she glanced out at the cove. Her heart caught in her chest. There, barely visible in the starlight and the dim glimmer thrown by the distant fire, she saw a figure, dark and cloaked, on the beach.

She blinked to be sure, stared at the unmoving blackness, felt in the dark for Saiyuqa's sleeve, and, giving it a tug, pointed at the figure.

"Hawkins," Saiyuqa said, again hopeful.

# Chapter 28

Youthful, adventurous, full of piss and vinegar — the midshipmen where a rambunctious lot, and, to their chagrin, their days were now filled with mundanity. Cartography was their raison d'*être*. Hour after hour they plotted bearings, degrees of arc, distances from known positions, soundings, elevations. From beneath their tight, cramped hands emerged parchment promontories, islands, channels, rocks, and reefs. By day they sniffed the compass rose. At night they dreamt in fathoms, in minutes and seconds of Lat. and Long.

Joseph Whidbey spent an hour in the hold thinking about where he'd stow the supplies from *Daedalus*. With the uncertainty over *Chatham*'s seaworthiness, it still wasn't clear how much of them *Discovery* would even take aboard. Only when that was decided could the work begin, and of course it would have to be done in a blessed rush.

Old Joe was frowning at this thought as he climbed the forward companionway onto the main deck. He blinked at the light and squinted up at the sky. It was sunny and the moon was visible; conditions were perfect for celestial observation. He would go ashore for the noon sighting, but until then he would enjoy some fresh air. He arched his back and cast his eye around. There were two drafting tables on the quarterdeck, two more on the main. A cadre of midshipmen, the best draftsmen and the luckiest of the rest, worked at them. The rest of their number worked in the dimness below deck.

Whidbey arched further, and his eyes ascended the mainmast. Fists to lumbar, he held the stretch. The yards had yet to be refitted, and when that was done the work of re-rigging could begin. In a blessed rush, of course.

"Has it grown, Mister Whidbey?"

Whidbey straightened. Midshipman Ramsay was peering up the mainmast, holding a pose very like his own.

"I noticed Doctor Menzies watering around it yesterday. I thought perhaps..."

"You have time for japes, Mister Ramsay. I take it the charts are done."

"Ah, well, not quite. I needed a stretch. And then I saw your fine example."

Whidbey grunted.

Ramsay continued in a softer voice. "I thought you might need some help at the observatory, Mister Whidbey. You are headed there shortly, I think."

"I wasn't born yesterday, Dick Ramsay."

"We are like monks in a scriptorium, Mister Whidbey," the midshipman lamented.

"Hard cheese, boy." Whidbey's eyes were now on the fo'c'sle and the waist of the ship. He massaged the ball of his shoulder with his hand. He tilted his head this way and that, swivelled right and left from the hips.

"I shall wait here for your summons when you change your mind."

Whidbey stopped his exercises and laughed appreciatively. "Yes, Mister Ramsay, I'll show you just where to wait." He walked him to his table and clapped him on the back; then he climbed onto the quarterdeck, where Midshipmen Roberts and Hawkins were at work. He perused their charts while performing another set of twists and stretches, manipulations that produced a series of soft cracks, as though the vessel of his body had grounded on the reef of his spine. He grunted with satisfaction.

Roberts and Hawkins exchanged glances.

"Show me your variation calculation for this area."

Roberts showed him and he nodded.

"Good. Very good. Ah, Mister Baker. Your apprentices have been educating me on magnetic variation..."

An hour later, Jim Hawkins completed the chart he'd worked on for two days; for the first time he pondered it in its entirety, thinking about its origins, those long days in open boats, the nights huddled on rocky shores or in the boats themselves. Hardship, deprivation, fatigue. He yearned for that, and rued this present slog.

He rolled it up and descended to the main to deliver it to John Dorsey for copying. As he spread it out across Dorsey's table the other mapmakers gathered round. He glanced around at their faces. "How is it going, fellows?" he asked, tapping the chart as if pointing something out.

Dorsey cursed creatively, keeping his voice low. "At least *you* get some variety. *Copying* these things is like tea at Granny's." He leaned over the chart and navigated a channel between two islands with his finger.

Lieutenant Puget passed close by. "Be careful when you transcribe these soundings," Hawkins said, pointing on the chart. "Here. And here. Look how close this shoal is to the deep-water passage."

The midshipmen nodded attentively. Ramsay leaned in and traced the shoal's outline with his middle finger.

Puget climbed the steps onto the quarterdeck.

"Who gives a shit," Dorsey said when he was gone.

"Clerk's work," Pitt said.

"Best done drunk," Lincoln said.

Dorsey looked up hopefully.

A shadow fell across the table. Lieutenants Puget and Baker stood at the edge of the quarterdeck, directly above.

Hawkins tapped a point of land. The others faked interest in what he pretended to show.

"Mmm mrmm mmm mnning briefing. Watch yrrr mmm mmnr mmr," Puget told Baker.

"Why's that?"

"The Old Mmn. In a mmmm mrrm."

Hawkins chanced a glance and saw they were paying the midshipmen beneath them no heed. Baker looked up the mainmast. "I thought he was rather cheerful after his interview with Duffin."

"Mrmm hmm yestermm mmm mrmm. Not today. Umm hrmm mm state of repair mm uhmm rubbish for supplies mm hmm mmm hmm bloody cuttings on the quarterdeck —"

Both lieutenants laughed.

The rest of what they said was completely inaudible. Puget took his leave of Baker and descended to the main, passed the table where the middies were clustered, and strolled forward. Mid-deck he hailed Menzies, who had just emerged up the fore-hatch ladder.

Hawkins could feel Baker's gaze on his head. The lieutenant made a sonorous show of clearing his throat.

"Officer of the deck!" a watchman called. "Starboard quarter!"

Baker strode aft to look. The midshipmen moved to the gunwale rail and craned to see from there. Three canoes had rounded the headland at the north end of the cove and now drew smoothly past the Portuguese snow in the outer harbour.

They were the biggest canoes any of them had yet seen, each with a carved prow extending six feet above the water. Maquinna stood at the centre of the lead vessel, his still form seeming to glide across the water. Twenty men propelled him in perfect unison. The other two dugouts held steady station on his.

"Well, well, well. Come to answer for murder at last," someone said.

"About time."

Murmurs of assent, exchanged glances. Hawkins kept his eyes on the canoes.

"I'll wager he didn't do it himself," Ramsay said.

"One of his people, though."

Hawkins felt a sick chill as he watched the chief's procession.

"It doesn't add up," Ramsay said. "Everyone liked Francisco. And he *knew* the Indians. Why would they kill him?"

The canoes slackened pace.

"A savage needs no reason," Lincoln said. "They killed him, plain and simple."

Ramsay wasn't buying. "They stayed here until he was found. Scotty

MacMenzies told me he'd been dead a couple of days by then. It's like they didn't know."

"It only takes one," Pitt said, "and he wouldn't be talking, would he? What about his mate Copaza? We saw his temper for ourselves."

Dorsey spat over the side.

"He was always skulking around," Lincoln said.

"Someone must have seen something. Someone must have seen him that last day or —"

"Save your breath, Dickie," Pitt said. "He forgot where he was and it got him killed. It's just as well we're stuck on board. We're safer for it. Soon we'll leave these miserable people, and good riddance, I say."

"He was..." Hawkins began.

"A character!" Ramsay said.

"... a decent fellow," Hawkins finished, his voice cracking.

"*I* wouldn't know," Dorsey said. "You fuckers went off with him for a fuckfest at the fucking spa and fucking left me here."

"He wasn't there," Ramsay said. "He never made it."

"Look, we hardly knew the chap," Pitt said. "He served a different king, a different country."

"That's not —" Hawkins began.

"Oh, shut up," Lincoln said. "You're moaning like he was one of us."

Whether intended or not the nudge he gave Hawkins was hard. Hawkins pushed back harder.

"Links. Jim. That's enough. Let it go," Pitt said.

Neither Links nor Jim looked like they wanted to let it go. Pitt stepped between them, his voice a murmur. "Get a grip, you two. A scrap on deck's the last thing any of us needs."

The two angry midshipmen glared at each other until Pitt laid a hand on Lincoln's shoulder. It was a friendly gesture — until he dug his thumb into soft flesh.

Lincoln winced and brushed his hand away, scowling fiercely, enraged. Pitt gave him a cold stare. It took Lincoln a moment to see sense and calm down; his scowl slowly dissolved, and he turned his gaze back onto the canoes. "You're right, Tom. I know you're right. It's these bleeding charts. The pressure we're all under. I hate it." He shook his head and grinned sheepishly in Hawkins's direction. "Jim, that was unconscionable of me. And rude. Accept my —"

"Doctor Menzies," Ramsay said. "It's quite the spectacle."

"That it is." The surgeon joined them at the rail. "It appears Maquinna's entire court has come along tae witness his parley wi' Don Quadra."

"Tae witness his parley — air tae fight?" Lincoln said. "Which will i' be?"

Ramsay gave him the cut-eye to stop. Menzies merely glanced his way. "They'll no' fight today, Mister Lincoln. If they were guan tae attack they'd no' arrive like this."

"They're too sneaky for a direct attack," someone opined.

"The more I think of it, it's that sneaky Copaza did it," Lincoln said. He reached and clapped Hawkins on the back. "I'd bet you your prize farthing on that — if you could bear parting with it."

"They're heading straight in," Ramsay observed. "Why aren't they circling?"

"Aye — they do tha' circuit when they visit another chief, tae show they're friendly. But Maquinna feels this place belongs tae him. There's nae reason for ceremony when he enters his own village."

They watched the canoes advance toward the beach.

"Well, let's hope tha's the case," Menzies continued, "or we're like tae see a wee bit o' trouble. We can all agree this is no' a pure social call."

The captain appeared at the top of the companionway. "Mister Baker. Report."

"It's Maquinna, sir, arrived for his conference with the dons."

Vancouver's eyes found the canoes. "Marines to muster. Do it quietly, Mister Baker, but do it *now*. Signal *Chatham* and *Daedalus* to do the same."

"Sir."

"Mister Mudge, see the swivel guns charged and loaded with shot." He looked down at the plotting tables on the main deck. "Those will have to be moved below for the time being. These also." He indicated the tables on the quarterdeck. "The young gentlemen will have to work down there while we see what unfolds ashore."

He turned to see how the Spanish were responding, and saw soldiers forming up in parade ranks on either side of the entrance to the Big House. The Spanish commandant, followed by his officers, was at that moment descending the path to the landing, his pace serene, matching perfectly that of the approaching canoes.

# Chapter 29

The last of the visitors filed in and gathered behind Maquinna. The great hall grew eerily silent. Stillness fills a void just like hunger does an empty stomach.

Maquinna sat on a bench at the centre of the hall, flanked by his advisors Natzape and Quatlazape, who were in the middle of a heated discussion. Old Natzape leaned forward on his walking stick and spoke with some passion. Quatlazape murmured a reply. The chief kept his gaze on the far wall, just above the heads of the Spaniards who faced him: Quadra, between Alberni and Caamaño. At a table to the side sat Moziño and Cepeda. In that whole vast room, the seat of the Spanish province of Neuva California, there were just four soldiers — two standing ceremonial guard beside the flags on the inner wall, two more at the door to Quadra's bureau. All were conspicuously unarmed.

Maquinna's gaze dropped to rest on Quadra. They held eyes for a moment before he stood and gestured to his shaman, Tsakwasap. The old man shuffled into the gap between the benches. His face was painted, and he was dressed in a fur cloak. He held a small bowl close to his chest and fanned it with his fingers.

Alberni leaned in to whisper to Quadra.

A smoky tendril escaped the bowl. The shaman fanned it further, watched it thicken and rise, then reached and gathered it in, cupping and sweeping it around himself as if drawing water from a gravity-defying river. He chanted as he bathed, his voice high and strained, that of an ancient.

When he was done he moved to stand in front of Maquinna, who stood and reached with both hands to gather smoke and bathe as the old man had. Natzape and Quatlazape stood in turn and smudged also.

As soon as Quatlazape finished, Quadra rose to his feet. Tsakwasap hesitated, glanced at Maquinna, and moved to stand before him. He offered the bowl, and Quadra bathed in its smoke. Alberni and Caamaño followed.

Tsakwasap turned in a circle, pausing at each of the cardinal points to intone a prayer and waft smoke into the air. Then, with his eyes seemingly closed, he returned to his place behind Maquinna.

The chief stood again and beckoned to Pedro Alberni, who rose and went to his side.

"My people who were here told me what happened. I offer my condolences. It is an appalling crime. A senseless death."

Alberni translated. Quadra nodded.

"They told me that your men were angry, that they wanted to detain and punish mine, but you allowed them to leave because you knew they were innocent."

Maquinna waited for an acknowledgement. Quadra did not provide it.

"They told me you believe I am responsible. That I plotted and ordered the boy's death and therefore committed the murder myself."

At the table, Felix Cepeda scribbled furiously.

"I believe these suspicions cannot exist in your heart, that when you examine them, you will know it cannot be so, for I have a thousand obligations to be your friend. You gave me copper to share among my kin, and abalone to distribute to my people. Yours are the cloth, the beads, the coats of mail, and the instruments of iron with which I am provided. You have paid me kindnesses and honours too numerous to mention, though I have not forgotten a single one."

The great hall, so vast and full, was still, save for Cepeda's rapid motions, quill to ink to paper. Scratch, scratch. Repeat.

"Our trust in each other is such that I have slept in your lodge and you in mine — where you had no arms or soldiers to defend you. If my friendship were capable of betrayal, I could have taken your life any number of times. You must think very low of me if you imagine that I, seeking to break our friendship, would order the murder of a defenceless boy."

Quadra stiffened.

"What purpose would be served by killing this boy? Could it be an act of war? Do you think that if I chose to make war, I would start by killing a boy and not his chief? No, if I made war I would place my full force against my enemies and battle them. I would not come into their midst as I do today. Yet here I stand, unarmed, in the place where you are strongest. My nobles here, my *masicim* outside, are unarmed. You could set your soldiers upon us and kill us all. Is my behaviour that of a chief at war?"

Maquinna's voice, Alberni's translation, the hypnotic scratch of Cepeda's pen. Those were the only sounds.

"If we were enemies you would be dead already. You know this. My kinsmen Wickaninnish, Cleaskinah, and Tatoosh would fight at my side. They have guns and powder and shot. Our people united far outnumber yours. Be assured, if I waged war on you, I would do so with overwhelming force and speed and purpose. I would be victorious — or I would lie dead on the field of battle."

He let silence linger before he continued. "The boy's murder was not an act of war. So what was it? What did he have that could incite greed in me or any of my people? And to this I reply: are not the Spanish safe in my territories? Have not your brothers" — he indicated Alberni beside him, and Moziño at the table — "been alone in my lodge, or in those of my kinsmen, with all their belongings, their instruments, medals, rings, and adornments? What harm has been done to them? Who of my people has insulted them, let alone hurt them in any way? You yourself have gone unaccompanied among my *masicim* and been surrounded and overcome — yes, overcome! — not by treachery, but by countless examples of friendship and goodwill."

Maquinna turned to look at his tribesmen. His eyes fell briefly on Tsakwasap. He turned back to Quadra. "How, then, can you let your men say *I* commanded the death of this boy? How can you believe *I* am capable of murder?"

He extended his arms wide. "Let it be known by your men that Maquinna is a true friend, that he is far from harming the Spanish. Make them understand that Maquinna returns friendship with friendship. Make them know that Maquinna played no part in this murder, and that his people are innocent. This is the word of Maquinna, which is the truth."

Maquinna held Quadra's eye and iced the cake with the trick of silence. Then he returned to his seat between Quatlazape and Natzape.

Quadra looked into the faces opposite him, then at those gathered around. He nodded thoughtfully and stood.

"Great chief," he began, "great prince and friend. You have acted always with honour and integrity towards me. Neither I, nor any Spaniard, has anything to fear from Maquinna of the Mowachaht."

He bowed to Maquinna, who nodded.

"Yet someone killed this boy."

He paced slowly in the space between the benches, hands clasped behind his back.

"That doesn't sound right — 'this boy.'" He stopped and faced Maquinna. "'This boy' had a name. Let us use it. Francisco Almeida was his name. Francisco Almeida. He had a name and a father and a mother, this boy. He had a bright future, a life ahead of him."

Paper rustled as Cepeda reached the bottom of a page, set it aside to dry, and began a fresh one.

"He served my master, the King of Spain, to whom he was not a boy but a man — a man for whom I am responsible. *Someone* killed Francisco Almeida, robbed him of his life, cut him up, and cast him on those rocks." He pointed through his office towards the harbour. "*Someone* butchered Francisco Almeida, and I have lost a man, a member of my complement. Someone I admired. Someone with great potential. Someone I viewed as a friend."

He paced, turned. Paced back. "Your people, too, have lost a friend — a friend who loved and understood them." He stopped at Cepeda's table to pick up a sheaf of papers and returned to stand in front of Maquinna.

"You say I have been just, that I have been a friend to you and your people. Then you know that I will allow no innocent to suffer. I will not lash out blindly to strike the blameless." He held up the papers in his hand. "I have already spoken to others and learned things that trouble me. But I still do not know what happened. That is why, my friend, I ask you to help me identify the killer of Francisco Almeida and bring him to justice."

He returned to his bench and sat.

Silence hung from the rafters like a curtain. Maquinna looked at his two advisors. Quatlazape sat impassively, his dark eyes signalling nothing. On his other side, Natzape polished the handle of his walking stick with his palm.

"I have said that no one among my people is guilty."

"Francisco spoke your language. He had many contacts with your people. He was well known. He had friends."

Maquinna's eyes did not leave Quadra's face as he listened to Alberni's translation. "He was known among my people. He had friends. Friends do not commit murder."

"No." Quadra indicated the papers in his hand. "Copaza was seen with Francisco on the night of the murder."

Maquinna's expression was poker-game stoic.

"I wish to question Copaza. He may be able to tell us something about what happened that night."

"He is not here. He is away hunting. But you have the word of Maquinna that he is innocent." Maquinna pointed at Cepeda. "And now you have it for your king."

"But Copaza was there that night. And there were others."

Maquinna did not respond, but behind him old Tsakwasap chose that moment to brandish his ceremonial rattle and chant an incantation. Maquinna turned and glared. The old man ignored him and took his own sweet time to finish.

Alberni, standing with the chief, gave the commandant an almost imperceptible shrug.

Quadra again held up the papers in his hand. "There were girls, that night, in the dark. Two of them. The writing says —"

"They are innocent." Maquinna crossed his arms in a gesture of finality and held the Spaniard's gaze. The moment was exquisite, the wait for one to blink. Neither did. In the harbour a bell sounded: three strokes of two and a solo, seven in all.

"Then who?"

Maquinna continued to hold his eye.

"My friend, I only want the truth."

"My friend, the truth is that a chieftain cannot command all things and all people."

THE WIND FROM ALL DIRECTIONS | 251

Quadra finally blinked.

Maquinna glanced at his counsellors. "Your people need not fear harm from mine. But I do not control the followers of others. You must look among them."

"Who? Who must I look among?"

Maquinna looked at Natzape and Quatlazape; he turned to survey the elders grouped behind him. He even sought out Tsakwasap's eye. "The guilty hide in plain sight behind their own chieftains."

"I don't understand."

The chief's expression was unreadable. He took a long time to respond. "I am certain the Hesquiaht are responsible."

Natzape's stick slipped out of his hands. He reached to pick it up. Again Tsakwasap mumbled an incantation. This time Maquinna ignored him.

Quadra's shoulders slumped. "The Hesquiaht," he said.

"Since long before my father's time, my people have fought them. They are bandits, and they covet our lands. We know them to be cruel. They are capable of barbarities such as this."

Quadra exchanged glances with Caamaño and Alberni. "But who? Who among them is guilty?"

"That is not known to me, only that they shelter there. The Hesquiaht will deny it, but they are two-faced and treacherous. Lend me five or six of your swivel guns. I will assemble the fiercest of my warriors and attack the Hesquiaht. I will clear them from their nests along the coast. Send whichever of your men you choose, and we will attack together — so that all will know that Maquinna is one with Quadra, and Quadra with Maquinna."

A murmur arose from Maquinna's tribesmen. Quadra gave no reaction at all. His eyes seemed unfocused and unseeing. Watching him from the table with Cepeda, Moziño grew alarmed. He was about to stand and go to him when the commodore drew a breath, sighed, and glanced at his subordinates.

"My friend," he said, standing. "I thank you for coming to meet me, and for your expressions of condolence. By these, you have proven your friendship. I have but one regret from our meeting today: that I do not yet understand the circumstances of Francisco Almeida's death." He held up the papers in his hands and gestured at the ones in front of Cepeda. "Now I must consider what you have said."

Maquinna nodded.

They escaped into formalities, exchanged solicitous words. Quadra extended an invitation to Maquinna to stay for the night.

"This is not the time," Maquinna replied. "Your loss weighs on you and you must grieve, for he was a son to you. I will return in a few days. We will speak then."

Quadra offered his hand.

As those around them began to mingle and converse, Quadra still gripped Maquinna's hand in his. "I believe the killer took a trophy," he said, loud enough for only Alberni and Maquinna to hear. "If you find the silver medallion Francisco wore around his neck, you will find the killer."

For a moment Maquinna looked confused. "I have said: your people are safe among us with all their belongings. My people are innocent. No one among them stole his medallion."

"I ask only that you help me find the truth, so that justice can be done."

"The truth is always complicated, and justice is never perfect. I have heard your words. When I return we will speak again."

Caamaño had already escorted Maquinna's followers down the stairs and into the noon glare, leaving Maquinna and Quadra in the gloom of the great hall. Natzape and Quatlazape had waited for their chief. As soon as Maquinna turned away from Quadra, they drew him aside to talk. Alberni and Moziño stood with Quadra. Moziño had never seen Quadra so subdued nor Alberni so angry.

"Vague words. Assurances of undying friendship," Alberni sputtered, "and a kind offer to join in a fight against his enemies! He's playing us. We know nothing more than we did yesterday."

"No," said Quadra.

"'Copaza's gone hunting.' What horseshit. Don Juan, I'll take twenty men and go find Copaza and drag him back here for questioning. He knows the truth."

"I can't do that."

"They do know something, Don Juan," Moziño said.

"I know."

Alberni's face was flushed. "I'd rather get kicked in the *cojones* by a mule than go through a charade like this again. You keep saying Spanish justice will prevail, Don Juan, but this is making a mockery of —"

"Captain. That's enough."

Alberni clamped his mouth shut. His brows were knotted, his big fists balled in anger.

"Your Excellency?" It was Cepeda. He handed a document to Quadra. "If it is possible now?"

Quadra stared at the paper without seeing it. At last he focused on it. His expression changed as he read. He looked up, nodded at Cepeda, clapped scowling Alberni on the back, and pulled him towards Maquinna. "Translate, Pedro," he said. "My friend: will you remain a moment longer? There is another matter I would discuss with you. Yesterday, Captain Vancouver provided me with the testimony of Señor Robert Duffin, an English trader who arrived here a few days ago." He gestured in the direction of the harbour.

"I remember Robert Duffin."

"Señor Duffin swore a statement about the purchase of land from you by Señor Meares four years ago."

"Meares is a liar," Maquinna said. "I never sold him any land."

"Duffin says that Meares told the truth." Quadra held up the document. "In this document Duffin says you sold the entire village."

"Then Duffin is a liar too. You know that the act of writing words does not make them true."

Quadra winced. "I would like to read you this, to get your response to his words."

"Say his words, then. And I will give you my response."

# Chapter 30

A tight smile played across Van's face. Looking out over the heads of his oarsmen, he reflected on the number of occasions he had pressed his counterpart in writing, in person, ashore and afloat, for his final position. To say the least, the man's proposals were fluid.

Eventually, they had solidified around his refusal to cede Nootka Sound, based on testimony he had personally collected that summer from three traders. All three — two Americans and a Portuguese — had been present in Friendly Cove in the years 1788 and '89 and had witnessed the events at the heart of the dispute. All three acknowledged that Meares had erected a modest temporary structure in Friendly Cove during the summer of '88. And they all insisted there was no trace of it remaining the following spring. When Martínez arrived, he'd asserted Spanish sovereignty in good faith.

Robert Duffin, who had also been in Friendly Cove in '88 and '89, contradicted their statements. He claimed that Meares's post had been both substantial and permanent, and had stood on land he'd bought outright from Maquinna.

Van had forwarded Duffin's deposition to Quadra the day he took it. Quadra had written back the next day, restating his previous position; he had not even mentioned Duffin's evidence.

So Van had decided: Enough with the letters. He was on his way to hash it out in person. Armed with Duffin's testimony and a flimsy technicality, he would take one last go at establishing the supremacy of Britain's claim to sovereignty over Spain's.

At a considerable altitude above his head, I saw below me rotting lodge timbers abandoned decades before, the millennia-old midden slope that led to the Big House and, beyond, the island in the lake with its hidden shrine and ancient relics. I wheeled, folded, turned head down, and dropped into a spiral, then flipped and used vortex drag for lift to complete a loop. As I righted, I extended fully and rode a current higher, my heart pounding, bursting with the joy of flight.

Quadra was standing with Cepeda at a cluttered table. "Captain! Señor Dobson! Your timing is perfect. Look what you've saved me from." He indicated the paperwork. "Please, sit and drink a coffee. Felix, join us."

They took seats around a side table, the two commissioners exchanging comments about the weather and mild complaints about administration while a steward poured coffee and left them with the pot and a plate of shortbread.

Dobson eyed the pastries — polvorónes, a little far to reach. He sniffed his coffee, took a sip, and burned his mouth.

"I have your latest letter," Vancouver said. "With the...ah, matters at hand, I expect you had no time to consider Robert Duffin's affidavit."

Dobson put his cup down hurriedly to translate. Quadra smiled at him and returned his gaze to his counterpart.

"That is quite understandable in the, ah, circumstances. But the affidavit is material to the issue. Duffin has confirmed Meares's account — that they built a substantial building here four years ago."

Quadra took a sip of coffee and gently set his cup and saucer down. "I did receive his statement and I have considered it. Sugar?" His eyebrows rose in inquiry.

Vancouver declined with a wave.

"Señor Duffin was Señor Meares's mate. He cannot be considered impartial. He has a clear interest in the original matter. One cannot place the same weight on his testimony as upon that of several independent witnesses."

Vancouver pursed his lips. His cup lay steaming and untouched on the table. "Your *three* witnesses all speak about the absence of a factory in Friendly Cove in 1789, when Martínez seized Meares's ships. Their accounts on that are consistent, but the issue is not the factory's absence in 1789 — it is its presence in 1788. All four witnesses say that John Meares built a structure here the year *before* Martínez arrived. There is disagreement as to the size and permanence of the structure, but there is none over its existence. And therefore, being that it existed on land previously possessed by Maquinna, the structure had to have been *sanctioned* by Maquinna, or it would not have been constructed at all."

While Dobson translated, the Spanish commissioner brought his saucer to his chest. A faint tendril of steam rose from his cup. His eyes narrowed as he breathed it in. Meanwhile, the British commissioner reached inside his coat and removed a sheet of paper. He waved it now for emphasis.

"Mister Duffin confirms that John Meares bought a site in Friendly Cove before the building was constructed. That is the central issue: his ownership of land here in 1788. None of the evidence you have compiled, none of the statements provided by your witnesses, actually refutes the purchase and ownership of land by Meares."

"I agree that Señor Duffin's assertion on that point is clear. However, there is no agreement on the facts. Duffin says Maquinna sold the whole of Friendly Cove. Meares said he bought a 'spot of ground.'" Quadra spoke the English phrase, accented but unmistakable. "Duffin testifies that the price was several sheets of copper and other trade goods, while Meares claimed it was a couple of pistols. They were both here. They both witnessed the same events. For such an apparently black-and-white transaction, their numerous contradictions are troubling,"

"I care not a fig about the price. I care only about the substance of the claim. Here" — Vancouver held up the page again — "is sworn testimony by Duffin that Meares purchased land in Friendly Cove."

Quadra stood and went to his desk. He picked up a sheaf of papers and looked through it. Cepeda joined him; they conferred quietly, and Cepeda handed him another sheaf. For a moment he perused it, seeming hesitant, before returning to his seat. "Beyond the obvious small discrepancies between Meares and Duffin, there is a more substantial dispute. That is, whether there was any sale at all. When Maquinna was here yesterday I asked him to respond to Señor Duffin's testimony." He held up a page of his own. "This is Maquinna's statement that he did not sell land to Meares. He says he traded furs for copper — nothing more. He is adamant that he sold no land. His statement" — he proffered it to Vancouver — "was translated into Spanish by Alberni. If you feel it necessary, I will ask Maquinna to speak with you directly when he returns, to confirm its substance."

Vancouver took the page by an edge, as though it were unclean, and handed it to Dobson without a glance. Instead, he held Quadra's gaze. It was quiet in the room and in the great hall beyond the closed door. Outside, beneath the balcony, a Spanish soldier shouted to another on the landing.

Dobson held Maquinna's statement and waited for either commissioner to speak. By habit, almost absently, he translated the shouted conversation:

"Sanchez — you twat! What the fuck is that?"

"What's it look like, you whoreson arsehole? It's a fucking Indian boat!"

"You poxy bunghole! Don't you think it warrants a hail to the fucking guard?"

"Why don't you..."

Dobson's schooling in Spanish had been formal and commercially focused. His recent duties as a translator had been demanding, and he'd been very rusty to begin with. Yet, with intensive daily practice, the language had returned; indeed, his command of it had grown. Now here was a lesson in the common vernacular — to which he had had little exposure — and he understood it all! He smiled to himself, delighted.

Quadra held up another page from the sheaf in his hand. "This document was also executed by Maquinna. It is a grant by him to Spain of the land comprising the *establecimiento* of Santa Cruz de Nuca. It is a deed of land, Captain, and puts the controversy to rest. There cannot be two deeds for the same land."

Vancouver's face drained of colour. He took the document and saw it was in Spanish. He peered closely at the signatures.

"Who is this?" he asked, extending the page to Quadra. "A witness?"

Quadra looked. "Captain Barras Andrade, of the *São José o Fénix*, the

Portuguese vessel that arrived recently."

As Vancouver studied the page Dobson observed his pursed lips, his heavy-lidded eyes. The captain, he realized, looked fatigued. His face seemed bloated. He wondered if he was unwell.

Vancouver looked up at Quadra. "And this?" he said, pointing.

"Yes. Captain Magee and his mate, Señor Pruitt. They both speak Spanish and were ashore, so I summoned them to witness the grant as independent observers."

Vancouver stared at the signatures. Now his brows arched. Colour returned to his face. And then some. "As independent observers," he repeated. His eyes remained on the document for a long time before he dropped it onto the table. "I am..." He coughed and cleared his throat.

Dobson's gaze fixed on George Vancouver. He had heard stories about the captain's temper. Until this moment the diplomatic discussions in which he'd performed a supporting role had seemed dusty, arcane, and theoretical. Now he saw what was at stake, the forces these men represented and might consciously or unwittingly unleash. Suddenly the confrontation between Martínez and Colnett was not so dusty and arcane after all.

"I am *dumbfounded*," Vancouver said, "that your *independent* observers are again two American traders and a Portugee; and that in a matter of such import I, in my capacity as representative of His Majesty's Government, which has an avowed interest in this matter's resolution, was not provided notice to attend. As I was but ten minutes away, it strikes me as...*unfortunate*, sir. Very *unfortunate*."

The flat of his hand struck the table for emphasis, jangling the cups and saucers. He waited while Dobson translated. By the time the young man finished, the scowl on his captain's face was gone, dissolved like fog on a pane of glass.

"Nevertheless," he continued coolly, "I must acknowledge the differences in the testimonies we have at hand. But as to our original mission, with respect to the Convention negotiated by our governments in Madrid, your witness statements, and the, uh, *recent* concession of land, matter not a whit. My instructions are clear: to receive from you the territories specified in the Convention."

He waited for Dobson to catch up.

"I expect, however, that you will adhere to the principles contained in your last letter."

Quadra allowed a brief silence. "I shall."

"Then I shall consider Nootka a Spanish port while the matter is referred to our superiors. I request your permission to carry on our necessary employments on shore until we are ready to depart."

"Granted, Captain, of course — along with any assistance I can provide."

They nodded, and both reached for their coffee cups. A bitter toast to seal a bitter bargain, Dobson thought. He sipped his own. It was tepid. He looked wantonly at the sugar bowl. It remained just out of polite reach.

"As we are now, after a manner, resolved," Quadra said, "we must both see to our separate plans. The *Activa* will be ready for sea in a few days. When I sail, I will leave Caamaño in charge until Fidalgo returns from Juan de Fuca. Caamaño will then follow me to California."

One of Vancouver's thick eyebrows arched like a breaching porpoise. "Fidalgo will withdraw from your post inside the Strait?"

Quadra reached to pour more coffee. "It's a simple case of logistics. Over the winter, it is easier for me to maintain one post here in Neuva California than two."

*Neuva California* was a new one for both Britons.

"Quite," Vancouver said, rubbing his chin.

"Sugar?"

This time Vancouver accepted. He stirred it in with one of Quadra's silver spoons, then closely examined its handle. Dobson thought there was a hint of a smile on his lips. A moment later it was gone. He looked at his own spoon and saw it was engraved with the words *Plus Ultra*.

"Señor Dobson?"

Dobson helped himself to sugar too and accepted a polvorón.

"Have you told Maquinna that you're leaving?" Vancouver asked.

"I will tell him when he returns."

They sipped coffee. "On another matter," Quadra said, "when should I expect your charts?"

Vancouver placed his cup in the centre of its saucer, which he deposited carefully on the table, and sat back, rubbing his palms together as though he had just hauled up a pennant in a windstorm. "I'm pleased to say we've resolved our technical issues — all my midshipmen save Mister Dobson here are drawing charts as we speak. We are making very good progress."

Quadra waited, but Vancouver seemed disinclined to say anything further.

"Yes?" Quadra prompted at last. "So when will you deliver them?"

A rueful smile appeared on George Vancouver's face, one that was so out of character that it unsettled Dobson. "Not as soon as I had hoped. We still have a substantial backlog of data to get through, and once that's done, I want to check and confirm our plots. I still think it best we give you the lot in California. Better yet, when we return here next spring. If we have the winter to review and correct them, we can ensure their quality."

This was greeted by a short silence.

"Captain, I must have those charts when I leave. Those are my orders from the viceroy himself. If there are still corrections to be made, make a note on the margins. Just deliver them to me before I sail."

"They will be all the more reliable if we take the time —"

"I must insist, Captain. Deliver the charts before I depart."

Vancouver's hands lay flat in front of him as if he was ready to rise, but only his thumbs lifted from the table. "As you wish."

Quadra nodded and made to stand.

"Before we part, may I ask about your investigation?"

The Spaniard slumped back into his chair. For a moment he said nothing. "We don't have the complete story. There are conflicting accounts. To be frank, I'm uncertain how far to push my enquiries. I'll be forced to make compromises I'd prefer not to make. Justice tempered by the circumstances..." He straightened and stood. "I remain hopeful that Maquinna will tell me more when he returns. Above all, I want the truth. Then I must decide if I can act upon it."

In the cutter on the way back to the ship, Van considered all that remained to be done. *Discovery* was seaworthy, though not yet fully rigged; her supplies still needed to be brought aboard, along with wood and fresh water. *Daedalus* was ready for sea, but *Chatham* was another story. This day Broughton would land her ballast to lighten her to the greatest extent possible. Tomorrow there was a spring tide, and at its height the ship would be floated ashore, hove onto blocks, beached, and tipped over for the all-important repairs to her keel. If she wasn't refloated before the end of the spring tide it was two weeks till the next one.

He glanced up at the sky as if looking for evidence of winter's imminence. There was none — it was another unblemished day, the latest in an unbroken string. A string that would soon, inevitably, end.

The boat passed alongside Caamaño's *Aranzazu*. Its launch had just put off and was headed for the mouth of the cove, full of soldiers to relieve the guard at the fort. Vancouver studied the boat, turned back, and appraised *Aranzazu* and then Quadra's flagship, *Activa*, which lay close by *Discovery*. A smile played at the edges of his mouth.

Sometimes at sea, to pass an evening, he played chess with Joseph Whidbey. He usually won, for he could read the master's thoughts before they became moves on the board. He understood the limitations of his own game; he knew he was only a move or two ahead, which was just enough with Old Joe. And here we are, he thought, at the edge of the world, playing another game. The move he was watching was a ruse, a feint made by necessity and easy to miss — unlike his own clumsy effort with the charts. *A simple case of logistics*, his counterpart had called it. *Easier to maintain one post than two.* They were barely managing one, maintaining the appearance of strength with deceit and pretense.

He turned his attention back to the harbour. In the outer road, the Portuguese snow bobbed tightly at its moorings. In the very middle of the anchorage, two English traders lay close by two American brigs, all moored as well — there was no room to swing on a single anchor. The harbour is tight for the traffic it receives, he thought. This reminded him of something, and he craned aft to see the shore. Magee's shallop was still on the construction stocks. It would add to the crowding when it was finally launched.

He noticed a single Indian canoe drawn up on the shingle where *Chatham* would soon be careened. A couple of days before, he had watched Maquinna lead a grand withdrawal after his conference with Quadra. There had been no Indians present in the cove since. He twisted for a better view. A small group of Indians filed slowly up the rise to the Big House, men and some women, led by the elderly war chief, Natzape, leaning on his stick.

"Things are getting back to normal, Mister Dobson," he told his cox'n.

"Sir?"

"There are chiefs making social visits again. So it's back to normal here in Neuva California."

Dobson laughed. "It's a grand ambitious name, sir, isn't it?"

"It is that."

When he boarded *Discovery* he ordered a signal hoisted to summon the commanders of *Chatham* and *Daedalus*. Within twenty minutes they had congregated in the great cabin to receive their orders and discuss preparations for departure.

# Chapter 31

You are wondering about that canoe, and what Natzape and his delegation had to say, and whether Copaza was guilty or innocent, patsy or perp, fall guy or fiend.

In due course I'll take you to the Big House. First, though, witness with me the actual events of that fateful night.

⧗

"Hawkins," Saiyuqa said hopefully.

Matuateh was sure there was someone there, too.

"Shut up," Copaza snapped.

Francisco was still at the traders' fire. The conversation there went on for a long time and seemed animated. Finally, Francisco pulled his companion away and out of the circle of light. They came towards the ridge, where the three of them were waiting.

"Stay here," Copaza said, and climbed down to meet them. They stood profiled against the traders' fire, and Matuateh strained to make out Francisco's companion. She went cold: it was the big dark Spaniard, Carlos, a rough, frightening man. She had seen how Francisco jollied and joked with him, but he still made her nervous. She looked back at the indistinct figure on the beach. For Saiyuqa's sake, she hoped it was Hawkins.

She heard Copaza say, "Two. You wanted two." There was irritation in his voice.

Francisco pulled Copaza away from Carlos, spoke to him, handed him something. Copaza looked down at it and up to Matuateh and Saiyuqa. He said something terse to Francisco and started towards the traders' fire.

Now Francisco and Carlos spoke. Carlos seemed angry. Francisco's tone was soothing. Matuateh listened to their Spanish babble and watched Copaza enter the firelight and speak to the traders. One of them went inside their tent and returned a moment later. Copaza started back.

The heat was gone from the discussion below. Francisco and Carlos fell silent and watched Copaza approach. He had a sack, and Francisco took it from him, fished inside, and pulled out a bottle. He held the sack out to Carlos, who grabbed it from him. There was a loud clink, and Francisco gripped his arm and spoke angrily. Carlos shook him off, and they stood staring at each other. Matuateh watched from above, her heart pounding. Finally, Francisco spoke, his voice calm, first to Carlos, then to Copaza. Matuateh could not hear what he said. Copaza looked up towards her, eyes seeking her blindly. Then he turned to Carlos and gestured for him to follow. They circled the traders' fire, staying in the shadows, and when they reached the edge of the forest they stopped. For a moment Matuateh thought they were going to return. Instead, they disappeared into the trees.

Francisco peered along the beach and called out softly.

The indistinct figure in the dark moved closer. Matuateh still could not see who it was. Next to her, Saiyuqa leaned forward, straining to see.

Francisco walked out to meet him and stopped in his tracks. The two of them had a rapid-fire exchange in the middle language the whites used between their tribes. Next to her, Saiyuqa whispered: "It's Hawkins!"

The two men conferred at length. At last, they turned together and came to the foot of the rocks. Hawkins, Matuateh saw, wore a cloak. Francisco looked up to where he knew the girls to be. His easy grin came to his face, and he called softly, "Come down, pretty girls. Pretty girls, come down."

Matuateh and Saiyuqa exchanged glances. They climbed down and stood awkwardly. Francisco and the cloaked man came closer. The girls finally saw his face. It was not Hawkins, but another of the Englishmen, the tall, curly one named Pitt.

"Copaza is a *liar*," Saiyuqa said to Matuateh. "He's not even a trickster. He is the droppings of a trickster."

"There's been a mix-up," Francisco said. "Please understand. It's not Copaza's or anybody's fault. I gave this gentleman a message for Yim Hawkes, but Yim Hawkes was sent back to his ship. This gentleman has come in his stead. He is the son of a great *tyee*, and he will be as gentle and as generous as Yim Hawkes. He is prepared to be very generous," he said, emphasizing the *very*.

Saiyuqa had known only the life of a *coulz* and was somewhat mollified by the promise of generosity for her gentle favours. But she was still angry and unsettled by this unexpected turn. For her, it wasn't a matter of choice.

Matuateh was thinking only of herself, of her happiness at being with Francisco — who enveloped her now in his arms and kissed her.

Down the beach there was movement. A stumble, a voice.

"What was that?" Matuateh asked.

Another vague shape appeared from the darkness. It called out, and Pitt called back quietly. It came nearer and materialized into another of the English from the hot springs. He greeted Pitt loudly and Pitt shushed him again, hurried to him, pulled him close to speak.

It was the one called Links. He grinned and swayed as he listened to his friend. He had a bottle, which he held by the neck.

"I don't like this one," Matuateh told Francisco. In her mind she saw him, spotted and mottled like a snake, in the water, blubbering, while two of her friends bled and wept.

"I won't go with him," Saiyuqa said angrily. "I won't."

Francisco looked like he didn't like this turn of events either. He addressed Pitt, then Links directly. They both replied, though Pitt did most of the talking. It was a lengthy back-and-forth. Finally, Francisco turned to Matuateh and Saiyuqa. "Don't worry. His friend invited him along to drink. Just to drink. See, he brought his own bottle. In fact, I think he's drunk already." His eyes rested on Saiyuqa. "You don't have to be with him. I promise."

Saiyuqa was not happy with this development. Nor was Matuateh, though she spent scant time thinking about it. She held Francisco's sleeve possessively until he said, "Let's go."

Copaza had landed their canoe in a tiny bight behind the ridge. When they got to it Links uncorked his bottle and drank. Pitt said something to Francisco, who handed him the bottle Copaza had bought. Pitt uncorked it and took a swig. The liquor caught in his throat and he sputtered and coughed. Links laughed. Pitt scowled and took another pull, forcing it down.

Francisco accepted the bottle back and took a swig himself. When he swallowed he grunted, grimaced, and shiver-shook like a dog. Links and Pitt both laughed, and Francisco grinned good-naturedly. He moved to cork the bottle, but Pitt said something. Francisco looked at him for a moment before wiping the bottle's mouth and offering it to Matuateh.

She looked from it to him.

"Try it," he said.

Matuateh had never tasted whisky. It burned her throat and she choked and coughed. Saiyuqa did too. The three young men laughed at their reaction and took additional swigs themselves to show their own fortitude. Then they dragged the heavy dugout into the water, scraping it across the wet stones that marked the tide's retreat.

When it was afloat in the shallows the boys toasted its launch.

They set out with Francisco in the stern and the two girls paddling with him, the English content to ride. The canoe hugged the darkness of the north shore and quietly passed the dimly lit ships moored nearby. When they reached the mouth of the cove, they turned north and left Yuquot behind a point of land.

They were now in the darkness of the Sound. Matuateh studied the shore on their left and soon spotted what she was looking for. They paddled into a narrow crevasse and hauled the canoe up so it was out of sight. The boys drank again. Somewhere above an owl hooted; then all was still.

Matuateh led them up the bed of a dry rivulet that fed the crevasse in rainy weather. It was a steep slope, and as they climbed stones grated and shifted underfoot. After a few minutes the rivulet crossed a rough path that followed the contour of the land. She waited there for everyone to catch up. When they did they paused for breath and a drink, for they were huffing and hot from the climb. Matuateh wished the stream was flowing; she would have preferred water to whisky. She took another wary sip from the bottle. Her tongue and mouth burned and it stung her throat.

"These are the paths of deer," she told Francisco. "This way."

The others followed her, waving insects away. The path was narrow; brambles reached close to scratch as they passed. Other paths intertwined with theirs, heading off in many directions, but Matuateh knew the way. They wended on through the dark forest until she heard water trickling down a slope. She knew they were close now. A minute later the path wound around a large boulder and ended on a grassy ledge.

Below them lay the cove at Yuquot, with the lights of the ships glimmering softly, those of the Spanish village and fort shining faintly beyond.

Francisco strode to the edge to take it in. "It's perfect," he said.

The English jabbered among themselves. Links laughed, took another drink from his bottle, and spoke to the ships in the harbour. Matuateh heard Macubah's name. Pitt laughed and drank and handed Francisco the bottle. As Francisco drank, Pitt moved towards Matuateh, suddenly grabbed her hand, swung her to him, and caught her by the waist.

She tried to push him away, but he held tight. She called out in alarm, and Francisco was beside her instantly. He said something curt and Pitt let her go. Francisco drew her away by the hand. Matuateh could see their faces. Francisco was angry. Pitt laughed, shrugged, said something, and drank again, forcing a mouthful down. Then he handed the bottle to Francisco. Relief swept over Matuateh. It was a peace offering, a gesture of contrition, and when the bottle came to her she drank too. The liquor blazed in her mouth and throat.

They were hot from the climb through the woods, and a gentle breeze now blew off the cove, cooling their sweat. They sat on the ledge and admired the view. The three boys were all getting along again. They spoke among themselves, gestured at the ships, laughed quietly. The bottle was passed around again, and this time Matuateh did not drink. She felt her tongue and throat burning from what she had taken already. It did not taste or feel good to her. She did not like the effect it gave, the night spinning slowly, the confusion in her head. She decided she would take no more.

"Matuateh," said Saiyuqa. "Sister."

Matuateh peered and saw her anxious face. "Do what you have to do. Francisco promised it'll be all right."

Saiyuqa's eyes narrowed. She drank from the bottle as it came to her, squeezing her eyes shut and dipping her head, her chin pointed, as she swallowed hard. Pitt came to sit beside her.

Francisco led Matuateh a short distance from the others. The breeze had chilled them now and they sat close together, he with his arm around her. She nestled into him and he whispered to her, his voice a little slurred. He made her laugh, and she spoke mock-Spanish back to him and he laughed back. She was heedless and happy; they were together and that was all that mattered. He touched her cheek, lifted her chin. She felt his lips' caress. They lay beneath the stars in each other's arms, aware of nothing but this moment. The night spun around them. A chorus of crazed crickets screamed in her head, but she was with Francisco; that was all that mattered.

She was brought back by a noise from a great distance. It echoed in her head, grew to something louder. Rustling. Footsteps. Someone was approaching. Copaza, she thought, alarmed. Both she and Francisco sat up quickly. But it was not Copaza. It was Pitt. He thrust the bottle into Francisco's hand and stood over them, rocking slightly, leering. Matuateh covered herself, and he laughed and spoke in their white middle language. Francisco stared up at him before he drank. He grunted as the liquor reached his stomach and handed the bottle back. Pitt handed it straight to Matuateh, and she took it, unsettled by his presence, so close, in the space that had been theirs. She drank, though she did not want to. Her vision was swimming and her head was impossibly heavy on her neck. She swung it with effort to look at Francisco, then at Pitt.

Francisco grabbed the bottle away from her. "No more," he said. "It's not good, this rum." He said something to Pitt, who laughed dismissively, took the bottle back, and staggered away. Matuateh's head was spinning, her thoughts confused and disconnected. She was very tired. Her eyelids, dragged by the weight of her drooping head, closed.

She awoke some time later to a commotion that broke through the thump of her own heart in her head. Her stomach was afire. She was on her side and felt Francisco's body curled into hers, his arm around her waist. She was uncertain where she was. And then she remembered. She wondered how long she'd been unaware.

Lightning stabbed her between the eyes when she sat up. Francisco stirred with her movement.

They were both conscious now, aware of noise and movement yet unable to rouse themselves or comprehend the scene on the other side of the little clearing.

Pitt lay spread-eagled on his back, as though he'd fallen from the sky. Next to him lay Saiyuqa, on her side, stirring weakly. The other Englishman, Links, was standing shirtless, swaying unsteadily over her, now hectoring her, now mumbling to himself, now addressing the night. He stumbled away from her, swung around to take in the harbour, guzzled from the bottle he held in one hand, stumbled around and back to address Saiyuqa again. He gestured with the bottle.

Saiyuqa shifted feebly and tried to crawl away.

Links became angry at her unreasonableness. He reached for her hair and tugged her into a sitting position. From where Matuateh lay, seemingly paralyzed, she saw Saiyuqa's eyes roll white. Her head drooped and she would have fallen back prone if Links had not held her hair. He stooped and nuzzled her neck, his bottle held wide from his body for balance. Matuateh saw that Saiyuqa was comatose now and beyond response. Links swore and gave her hair another tug that tilted her head back and raised her chin. Her mouth fell open and the pain was enough to bring her eyes back from within her skull.

Links tipped the bottle and poured whisky down the funnel of her throat.

At first it flowed without resistance. Then she gagged, for the liquid was backing up, unable to flow through the constriction of her gorge; she coughed and sputtered, her body struggling to expel it, but Links still held her hair. She was choking, drowning on whisky. Her hands went to her throat. She clawed at her neck and mouth in a desperate, flagging frenzy. The whites of her eyes returned. She ceased struggling.

Matuateh watched helplessly, unable to rise, frozen in her stupor.

Links laughed.

She felt movement at her side. Francisco rolled to his knees, rose to his feet — and launched across the clearing. He barged into Links, shoving him hard and driving him back, away from Saiyuqa. The Englishman stumbled and nearly fell, yet with the uncanny agility afforded by drink, his arms flailing and feet shuffling wildly, he regained his balance without dropping his bottle. He stood and swayed, drew himself up, and peered at Francisco, who ignored him and knelt to attend to Saiyuqa.

With exaggerated care Links put his bottle down on a patch of grass. He moved closer to where Francisco ministered to the unconscious young woman, as if to observe — and then he lunged. His momentum carried all three forward onto the ground. Saiyuqa went down and lay still. Francisco sprawled flat on his back. Links rolled into a crouch and made to stand.

Francisco kicked him hard in the chest with both feet, and he went reeling away. Once again, drunk as he was, he kept his footing.

It was at the farthest reach of his staggering dance that he stopped and pulled his knife from the scabbard on his belt. He leaned into a crouch and flicked the blade in the air, as if inviting Francisco to repeat his last manoeuvre. Francisco was on his feet now, and he crouched too, and they circled each other, round and round again, Francisco murmuring, "Auggie, Auggie," in a soothing voice.

It was clearly a call to sense, but it had the opposite effect. Links, his face contorted, sprang. Francisco dodged out of his path and swung an off-balance punch that hit home. Links lurched sideways with the blow, recovered, and swung at Francisco, who had lost his balance with the momentum of his punch. The knife's blade sliced across his chest. Blood welled instantly along the line of the cut. Matuateh heard him grunt and saw him look down — there was no pain in his expression, only surprise. In that moment, Matuateh thought, That will end it; the Englishman will come to his senses. Francisco must have thought the same thing. He straightened, said "Auggie" — and Links lunged. His blade struck, this time not as a wild swipe but as a thrust. Its force propelled Francisco backwards. He fell, and Links fell on him, and his blade thudded into Francisco's torso. Again, and again, and again.

The rate of the blows slackened and eventually stopped.

Links looked down at Francisco's body. Matuateh thought there must now be a return to sanity, a realization of what he had done. The blade resisted as he pulled it from Francisco's chest. He stared at it, rose to his feet, stood shakily, and looked again at the body. He looked at Saiyuqa, who was still prone. Then he looked across the clearing to where Matuateh lay propped, still disembodied by drink, helpless witness to his act of madness.

The moment their eyes met, fear replaced horror in Matuateh's mind. She rolled and crawled to her knees, rose unsteadily to her feet, and faced him.

He took a step toward her.

Her blood froze as she realized she was going to die.

A hoarse voice broke the spell. "Links," it said. "Links."

Pitt's eyes were open. The fight had gone on around him. He, like Matuateh, was too stupefied to move. His voice was weak. Links went to him, knelt, listened.

Matuateh backed away, then remembered Saiyuqa. She froze again.

Swaying, Links stood and turned to her. Pitt spoke again, this time in a stronger voice — there was a note of urgency in it. Links looked down at him and nodded, advanced towards Matuateh, and stopped over Francisco's body. With the blade of his knife, he pointed at Saiyuqa, then at Matuateh, and held his hand over his mouth.

He dropped the hand away, brought the blade towards his own throat, and made a slicing gesture across it in the air.

He addressed her in English, but she recognized some of the words. King George. England. Nootka (gesturing around him). King George Macubah (gesturing towards the harbour). Nootka, England, Macubah. Spain (indicating Francisco's body).

He pointed the blade again at Saiyuqa, then at Matuateh, and repeated the cutting gesture near his own throat. Then he pointed at them and covered his mouth. His face was smeared with Francisco's blood. For a moment he glared at Matuateh, then gestured dismissively into the night, as though shooing a dog. He turned towards Pitt, took a step in his direction, but stopped, turned back, and bent to the body to pluck a medallion from Francisco's nearly severed neck. He gave it a cursory glance and pocketed it. Then he staggered to Pitt and knelt to prop him up.

A bottomless chasm lay before her. She felt horror and grief at what had befallen Francisco, revulsion towards the Englishman, fear, disbelief at the sudden senseless violence — and disgust with herself, at her helplessness. She was angry and frightened and weeping, all at once, and for a moment she forgot the burning in her mouth and throat and belly, the strange spinning of the night around her.

"Crazy white man," she sobbed. She could think of no other words, so she kept repeating, "Crazy white man...you *crazy* white man," as she moved to help Saiyuqa, sobbing in sorrow and fear and anger. She shook Saiyuqa into semi-consciousness and got her to her knees, still crying and repeating the only words she could summon. She pulled Saiyuqa's arm over her shoulder and dragged her until her feet began to move. As quickly as Matuateh could manoeuvre her, they staggered into the woods.

They crashed along a deer path, Matuateh's only thought being to put distance between them and Links. She veered onto another path, then another, to ensure they could not be followed. She knew the paths but she had no plan, no destination. Just away. Saiyuqa was a dead weight and Matuateh was breathless from the exertion. She stopped to rest. Saiyuqa was partly conscious now, woozy and disoriented, still unable to walk by herself. Matuateh took her weight again and moved on, taking a new trail whenever she could, thinking only of putting the safety of the forest between them and the English. She had to stop frequently to catch her breath and find new energy.

It was during one of these rests, when her breathing had subsided and the pounding of her heart had faded in her ears, that she heard the first sounds of predawn, the birds that foretell day's advent; and the unmistakable sound of a creature, man or beast, stumbling along the trail behind her.

Her stomach clenched, her hackles rose; and that strange energy that courses when danger threatens charged her limbs and cleared her brain. She was instantly sober, assessing choices for survival. She looked around and seized upon a heavy stick.

"Be still," she whispered to Saiyuqa. "Roll off the path and keep still."

She helped Saiyuqa, then moved off the path herself, crouching.

A figure came into sight. Shambling, fast. Matuateh waited until he was nearly abreast of them before she swung her club. It struck across his midsection and dropped him to the ground.

THE WIND FROM ALL DIRECTIONS | 273

"*Uhhhh,*" he gasped.

She leaped out and raised the club to smash the crazy white man's skull.

The black of night had ebbed into dimmest dawn. She locked eyes with him. She lowered the club. "What are you doing here?"

Copaza peered up at her from the forest floor. "Looking for you." He sat up, rubbing his chest. As he reached a sitting position he groaned and cradled his temple.

"He's dead," Matuateh said. "Francisco's dead. Killed by the English."

Copaza cursed. "The whisky," he said, now holding his head.

"No, the English," she said.

"It's poison. It's not supposed to be like that. I came to find you, to warn you." He glanced around, saw Saiyuqa prone on the ground, thought for a moment. "Where's Francisco?"

"He's dead." She began to cry. She had been composed until then, during their escape. "Dead," she said again, sobbing. "The English."

He reached out in the fading darkness and gently, tentatively, touched her shoulder.

"Then I'm too late," he said.

He sat with his arm extended awkwardly towards her while she cried. Eventually, he drew her close and held her. When she composed herself he allowed her to draw away. He looked around at their surroundings, thinking. "We'll be blamed for this," he said. "We have to go."

She looked at him.

"Carlos. The other Spaniard. He may be dead too."

"Did you kill him?"

He looked at her strangely. "No. It's the whisky. It's poison."

"Is he dead?"

"I don't know. I left him to come for you. He's in bad shape. I'm not...I'm not too good either."

Saiyuqa was completely still. Matuateh pressed her palm to her chest to feel her breathe. "I won't leave another to die."

"We have to leave him. I can't make it back there. It's a wonder I found you."

"Where is he?"

Copaza stared at her. As far gone as he was, he saw she was determined.

"I left him on the outer shore, at the top of the bay near the big rock."

"Stay with Saiyuqa. I'll come back here and we'll take the canoe. The English won't find where we hid it."

She went in the direction from which he had come; and as she looked around, she who had run blindly in the dark now recognized where she was. She found a path that would take her to the outer shore. Soon she heard breakers. She emerged above the beach. The sky was brightening. She walked along the grass verge separating the stony shore ridge from the forest, looking for a body, listening for sounds of life above those of the sea. The ocean air was fresh in her face and she felt better for it — her mind was clearing. But she thought of Francisco and had a blinding vision of the knife plunging into his torso while she lay paralyzed, unable to act or even speak. She began again to sob. Her eyes streamed, her face tightened into a mask of grief; she took great racking gulps of breath. She was on the verge, she felt, of shattering into bits. She saw her broken shards scattered on the beach, raw edges forever jagged, never rounded by the ceaseless roll and recession of the waves. This was the future she foresaw: solitude on a tragic shore, the waves, an infinite cycle of suffering.

She found Carlos sprawled face down against a driftwood log, covered in his own retchings, curled up with his arms across his middle, moaning pitiably. As she rolled him over, she felt a stab like a flash of lightning, a white pain echoing inside her skull. Poison, Copaza had called it. She untied the kerchief Carlos wore around his neck and used it to mop his brow and wipe his scarred face. His eyes fluttered open and in them she recognized the blinding pain she felt herself. She spoke to him tenderly, as Apanas had comforted her when she was a small child, as her own mother had comforted her before Apanas. She wiped his brow, his cheek, his chin.

He mumbled and closed his eyes. Then they fluttered open and he smiled and reached a hand towards her. She drew back fearfully. His hand stopped in midair and made the sign of the cross. He drew it on her from the distance between them; then his hand fell back to the ground. His eyes closed.

She heard a sound. With a fright she saw two figures emerge from the forest to walk on the firm ledge above the beach. The Englishmen. One supported the other, as she had supported Saiyuqa. Neither looked around. Neither saw her. She watched them in the bleak dawn light as they stumbled in the opposite direction, away from her, towards the Spanish village and the white men's world.

Shhh, she said to Carlos, shhhh. She held a finger to his lips. His eyes fluttered open, then shut again. Matuateh rose and returned to the forest.

A moment later I landed on the driftwood log to get a closer look at Carlos. His eyes opened briefly at the sound of my wings. He would live.

There was nothing for me there.

Nothing *there*, but there were plum pickings on a nearby grassy knoll. I crouched and pushed off and caught a tailwind off the sea.

# Chapter 32

Matuateh returned to Copaza and Saiyuqa and they fled in the canoe. They were too feeble to travel all the way to Tahsis, so they landed a short distance from Yuquot, concealed the canoe, and hid in an old hutch in the forest that Copaza knew from his days of *osumich*. There, with the passage of the hours, their physical agony subsided and they recovered their senses. Matuateh was the least affected. She tended the others through that long day and night.

"I didn't want this," Copaza told her. "Any of it. What happened..."

"I know," Matuateh replied.

In a day they were well enough to make the journey to Tahsis. They paddled in silence, grateful for the cleansing distraction of physical exertion. Matuateh's mind roiled with thoughts of Francisco and the calamity of which she was a part. Visions of that night, details she had forgotten or willed away, came unbidden.

At Tahsis, everything was unsettlingly normal. Word of Francisco's murder had yet to arrive; his body was only discovered in Yuquot that morning.

They went to Apanas and told her everything. Matuateh sobbed in Apanas's arms as the older woman cradled her like a child. Copaza looked on, and Saiyuqa said nothing. She had closed like a clam since their escape.

Apanas made them bathe and eat a meal, their first in days; then she led them to Maquinna.

Maquinna listened to what they had to say and summoned his counsellors.

"We will be blamed," Quatlazape said.

"We will be blamed unless we say what we know," Natzape countered. "The truth protects us."

"The truth is on our side," Maquinna said.

"Quadra is a white man," Quatlazape said, "We will still be blamed. He will never believe it was anyone but a 'savage.'"

"Quadra will believe you," Natzape told Maquinna. "He is fair. He has always spoken of the fairness of Spanish justice."

"This is what comes from being the white man's dog," Tsakwasap said.

The look Maquinna cast him was withering.

"The truth is our best protection," Natzape said.

"That may be so," Quatlazape told Maquinna, "but if you blame those two English, you will be taking sides between the whites. You've always avoided that. If you choose a side now, is it the best one for us? Despite all Quadra's nice words, his assurances and his promises — and I grant you he is a good man — he has already sent half his men away. If the Spanish leave, we will be at the mercy of the English. It will not go well for us if we have accused one of their own of murder. We'll pay for it many times over."

"Macubah has been fair in all his dealings with us. We heard that also from the Salish and Kwakwaka'wakw who encountered him. He attacked no one, harmed no one, took nothing. He punishes his own men when they go against his commands. He is like Quadra."

"I have come to know him a little," Comekala said. "What Natzape says is true."

"Macubah will not be here forever."

It went back and forth like this until Tsakwasap interrupted with a shake of his rattle. Everyone expected him to chant or call upon the spirits. Instead, he said, "You all speak of sides. The only side for the Mowachaht is our own."

Maquinna's eyes held the shaman's. "The people's welfare is my only concern."

"It is not taking sides to tell what we know is the truth. And it isn't the English side that killed the boy," said Natzape. "It's one Englishman."

"The son of their great chief who rules under their king — *he* was there," Quatlazape said. "They won't acknowledge any wrongdoing on his part —"

"Where is his guilt?" Natzape asked. "Matuateh says —"

"What if it *was* him?" Quatlazape interrupted. "There is only Matuateh to say, and she was under the spell of whisky. She herself admits that. What if she is mistaken? They will call her a liar anyway. What will they say of her motives? She was *there*. She was *with* the dead Spaniard." Matuateh's head fell to her chest and she began to sob again in Apanas's arms. Quatlazape cast an eye at Copaza, whom he had treated with contempt since the boy's failed apprenticeship with Tsakwasap. "Who sanctioned her congress? No one. And we all know what she is."

Apanas glared at him. "She is my *daughter*."

Tsakwasap broke the silence that followed with another shake of his rattle. The sound jarred, like gravel cast onto drum-skin. Maquinna glanced at him, but this time the old man closed his eyes and intoned an appeal to the spirits.

"Even if Quadra believes it was not one of us," Quatlazape continued, "even if he believes the story of a drunken child" — here he gestured and scowled at Matuateh — "the English will not give up a member of their *tyeeclati* for punishment by the Spanish. These two tribes of white men, they hate each other. They will fight a war before they ever do that. Even though Quadra and Macubah behave as friends, their nations are enemies. We cannot allow ourselves to be caught between them."

Maquinna listened to everybody's opinion and made no pronouncements on what he would do.

Later that day, the Mowachaht who had fled Yuquot upon news of the murder arrived with the message summoning Maquinna. They confirmed what Quatlazape had predicted, that the Mowachaht were being blamed. The counsellors convened again. Maquinna listened to their deliberations in silence.

Many thoughts exist in the mind of a leader, because many considerations must be weighed in the balance. Perhaps Maquinna had not decided what he would say to Quadra when he left for Yuquot the next day. Maybe he had to think about it on the way — the consequences, the implications, those who would suffer. Did he sleep on it at Marvinas Bay, the night before he entered Yuquot? Perhaps he was still mulling his decision on the final ride into Friendly Cove. It could be that he decided what he would tell Quadra only when he stood before him in the great hall, when he denied his people's guilt (true) and blamed the

Hesquiaht (which was, as you now know, a statement at liberty from fact). Regardless, what he said served his ends. The actions of a great and noble chief are not always great and noble.

The alliance with the Hesquiaht that Calicum's marriage to Apanas was intended to secure had never materialized; the Hesquiaht had remained close with Maquinna's rival, Wickaninnish of the Tla-o-qui-aht. The circumstances (unfortunate as they were) now offered Maquinna an opportunity to take the Hesquiaht down a notch, and Wickaninnish with them. Give me arms, he told Quadra. Lend me your support, and with it I will punish the Hesquiaht.

When Maquinna returned from Yuquot, Apanas heard what he had said, and grew alarmed for her kin. She went to Natzape and begged him to intervene with Maquinna.

"He has spoken," the old man said.

"Then I will go to speak with Quadra myself."

Natzape looked at her. "Woman, you should not do that."

Apanas wore him down. He had a fondness for her. His wife had died two years previous, and the embers of youth still smouldered in the old fellow.

"I will do as you ask," he said eventually. "But it is against the will of Maquinna. He must never know that we have spoken to the Spanish. You will come with me, Apanas, and Matuateh must come too. We will speak to Quadra together. I will tell him that we will trade the truth for a promise. Only when he gives his word that he will hold what we say secret — only then will Matuateh tell her story. Quadra is a just man and will keep his word once given. He has told us this himself."

⧗

Natzape travelled with Matuateh and Apanas to Yuquot to meet Quadra. In the Big House again, this time in Quadra's office, without benefit of smudge or shaman's rattle or the presence of the assembled elders of the Mowachaht nation, Natzape explained that he was defying his chief, as a *masicim* should never do, to prevent a grave injustice. He proposed his quid pro quo: the truth, for Quadra's word that he would hold it forever in confidence.

Quadra's expression was inscrutable. He remained silent for a long time as he thought about Natzape's terms. At last he consented.

When Matuateh finished speaking, Quadra's face was drained of colour. He looked, Apanas later said, like a man who had looked directly at a *chi'ha*, the consequence of which is certain death.

There was a long silence in the room. Finally, Quadra spoke; but his words were not addressed to Natzape, or Apanas, or Matuateh. Nor to Alberni or Caamaño, sitting sombre and silent beside him. These words he spoke to himself, and Alberni, looking at his chief, did not see fit to translate them for the visitors; and so they were lost to Matuateh — all, that is, except one, which she remembered always, as if it were tattooed upon her soul. It was a word she had learned from Francisco on the very day they met: *perdido*.

Lost.

# Chapter 33

For the British contingent, the next several days passed as a whirlwind. *Chatham* was floated ashore and tipped on her side. Crewmen from all three ships swarmed over her hull like ants at a picnic, inspecting seams, caulking, replacing timbers. They repaired and coppered her damaged keel, removed her rudder, and rebuilt it on the beach. Two days later they righted and refloated the brig and began the laborious task of reloading and re-rigging. On *Discovery*, repairs and rigging were completed, and fresh sails were bent on. The supplies delivered by *Daedalus* were finally divided between her sister ships and stowed in their respective holds.

The midshipmen missed these many acts of busyness. They did nothing but plot maps or copy those plotted by others. All three ships needed complete sets, and multiple duplicates were needed for dispatch to the Admiralty. One set would be borne on *Daedalus*, which was bound for Port Jackson in Australia; another was produced for dispatch via a China-bound merchantman that had yet to be identified. And then there were the copies intended for the Spaniards; it did not go unnoticed that the poorest of the draftsmen were assigned to produce those.

It was meticulous, tedious work. Tensions simmered among them and frequently boiled over. Amid the general strain and botheration, no one noticed those among them who were edgier, cockier, quicker to lash out. It is striking how guilt can hide in plain sight. The devil's best trick is convincing others he does not exist.

It had been more than a week since Francisco Almeida's murder, and the consensus in the cove was that Copaza had done it — or, if not him, some other Indian; it didn't matter who. There had been no arrests or reprisals, and there were grumbles that the Spanish commandant had done nothing to punish those responsible — that the savages needed to be taught the value of a white man's life.

These complaints rankled Jim Hawkins. He had seen Francisco and Copaza together. There had been no animosity between them. They had acted like friends. He felt sure that if the facts were assembled — methodically, like a chart drawn from a hundred independent observations — the truth would be revealed and Copaza would be exonerated. At his drafting table, and on the few occasions he left it, and at night in the midshipmen's mess, he spoke to those who had been ashore in the days before Francisco's death, whether on a work party, as a coxswain or messenger, or on duty at the observatory, even those who had been at the infirmary. Had they talked to Francisco? Seen him? Seen anything odd?

No one wanted anything to do with his questions. They were treated as an annoyance, a waste of time, or — worse — a reminder of the danger that lurked in *terra nullius*. Hawkins half-believed them when they told him he was wasting his time — yet he persevered.

He had been ashore only once since Francisco's disappearance — and that just to helm a boat. On the beach he encountered Ensign Ortiz, who told him what he knew about the Spanish commandant's investigation — which was only that Carlos Libertad had somehow been exonerated, though he would be confined to *Activa* until it sailed.

There was talk about the expedition rendezvousing with Quadra in California. Hawkins resolved to seek out Carlos there.

His mind kept returning to the facts as he knew them, the events leading up to that night. He made notes in his journal and kept talking it through with his shipmates, thinking he might work it out and stumble onto the truth. Roberts, with whom he shared a drafting table, looked at him sympathetically and kept his thoughts to himself. Others were less patient. "Jim, you're getting a little obsessive," Ramsay told him. Lincoln scowled darkly, clearly annoyed with his incessant questions. "Jesus, Hawkins," Dorsey said, "just let it fucking go."

A few days after his final meeting with Quadra on the diplomatic issue, Vancouver responded in writing to the Spanish commander's last letter. It was a letter for the record, confirming that they had agreed to disagree. Accompanying it were the charts his counterpart had repeatedly requested.

The next day Quadra sent a note acknowledging receipt of both the letter and the charts. This marked their last official exchange in Nootka Sound. *Activa* was ready to depart. It would sail next morning.

That same day, Maquinna returned to Friendly Cove as promised. He came in a single canoe, and its progression through the harbour elicited keen interest among observers on *Discovery*. He spent a long time at the Big House and departed before dark. Quadra accompanied him to the landing to see him off, and it was clear to all those watching that they parted with profuse expressions of friendship and affection.

# Chapter 34

That night, Quadra and his officers came aboard *Discovery* for the final time before *Activa*'s departure. They and their British counterparts crowded into the great cabin, where a head table was set for the seniormost of them, and smaller ones squeezed in for everyone else. George Vancouver gave a short speech and toasted their respective monarchs. Quadra responded with a laudatory toast to Vancouver and his officers and men. This begat another toast to return the compliments. A number of spontaneous toasts followed, offered up by various officers from both sides. The mood in the cramped cabin grew boisterous, the company raucous. The two commissioners conversed congenially and held themselves apart from the developing bacchanal.

Midshipman Tom Dobson focused on their exchanges and could not translate those of others; so, as the evening wore on, everyone made do. The French speakers at the head table had the easiest of it. The warrant officers, midshipmen, and master's mates of both navies, all mixed in at jury-rigged tables and crannies, used whatever worked. Liquor flowed generously and efforts at polite conversation gave way to shouts and gestures and, all else failing, backslaps and glasses raised and drained in unison. They revelled in the grand camaraderie of the sea. No mere language barrier could keep them from communing as equals — indeed, as brothers.

The sweet was served, the table cleared, and the port circulated. Vancouver called "Gentlemen! Gentlemen!" and waited for quiet.

Pedro Alberni, seeking to help, tinkled a spoon on his glass. The cabin instantly fell still.

He looked around and registered that every British eye was upon him. "*Qué?*"

"It's a, um, tradition, Captain," Zach Mudge explained. "Actually, an old superstition. About luck. We don't..." — he made the motion of striking his glass without actually striking it — "on a ship."

Indeed (he didn't say, but I well knew), it tolled the death of a sailor.

As Dobson translated, Alberni rubbed his chin. In the sudden quiet, the scratch of his stubble was plainly audible. "*Mis disculpas,*" he said. My apologies.

This was the customary moment for the toast of the day, which in the British Navy marked the formal end of dinner. By tradition, the toast was given by a junior officer.

Vancouver looked lengthwise down the table that T-boned his own, scrutinizing the faces of the midshipmen at its end.

"I believe it's Mister Pitt's turn, sir," said Mudge, whose job included keeping track of such things.

Vancouver's eyes rested on Pitt without enthusiasm. "Yes. Mister Pitt. Will you honour us with the toast of the day. I think we will dispense with the *usual* toast tonight. I am in the mind for a *Sunday.*"

This was a point of discretion on Vancouver's part, for there was a different toast for every day of the week, and while most were wholesome and sentimental — to absent friends, to wives and sweethearts — a few were bawdy or bellicose; these were avoided in mixed company, whether the mix included members of the fair sex or representatives of a frequent enemy such as Spain.

Old Joe Whidbey, sitting outside the inner circle, had kept an eye on his boys all through dinner. They had been enjoying themselves and drinking heavily, Pitt as usual their ringleader. Old Joe had noticed him casting looks at the dignitaries at the head table; he'd seemed curious about the captain's interaction with the Spanish commandant. Whidbey studied the lad's face to see if he'd caught the captain's drift. It seemed he had, for he nodded, inclined his head, and picked up his glass. Everyone else raised their own expectantly.

"Gentlemen."

Pitt extended his glass towards the two commanders, lifted it high, and held it motionless. The cabin was still. "We are, all of us, servants of the naval profession, and disciples of Mars. We are thus of one mind. One sentiment. One fervent wish. And so, a toast — to a willing foe and sea room."

Whidbey's head swivelled from his glass to Pitt. The boy had given the Friday toast, and while it *was* Friday, Vancouver had clearly signalled he did not want the Friday toast delivered. It was meant for nights of boastful swagger among one's peers, not for a diplomatic occasion. It was certainly not for utterance in the presence of foreign naval officers whose predecessors had been their predecessors' principal foes for two hundred years.

Whidbey glanced up the table at the expectant faces of the Spaniards, at Vancouver's ruddy glare. The Spanish officers sat with glasses in hand, politely awaiting the translation. Quadra's expression was unreadable. Broughton cleared his throat. Puget shifted uncomfortably in his chair. The rest of the British officers sat frozen with glasses raised. Everyone recognized it as a faux pas. Everyone, that is, except Tom Dobson, who was newly enrolled in the navy and unschooled in its traditions. And though he did not know that there were seven distinct toasts, much less how Friday's differed from Sunday's — he sensed the sudden tension in the cabin.

Still, having grown accustomed to the awkwardness of a conversation, nay an entire relationship, reliant upon a single point of contact — *him* — he felt obliged to translate Pitt's toast into Spanish verbatim.

"To a willing —"

"Mister Dobson," Vancouver interrupted. "You will please translate the Sunday toast. It is 'to absent friends.'"

"To absent friends," Dobson intoned immediately in English, his glass raised high as if it were his toast, not Pitt's. He repeated the words in Spanish.

Quadra raised his glass higher to Vancouver, then to the others, finally settling its rim and his gaze on Pitt. His eyes narrowed at the distance. He downed his glass in one go. Everyone else followed his lead.

"That is a poignant sentiment," he said in reply, his eyes still on Pitt. "Yet among friends such as we have become, among brothers such as us, one feels less distant from those for whom it is intended."

"Hear, hear," Vancouver said when he received the translation. "Well said."

Broughton and Mudge nodded. Puget and Baker exchanged looks. Whidbey glanced at Menzies, who raised one eyebrow back. Whidbey was sure Pitt would receive a tongue-lashing after the Spaniards disembarked — this time with justification. This was a glaring example of the lad's inattention to his studies, and the captain was clearly not pleased.

Well, the lad would learn eventually.

The formalities were over, and the diners rose to mingle. They soon migrated to the quarterdeck, where it was cooler and there was more room. Stewards circulated among them, topping up glasses, and the midshipmen sought to be well topped up. A few glasses later, Jim Hawkins noticed Archibald Menzies chatting with his Spanish counterpart, Moziño. He slipped away from his mates and edged through the crowd towards them, realizing only then that he was a little drunk. He moved carefully to compensate. Menzies was showing Moziño the newly installed glass cover on his plant enclosure's frame. They glanced up at his arrival, nodded, and continued their conversation in French. Hawkins, swaying a bit, had the presence of mind to realize theirs was a professional discussion; he moved on. Ned Roberts was nearby with Ensign Ortiz, Ortiz leaning close and gripping Ned's sleeve as though conveying a confidence. Hawkins understood that they too would be conversing in French, and passed them by.

And there was Old Joe smoking a cheroot with Pedro Alberni. Hawkins was suddenly overcome with affection for the grizzled Spaniard. He slow-walked towards him, thrust his hand out, and fervently wished him a bon voyage and good health and good digestion too, because he wondered if the meat at dinner might have been a little off. Alberni understood none of what he said, yet he nodded and grinned and returned the handshake; and when Hawkins finally stopped talking he began to reply — but at that moment Hawkins belched wetly, clapped a hand across his mouth, and reeled to the railing to throw up into the harbour.

The retches that followed rid him of his recent meal, and brought him closer to self-awareness. He wiped his mouth, cleaned his hand on his breeches, and glanced around. In the general clamour of the party, no one paid him any attention. No one, that is, except Alberni and Whidbey.

Alberni gave him thumbs up and winked.

He turned away in embarrassment. There was a sour taste on his tongue. Water, he thought. With exaggerated care, he descended the quarterdeck ladder to the main and stumbled to the scuttlebutt that stood in the shade of the foremast. It was quiet there, well forward of the revellers. He filled the ladle and drank. Cold water sluiced through him like an avalanche. He felt better immediately. No more for me tonight, he decided. He drank another ladle — and realized his bladder was full. He turned and edged past the windlass to go to the head at the bowsprit.

It was then that he noticed the Spanish commandant below the fo'c'sle with another man. He took a step closer and saw it was Tom Pitt. Dobson was nowhere to be seen, and they were doing fine without him — they were having a decidedly serious conversation. Hawkins wondered if Pitt was apologizing for muffing the toast. Yet Pitt did not look at all contrite, and Quadra looked angry. Pitt shrugged, turned, and walked away without so much as a backwards glance. He went aft along the starboard gunwale and did not see Hawkins in the dark.

That was some balls, thought Hawkins — and all over a silly toast.

Quadra watched Pitt go, and his eyes fell on Hawkins — who looked away, embarrassed to be perceived an eavesdropper, and suddenly saw there was someone else lurking in the dark in the lee of the foremast. Hawkins glanced back at the Spanish commandant and saw he had followed his gaze and seen him, too.

Perhaps Lincoln had also come forward to use the head; now, as he realized that Quadra and Hawkins had both caught him skulking, he bowed theatrically, spun around, and started aft. As he passed Hawkins, though, he lunged unexpectedly and grabbed him by the lapels, pulled him close, and hissed, "Out of my way, arsehole. Stay the fuck out of my way." He shoved him hard and continued aft to disappear among the revellers.

Hawkins barely caught his balance before he felt a violent internal roiling. The water he had downed with relief was returning with a vengeance. He spun to the railing and once again spewed into the harbour.

"Well, *there* you are!" rang the captain's voice.

He was not addressing Hawkins, whom he did not even see, but the

Spanish commandant. He came forward with Dobson, exchanged a few pleasantries with his counterpart, and guided him aft.

Hawkins dodged out of sight around the fore-hatch spar gallows and continued his thwarted journey to the head.

⧗

Joseph Whidbey lingered with Pedro Alberni. Language stood between them, for the soldier Alberni knew little of the port pidgin mariners learned on their voyages. Yet Whidbey knew him for a good man, and so, lubricated by drink and companionship, they conversed as best they could.

"Good," Whidbey said, indicating the cigar Alberni had lit for him.

"Cuban," Alberni said, puffing.

"Ah. Good." Whidbey puffed appreciatively. "Cuban?"

"*Si*. Good, Cuba."

"Never been...*no va. No va.*"

"No." Alberni puffed. "*Política*, hmm? Nice place. *Hermosa. Caliente.* Good *gente*...ah...good pee-pul."

Whidbey sensed Alberni studying him. He drew on his cigar and looked up at the stars.

"Whidbey? José?"

Whidbey peered at Alberni in the semidarkness, and saw that his expression was serious. He looked like a man who needed to get something off his chest. He began to speak, earnestly and at some length — but to Whidbey it was rapid-fire dago, and he leaned closer, trying to catch the soldier's drift. He understood a few words: '*diplomacia*,' 'Francisco,' '*inglesa*,' 'Don Juan,' and then '*diplomacia*' again.

Whidbey suddenly understood what his friend was saying. "Yes — Francisco! Before long we'll meet again in San Francisco. Let's you and me smoke another cigar there, eh, Captain? A Cuban." He raised one hand to indicate the cigar. "And raise a few glasses." He made a tipping gesture. "For *diplomacia, si*?"

The Spaniard searched his face. He spoke again, but it was entirely in Spanish. His limited pidgin, and English, and all other alternatives he could think of had failed him.

Whidbey held out his hands encouragingly, as if to gather his words in. "Sorry, my friend. Try again."

It was no use. Whatever he wanted to say was too complicated for him to convey, or for Whidbey to understand. "Fucking politics," Alberni said, resorting again to his spotty pidgin. He took a pull on his cigar. Its tip glowed red in the dark. "Fucking politics," he exhaled.

"Aye," Whidbey agreed. "*Si*, Pedro. Politics." He puffed on his own cigar, happy to communicate at least as well as this.

Quadra and Vancouver, trailed by the ever-present Dobson, climbed back up onto the quarterdeck and passed them, headed aft. Whidbey and Alberni each took a final puff on their cigars, tossed them over the side, and followed their commanders.

Soon, amid mutual assurances of friendship and expressions of deep regret at parting, the Spaniards went ashore. *Activa*, with Quadra, Alberni, and most of his soldiers, sailed for California before dawn.

# Chapter 35

In the days that followed, preparations for their own departure continued apace. *Chatham*'s crew dismantled their shore accommodations, emptied their temporary storehouses, and moved back aboard. *Chatham* and *Discovery* were both rigged for sea, their supplies securely stowed. Work gangs cut firewood in the forest, water parties filled kegs at the Spanish wells, and coopers repaired broken barrels and casks on the beach, while a carpenter's crew fashioned staves for them and spares for the voyage. Just before departure, *Discovery*'s small menagerie (chickens and a goat) would be separated from the Spaniards' livestock and boarded. The infirmary and the observatory would be the last of their shore outposts to be dismantled. When all else was ready, the sick would return to their ships, and the marquee, tents, and navigational gear would be brought aboard.

George Vancouver spent most of that week sequestered in *Discovery*'s great cabin, poring over paperwork. He now had a firm deadline to complete his dispatches. The Portuguese vessel on which Robert Duffin served would depart shortly for Macau, and he had secured a berth on her for Zach Mudge. In China, Mudge would arrange passage for England. He would carry Vancouver's reports, the charts they had produced since their departure eighteen months before, and a lengthy epistle outlining his negotiations with Quadra and the rationale behind his decision to decline possession of Nootka Sound. Vancouver was worried about how the latter would be received in London — this was why he had taken the extraordinary step of detaching his first lieutenant to deliver it. He trusted Mudge and was confident he would answer the politicians' questions regarding his handling of the affair. Mudge presented well, and he had connections that lent him credence. Van was no politician, but he knew how to cover his posterior.

During that week, in addition to his admittedly defensive epistle, he wrote reports on the survey, the state of his ships and their supplies, the health of the men, and tended to sundry bookkeeping, personnel, and administrative matters. The weather closed in, delaying the *Fenis and St. Joseph*'s departure, which proved fortuitous, because all that documentation took time to prepare.

On the morning of the first of October, the Portuguese snow finally warped out of Friendly Cove bearing Zach Mudge and his captain's dispatches and charts. It would take Mudge nine months to reach England; it would take Van barely ten minutes from the moment he saw Mudge off to step ashore for the first time in days.

He had arranged to meet Broughton and their respective sailing masters, Whidbey and Johnstone, at the observatory, to discuss the voyage south. It would not be a simple coasting cruise; there were gaps in the charts that he intended to fill. By mid-afternoon, they'd agreed on their course of action, and when the others dispersed, Vancouver remained. He was in no hurry to return to the ship's close confines. He put the two midshipmen he'd brought ashore with him to work checking the recent estimates of his chronometers' errors, while he reviewed the longitudes determined from the previous week's sightings. He was stooped over a table engrossed in this when a marine leaned inside the tent and announced a visitor.

"An Indian, sir," said the corporal doubtfully. "Says he's here to speak with you."

Vancouver marked his place and stepped outside.

The other sentry stood blocking a native man from coming closer.

"Comekala."

The marine held his ground.

"It's fine, Private. Thank you. He is a friend."

Both marines retreated a few paces and watched warily as their captain greeted the young Indian. The corporal murmured to the private, who began a circuit of the observatory's perimeter. The corporal stayed put.

"I'm very glad to see you. I thought perhaps we would not meet again before my departure," Vancouver said.

"I must talk with you, Macubah. Walk with me. Please."

Vancouver glanced back. The corporal held his eye, stone-faced. Behind him, both midshipmen had come to the tent's entrance to look out. "I'll be back shortly," Vancouver said. "Mister Ramsay, will you go over the gain rate estimates for Kendall's K3. Mister Pitt, do the same for Arnold's 176. We'll discuss them when I return." He turned back to Comekala and saw an odd expression flit across his face. The young man abruptly turned and started away.

They walked north along the shore.

"You and I have talked of many things. In Tahsis and also here. You said once that wrongs cannot be undone, but we can learn from them. Understanding can prevent further wrongs. That is what you told me."

Cook's wild rampage in Tahiti, his death in the Sandwich Islands — both had begun with unknowns and escalated beyond the control of any man. Van gave a nod.

"My brother is Copaza, the one they accuse of killing the Spaniard Francisco."

(Such beautiful eyes, I thought wistfully, feeling a sudden pang of hunger. A strong wind gusted off the open ocean, making it difficult to circle, so I fluttered onto a nearby log).

"Copaza is many things, but he is not a murderer. He didn't kill Francisco. My uncle told Quadra that."

"Quadra told me this. Also that your uncle would not tell him who *did* kill him —" This was not quite accurate. Maquinna had blamed the Hesquiaht. "— specifically. And so the killer goes unpunished."

He was certain Quadra had been right in not retaliating against the Hesquiaht. A people should not suffer for the act of an individual.

"By the time he left," Comekala said, "Quadra knew the truth — because my mother learned what happened and told him. She is Hesquiaht and did not want her people to suffer. So he knew everything and did nothing about it. He had his reasons, but the result is that the killer is free today. This should please no one. Certainly no one in my family because, while Copaza has been exonerated, and the Hesquiaht will not be punished for something they didn't do, Francisco the Spaniard is dead, and Matuateh, a girl who is a sister to me, is a widow now, before she ever wed."

Pause.

"I see how she suffers and am sad for her. I am also sad there is no justice for Francisco — or for Matuateh either. It hurts me to see this, but I must obey my chief. You know what duty demands of a man."

"Yes."

"My wife Keiskonis also looks upon Matuateh as her sister. Keiskonis does not see my duty the way I see it."

Van remembered the young woman with the fiery eyes and dazzling smile. Menzies had seemed deeply affected by the memory of her friendship and, if Van were to judge, not a little beguiled. He said, "I don't understand."

"My wife is a persistent woman. There is no peace for me if I do not listen to her."

Vancouver smiled.

"Keiskonis tells me you must know what Quadra knew before he left. Macubah, the killer is on your ship. He is one of you."

⧗

It is often said that information is power, and that is generally true. This knowledge, though, did not make Van feel powerful in the least. It placed him squarely between a rock and a hard place.

And so, in the darkness that night, he sits at his desk in the great cabin and considers his course.

There is a murderer aboard *Discovery*.

The victim is a Spaniard, and the Spanish know who did it.

There is a witness.

She is an Indian.

She can easily be discredited, for she is an Indian; and she has accused an Englishman, who will deny it. There is another Englishman who will undoubtedly back his countryman's account.

In any event, the girl has come forward in defiance of her chief's wishes. Her testimony must be held in confidence, at least locally, to protect her.

THE WIND FROM ALL DIRECTIONS | 295

Leave aside the fact the chief's territory is at the centre of a broader territorial dispute between the Spanish Crown and His Britannic Majesty's Government, one that *he* has been delegated to resolve, which he has thus far failed to do, though not for want of trying.

Turning to the villain. Augustus Lincoln was not chosen for the voyage, but rather foisted upon it by high connections. He has not distinguished himself in any way since departing England other than by contracting an incurable malady, and by glomming onto Pitt, and Pitt to him, and here is the *real* problem for George Vancouver.

Pitt is a witness, an accessory, maybe even an accomplice to the crime — and he has been a thorn in Van's side, yea, rump, since early in the voyage. He is a troublemaker, a shit-disturber, the self-appointed *spokesman* for the midshipmen (as if that is a Thing in His Majesty's service), an irresponsible, thin-skinned, dissolute, lazy, prideful, boastful narcissist. He is also the scion of the most powerful family in England. His father is a peer of the realm, rich beyond imagination; one cousin is the prime minister, another the first lord of the Admiralty. Lord Chatham, born John Pitt, had issued Vancouver's orders for the present voyage and had, at the behest of the secretary of state, Lord Grenville (yet another Pitt cousin), inserted an instruction to avoid doing anything that might create conflict with any foreign power (read: Spain), and another that Van does not need to look up for he can recite it verbatim: "You are hereby strictly charged to use every possible care to avoid disputes with the natives and to endeavour to secure their friendship and confidence."

Simultaneous with the issuance of these definitive directions, family influence had secured the Honourable Thomas Pitt a berth on *Discovery*.

Well, Van, he thinks, what an un-pretty pickle is this. Don't offend the Spanish. Don't offend the Indians. Take care of our lad and make sure he has a nice trip.

Alone in the creaking silence of the great cabin, feeling the damp chill of night off the harbour, he contemplates his conundrum.

He has knowledge of a contemptible crime affecting foreign parties, with a conspicuous nexus to the nation's Powers That Be. And he is bound by the dictates of honour and duty, unable to turn a blind eye to what he knows.

Oh fuck honour, you say. Fuck duty. Why court ruin? A man who was politic and calculating, a climber, one focused on advancing his career and status, would let it go.

Alas, George Vancouver is not such a man.

# Chapter 36

Oppressive skies, clouds sagging to earth. The weather had now undeniably turned. The temperature plummeted, winds blew at gale force, and torrents of rain descended, delaying the Britons' preparations for sea and, ultimately, their departure. Finally, on October 12, the very day on which the Tammany Society of New York celebrated the first Columbus Day (it being the three hundredth anniversary of the great navigator's discovery of America), the weather cleared, and members of the Mowachaht nation saw a party of *their* discoverers off. The remnants of the Spanish garrison, now led by Salvador Fidalgo, erstwhile commander of the abandoned outpost of Nunez Gaona, also waved goodbye to Vancouver's doughty squadron and hunkered down for a cold, wet winter in Nootka Sound.

On the voyage south, the explorers probed every promising bay and potential harbour on the coast, as well as the mouth and navigable reaches of a great river, the Columbia, which took them a hundred miles inland from the Pacific. They found not the Strait of Anián, nor Maldonado's Passage, nor any other sea route linking Asia and Europe, but a continuous shore, the western margin of a land mass that had yet to be traversed by any European north of New Spain.

This will soon change. In July of the following year, Alexander

Mackenzie will descend to Pacific tidewater via the Bella Coola River and become the first white man to cross the continent. He will miss George Vancouver, back on the coast that spring to resume his northern exploration, by just forty-eight days. Mackenzie will hear stories from the Nuxalkmc of blue-coated men who came by sea and were led by one called Macubah.

That was all in the future, on the day *Discovery* limped through the Golden Gate into San Francisco Bay. She was sea-battered, her crew exhausted. Gales had buffeted her south of the Columbia. At one point, a seaman aloft in the rigging was swept overboard. It happened during the day, and the watch reacted instantly. The ship hove to, a boat was lowered, and the man was plucked from the water no worse for wear. Everyone was relieved, and grateful (for once!) for the regular lifesaving drills their captain insisted they perform, for it could have been any of them in the drink. Sadly, one man *was* lost on the voyage. He disappeared overboard at night. It was never clear whether he'd slipped or been swept away. Some speculated he'd done himself in. In the dark, no one saw a thing.

*Chatham* arrived in San Francisco a week later, and together they sailed for Monterey, where Quadra was waiting and *Daedalus* had already arrived. Once again, the Spanish commodore offered his counterpart assistance; once again, Vancouver needed it. It was now December, and his three ships had long, arduous voyages ahead of them — *Daedalus* for Australia, *Discovery* and *Chatham* for Hawaii. They all needed repairs and provisions.

Quadra provided shipwrights and labourers to work alongside the Britons on their refit, arranged supplies, delivered fresh food. As he had in Nootka Sound, he invited the British officers to dine with him daily at his quarters in the *presidio*. And he arranged excursions for them: horse races and a bullfight, riding, hunting, even forays to other Spanish outposts. George Vancouver used these outings to note the characteristics of the region, its topography and agricultural potential, the size of its settlements, its garrison strengths and fortifications. He compiled these observations into an assessment of the Spanish situation in California, a report that would be invaluable to his superiors in England. Alas, it would be stale toast indeed by the time it reached them — he had no means of delivering it any time soon.

He had another report to convey, one he believed to be as pressing and urgent as that he'd prepared on California. It was in the form of a private letter, summarizing what he had learned from Comekala about the murder of Francisco Almeida and the roles of two of his midshipmen, the conditions of confidentiality under which that information was conveyed to him, and details of a subsequent event he felt sure was connected. "I feel duty and honour bound," he wrote, "to convey this information fully and faithfully to you and you alone. I place my trust in your judgment and do not intend to act until I receive instructions on the course of action I am to pursue."

The letter was not yet addressed. He was unsure to whom it should be sent. Lord Chatham, the first lord, or the foreign secretary, Lord Grenville? They were peers and ministers, and he considered them honourable men — yet they were relatives of Midshipman Pitt. Philip Stephens, the secretary of the Admiralty, and Evan Nepean, the undersecretary of state, were personal acquaintances; he knew them both to be honourable. Still, they were servants of the Crown, functionaries who served at the pleasure, et cetera. Might they be beholden to others? Coerced or silenced by them? He racked his brain for other independent possibilities. Sir Alan Gardner, now lord commissioner of the Admiralty, had been a mentor to him in Jamaica and a supporter since. Might he have the influence and discretion to guide this thorny mess to a just resolution? And what of Joseph Banks? He was influential, a man of repute, though certainly no ally of Van's. Could he set their past animosity aside in the interests of justice?

Who else was there?

The only thing of which he was certain was that the information he possessed was sensitive. No — what a gross understatement! — it was sensational, and it would precipitate a scandal if it became public. It had to be held private until prudent decisions could be made and discreetly acted upon. He felt sure it was best to deliver it into the hands of a single trustworthy and honourable man. The question remained: who?

The letter would have consequences. He knew they could be adverse for him. Already he felt vulnerable. He had not resolved the diplomatic matter — that could be construed as a failure on his part. Add to this the resentments and grievances that accumulated over a long voyage; it was certain that one-sided stories, spiteful gossip, and petty complaints would reach home — to his detriment, if people wanted to damage or destroy him. Who knew how circumstances had changed in the months since his departure? If the political winds had shifted, it might be convenient to hang him out to dry.

⧖

The question of *how* to deliver the letter was answered by his amiable host.

After a pleasant lunch on a shaded balcony at the *presidio*, the Spanish commodore leaned back from the table and considered his British counterpart. "George, I have been thinking. The letters you send on *Daedalus* will take a very long time to reach home. I have an alternative. We have ships sailing regularly to Cádiz from Veracruz. I can forward a packet for delivery to your ambassador in Madrid. It would be in London before *Daedalus* even reaches Australia. Your men's loved ones could receive letters from here months before Lieutenant Mudge arrives with the ones from Nootka."

Stewards bustled around the long table, clearing plates, pouring coffee and brandy. Vancouver waved away a refill. His eyes narrowed, his lips puckered as he considered the proposal.

"Assemble a packet, and include your dispatches if you wish. I will ensure it is given diplomatic treatment."

Joseph Whidbey sat back in his chair, thinking this a most accommodating offer. He picked a tooth with his finger and waited for his captain to accept. A signal gun sounded from Point Pinos. As it echoed in a sudden silence, it occurred to Old Joe that his captain's dispatches would make interesting reading for Spanish eyes. Very interesting reading.

"You make a kind offer, Don Juan," Vancouver said at last. "I know all hands will appreciate it. And what's more, that shorter route could hasten the resolution of our dispute. Our governments could send us both fresh instructions by next spring."

"Yes. I hope they do."

"And that is why I will ask Mister Broughton here to bear the packet himself."

As Dobson translated this, Quadra's eyes did not stray from

THE WIND FROM ALL DIRECTIONS | 301

Vancouver's face, even though Broughton, sitting next to his superior, startled visibly before going rigid in his chair.

"You would detach *Chatham*'s commander to carry dispatches?"

"No, no. Let me explain. I'm no politician or diplomat." A sheepish smile spread across Vancouver's face. "I cannot anticipate all the questions my superiors will raise about our deliberations in Nootka Sound. I simply cannot represent everything in writing. Mister Broughton has been party to our discussions. He is familiar with the issues. If he is there in person, he can answer questions and clarify matters for them. It is in both our interests, yours and mine, that we receive clear, well-informed direction on how to resolve things once and for all." His eyes swung onto Broughton. "Mister Broughton will be my emissary. I have complete confidence that he will represent matters fairly and accurately."

Broughton said nothing. He looked stunned — concussed even, like he'd struck his head on a beam.

Quadra glanced at Caamaño and Alberni. Now it was his turn to think. After a moment he nodded. "Very well. Captain Broughton will accompany me on *Activa* to San Blas. I will see that he's given passage to Veracruz from there."

"Your kindness, as always, overwhelms." Vancouver looked down the table at Lieutenant Puget, whom he had appointed to replace Mudge as his First. "Peter, we'll need to prepare that packet and put out a call for personal letters. And we'll need to finish the charts from the autumn survey as soon as possible. And copy them for Don Juan, of course."

"I'll see to it when I get aboard, sir."

"There we are. All is arranged." Vancouver looked back at Quadra. "Once again, Don Juan, I thank you."

Quadra acknowledged this with an incline of his head.

Whidbey thought he looked tired. There were rumours he was not well, rumours Menzies (who had recently examined him again) would neither confirm nor deny. The surgeon was as tight-arsed as a Presbyterian vicar when it came to patients. Old Joe glanced across at him and found him studying the Spanish commodore's face.

Vancouver was doing the same. Rather intently, in fact. "Don Juan, there is a matter I would discuss with you. In private."

"Of course, George." Quadra rose from the table. All the other officers present rose with him, mingled briefly, and dispersed. Tom Dobson stayed back. The three of them were now alone on the balcony. Vancouver looked inside to confirm everyone was gone. There were Spanish stewards waiting to finish clearing their table, but no officers from either side within sight.

"Mister Dobson. I will take it from here. Will you please wait for me inside."

Dobson's face was a study in confusion. He opened his mouth to speak, stammered something, read Vancouver's expression, and clamped it shut. His eyes flicked from face to face uncertainly.

"I have this, Tom. Just wait inside."

⧗

For the first time in their acquaintance they were alone. Vancouver wondered if this was wise. He decided wise did not matter. It was right.

"You and I were given a difficult task," he began in French, speaking haltingly. He had thought about what he would say, even rehearsed a little. "I speak of the diplomatic issue."

The Spaniard observed him curiously.

"I have tried to do my duty. To be a loyal servant of my king. I know you have done the same. In the circumstances, it has required...ah, creativity of both of us. We have not always been completely forthright with each other. For my part, I regret that."

Quadra waited.

"After you left Friendly Cove, Comekala came to speak with me."

Surprise flickered across the Spaniard's face.

"I know what happened in Friendly Cove."

Quadra stood completely still. These last words, still spoken slowly by Vancouver, had been in English.

"Comekala spoke to me in confidence, and obviously there are certain...considerations locally. Yet I cannot stand by and do nothing. I cannot remain silent with this knowledge. I have prepared a private letter, which Mister Broughton will carry to England. It contains everything

THE WIND FROM ALL DIRECTIONS | 303

Comekala told me. Mister Broughton will not know its contents, but he will deliver it into the hands of a man of importance. A man of great influence. Through him, it will be known in England, in the corridors of power, what these…” A pause, while Vancouver searched for a word. “… villains have done. I do not know what they will do with the knowledge. Yet I give you my word I will convey it.”

Quadra's face was a mask. He turned away to look out over Monterey Bay.

“Don Juan.”

Quadra turned back to him. Vancouver continued in French. “Before we depart I will give you corrected charts of our summer survey. I was never happy with those I gave you in Friendly Cove. Now I feel I must rectify my…error. The charts you receive will be of the highest quality.”

“*Merci, Georges. Votre diligence est appréciée. Comme c'est votre honneur. Et votre amitié.*”

They stood together looking out at Monterey Bay. Van felt relieved. He had said what he had to say, made amends of a sort. He thought the discussion over.

“He wore a small silver medallion,” Quadra said in French. “It was not found with his body. A Cuban version of the Virgin Mary. It might have been taken as a trophy.”

Vancouver stared at the Spaniard, who kept his own gaze on the bay. After a moment Van too returned his gaze to the fore, and they stood together, immersed in their individual reveries about the possibility of justice, the nature of man, the inevitable end of youth, ambition, life.

⧗

Early next morning, *Discovery*'s midshipmen were mustered without warning and sent ashore en masse. On the pier below the *presidio*, they met their peers from *Chatham* and *Daedalus*, as well as their Spanish counterparts. They were there, Peter Puget announced, for a contest. They assembled into boat crews, and for the next four hours raced in heats across the harbour and back. The heats led to more races, which led to a final one — the best against the best. Vancouver had given leave to his officers, petty officers, and a bevy of crewmen to go ashore, where they enthusiastically cheered on their snotties and (with a somewhat more critical eye) wagered privately on every heat.

Vancouver, though, begged off the fun himself; he remained aboard to attend to business. He ordered the lower deck and well smoked while his people were ashore. Before you light the pitch, he told the bosun, I will inspect the area.

He took with him on his rounds trusted men upon whom he impressed the necessity of absolute secrecy. They were his clerk, Orchard; Wilcox, the master-at-arms; the ship's corporal; and the marine sergeant, Flynn, who posted a marine at the top of each ladder before they went below.

They went straight to the midshipmen's cockpit. Flynn stationed himself at its entrance in case anyone slipped past his men up top.

"Search everything thoroughly. Every sea chest and hammock, and look through anything hung against the bulkheads or hull. Look for things tucked away in a crevice, between planks, under the table. Check the deck and deckhead for recesses."

"Is there something specific we should look for, sir?"

"Anything untoward, Mister Orchard. Contraband. Liquor. Pilfered supplies. Oh! Yes. A silver medallion. Possibly on a silver chain. Religious, depicting Mary, the Mother of Jesus."

"A secret papist we've got among us, is it, sir?" said Master-at-Arms Wilcox, grinning.

Vancouver returned him a cold stare. Wilcox, who despite his sometimes-grim duties had a reputation for wit, was unsettled by it.

"About this medallion. Perhaps it will be part of a collection. Well, get to it, men. Be thorough, and mind you don't tear the place apart. Put everything back the way it was. I want no indication that a search was conducted."

He stood back and watched, attempting not to show interest in any particular midshipman's belongings. They worked methodically, the ship's corporal concentrating on the hammocks and hanging gear, Orchard and Wilcox combing through sea chests. Orchard eventually searched Pitt's. Wilcox went through Lincoln's.

The searchers found no liquor, contraband, or pilfered items. The midshipmen had collected many souvenirs and keepsakes, but there was no medallion featuring Cachita, Our Lady of Charity of El Cobre, heavenly protector of Cuba, in anyone's belongings.

"Young Mister Lincoln's got an eye for knickknacks," Wilcox said. In his palm were several trinkets nestled within a handkerchief.

Vancouver had watched him search Lincoln's chest, aching to do it himself. "Let's take a look."

There was a thin copper bracelet, engraved with the types of animal figures favoured by the northwest natives. A George II farthing dated 1754. A small silver spoon engraved with the words *Plus Ultra*. Vancouver's eyes narrowed at it. They narrowed further at the next item he picked from the cloth. A small optical lens, cracked and useless, missing its brass rim. He rolled it in his fingers, his expression clouded. Could it be?

He dropped it back into Wilcox's palm.

There was one other item that caught his attention. A fine copper ring with a tiny strip of something attached, crisp like parchment, stained rusty-dark. A scrap of skin from an animal, thought Vancouver, though it was hairless.

"That's it?"

"Aye, sir."

"Look through his things again. All his things. One last time."

Wilcox laid the handkerchief open on the midshipmen's mess table and went back through the trunk. While he and the others searched, Vancouver stood and stared sourly at the table, at that lens, remembering how in Tahiti he had raged at the islanders over the theft of a telescope it would fit perfectly. How close he had come. How close.

Lincoln was obviously a collector, but the medallion was not among his belongings. This search was all for naught.

⧗

But why, Dear Reader, *why*? You saw Cachita in his bloodstained hands. Why isn't it part of his tickle trunk trove?

Flash back to the beach the morning after that fateful night. Matuateh tends insensate Carlos. She hears a sound, sees two figures emerge from the forest and walk along the shore. It is them — Lincoln and Pitt, propping each other up, none too spry after the night they've had.

Shhh, Matuateh tells Carlos, and slips back into the forest.

A moment later I land to check on Carlos myself. His eyes flutter open. Nope. I resolve to drop in on Francisco before some opportunist beats me to him.

I take off — and am struck by a thought. Pitt and Lincoln look like death warmed over. I wonder if...you know. I veer back towards them just in time to see Pitt collapse on the beach.

Lincoln tugs him by the arm, tries to pull him to his feet. "Keep moving, Tom. We've got to keep going."

"Wait," Pitt moans, his voice pitiable. Down on all fours, he retches. Lincoln sinks down next to him and pulls himself up against a log. That is all he can do. Pitt dry heaves and goes still. Lincoln's eyes shut too. They are both in bad shape, but I can tell they will live.

And then Lincoln's hand falls open.

Overhead, I catch a glint. There, in his palm, a shiny bauble glistens in the morning light. It's Cachita, and she's beautiful, and I focus on her, feeling delicious desire, greed, the compunction to *have*, course through my hollow bones. I reduce altitude, circle tightly, flutter in, and grab her in my claws. Feeling my sudden weight, Lincoln's hand closes reflexively, but I've performed a classic touch-and-go, and I'm gone baby gone, soaring already, and thinking, Cachita's *mine*, all mine, and besides, she's no use to Francisco anymore, is she?

This reminds me just how much I liked that young man. I wheel and set off to eat his eyes. On the way I cache his medallion in a tree.

⧗

So, yes, I took it. It was shiny and bright. It was beautiful, and it pleased me, and I wanted it. I took it because I could. Does that make me any worse than Vancouver or Quadra? Or England? Spain? Or the Mowachaht, who took from others when it suited their purpose? Humans are not above ravening when they want something from somebody else.

I seldom suffer regret. Here, though, things might have turned out better, more just for all concerned, if I had resisted my nature, there on the beach, and Van had found Cachita that day in Monterey.

THE WIND FROM ALL DIRECTIONS | 307

While the ships' companies worked flat out on repairs, the midshipmen were mobilized to prepare the contents of Broughton's packet, which would contain handwritten duplicates of the reports sent with Zach Mudge weeks before (in case Mudge and his packet were lost at sea), as well as reports on the busy period since. And charts of all their discoveries since departing England. Yes, everything they'd produced in Nootka Sound had to be produced again, updated and corrected accordingly, and copied for the Spaniards.

Joseph Whidbey was busy with work of his own, readying *Discovery* for sea. Still, he noticed a distemper among the lads. They grumbled and squabbled among themselves. They all wanted to be ashore, experiencing the marvels of California, not stooped over a chart table or chained to a desk.

"Hard cheese, Mister Pitt," he told one griper. "This is the hand you've been dealt. Follow suit and play, boy, and stop your infernal grousing."

Truth be told, Whidbey sympathized with young Pitt. The captain had specifically directed that he, along with Lincoln, copy ledgers and general correspondence for the packet, the most tedious of all the tasks to be performed. It was done below deck, unlike the chart work, which was conducted under the glorious California sun. Whidbey wondered what those two had done to deserve this punishment, for punishment it surely was. Even before *Discovery* departed Nootka Sound, they'd been confined to the ship. No doubt, out of youthful high spirits, they'd transgressed, broken a rule, or crossed a line — and the captain had noticed.

Whidbey had heard grumbles about their treatment from the denizens of the midshipmen's mess.

At least, he thought grimly, that cramped space was not as crowded now as it was before.

Young Jim Hawkins had disappeared on the voyage south. No one knew what happened to him. It seemed likely that he had fallen overboard, that the sea had taken his body, and all his considerable promise, without a trace. But could he really have fallen? It had not been the worst night of the voyage, though there'd been a gusting wind, a heavy swell. It was *possible* he'd slipped, yet it seemed unlikely. He had his sea legs; he'd lived through much worse. A rumour quickly spread that it was suicide. This was bolstered by the fact that his journal was missing. Everyone knew he kept it diligently. The theory went that he took it with him into the sea, leaving no clues as to his state of mind.

If that were true, what could have driven him to do such a thing?

When he was discovered missing, after they'd fruitlessly searched the ship, one of his messmates volunteered that he'd not been himself for months — since June, when he was reprimanded for getting lost on a boat expedition. After that, he'd seemed depressed; he'd become temperamental and remote. Lincoln had not been the boy's best mate, but he'd been close by him all those months. He'd noticed the change.

When he volunteered his theory, a look crossed Vancouver's face that struck Old Joe to the core. It was raw fury and something more: a dark certainty. Whidbey wondered if it was guilt. Did George Vancouver feel responsible for Hawkins's depression and miserable demise?

Perhaps the captain's rebuke was a factor in the boy's death, yet in his heart Whidbey held himself to blame. Back in Nootka Sound, he had put Jim forward as a mapmaker. He had extolled him for his technique, his attention to detail, his aptitude. While others of the youngsters had been given lesser tasks and more variety, a chance now and then to lead a work crew ashore or to spend a night at the observatory, Hawkins had had little respite from shipboard duty, no time for a proper rest.

It must have broken his spirit. The poor fellow, seemingly so steady, had become unhinged by the unceasing toil, the pressure to excel. It was unlike the boy he thought he knew; and yet it was possible.

Or maybe he *had* slipped and fallen overboard. The sea is a cruel master and oh, so tricky.

As always, Old Joe needed to attend to *Discovery*'s seaworthiness: her rigging, sails, the stowage of her hold. And there were observations to make with the captain, and cartographic challenges to work through with Baker. Yet despite his heavy workload, the tensions on board, and his regrets over Hawkins, he found himself in a most agreeable frame of mind. The pleasant warmth of California's climate seemed to cure his perennial aches and twinges, the stiffness in his back, the cracking in his shoulders, hips, and knees. He was long accustomed to what Menzies called his "barometric condition," his every ache a portent of tomorrow's weather. Yet here in Monterey, he was energized and completely free of pain. He revelled in it.

"If you could bottle this place," he told Menzies one morning, stretching comfortably in the warm sunshine, "you'd have a miracle cure on your hands. And it would make a tastier tonic than any of your foul elixirs."

They were waiting for the captain to emerge from his morning session with Puget. They were going ashore for a visit to the Franciscan mission at Carmelo. Commodore Quadra would accompany them himself.

"Aye, if I could bottle California, I daresay I could cure scurvy, typhus, and tuberculosis combined — and gi'e the pox a run for'ts money, though I doubt it would permanently cure *your* numerous complaints, Whidbey. I'll wager after a day or two at sea, ye're back tae your regular oracular self — good as ever before."

"You are a font of comfort, Doctor," Whidbey sniffed, a bit put out. "Though I warrant your bedside manner could be improved upon."

"Aye, I ken that in your case. I dinnae employ it for patients in your current happy condition."

Whidbey rotated his shoulder blades, enjoying the absence of twinges or cracks. Twenty, he thought; I feel twenty again.

Menzies watched him with a sly look on his face.

"Do ye know, Whidbey — in Africa, the witch doctors of the Hottentot foretell the future by casting bones upon the ground. If they cannae discern a pattern on the first throw, they scoop them up and cast them till they do. But when ye're back tae yourself, Joe — right as ever a Whidbey was — ye'll do us better than tha'. We Discoveries won't have tae roll *your* scrawny bag o' bones across the deck. Ye'll again foretell the weather a day in advance by the creak o' your elbow or the twinge in your big toe, or I'm a Frenchman."

"Perhaps you are, Menzies," Whidbey said. "I've often wondered about that *foreign* accent of yours." His eyes narrowed. "And don't get me started on witch doctors."

But try as he might, he could get no rise from the surgeon. Menzies took his jibes with equanimity, until George Vancouver emerged from his cabin and strode purposefully towards the gangway. Menzies and Whidbey climbed down ahead of him into the boat and moved forward to leave him room on the back thwart, where Midshipman Ramsay waited as coxswain to ferry them ashore.

# Chapter 37

Juan Francisco de la Bodega y Quadra will never return to Nootka Sound. Within fifteen months of those companionable days in Monterey, he will be dead, felled at fifty-one by the cumulative effects of a life at sea.

George Vancouver will return to the Sound in the spring. His survey of the northwest coast will consume two more years, after which he will lead his expedition safely home, having placed a great swath of territory upon the map of the known world and proven there is no navigable route linking the Atlantic and Pacific within temperate latitudes. Thereafter, the search for the Northwest Passage will shift to the Arctic, culminating in Franklin's doomed expedition fifty years hence.

Within three years of the end of his voyage, Vancouver will also be dead — though not before he is publicly maligned and humiliated, the target of a campaign of whispers denigrating his character and accomplishments and accusing him of cowardice, corruption, and cruelty. His former subordinate, Thomas Pitt, will play a pivotal role in his vilification. Pitt will impugn his honour, stalk him, insult him, physically accost him in the street, and demand satisfaction in the form of a duel. The ailing Vancouver will not take the bait; rather, he will seek exoneration from the scurrilous accusations made against him. He will ask his superiors to convene a panel of his peers to conduct an impartial review of his behaviour on the voyage. His request will be denied.

By then, Spain and Britain will be embroiled in a conflict that will make their near-war quarrel over Yuquot seem trivial. Both powers will abandon their dispute in the northwest and leave the Mowachaht to the traders, who will themselves depart when the sea otter reaches the brink of extinction. Only then will the Mowachaht return to Yuquot, few in number, lungs bleeding, faces pocked like the surface of the moon.

Against all odds they will survive; and at their home fires their children will hear the legends of their people, the stories of their ancestors; and *this* story too will be told — to one child at least, when she is very young, by her mother, Matuateh, and by Copaza, who will be like a father to her, and who will become Tsakwasap, successor to old Tsakwasap, in the tradition of the Mowachaht.

⧗

Fly with me now to another place and time — to England in 1804. It is predawn in a Kensington meadow. Two men stand afloat on mist. They gaze upon the vague profile of Holland House, at dripping bare branches, and up at the sky; anywhere but at each other. Their bearing is stiff, their posture resigned.

Dawn brightens. In the wet grass beneath the trees bordering the meadow, sparrows flutter and forage. Starlings strut among them. A dark bird of carrion lands noisily on a branch above them and shuffles edgewise, flapping and folding its wings.

Two other men conferring nearby glance up at the sound. They are seconds to the principals, and there is little for them to discuss — the *code duello* specifies all quite clearly. They rejoin their companions. In a tight voice one of them announces the terms: twelve paces, on his signal. His counterpart, moving woodenly, proffers an open pistol case to one, then the other, of the duellists.

Long barrels tilt at the lightening sky as they examine their weapons. This moment stretches on and on. Are they thinking of a way out of the meadow, a path that will spare both dignity and life? One of them, slim and of middle height, stares at the pistol he has chosen. Thomas Best cannot believe the circumstances — a petty squabble over a woman of doubtful virtue. He seeks his opponent's eyes and finds them already on his face. Their owner, a tall, powerfully built young man with bushy mutton chops, cocks his pistol.

Best hesitates before following Thomas Pitt's lead.

Elbows crooked, barrels tilted to heaven, they walk off the distance and turn to brace, one foot forward, one back. At a word from the designated second they take aim, weapons levelled at arm's length.

Pitt sees that Best is aiming to the side and not directly at him, a signal he intends to delope.

"Best, that's not on. It won't do," calls Pitt, now Lord Camelford.

Best rectifies his aim.

They stand frozen thus, waiting for the signal. Harsh grey light gathers around them. Stillness and silence prevail between the men, broken only by the peeping and fluttering of the sparrows. The fetching ebony stranger in the tree tilts its head to make an announcement.

"*Quork.*"

The man who will give the signal looks from one duellist to the other. Camelford looks sidelong at him and clears his throat; his eyes return to his opponent.

The second still hesitates, looks again at Camelford, but his glance is not returned. At last, prisoner to obligation, he utters the word. There is a single flash, an ear-splitting crack. Camelford has fired. The meadow erupts in a clamour of beating wings and panicked chirrups — the little birds take flight. I am already aloft. An instant later there is another flash and crack, then stillness. Smoke rises from the pistols. The seconds wonder if there have been two misses, if honour has been served and the rapprochement they have urged upon their friends is now possible. They will laugh at this folly over a hearty breakfast, one tasting of continued life and vigour, sweet with camaraderie, seasoned with relief. As if in contemplation of this prospect, Camelford lowers his weapon and gazes down at the ground, before his knees buckle and he crumples into the grass.

The others rush to him — only then do they see the stain spreading across his waistcoat, a red horde of conquest on a snowy plain.

Thus is settled a trivial matter of honour.

He breathes — he is alive! Hope swells among them. Camelford reaches for his fellow duellist — a drinking companion in happier times

— clutches him by his vest and pulls him close. Now just inches from him, he speaks, his voice gut-clenched; he forgives Best, declares him innocent of the accusations he himself had made. He urges him to depart the scene for his own safety. He urges their seconds to do the same. They must all avoid complications.

They refuse to go. They lean in to lift him.

"Stop — *stop!*" he cries through a surge of pain. "Listen to me...I have been...the aggressor in this matter. I...I alone...must pay the consequence. No harm will come...to any of you from this." He looks from face to face. "Rest assured...I will not...reveal your identities...upon my honour...Now go. You must go."

High above their heads, I spot it — that notion of honour, so firm, so fluid. I wheel to observe the spectacle beneath me, then veer away. So do the wounded man's companions; they vanish into a crowd that is gathering, drawn by the shots.

Thomas Pitt, Lord Camelford, is carried to a nearby house. A surgeon is summoned; his diagnosis is grim. The ball has entered his lordship's chest, shattered ribs, punctured a lung, severed his spinal cord. The wound is pronounced mortal — yet the young peer does not die. He lingers in great pain, suffering resolutely, courage evident in his fortitude. Relatives and friends, among them former shipmates, rush to surround his bedside to comfort him and hold grim vigil.

Two long days and nights pass.

The end approaches and he knows it. He becomes repentant. He admits he has led a dissolute life and voices hope that his current suffering, combined with whatever good he has done in his twenty-nine years, may atone for his sins. On the cusp of eternity, he locks eyes on a friend, a one-time shipmate who shared his experiences on a voyage of youthful adventure and notable accomplishment.

"*Tanash mamathi,*" he murmurs, and dies.

The room is full of grief. Those gathered at his bedside mingle and console one another. "That moment at the end," one man says to Augustus Lincoln later. "What was it he said to you?"

Lincoln merely stares at him. There is something off-kilter in his expression that unsettles the well-intentioned mourner. In the awkward silence he turns to Robert Barrie. "Did you understand it?"

Richard Ramsay sees that Barrie is overcome and feels compelled to speak.

"I can't be certain I heard it correctly. It sounded —"

"It was *tanash mamathi*," Lincoln interrupts. "It is how the Nootka Indians describe the soul, which they liken to a bird."

The gentleman looks at Pitt's body, now restful in repose. "That's a beautiful image. It's a blessing he could dwell on it at the end. And to think it is a savage concept."

Lincoln returns a smile that is remarkably cheery in the circumstances.

Crazy, daft bastard, Ramsay thinks. He never liked him as a youth. Nor does he like him as the man he has become — war hero or no.

⧗

I'm tired of circling and I'm getting hungry, and when that happens I get shirty and short. Let's keep moving. We are near the end. Join me for a final flight, a return through time's frontier to Yuquot in the future. If you look down now, there, at one century's distance exactly…It is 1904, and an angry wind is blowing in Nootka Sound and all along the coast. The children of the Mowachaht, as well as those of the Hesquiaht, the Tla-o-qui-aht, and the Cheklesahht —indeed, of all the other *ahts* — have been seized and sent away to be *schooled*, in the course of which they will have the Indian beaten and bejesused out of them. In this very year, the Mowachaht's most sacred treasure, which will come to be known as the Yuquot Whalers' Shrine, will be sold, packed up, and shipped to New York, where it will be forgotten in the basement of the American Museum of Natural History. We won't linger — it's too sad, and yet these hardy people will survive even these indignities.

Don't think to land — I said keep moving. We are in the right place, but we have a long flight ahead, another century exactly, to the summer of 2004.

⧗

Roost and feel the heat. The sun beats down from an unblemished sky. Below us, a man walks with a little girl towards the house at the water's edge, on the far side of the cove from the lighthouse. He is nervous.

He has come here to research a book and brought his family with him. They have been here for four days, renting a small cedar cabin lacking in mod cons but boasting a magnificent view of the open Pacific. While he pursues his research, the girl's mother has claimed its deck.

The girl has gone with him on his tromps, and he has told her about James Cook, sea otters, the Northwest Passage, and the meeting of Quadra and Vancouver at this very place in 1792 — the pageantry and diplomacy, the fraternization, the murder. The two of them have been all over the site of the long-abandoned Spanish outpost, though there is nothing of it left to see. The forest and the Mowachaht reclaimed it long ago.

"Quadra's headquarters stood right where we're standing," he'd said at one point. "The British called it the Big House. From the balcony up on the second floor — imagine it just above our heads — he could look out *there* into the harbour. Imagine it full of ships, men-of-war, schooners, brigs, Indian long canoes bustling back and forth."

The little girl's eyes had shone as she visualized the scene.

"First Nations," she'd said after a moment.

"Pardon?"

"They're not Indian. They're First Nations."

I like the kid, but this man, this "writer,"‡ bugs me with his gonzo enthusiasm, his nerdy penchant for detail. Approximately right is close enough in *my* book. Truthful hyperbole makes a better story. You'll sway more people with it than Joe Friday here, or the failing *New York Times*, with all its so-called facts.

Anyway, that's what he's been like, this guy, this writer, his whole time in Yuquot. Tromping around, making notes, imagining what really happened. Just make shit up, for crying out loud.

His visit has coincided with the local First Nation's annual summer festival, and many Nuu-chah-nulth people (as they are known in modern times) have come to Yuquot for it. There's been a party atmosphere, a celebration with drumming, chants, dancing, a feast.

"Do you know what '*tanash mamathi*' means?" the aspirant scribe asked everyone he met.

---

‡ This *wannabe* writer — he has never actually published a word; he fancies himself a post-modernist, and that may be true, what with his personal MacGuffins and weakness for unreliable narrators. He's just the type to put himself in his own book.

Several people instantly recognized the term *"mamathi"*; no one recognized *"tanash."* Talk to Ray, they told him, referring to Ray Williams. He and his wife are among the few elders who speak the language of their ancestors. They are also the only people who live permanently in Yuquot these days. "Maybe Ray knows what *tanash* means."

Hearing this, our Hemingway hesitated. The Mowachaht had lived in this place for millennia, and he wanted to know about the dying words of an English dilettante who spent mere days here two centuries ago. Of all the things he might ask an elder of these people, this was trivial indeed. Insulting even.

He recognized his folly and saw himself at last for what he was: an interloper, irrelevant, ridiculous, a joke. And so he held his tongue.

Until now. It is his last day in Yuquot, and the MV *Uchuck III* is approaching to take him back to the mainland. He is on his way with his daughter to speak with Ray Williams, his reluctance to ask such a strange and selfish question finally trumped by his selfish unwillingness to depart with half an answer.

"According to his biographer, Pitt's dying words were *'tanash mamathi,'*" he tells the girl for the umpteenth time. He is practising on her.

Really, I've had it with this guy. The girl must have too.

"... but that doesn't make sense. He spent a grand total of fifty days in Nootka Sound in 1792 and '93..."

All right, that does it. I'm fed up now. It's been a long journey, and it's hard work passing through the walls of time to show you the truth. I'm really hungry, and this idiot's droning on. As if he'll ever get published.

They knock on the door of the Williams house, which doubles as a gallery for their son, a master carver. Ray is called.

"What do you want?" he asks bluntly.

He listens to the writer's preamble and invites him and the girl inside. There he listens to what the man has to say about the English lord and his dying words. He confirms the definition of *"mamathi"* that others provided, and clarifies the pronunciation. But he is stumped by *"tanash."*

He takes a moment to think, considering the circumstances. If a man were dying, he might not speak clearly. He might mumble or miss a syllable. Besides, he might never have heard the words right in the first place. The same might be true of all those gathered round him when he died. "*Tanash*," Ray Williams says, was likely "*wikhtinish*." And he explains what "*wikhtinish*" means.

So here was the longed-for answer. "*Mamathnhi*" is the Mowachaht word for white man; and "*wikhtinish*" means crazy. "*Wikhtinish mamathnhi*," then, translates as "crazy white man."

The writer can't help himself — he gives out a guffaw of delight before he recovers, thanks Mister Williams, and bids him goodbye.

Walking towards the dock where his wife is waiting with their gear — the *Uchuck* is now in sight and chugging nearer — he won't shut up. "Mystery solved!" he bubbles, laughing and doing a little dance. "The strange case of a dying man's last words! Riddle cracked — I did it!"

Oh, I am *done* with him. As if *he's* done anything that affects the price of steak. I'm famished, and hunger makes me ornery, and I've come a long way, and this denouement is taking way too long, and I'm *not* going to take any more of his nonsense. I'm perched on the bare branch of a tree, and as I crouch to take off the kid looks up and sees me. We make eye contact. Then I'm in the air. I do a tight circle, not too high; there's no wind (for once) in Yuquot, and I have to work at it, my wings beating while I simultaneously calculate speed, mass, acceleration. It's a simple calculus, I've done it countless times before, and I reach the optimal elevation, the point at my end of the vector, and I let go, swing around, gliding now to watch, hearing the exultant voice of Slim Pickens as Major Kong screaming, "*Yahhh hoooo!*"

Nothing for a delicious moment. Then comes an "*Uaahg!*" from the man.

They both stop in their tracks.

"*Oooh...*" says the girl.

He glares at his shoulder, reaches up to touch it, and stops himself.

I told you what I'm like when I'm hungry.

The girl is about to laugh, but, seeing his expression, she scrunches her lips into a serious face.

He grunts again and looks up at the sky. Circling high above, I give him a beady stare, but you think he notices? None too observant, this one. And he calls himself a *writer*.

"That's good luck," she says, and hands him a tissue. "I read that in a book."

I like this kid.

My work here is done. I catch a draft and rise, circling wider to veer away. Of course, the wind is back, gusting from all directions. It carries me. I soar.

⧗

So there you have the truth, Dear Human — *my* truth, and I've seen it all.

Maps are made and lines are gouged upon them.
Empires rise and fall.
Character is fate.
Boys will be boys.
All things die.
Nature prevails.
What's a hungry raven to do?
I think I'll grab something to eat.

## A NOTE ON SOURCES

*The Wind From All Directions* is based on historical events. Vancouver, Quadra, and Maquinna did indeed meet in Nootka Sound in 1792; and there *was* a murder. It was but a footnote to the negotiations, ceremonies, and preparations for sea in which those who recorded it were engaged. When I came upon that footnote, I knew I had my story.

I reviewed many historical sources to create this fictionalized account, and recommend the following in particular to anyone seeking insight into the characters and nations involved in the events (real or imagined) related in this book:

On Vancouver and the British: George Vancouver, *A Voyage of Discovery to the North Pacific Ocean and Round the World 1791–1795*, Volumes I and II, edited by W. Kaye Lamb (London: The Hakluyt Society, 1984). Kaye Lamb's introduction in Volume I is an excellent summary of Vancouver's life, his accomplishments, and the diplomacy he engaged in with Quadra. Volume II covers the events of 1792 in Vancouver's own words.

On Quadra and the Spanish: Warren L. Cook, *Flood Tide of Empire: Spain and the Pacific Northwest, 1543–1819* (New Haven and London: Yale University Press, 1973). Cook provides the background to the negotiations — the fur trade, Spanish–Indigenous relations, the Martínez–Colnett incident in 1789, and Spanish strategy — as well as an exhaustive narrative on the events of 1792.

On the Mowachaht: Aldona Jonaitis, *The Yuquot Whalers' Shrine* (Seattle: University of Washington Press / Vancouver: Douglas & McIntyre, 1999). Jonaitis describes the rich culture of the Mowachaht and summarizes their history before and after 1792.

# ACKNOWLEDGEMENTS

I am grateful to the many who provided feedback, advice, or support over the long course of this book's evolution. They include Beverley Dowling, Kathryn Shailer, Mark Hume, Laurie Leclair, Jim Blackmore, Bobbi Ackerman, Nancy Kay Clark, Murray Glow, Philip Slayton, Steve Nash, Shane Carmody, Mary Delmau, Chris Temple, Terry Vulcano, Lorna Clark, and Jeannie MacPherson. In the final stages, I am particularly thankful to Bill McCutcheon, Kaitlin Thompson, and Mary Stinson, whose comments were insightful, constructive, and gently, deftly delivered. Jennifer McIntyre, my editor at Double Dagger, provided invaluable input and advice and was a delight to work with.

Several years prior to the book's publication, John McKay and Robert Griffin kindly responded to my queries regarding Vancouver's vessel, HMS *Discovery*. Mr. McKay provided me with inboard and outboard profiles of HM Sloop *Discovery*, which he produced from original research. He is the author of the excellent *The Armed Transport Bounty*, part of the Anatomy of the Ship Series (London: Conway Maritime Press Ltd., 1989), to which I also referred for details on eighteenth-century vessel configurations. Dr. Griffin, then-manager of Human History at the Royal British Columbia Museum in Victoria, BC, provided me with copies of drawings of HM Bark *Endeavour*, Captain James Cook's command on his first global circumnavigation. The RBCM's long-time exhibit on *Discovery* was actually based on *Endeavour*, which was a similar vessel with origins as a Whitby collier. I have also made much reference to

Karl Heinz Marquardt's *Captain Cook's Endeavour* (1995, revised 2001), another title in the Anatomy of the Ship Series published by Conway Maritime Press.

Regarding the troublesome character of Thomas Pitt, who came to occupy more of this story than I originally intended: the events of his life are related in *The Half-Mad Lord: Thomas Pitt, 2nd Baron Camelford (1775–1804)*, by Nikolai Tolstoy (London: Jonathan Cape, 1978). As with all my characters, by necessity I have taken fictional liberties with the historical personage. However, with regard to Pitt's dying words, I have not. Those words were mistranslated at the time of his death in 1804. They were corrected at last in 2004, when Mr. Ray Williams of Yuquot provided me with his thoughtful translation. I am grateful to Mr. Williams for his help. The account of my meeting with him, contained in the last chapter of the novel, is materially accurate — save for the actions of the irritable raven. That event is entirely of my own creation, a just comeuppance for my compositional sins.

Much of the story told in this book occurs in the territory of the people today known collectively as Nuu-chah-nulth. Several Indigenous First Nations comprise this group, including the modern-day Mowachaht/ Muchalaht. I am grateful to Ms. Margarita James, president of the Land of Maquinna Cultural Society, for advice on elements of this book.

For detailed insight into the lifestyle, culture, myths, stories, and whaling practices of the Mowachaht and other peoples of the Pacific northwest, I referred to various ethnographic works, such as Philip Drucker's *Cultures of the North Pacific Coast* (New York: Chandler Publishing, 1965) and *Indians of the Northwest Coast* (New York: McGraw-Hill, 1955), and Edward S. Curtis's *The North American Indian, Volume 11 – The Nootka. The Haida* (Norwood, MA: Plimpton Press, 1916). The latter is but one volume of an epic twenty volume, twenty-year endeavour by Curtis, a photographer, to document the lives of the Indigenous peoples of North America. While Curtis has been criticized for the artistic licence with which he depicted his photographic subjects, in recent years his work has been reassessed. For example, he produced film and sound recordings of ritual Kwakwaka'wakw dances and songs that were banned from performance at the time or at risk of being lost. Today, these recordings attest to the richness of Indigenous cultures in the Pacific northwest and their capacity to endure.

I have striven for authenticity in the setting of this novel and the depictions of characters appearing in it, whether historical or fictional. I have endeavoured to be respectful to all characters, parties, and nations represented. If I have not succeeded in these ambitions, it is my failure alone.

## ABOUT THE AUTHOR

Ron Thompson was born and raised on the Canadian prairies. After serving in the army reserve and as a naval officer, he spent two years as a development worker in southern Africa. He subsequently pursued a career in Canada and internationally as an economist, investment banker, and consultant.

Ron's historical commentaries have been published in the *Burney Letter*, his short fiction in *Canadian Voices*. His first novel, *A Person of Letters*, was published in 2015. His second, *Poplar Lake*, followed in 2018. While *The Wind From All Directions* is his third published novel, it was begun before either of his previous books. It has taken him twenty years to see it into print.

Ron is a Chartered Financial Analyst and a graduate of the University of Saskatchewan, the University of Toronto, the London School of Economics, and the Humber School for Writers. He lives in Toronto.

POPLAR
LAKE:
RON
THOMPSON
POPLAR LAKE

## PRAISE FOR RON THOMPSON'S POPLAR LAKE

"In *Poplar Lake,* Ron Thompson has written a captivating story, rich with humour and heart. I didn't want it to end."
   - Terry Fallis, two-time winner of the Stephen Leacock Medal for Humour

"Thompson's got everything here to make a great Canadian novel, and he goes a long way to writing just that. After years of living in the shadow of an edifice called Canadian Literature, in which its many settler novels featured no First Nations people, as if the land was simply empty and hard-working immigrants were given a stake in it by a beneficent government, writers such as Thompson have woken to a new day. In the light of the Truth and Reconciliation hearings, these writers want to include First Nations people in their narrative, and Thompson does."
   - Bill Robertson, The Star-Phoenix/Post Media

# DOUBLE‡DAGGER
## — www.doubledagger.ca —

DOUBLE DAGGER BOOKS is Canada's only military-focused publisher. Conflict and warfare have shaped human history since before we began to record it. The earliest stories that we know of, passed on as oral tradition, speak of war, and more importantly, the essential elements of the human condition that are revealed under its pressure.

We are dedicated to publishing material that, while rooted in conflict, transcend the idea of "war" as merely a genre. Fiction, non-fiction, and stuff that defies categorization, we want to read it all.

Because if you want peace, study war.

www.ingramcontent.com/pod-product-compliance
Lightning Source LLC
Chambersburg PA
CBHW022013310726
48972CB00006B/1627